PRAISE FOR JOEY W. HILL'S VAMPIRE QUEEN NOVELS

Beloved Vampire

"Lock the door, turn off the television and hide the phone before starting this book, because it's impossible to put down! . . . The story is full of action, intrigue, danger, history and sexual tension . . . This is definitely a keeper!"
—*Romantic Times*

"This has to be the best vampire novel I've read in a very long time! Joey Hill has outdone herself . . . [I] couldn't put it down and didn't want it to end."
—*ParaNormal Romance*

A Vampire's Claim

"*A Vampire's Claim* had me in its thrall. Joey W. Hill pulled me in and didn't let me go . . . I Joyfully Recommend that everyone should sink their teeth into [this book]."
—*Joyfully Reviewed*

"*A Vampire's Claim* is so ardent with action and sex you won't remember to breathe . . . another stunning installment in her vampire series."
—*TwoLips Reviews*

"Hill does not disappoint with the third book in her well-written vampire series . . . Sure to enthrall and delight not only existing Hill fans, but also those new to her writing."
—*Romantic Times*

"A great vampire romance . . . [an] enticing, invigorating thriller."
—*The Best Reviews*

continued . . .

The Mark of the Vampire Queen

"Superb . . . This is erotica at its best with lots of sizzle and a love that is truly sacrificial. Joey W. Hill continues to grow as a stunning story-teller."
—*A Romance Review*

"Packs a powerful punch . . . As the twists and turns unfold, you will be as surprised as I was at the ending of this creative story."
—*TwoLips Reviews*

"Joey W. Hill never ceases to amaze us . . . She keeps you riveted to your seat and leaves you longing for more with each sentence."
—*Night Owl Romance*

"Dark and richly romantic. There are scenes that will make you laugh and cry, and those that will be a feast for your libido and your most lascivious fantasies. The ending will surprise and leave you clamoring for more."
—*Romantic Times*

"Fans of erotic romantic fantasy will relish *The Mark of the Vampire Queen*."
—*The Best Reviews*

The Vampire Queen's Servant

"This book should come with a warning: intensely sexy, sensual story that will hold you hostage until the final word is read. The story line is fresh and unique, complete with a twist."
—*Romantic Times*

"Hot, kinky, sweating, hard-pounding, oh-my-god-is-it-hot-in-here-or-is-it-just-me sex . . . so compelling it just grabs you deep inside. If you can keep an open mind, you will be treated to a love story that will tug at your heart strings."
—*TwoLips Reviews*

VAMPIRE TRINITY

Joey W. Hill

HEAT
New York

THE BERKLEY PUBLISHING GROUP
Published by the Penguin Group
Penguin Group (USA) Inc.
375 Hudson Street, New York, New York 10014, USA
Penguin Group (Canada), 90 Eglinton Avenue East, Suite 700, Toronto, Ontario M4P 2Y3, Canada
(a division of Pearson Penguin Canada Inc.)
Penguin Books Ltd., 80 Strand, London WC2R 0RL, England
Penguin Group Ireland, 25 St. Stephen's Green, Dublin 2, Ireland (a division of Penguin Books Ltd.)
Penguin Group (Australia), 250 Camberwell Road, Camberwell, Victoria 3124, Australia
(a division of Pearson Australia Group Pty. Ltd.)
Penguin Books India Pvt. Ltd., 11 Community Centre, Panchsheel Park, New Delhi—110 017, India
Penguin Group (NZ), 67 Apollo Drive, Rosedale, North Shore 0632, New Zealand
(a division of Pearson New Zealand Ltd.)
Penguin Books (South Africa) (Pty.) Ltd., 24 Sturdee Avenue, Rosebank, Johannesburg 2196,
South Africa

Penguin Books Ltd., Registered Offices: 80 Strand, London WC2R 0RL, England

This book is an original publication of The Berkley Publishing Group.

PRINTING HISTORY
Heat trade paperback edition / September 2010

Library of Congress Cataloging-in-Publication Data

Hill, Joey W.
 Vampire trinity / Joey W. Hill. — Heat trade pbk. ed.
  p. cm.
 ISBN 978-0-425-23670-3
1. Vampires—Fiction. I. Title.
 PS3608.I4343V363 2010
 813'.54—dc22   2010012982

PRINTED IN THE UNITED STATES OF AMERICA

10 9 8 7 6 5 4 3 2 1

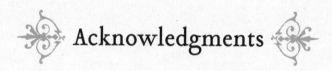 Acknowledgments

I'm always grateful for the insights of my editor, Wendy McCurdy, and my critique partners Sheri Fogarty, Ann Jacobs and Denise Rossetti, but they deserve special thanks this time. Gideon, Daegan and Anwyn's story started out as one long book, but it needed to be two in order for their relationship to evolve the way it should. Though my faithful readers know this isn't the first time that has happened to me, sometimes an author can't see the forest for the trees. I couldn't have figured out how to make it into two fulfilling stories without the help, guidance and encouragement of Wendy, Sheri, Ann and Denise.

I also send thanks to Susan Allison, who made the executive decision to allow it to be two books. Your support of my work is a continued joy. Finally, a particular thanks to Ann Jacobs, who was the one who saw that the ménage relationship needed to have two distinct phases of development, and therefore allowed me to devote more time and richness to the way these three fell in love.

I hope the readers will love them as well, but if there are any shortcomings in either book, that responsibility is all mine, as always.

Last, but not least, thanks to Rachel for "God's roadmap"; for the guidance it provided to Gideon, Daegan and Anwyn, and for the validation it provided to me.

Vampire Trinity

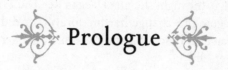

Prologue

"INSATIABLE," one of her favorite songs, was weaving its magic through the shadows and flashing lights of Club Atlantis. Bodies moved in sinuous silhouette on the dance floor to that sensual underbeat, somewhere between slow and fast. Her attuned senses detected a variety of things. Perfumes and colognes, the musk of arousal and perspiration. Provocative laughter, the rush of a hundred different conversations and stories. Club Atlantis was a cauldron of life tonight, the sexual heat rising by the moment.

The sharp snap of a whip. A cry of pain, mixed with lust. She cocked her head. Someone was using a single tail in the public play area. Someone closer, probably along Pleasure Alley, was caning their slave, that sharp, brief slice through the air that most wouldn't hear, lost in the dance music or other crowd noise.

But she heard it. This was a dream, and in dreams the senses detected whatever the dream demanded. However, even if she really stood in Atlantis right now, she would hear, smell and see everything as acutely. The aromas, the variations of light and shadow, even the currents of air, stirred by the movement of bodies dancing, writhing, fucking or kneeling, would swirl along her skin and leave invisible imprints like intricate tattoos.

In dream or reality, she could experience all those things now, because she was a vampire.

In this dream, however, she was still her human self. It was one of her favorite dreams, and it had been coming more frequently of late. It was five years ago, the night she met Daegan Rei. Did a moth know that the flame was going to change her life forever, or did she simply fly toward that heated embrace, knowing it would offer her something she couldn't give herself?

In the end, the answer didn't really matter. The moth had never wanted the choice.

~

Making her rounds through Club Atlantis on a busy night gave her a deep, abiding pleasure. Feeling the energy spun by all the people here, come to satisfy their craving to Dominate or be Dominated, knowing that she'd contributed to almost every detail of the setting and atmosphere for that experience—there was nothing like it. As she moved through the club, she watched faces, emotions, body language. She'd zero in on anything that wasn't quite right, someone who wasn't getting the experience they desired. She worked the floor, providing guidance where needed, a warm word, a subtle suggestion, a light touch to direct attention in the right place.

A Mistress herself, she was aware of the gazes of unattached submissives following her, hoping she might choose one of them for a session, as she sometimes did. She also felt the speculative glances of Masters and Mistresses who'd like the chance to share a sub together, learn from each other's techniques.

The desire to maximize a customer's experience wasn't about money, though Club Atlantis's success spoke for itself. She understood what each unique soul sought here, and whether she could provide it. It was a skill she loved having. Her heart beat inside Atlantis, because it was who she was, what she wanted.

At times, in her bed at the end of an evening, she'd feel that heartbeat slow, and a yearning would settle into her, to find what others found within her walls. She knew her needs were more complex than most Mistresses. She wanted someone to belong to her, to be her slave exclusively, his heart, soul and mind willingly surrendered. However, there was an additional, vital component to her need as well, one that seemed beyond her power to describe. When it at last stood before her, in whatever manifestation met her deepest desires, she knew she would understand it.

That night, her intuition and her yearning clasped hands and gave her that miracle. A gift and curse at once, as Fate often was.

She drifted along the eastern wing of the club, with its wide platform view of the bar, the dance area and one of the public play areas that was crafted like a metal undersea world. Cages were designed as a coral reef, submissives bound there with restraints like seaweed. The St. Andrew's crosses were weathered driftwood and embedded in the side of a partial shipwreck. More slaves were bound upon them. Gold pieces of treasure were scattered over the sandy ground and caught the flickering torch-light. Over the darker area of the shipwreck, a shadow lamp made it look as if schools of colorful fish, sharks and manta rays were passing over the mostly naked bodies restrained there.

The center feature of that public play area was a large water tank. A staff submissive was on display, her long hair floating free, her upper body bare except for ropes that created a shibari-style harness. It bound her wrists beneath her breasts. Her lower body was wrapped with tight latex to form a jeweled and slick mermaid's tail. A waterproof vibrator was inside her, and the control was on the outside of the tank, where guests could adjust the speeds, and watch her flounder and writhe like a graceful fish at the stimulation in the tank's confined space.

Since she of course didn't have the gills of a mermaid, she had a close-fitting, discreet oxygen mouthpiece beneath the jeweled mask she wore, the tank disguised behind the water ferns. In addition to that precaution, a Dom in a dark wet suit watched over her. He'd "caught" her and bound her in the harness, an intricate underwater rope perfor-mance, and now added to the torment the patrons were administering by touching her as he pleased, occasionally bringing her up to his mouth and giving her air in place of the mask.

It was a complex scene, but both were well trained. They also were husband and wife. The team of John and Tori had become a favorite attraction.

She moved onward, past the dance floor, and then to the mezzanine, where she could get a different view of the floor and the bar. While many BDSM clubs didn't permit alcohol, she knew it helped relax and stimulate. Plus, she had a large clientele who came to dance and be entertained merely as voyeurs. Those going to the underground level for rougher play knew that they would be required to take a Breathalyzer test. They had to prove they were sober enough for safe play in private. Knowing that, the patrons regulated themselves. And in the public areas, she had more well-trained staff that blended and kept things in line.

Her snug skirt hugged her hips, her stilettos placed precisely as she moved along the mezzanine. She was aware of the way her body moved, from the quiver of her breasts to the swing of her hips, the brush of her thighs as she tightened those muscles to walk sure and upright on the heels. James, her head of security, followed. They usually did these rounds together, because she gave him insight on who might need extra attention from his people. Being very good at what he did, he usually identified those trouble spots at the same time. But exactly because he was good, he wanted the additional set of eyes, the viewpoint of what he might miss.

So far, tonight's crowd was a good one. Of course, Atlantis didn't allow just anyone in their doors. Even a guest pass required thirty minutes with a staff person, discussing the rules of Atlantis. Anyone who gave off warning signals, or appeared to be paying lip service to those rules, didn't make it past the lobby. The vetting for the underground level was even more stringent.

She paused at the rail, scanning. Even as she assessed, she enjoyed as well. Watching the give-and-take between power and surrender. Whispering hands, bodies straining and needy. A slave's eyes glazed in lust, the Master's expression deep in the zone, registering every nuance of a submissive's reaction. Once stepping over the threshold of Atlantis, the shell was left behind. This was the sanctuary for the Freudian id, the primitive impulses and needs of the soul.

Impressions like those came at her in varying waves of heat, and she rode those currents like a shadow dolphin in the undersea exhibit, her attention wandering over the floor.

Then she felt something extraordinarily different. Turning her head with unerring instinct toward the source, she saw a man leaning against the bar.

Though he was all the way across the main floor, he locked gazes with her. In that brief second, he caught her breath, took it away from her with all the power of a black-and-white movie, though she couldn't explain why or how it happened. She'd been a Dominant all her life, recognizing it quickly after reaching sexual maturity. It was something she didn't doubt in herself, in her blood. Yet this male was no submissive.

In fact, he was pure, 100 percent Dominant in all aspects of his life. He would possess the woman he chose, body, heart and soul. Such a woman would have to be as strong as he was to hold her own and demand his soul in return. He would be satisfied with nothing less. He was looking for an equal, a Mistress. A unique, complex Mistress who would surrender to him and him alone, time and again, because it would simply be that way between them.

While all sizes and shapes of people came in here, she'd seen her share of devastatingly handsome men, both Masters and subs. With his dark eyes, close-cropped hair and powerfully built body, this one certainly had no trouble catching female attention. But she was barely aware of anything about him except his eyes in that vital first-impression moment. A moment that lengthened into a cycle of accelerating heartbeats as he straightened, left his drink and came toward her.

She was aware of every inch of her skin under his gaze. That heartbeat that slowed in the quiet hours, when Atlantis's lights shut off, was pounding as rapidly as the rock beat on the dance floor.

He was inevitable, the most devastatingly sexy word she'd ever applied to a man. When he stopped before her, the first words he spoke made it clear he understood it as much as she did. It wasn't a pickup line. The three words were command, intention and destiny, all at once.

"I want you."

That yearning she felt in the small hours of the morning, the answer was this man. When the third point of the triangle came, the one who would be her slave, who would surrender and utterly belong to her, she was certain that yearning would become something even sweeter, sharper, even more impossible to describe. Fulfillment, a three-point star so powerful its light would explode inside her, bringing unimaginable emotional and physical pleasure.

~

Of course, on the reality of that night, she hadn't had that clarity, but in the drifting fantasy of her dream, she knew it as truth, her desires meeting her memories.

She'd taken him to the Rose Room. It was remarkable that she'd chosen that room that night. Wall-to-floor-to-ceiling mirrors, the only prop a pedestal in the center with a vase of bloodred roses, a trail of petals scattered across the reflective floor.

He'd glanced into the room, a warrior's caution, but it hadn't given him pause. She'd barely crossed the threshold when his arms closed around her. She turned in that embrace, let out a small shudder of desire as he lifted her up against the wall and tore the side of her snug skirt all the way to the hip. She hadn't worn any panties under it, because of the tightness of the garment and because she liked to feel her thighs compressing her labia as she walked, that pleasurable friction of skin on skin.

There were inviolate rules about protection, safety, boundaries. She knew there would be none of that between them. When he lowered his hand to touch her, she arched with a moan. Finding her cunt, he pushed two fingers into soaking wet heat that clamped down on him, a shuddering spasm of response.

He freed himself from his jeans. She dug her fingers into his shoulders as he gripped her hips, pushed forward and pinned her deep and hard. He dove deep, to the hilt, and a sound between a breath, a moan and a cry wrenched from her throat. She refused to close her eyes, wanting him to see, to know that she did all of this willingly. That she was giving him control, not surrendering it.

His lips curled back from sharp fangs, a crimson flicker going through the dark eyes. The pupils were expanding, taking over the whites, those traces of hellfire threading through them. As he pressed her up against the smooth mirror, she realized she couldn't see him in any of the hundreds of reflections. It was just her, and yet she'd never felt more . . . not alone. His hand wrapped in her hair and exposed her throat. Crimson became flame in those wholly dark eyes, and then his fangs were there, sinking deep, just like his cock. Sensation exploded through every nerve ending, starting where they were joined.

That was all it took. She came hard on him, her fluids gushing over his thick length, her body wracked by convulsions as the pleasure gripped her in relentless hands, like his. He was still moving inside her, thrusting with brutal purpose, his mouth taking blood from her throat.

There was no opportunity or desire for games, no sense that she needed to prove to him that she was a Mistress, used to holding the reins. He knew all of it, knew all of her. It was frightening and thrilling at once. Handling him would be the challenge of her life.

She had no knowledge of paranormal beings, hadn't really given them any thought, but she accepted who and what he was as if she'd always known. Her heart had been waiting for a vampire.

~

As Anwyn slowly surfaced from the dream, her thighs were trembling, damp, telling her that she'd climaxed. Reaching behind her, she slid her hand down Gideon's rib cage and over the curve of his bare buttock, his thigh tucked up beneath hers. Listened to his even breathing. The third member of their uncertain triangle, he'd come five years later, to her present, whereas Daegan was currently absent, a hole in her heart she was glad she had Gideon to assuage.

He cinched his arm around her waist more securely, pressed his face in her hair, reminding her he was there, his heat and strength behind her. While she liked the tactile reminder, she didn't need to have it to feel his presence. Ever since she'd third-marked him, he was in her very soul, and she wanted him there. At a moment like this, she almost felt balanced, for Daegan's presence from the dream was still so close it felt as if he were in front of her, Gideon behind.

She'd hold on to the peace the temporary illusion gave her in sleeping hours, because peace was a far more rare commodity when she faced the reality of what she'd become. A vampire, turned against her will, infected by a schizophrenic sire with unpredictable seizures and dangerous surges of bloodlust. A vampire who might never have full control of her life again, who was dependent on a vampire hunter who'd become her third-marked servant by accident, and a powerful vampire she blamed for not being there when she'd needed him.

At least when she met Daegan in her dreams, she didn't carry the burden of his betrayal. The thousand small angers that had culminated in his leaving. In her dreams, she was allowed to simply miss him, and wish he'd come back. The insidious shadow creatures in her brain that sometimes followed her into her dreams had no power when he was there, which made his presence all the more welcome.

Every waking moment required her to accept her deepest fear. Her control, cultivated carefully over a lifetime, could now be scattered like bowling pins. The schizophrenic mood shifts brought rages, delusions and hungers. They swamped her systems and turned her into a force of destruction. Such episodes could come at any time. Some days it was every few hours. Occasionally she had the peace of a full day without one.

The fledgling bloodlust was a whole different ballgame from the seizures. The seizures were a physical ravagement of her systems, a mind-shrieking session of crazy, murderous madness. With bloodlust, she *would* have what she wanted, and anything that stood in her way was fair game. Now that Gideon was a third-mark servant, she had less fear of harming him irreparably, but she was grateful she'd fallen in with a male who'd lived so much of his life as a warrior. In her sensible moments, she was able to appreciate the complex choreography of defense and offense strategies that came so naturally to him. When Daegan was here, they'd coordinated their movements to help distract or restrain her, anticipate which direction her violence would strike and contain it before it happened.

I want you, no matter what you are. I always will. Never doubt it.

Daegan had said those words to her before he left. She remembered the touch of his long-fingered, large hands, the sensual, firm mouth. The unending strength of his body, surging into hers. She remembered his many expressions, the dangerous smile that always felt like a special gift for her. He hadn't smiled much, the days before he'd left, but there'd been less cause, for all of them.

In his absence, with Gideon here, she'd realized she didn't want to have it back the way it was. She wanted something better for them, for all three of them. Gideon was the missing piece that could make it work, mingling the past, present and future in a way that gave her hope in her dreams.

Unfortunately, Gideon was resolved that he was merely a temporary measure until she found a "real" servant. In fact, that resolve had grown steadily stronger. Since she had full access to his mind, there was no hiding from the harsh truth. The vampire hunter, who had become more dedicated and intuitive to her well-being every day for the past month, had no intention of being any vampire's permanent servant.

Ever.

1

Daegan had explained it was vital he get to the Council, that he was past due to report to them face-to-face on the events of the past couple of weeks. She understood that logically, but once Brian arrived, Daegan took his leave almost as soon as he discussed her condition with the vampire scientist and ensured he understood the role Daegan needed him to fill. Use his scientific skills to determine if there were ways to get the debilitating seizures and convulsions that didn't fit with a normal vampire transition under control, and use his strength as a vampire to help Gideon when she had those seizures, so she didn't cause harm to anyone, including herself.

Giving her and Gideon another look, Daegan had turned back to Brian. "Until I return, until this is managed, the relationship she has with her servant is exclusive."

"Damn right about that," Gideon muttered.

Brian's brow lifted, his gaze cutting to Gideon and then coming back. "Not my type," he noted dryly, with a hint of a smile at Gideon's scowl. "But I understand."

Before she could catch up on all the undercurrents in that exchange, Daegan put his large hands on her shoulders and gave her that look that said not to cross him on what he was about to say. It immediately stiffened her spine.

"Lord Brian is in charge until my return. Period. Follow his direction as you would follow mine." A grimness tightened his jaw at the look in her eye. "Perhaps better than that. I trust him and he is here to help you. All right, *cher*? If I have lost your trust, trust at least that this man can make things better for you, if you will let him."

He said it flatly, no inflection, but it sent a shard of glass through her heart anyway. She'd managed a nod, and because she knew he'd be gone in a few moments, she reached up, framed his face, her thumbs passing over his lips. *Don't leave me, don't leave me.*

Soon after she'd been turned, he'd taken her blood as a sire would, so he could speak in her mind or hear her thoughts as needed, but he'd vowed he'd do that only when essential to her well-being. He'd been well aware that bloodtaking had been another betrayal of past promises made. So she didn't know whether she was glad or not he'd apparently honored his vow and missed her involuntary thought.

Closing his hand over her wrist, he gazed down into her face. Those dark eyes were so unfathomable to her, and yet so absorbed in everything she was, she almost swayed into him. But she managed to hold her ground. He lifted his gaze to Gideon, standing just behind her.

Though Gideon usually told Daegan to fuck off when he tried to issue him a directive, Anwyn knew that Gideon shared Daegan's confidence in Lord Brian. He also seemed to understand this moment was not about that. "We'll be here," the hunter said. "Watch your ass and get it back here as soon as you can. She needs you."

Fucking handling her, the both of them, Gideon saying what she couldn't bring herself to say.

Daegan raised a brow. "And you, vampire hunter?"

"I need you like I need a chancre on my dick. Thanks for asking."

A cough came from the corner of their sitting room, where Debra and Brian were setting up a variety of equipment that looked like what she'd see in a private, well-funded hospital. Daegan sent Brian a quizzical look but the attractively built male with dark blond hair and direct green eyes straightened, nodded with a serious mien. "We'll do whatever we can for her."

Daegan nodded, looked back toward Anwyn and Gideon, but it was Gideon's gaze he met. "It turns out you are not the third wheel after all,

Gideon Green. Right now I am. Care for her. I will be back soon, but if she needs anything, you let me know."

His words appeared to stun Gideon. Anwyn didn't know what to say, but the vampire didn't seem to require her words. With an oath, he jerked her to him, tasting her mouth, rough and deep. It had barely started before he let her go, so suddenly she staggered back. With his exceptional vampire speed, he was already gone, Gideon's hands on her shoulders.

"That lacked some of his usual finesse." Gideon cleared his throat.

She locked her jaw against the surge of emotion that came with Daegan's abrupt absence, the immediate emptiness inside her. Instead, she let herself feel the tightening of Gideon's hands, his silent understanding. He always assumed that he was second fiddle to Daegan, but she knew that wasn't correct. She didn't know if she could explain it herself, however, or if she even wanted to do so. How could she explain that there was something in her, growing ever larger daily, that needed both of them in her life, for different reasons but no less strongly, not one over the other? Particularly when she was nursing a deep sense of inexplicable hurt toward one, and the other one considered this a temporary role at best.

Moving away, she turned and faced Lord Brian. She read people well, particularly men. She'd been braced for Lord Brian to be arrogant and overbearing, a less palatable form of Daegan. Perhaps it was the title, which she understood was given to all born vampires, or those awarded a Region. Brian was the former, the son of a British Region Master.

Much as she was reluctant to admit it while she was out of sorts with him, Daegan had understood her better than that. He had told her some about her new warden before the scientist arrived. Lord Brian was a rarity in his world. Though young for a vampire at eighty years, he'd shown no interest in becoming a territory overlord or Region Master. His ambition was wholly targeted toward a better understanding of the physiology of vampires. His studies included everything from the chemical makeup of the bond between vampires and servants to whether or not vampire vulnerability to the sun could be overcome. He also headed up project teams that were trying to cure the two diseases that affected vampires, Ennui and the Delilah virus.

His servant, Debra, was the first he'd chosen for himself, versus his parents' choice during his maturation. She appeared to be an exceptional lab assistant, quietly efficient, and yet from the way the two brushed as they moved, tuning the equipment, untangling leads and setting dials, it was obvious their intimacy involved the usual depth one would expect between vampire and servant. She was his, in whatever way he wanted her, and she didn't seem to have any problems with that.

However, Anwyn did detect a desire for something more in Debra. Though it wasn't evident in Debra's body language or expression, Anwyn didn't need a crystal ball to know what longing drove Brian's assistant. Being a servant required she give him everything of herself, yet accept however much or little Brian chose to give her, the right of a species that felt itself superior to humans. It was the root of the reason Anwyn had never capitulated to being Daegan's servant when she was human.

That thought made her gaze stray to Gideon. How, then, could she blame Gideon for fiercely maintaining that, third mark or not, he would not join her for a lifetime commitment in the vampire world? Would she want him to do so? See the proud man subjected to the things she knew happened there?

The vampire blood in her already clamored that it wasn't his choice, that it was hers. It scared her, how strong that voice was, how fiercely she wanted to hold on to that third-mark connection like an unbreakable chain She somehow already understood how Brian, born with such blood, didn't even question that his servant was his to do with as he wished, no matter that she seemed to be devoted to that purpose for him.

The human side of Anwyn, struggling valiantly to survive, wouldn't countenance taking that choice from Gideon. She didn't care what Daegan said about a third-marked servant being essentially trapped in the role for life, based on Council law.

But she didn't want to do without him, either.

Well, there was nothing she could do with that for right now. Higher priority was making sure she didn't drain Atlantis clientele during fits of bloodlust or rip off their heads. Complimentary drink coupons wouldn't make up for that little faux pas.

"So what do we need to do first?" she asked, trying to sound matter-of-fact instead of resentful and wary.

Debra produced a folded blue gown, the inevitable open-on-one-side degradation. "This is so we can have access to the leads we'll be taping at different nerve and pressure points."

It smelled like a lab, bringing the image of hospitals and silver, sterile instruments. Frightened lab rats, not knowing anything but cage walls and cruel procedures that denied their value except as tools.

"Anwyn. Hey." Gideon settled his hands on her shoulders again. "Can she wear an open shirt instead? Something familiar?"

"Certainly." Brian stepped forward. His voice was kind, firm, but his eyes were assessing her every reaction, increasing that lab rat feeling. "Miss Naime . . . or do you prefer Mistress?"

"Only if you want me to tie you up and shove a vibrator up your ass." She closed her eyes, fighting for calm, so she had no idea how he reacted to that. She needed to remember that Daegan had indicated many vampires didn't care for humor. They often took it for being a smart-ass. Which, in this case, would probably be a fair accusation.

"I want to call you what you'd prefer," he said smoothly. "I understand this is difficult. This is a partnership between us, to determine how to stabilize you during your transition and further, if needed. Even through the measures we may have to take to protect you and others during your seizures, you have my respect. We're here to help you."

"If anyone can help, he can." Debra's voice had her eyes opening again. The somber girl had a slim nose and a small mouth, her thickly lashed gray eyes packing a punch. Without those eyes, she might have been plain, a woman who dressed in comfortable shoes and slacks, which only accentuated the skinny body and long, narrow hands. But Anwyn's sharp eyes detected a decent figure, heavy breasts. With those eyes and the right clothes, her blond hair brushed out, she'd be impossible for any man to overlook. Except she appeared to have eyes for only one male. One who had delivered his polite speech and was now elbows deep in that piece of equipment again, brow furrowed and a lock of hair falling over his forehead as he muttered what sounded like expletives at it. Apparently, Debra was in charge of the touchy-feely hand-holding part of things.

Gideon had left her, disappearing into Daegan's room, and now he returned with one of his button-down shirts. Like most all of Daegan's clothing, it was black, but it was worn, soft and easy on the skin. "Will this do, Mistress?"

He used the title deliberately, she knew, always at the right moment, gauged to help her get a sense of balance. She'd known the first night she'd met him he was neither submissive nor Dominant, even though he'd come to her club in the capacity of a submissive. He'd come spoiling for a fight, looking for a way to exorcise the pain in his soul. He wanted to serve a woman, not a vampire. Unfortunately, his timing had landed him with responsibility for both, until she could get past this. His damn sense of honor wouldn't allow him to leave until then, no matter how much he abhorred what she'd become.

She was glad he wasn't in her mind for the bitterness that fountained in her at the thought. The two men to whom she'd felt the strongest connection in her life both had reasons to want to be away from her. She guessed she should be grateful they'd managed to stagger their escape schedules, Daegan taking his now, Gideon planning his for later.

When she went into the bathroom to change, it took an act of will not to put her fist through the vanity mirror that no longer had any function, at least in terms of checking her appearance. She changed in the bathroom without looking at it, feeling her blood pounding in her throat. At least one man in her life would never leave her. Barnabus, the vampire who'd done this to her. Her true sire. Her lip curled. Planting his residual schizophrenia in her, so his voice sometimes captured her throat, made her say all sorts of despicable things during seizures. Even when she wasn't having seizures, those shadow creatures in her head, the ones who supposedly weren't real, overrode everything else until she could barely see or think. She could only huddle in a corner, hands locked over her head, body rocking as she muttered and shouted at them to stop.

How many times had she passed homeless people lying in their nests of garbage, doing the same? No one else knew what it was like to have them in there, did they?

While she couldn't bring herself to feel pity for the vampire that had violated her on so many levels, there were times where she admitted enough empathy to agree with Brian's decision—though a hard-fought one with Daegan—to spare Barnabus for the time being. He'd been put in a temporary holding facility of Daegan's design so they had access to her "biological sire's" blood as long as they needed it. Once Brian had arrived, he'd agreed to take on custody of the vamp, employing some of his vampire and scientific contacts in the States to take over Barnabus's care from Daegan. Periodically he sent Debra to that undisclosed location to get more blood, Anwyn's anonymity carefully protected from Barnabus's new wardens. Brian had explained he wanted to study the way schizophrenia interacted with Barnabus's vampire nature, and assured Daegan he'd call him in for termination when those experiments were completed, unless he could rescue the vamp's mind.

She doubted that was possible. Just as a symptom of her turning, the voices were so integrated in her head. She hadn't been born with it in her genetic makeup, like Barnabus. Of all of them, Gideon understood those voices the best, because he'd stood in her mind, listening to them, watching them. But he could get in a car, drive out of range of her mind in a few hundred miles, and he wouldn't hear them anymore. The only thing that seemed to make them still and quiet for her was his presence in her head, or Daegan's, but the voices were always there.

Turning away from the mirror that showed no image of her, she left the bathroom. She knew she looked pale, strained, but before anyone could offer empty platitudes, she sat down in the chair Brian had positioned near the equipment for her.

"Just do what you need to do," she said.

The scientist nodded, began to attach sensors to her skin. Fortunately they were wireless, the equipment sensitive enough to pick up the necessary readings as long as she was within a few feet of it. Though his touch was relaxed and impersonal, it still made her tense. She didn't care for people touching her without permission. Even less these days, since it often felt like there were things crawling under her skin that jumped at outside contact.

Once again, though, Gideon and Daegan were different. They seemed to make that reaction lessen, instead of increase. Picking up on her needs, Gideon ran a hand down her arm, on the opposite side from Brian. "I'd have brought you one of mine," he said, nodding to the shirt. "But—"

"But you only have the shirt you're wearing." She tried to keep her tone light. "I guess one of these days we should go out and get you more than one change of clothes."

He grunted. "Not ready to be a kept man yet, thanks. I'll just grab one of Daegan's overpriced shirts if I anticipate ruining my T-shirt."

"I didn't realize he'd left that much behind," she said nastily. Debra glanced at her, but said nothing.

"He's coming back, Anwyn," Gideon said. "He doesn't know how to stay away from you." *Neither do I.*

He said that in her head, a quick voice caress, but she wasn't ready to be soothed. "You don't like vampires. You don't even want him to come back."

"I like you. And you do want him to come back. That's what matters."

"If you don't stop being so agreeable, I will punch you in the face. It's entirely unlike you."

He gave her his faint smile, a hint of the breathtaking appeal it gave his rugged features. "All right. I hope he trips and falls on the pointy end of all those stakes he's carrying. Gets a nasty, oozing infection that smells bad so you won't want him within twenty feet of you. How's that?"

"Better." When his fingers found hers, she tightened her grip in response. Inhaling the scent of Daegan's shirt, she felt the fabric against her skin and imagined it was his skin. This wasn't the first time Daegan had taken a trip away from her. As the Council's private assassin, he traveled quite a bit. She'd been fine with that, because her own life kept her pretty busy. Sometimes, though, she'd sleep in his bed the first day or two, absorbing his scent to tide her over while he was gone. Before, she'd never have revealed that kind of weakness for another, but of course the information was there for Gideon. He'd probably suggest they sleep in Daegan's bed tonight, because he picked up a lot of things in her mind, even though they'd made a privacy pact of sorts.

She and Gideon had a tacit agreement, that she would limit her forays into his mind, trying to keep it high level when she couldn't stay out completely, using the ability for conversation and trying not to probe his thoughts uninvited. It took practice and skill, somewhat like not using her vision when her eyes were open, but she was getting better at it. She couldn't do it during their more passionate encounters, but he'd seemed fine with that.

In turn, he'd agreed that when he was in her mind to monitor the indicators of her violent transition seizures, he'd practice mental "peripheral vision" to ignore other thoughts that might float by. Most vampires had the ability to restrict their servants' access to their minds, but most vampires didn't take full servants as fledglings, or deal with the unusual transition issues she had. She had to trust Gideon more than she'd ever trusted anyone.

Without probing his mind, she knew enough about Gideon to know he was out of sorts about Daegan's absence as well. He'd rationalize it, tell himself it was because Daegan was useful to help with Anwyn's transition. She didn't argue with him over it. With so many things uncertain right now, there was no sense goading Gideon, making him face possibilities that had only started to develop between the three of them before Daegan had left.

~

For the next week, Brian hooked her up to all sorts of monitoring equipment, but in the end she admitted she was glad she'd mostly held on to her patience. She'd had seven seizures during the first three days. Like those little balls sent up in the tornadoes to collect data, the monitors had given Brian a tremendous amount of data about predicting the episodes. He'd created the first cocktail and begun to inject it in her daily. Already it seemed to lessen the severity and frequency of the seizures, though he noted it likely wouldn't stand up against extreme stress factors.

He also couldn't predict if the injection was something she would need forever, or if, in time, the seizures would go away on their own. The shadow creatures in her head were something that the injections didn't change. Like the schizophrenia that had infected Barnabus's mind and spawned their presence in hers, only human drugs could address that, and her vampire blood would neutralize them. So that one she had to handle, but she could, with Gideon.

When he was in her mind, the shadow creatures tended to cower back into the shadows, not whisper so insidiously, as if they liked her best when she felt all alone. She'd lived most of her life adamantly independent, and probably the worst part of her transition was dealing with her dependence on others, her unpredictable loss of control. It was Gideon who had quickly recognized it could destroy what was left of her mind if some remedy wasn't found, and it was Daegan who had figured out the remedy. A third-marked servant, one who could balance and steady her, help her sort between what was real and those voices, while in theory she had command over him, a sense of control that dangerously wasn't a complete illusion.

A fledgling never took a third-marked servant, because they didn't have the control to keep the proper shields in between their two minds. Not only was it an etiquette issue, because no vampire was supposed to be that vulnerable and open to her human servant, but it also was hard for a servant to function if there were two running sets of thoughts going through his head at once. On a more serious note, if a vampire let her bloodlust run away with her, she might dive too deeply into the servant's soul, damage him psychologically.

Any one of those reasons would have kept her from marking Gideon, but mortally wounding him during one of her attacks took the decision away. Daegan made it for her, forced her to mark the vampire hunter. Gideon had made his peace with Daegan doing that. As for her, she didn't know if she was angry at the act, or if her anger was a cumulative net. She'd been blaming him for all of it, but was that just because she needed someone to blame?

Not only was she a vampire; she was starting out with three major handicaps in her scary new world. Number one: unstable, uncertain if the completion of her transition in another couple of months would bring the improvement it normally would, allowing her to take steps back into the nighttime world. Number two: a fledgling vampire with a full servant. Number three: a vampire who, more often than not, allowed her servant full access to her mind to monitor those seizures, and lend her mental and physical stability.

She did practice that curtain Daegan had taught her, to help screen her thoughts from Gideon so he didn't always have that running ticker tape of her subliminal thoughts in his mind. She also practiced increasing the thickness of the wall, because she knew there was no sense in not honing every skill she might need.

Sometimes, though, when Gideon slept in her bed, or with her in

Daegan's, his arms curled strong and sure around her hips, his head on her breast, lips so close to her nipple it ached for him in that nonstop carnality that seemed to plague and delight the vampire mind, she'd drift in his mind and see things there she wished she could forget.

As a human Mistress of a BDSM club, she'd already been a type of vampire. Feeding on the surrender of the males who came to her, the few who'd needed something extra special to let go of the reins and let her have them. She'd understood so many things about them without vampire senses, but now that she had those senses, it was almost irresistible to use that extra ability to forage that much deeper into a man's mind. Particularly this man.

His mind was as much a battleground as hers. Whereas her field of combat was between sanity and surrender to those voices, his was a siege force, clustered around an almost impenetrable fortress. His will to be what he'd always been was that fortress. The idea that he was becoming the antithesis of everything that had given his life purpose for the past ten years or so was an increasing horde outside the gate, growing louder and more insistent every day. It disturbed his dreams, even under her stroking hands. During their waking hours, his attention was all upon her, but she knew in the end, the battle in his dreams would determine the difference between temporal devotion to a cause and true loyalty, from his heart.

She'd been surprised, at the beginning, by how little her ability to be in Gideon's mind seemed to bother him. He encouraged her to do it if it would help her. But as she learned to navigate the pathways of his brain ever more deeply, she was chagrined to find out why. He felt he had few secrets she and Daegan didn't already know. He'd lost his girlfriend to a vampire in high school, and he had a brother who was now a vampire, as well as servant to one of the most powerful vampires known.

What he didn't realize, and what pained her, was finding how many of his thoughts and reactions were practically secrets to himself, things he'd buried far below his subconscious.

At different times, she'd pore over that buried treasure. Like when she hung in restraints, trying to get a grip on herself, or in the lethargic aftermath, when she lay on the couch, her head in Gideon's lap as he stroked it, lulling her into the deep sleep that the seizures often caused.

Like many men, he wasn't self-analytical. He knew what he knew about himself, and he assumed that was it. The inexplicable things he did didn't require any explanation, because that would require an examination of feelings. Amused, she thought it was fortunate men weren't required to do self-exams on their minds as women did for their breasts, because all manner of tumors would grow unchecked when they simply refused to turn their attention to them.

He didn't define his feelings about her. She needed help, and he helped her. That alone might have ruffled her feathers, not wanting to be some "damsel in distress" to him, but she saw other things. No matter how violent or ugly her attack, he hungered for the intimacy of the aftermath. Like when her head was in his lap, her fingers curled under his thigh, lashes brushing her cheeks, soft lips relaxed, coaxing his fingers to touch them. Every once in a while she'd nip him when he tried, playing with him when she felt good enough. But he wanted to touch her everywhere. He couldn't get enough of having her close. When she needed him so much, so clearly, there was no conflict for him.

Though it had been a long time since Gideon Green had had a woman in his life, he remembered with aching clarity what the casual intimacy felt like, as well as what it felt like to lose her. He would never again take for granted the ability to touch, flare his nostrils to take in her scent, or do any single thing to make her smile, to make life easier for her. Heavens above, he had his task cut out for him on that one.

She knew she hadn't accepted that this was the way the whole rest of her life could be. From that perspective, the lengthening of her life span wasn't a boon. She might need protection for the next few centuries to keep her from harming others. She might never again move freely down a city street, enjoying the night sounds and press of city crowds, go into Macy's and browse through lingerie or check out a new gallery.

Beyond her selfish interests, how could she ask them to commit their lives to this? Daegan, who wouldn't even leave to go get fresh blood when he'd been here, and Gideon, who'd become her shadow, sleeping right outside the cell they'd used for her seizures, until Brian had arrived. One very beneficial thing the scientist had brought with him were two sets of locking cuffs that couldn't be broken by her vampire strength. They allowed her to have the seizure wherever she was, rather than having to imprison her further. Being bound and caged was intolerable to her, but she'd had to bear it. Having only the restraints was at least an improvement.

She'd been able to go back to her bed during her daylight sleep, instead of staying in the cell. Still, with Brian's constant measurements and readings, and Gideon having to stick so close, there were times she intensely missed her solitude, her sanctuary from everything. Many mornings she'd lain alone in bed reading, listening to music, thinking over the night in the club, the adventures and banter of her staff. She'd taken that for granted, that freedom and ease of existence. The ability to truly be alone. How did she wrap her mind around a few centuries, when she couldn't conceive of living this way for a few months?

Daegan had told her the bloodlust would die down, become more manageable. Their "hope" was that the madness, Barnabus's schizophrenic shadows, would as well, when it wasn't fueled by that fledgling-crazed hunger or transition.

When it all became too much, she took advantage of the pleasure of her servant's body. How easy it was to use him like that appalled her in some ways, thrilled her in others. Gideon was generous with his body, as all men could be. She wanted to challenge him more, because she'd always required more than a cock and a pretty face. She wanted the soul as well. The first night they'd met, she'd made it clear that she would always ask more than he was used to giving, and he had responded just as she'd craved, with passion and fury both. Then she'd been turned.

If she could get past her fear of her new strength, her bloodlust, she would open that pleasurable battleground again. He would fight her—she knew it—for both her pleasure as well as his. He was a quick study that way. She'd always been very sexual, of course, but with a vampire's constitution, arousal was barely a thought away, and not in a damaging, addictive way. It was simply a part of her now, like her penchant for paintings of isolated landscapes and the fact she liked butter-pecan ice cream more than she liked strawberry. Desire was an ocean in her, always moving, always flowing.

Fortunately, a third-marked servant was well-disposed to keep up, even though she couldn't get past her fears to do much more than savage vanilla lovemaking, an edge to it that cut her to the bone, because she wanted so much more from him. The vampire hunter, with no clearcut mission or purpose now except seeing to her immediate needs.

It shamed her, her self-absorption. She wasn't the only one dealing with a radical transition to what her life had been. Gideon's conflicts could destroy him faster than a whole club full of vampires. He was her servant. She should be helping him. Though he always put her first, that dark side of him was getting stronger.

The Mistress in her had recognized it in him the first time he'd come into her club. A gravitational pull toward self-destruction.

If she didn't figure out how to face her fears, find a balance with the bloodlust and shadow voices, she wouldn't be the Mistress that helped him overcome that. She'd be the vampire that hastened it.

2

Present Day

THE phone by her bed was making a dovelike trilling. Belatedly, she realized it was the ringtone she'd programmed for Daegan's calls. Anwyn groggily groped for it, but a male hand reached over her, far more coordinated upon waking. Gideon was used to sleeping lightly, in case his enemies tried to gut him. She'd pointed out, more than once, that most would prefer to torture him first. Therefore, he could probably afford to sleep more deeply.

He opened the phone, tucked it in her hand and dropped a lingering kiss on her bare shoulder before sliding out of the bed, headed for the bathroom. He didn't always sleep with her during daylight hours, but yesterday had been a little rough. Brian had tried a different variation of the blood cocktail. It had worked in reverse, making her seize four times. Or was it five?

"*Cher*? Are you awake?"

"Yes." It took a moment to speak, and not just because she was having trouble getting conscious. That dream of their meeting had lingered, along with a tight ache of need for Daegan in her chest. In real time, that ache was wrapped up in the barbed wire of those things that still lay between them. Things that couldn't be resolved over a phone, damn it. "Is everything okay?"

"Yes." But there was a pause, as if Daegan was considering the answer. "I'll be here a little longer, but I wanted to check in, see how you were doing."

"Brian can give you a full report. Gideon has the spectator version." *Stop it*, she chided herself. God, what was it that turned her into a shrew every time she talked to him? In her dreams, she gave herself to him as if none of that was important.

"I'm sure. But I want to know how you are doing, *cher*." His tone, that deep timbre, sensual and stroking, rippled along her nerves. "I wanted to hear your voice."

She shifted to a sitting position, pushing her hair out of her eyes. "Lord Brian is helping me, just like you said. He's letting me work in my upstairs office for a couple hours each day, as long as I take these vital readings every fifteen minutes and keep my mind open to Gideon the whole time."

"I'm glad. It will keep getting better, *cher*. You're strong. Is Gideon taking good care of you?"

"He sleeps with me when it's bad. And he's always there . . . yes. He is helping."

A silence, full of too much being unsaid. It made her head hurt, made her want to curse, because she knew it was impossible to miss the resentment in her tone. She hadn't meant for it to be there. Goddamn it, yes, she did, but that shouldn't mean anything. "Daegan—"

"I'm glad he's there, and that Brian is making progress. I'll let you go back to sleep."

"Come home," she snarled. "And stop being such an ass."

She slammed the phone down on the night table, forgetting her strength. It still wasn't natural to her, having the ability to easily demolish an electronic device and split the cherrywood top of the table, sending a slender crack snaking six inches toward the edge.

"Damn it. Why couldn't I have found a typical, shortsighted, clueless male?" Anwyn pressed her fingertips to her temples, wondering how it was possible for her to be developing a migraine. Vampires didn't get migraines. Of course, her transition from human to vampire hadn't followed the usual pattern. With her luck, she'd still get the common cold and menstrual bloat. If that was the case, she would throw away her morals and kill someone. Being an unstable, schizophrenic vampire with PMS was too much to bear on top of it all.

"You called?"

She glanced up. Gideon was back in the doorway. He could be downstairs, or even out on the street, and still be in her mind, but he rarely strayed that far, knowing that Brian wasn't Daegan. When she lost it, she had to have Gideon close, had to have his touch. Gideon was hers, her servant, and somehow that made it more acceptable to her Mistress personality. As Daegan had predicted—damn him. Again.

The first time Brian had agreed she could try a short walk through the club during pre-opening hours, Gideon had been right with her, as had Brian. She'd been so nervous she'd sweated through her clothes. Those shadow voices in her head had mocked her the whole time, until she wanted to scream at them to shut up.

Her nervousness had been understandable. Up until that test walk, the last time her heels had crossed the polished floors and rich carpets, she'd nearly killed Gideon and herself. This time was much less eventful. A quick ten-minute stroll, where she couldn't remember what she'd said to anyone, and she had a seizure within minutes of returning to her apartment. She'd made herself repeat the process every day since then—every day Brian's readings said it was okay—until she could do a thirty-minute round of all the club areas, see and be seen, without the excessive perspiration and seizure marking the occasion. She never went over thirty minutes, though, immediately returning to her office or the underground apartment. Gideon never had to remind her of the time.

She had plenty of resentment and rebellion in her against what had been done to her, but she'd seen what could happen if she acted out. Sometimes she could still feel the blood on her hands, woke from nightmares where she was slamming Gideon against a wall, smashing his head against the steel support beam.

So she worked her ass off with Brian, cooperated fully with him and Gideon to get this under control. Obeyed Brian's direction because she couldn't handle the idea of hurting anyone. Big, bad Mistress, reduced to a cowering, insecure basement creature.

She couldn't visit the club during opening hours yet. The types of energies that swamped a BDSM fetish club during open hours were definitely something she wasn't yet stable enough to handle. She tried not to think about the fact she might never be able to handle it, might never again experience that rush of walking the floor during peak hours, except in her dreams.

Pushing that away, she focused on the man leaning in her bedroom door. The sight of him eased some of her irritation. He handled her tantrums, her short temper, understanding what they were, such that he even snarled back at her on more than one occasion, which actually made her feel better. Made her feel human, though she knew that phrase wasn't necessarily applicable to her anymore.

A few days ago, she'd made him sit still for one of the Atlantis staff, Chantal, to trim his hair, rather than letting him hack it with scissors himself. She'd shortened the shoulder length, but cleverly kept his dark locks a little longish over the brow, the lengths uneven so it fell around his strong face and corded throat with unruly strands. It framed the midnight blue eyes, that devastatingly handsome Irish ancestry only enhanced by the smoother cut. He was dressed now, wearing his T-shirt and jeans, boots and battered leather jacket with a warrior's grace on that lean, muscular body. He had about nine weapons cleverly concealed beneath the clothes, but she knew where they all were.

She'd had the pleasure of shoving him to her bed and stripping him, divesting him of every wooden and steel knife strapped to his calves or slipped into holsters under his arms and at the small of his back. She'd unbuckled the wrist gauntlets with their wooden arrows and taken away his jacket with the nine-millimeter. Tugged off the boots that held his toe blade.

She hadn't been a vampire long, but it was impossible to ignore the dangerous, erotic undercurrents of it, her stripping him of his weapons against her, him allowing her to do so, his ravenous, predatory gaze telling her he'd fight her only to give her the pleasure of overpowering him.

The first time she'd stripped him that way, she'd used one of the knives, tracing the trinity mark he now bore on his chest, leaving a rivulet of blood she could lick away. It made his hands fist in her hair, his breath draw in, that male groan of need wrenching from his throat. She'd reveled in his arousal at the stimulation of pain and pleasure both, even as she felt his emotional turmoil. He liked giving her blood, liked nourishing her, though he didn't want to feel that way.

When he'd first darkened her door, he'd craved a Mistress almost as much as he hated the part of himself that did. It made him unpredictable, sometimes hazardous in his lusts, but on that they were now well matched. She took a steadying breath. Though there were many things about her life she wished she could change, having Gideon here wasn't one of them.

"You called?" he repeated. "For a clueless, shortsighted male?"

She scowled. "It was better when he didn't have access to my mind. If I needed to be pissed off at him, but didn't really want him to know every detail about it, he'd come home, because he wouldn't really know how mad I was."

Gideon raised a brow. "So you want him to come back and let you be mad at him in person, where he can suffer the in-person effect of your state of pissed-off-at-him-ness?"

"You can't say that three times fast."

"I wouldn't try. The call didn't go well?"

"I've had less impersonal conversations with convenience-store clerks."

"Anwyn."

She closed her eyes. "Oh, Gideon. Why won't he come home?"

"You know why." Sitting on the edge of the bed, he took over the massaging motion on her temples with his large hands. "He's trying to take care of the Council's European to-do list so they'll give him what he wants. Time. Time for you to get past the transition, learn to manage it, before you have to appear before them for their validation bullshit."

"Yeah, that's all true. But I'm not wrong, either. He's staying away."

Gideon paused in his ministrations. "Does he know this is still his home?"

She looked up at him. "What does that mean?"

"You know what I mean."

Yeah, she did. Never mind that someone within the Council had betrayed Daegan, betrayed his location, something he couldn't have foreseen. Her life had been completely changed because he was a vampire, a vampire with enemies. For five years they'd been together, and he'd been the unthinkable, a vampire who had respected her wishes not to be marked as his servant, even though they'd been lovers all that time. Something she'd learned from Gideon was almost unprecedented. If he'd marked her, made her his servant, it would have protected her, perhaps even avoided this whole situation.

But she was a Mistress in her own right. Though she'd surrendered to Daegan, something in her responding to his superior Mastery over her, she hadn't been able to take that leap of faith, surrender fully to a third mark that would have given him all of her. Still, he could have seduced her into it. Hell, she'd been so in love with him, there really wasn't anything he couldn't have persuaded her to do.

Sure. If he'd had no respect for her will, who she truly was. *Goddess, listen to me.* A lifetime of self-determination, fierce independence, and the moment she was turned to a vampire, viciously raped and had her life turned upside down, she was looking for someone to blame.

What a candyass.

She tilted her head back into Gideon's hard abdomen, his fingers brushing her cheeks. "You're not supposed to be listening in."

"You're getting yourself worked up. I can feel it. So I decided to listen in. He understands, Anwyn. He's giving you time to work it out in your own head."

"Problem is, he understands too well. He thinks as long as I'm mad about it, he needs to stay away. I need him here."

"To torture him?"

"Yes." *No. I just need you both here. I can't explain it.* Gideon was her left foot, Daegan her right, and she was hopping like some off-balance rabbit, waiting for wolves to notice her. On the days when her seizures would come up on her fast and unawares, sometimes so fast even Gideon couldn't react to them quickly enough with his precognitive senses, it was worse. But the temperature checks and other measurements Brian had been taking were helping. As long as she stayed completely regimented, no deviations from her schedule, no stressors. At the first, she was relieved to have some predictability, but now she was starting to feel as if she were in a prison again.

Maybe she'd blame Daegan less if he wasn't hiding from her behind some pathetic excuse of looking out for her best interests. If he was here, with her, the way he should be. But all of it . . . He'd known she'd miss him. He'd known how badly she'd react to the choices he took away from her. Yet he'd done it anyway, to protect her, to care for her. To save her life and force her to want to live.

She was hating him for loving her.

The wry humor dissipated in that wave of despair that could come up and swamp her, make her limbs shake at the memory of what had passed, what she faced in the future. She knew enough about Daegan's world to know a vampire had to be in control of herself at all times. If she became the weak member of the pack . . .

"Hey." Gideon's hands settled on her shoulders. "Neither Daegan nor I are going to let anything happen to you."

"You know, I used to scoff at those biblical passages about 'pride goeth before a fall.' There's a fine line between confidence and dependence. I think somewhere along the way I went from being confident in my self-sufficiency to dependent on it, to define myself. And here I am, completely dependent on you, a man who doesn't want to be a vampire's servant; Lord Brian, who I didn't even know three weeks ago, and his Dr. Frankenstein experiments; and Daegan, who . . . I can't even think about without feeling so angry. While missing him makes it hurt to breathe."

"Good thing you don't have to breathe anymore."

"Yeah, it's all a fucking cosmic joke." She surged up, away from his touch, scraping her hands through her hair. "Don't look at me like that, like you're gauging when I'm going to have a meltdown, like I'm some freaking mental patient. I just . . . Damn it . . ."

Gideon was already moving toward her, that look on his face. He could anticipate the seizures sometimes as much as two or three minutes before they happened, sometimes five or ten, if they came upon her when she was calmed. He already had Brian's restraints in his hands.

Though she was furious, she had enough control left to thrust out her wrists. Gideon latched them, then guided her to the floor so he could put on the ankle ones. She could roll around this way, thrash, destroy her clothes with vomit, but she couldn't get free.

Tears she never could seem to hold back when this happened spilled out of her eyes. The other good thing about the restraints was Gideon didn't have to leave her alone in the modified dungeon cell they'd used earlier. Sliding down the wall, he brought her into the shelter of his bent thighs, crossing his arms over her chest as she latched her fingers onto his forearms. While there was some danger that she could break bones even with the strength in her fingers, he'd told her he was a third mark; he'd heal fast. No matter how angry she got, no matter what was happening before or after, he never denied her this when the seizures came to take her.

"Gideon." She spoke between clenched teeth, straining against it. The cacophony of voices rose. They would suck her down into their particular hell and make her into one of them, a mindless monster who wanted only blood and death. Making her feel like she'd never emerge from it, or if she did, she'd wake up among the carnage she'd created. "Please . . . don't let them . . ."

"Don't fight it, sweetheart. That makes it worse. Let it come. We'll talk when it's done. It's not real. I promise. It's not."

She knew that until she was inside of it, and then there had never been anything so real to her, rendering her desolate, a broken creature who would have to pull it all back together again. Until one day, her mind would break and not heal again. Just like Barnabus, controlled by those voices, killing the innocent, destroying lives . . .

"If we can't get this under control . . . If I can't ever be on my own again, I want you to—"

She'd promised she'd never ask it of him, but she'd learned untested promises meant very little. The madness swept over her, brought on by her stress about Daegan's absence and the sheer unpredictability of the blood, the painful need of that dream, so it remained unsaid. But she knew Gideon knew.

Before the seizure took her away from him, she wondered if that was the real reason he'd been brought into her life. Not to protect her or preserve her life, but to end it.

"**I** NEED a reading during coitus."

Dinner was almost over. Anwyn glanced up from the last swallow of her blood cocktail, neatly presented in a wineglass that picked up the candlelight on the table. She'd never done much entertaining in her apartment beneath Atlantis, but she did have a six-person dining room table off the kitchen. Most of the time, she'd used it for spreading out tax receipts and other projects related to running her business, but since arriving Debra had dug things out of storage she'd almost forgotten she had. Place mats, attractive dinnerware pieces she'd picked up in boutiques more for their pleasing appearance than a coordinated theme.

"Excuse me?" she asked, aware of Gideon's gaze snapping up from his plate. While she and Brian were taking blood only, Brian's servant had prepared an appetizing combination of steak and potatoes for Gideon, with a side vegetable casserole and salad for her. She'd made enough to share with Gideon, if he felt the need to ingest something green and reasonably healthy.

When they'd first started this dinner ritual, Anwyn had been bemused by the way Gideon offered to help Debra in the kitchen. It was as if a middle-class boy surfaced from the vampire hunter he'd become, recalling the manners of that long-ago life. She'd felt a twinge of something, not unlike jealousy, when he'd gotten a smile from the girl. He'd told her his cooking talents were limited to his McDonald's drive-thru navigation skills. So he'd been put to work setting the table, chopping vegetables and performing other less complicated domestic tasks.

"Lord Brian needs to get readings while you're having sex, Mistress Anwyn," Debra, the paragon of culinary efficiency, said now. It was as if there'd been an unspoken communication from her Master that it would be better for her to lead on the topic. "As you know, the worst convulsions are triggered by negative stressors. The body experiences a different yet just as volatile type of stress during orgasm. Therefore, he needs to see the variations so he can further tune the injection he's giving you. Having readings from all your daily activities will help with that."

"I see."

On the floor of Club Atlantis, submissives addressed Dominants when given permission to do so, but to impart information, not to instruct. Vampires and servants had a similar pecking order, and from Daegan she knew they were very cognizant of that. While Brian might be trying to help her, knowing her history and wanting to give her the reassurance of talking to a woman, she was allowing herself to be treated as less than a peer. It was a subtle thing, but one that frissoned through her vampire blood and told her she couldn't let that happen. Not in this new world. The information should be coming directly from Brian to her.

So now she turned her gaze to Brian, arching a brow. "Will masturbation provide the same data?"

He cleared his throat, giving her some small satisfaction at her reminder that on some things, at least, she didn't need kid gloves.

"Similar enough. And tonight would be preferable," he said, with just the right note of apology and concern in his eyes.

"All right. But I want to know something. The first night Debra made us dinner, when she pulled out the table settings, she stopped and looked at you, as if waiting for an answer to an unspoken question. You said, 'We'll all eat at the table. No games.' What did that mean?"

"Good memory." Brian nodded. "You remember Lord Daegan said you and your servant were exclusive until your transition was complete and he returned?"

Dear Goddess, let him come home before the transition is complete. That could take up to three months. If she had to wait three months to see him, she might completely lose it. But she nodded. She felt Gideon's gaze on her, knew he might have heard that thought.

"Vampire social gatherings always involve sexual games with the servants. It's required by etiquette, and there are many political strategies worked out through such games. Though it's also for the pleasure of the diners."

Brian lifted his wineglass without glancing toward Debra. Putting down her fork, she immediately rose, took it from his hand and went to the sidebar to pour him another glass. "During a typical social gathering," he continued, "a vampire's servant either stands behind her Master's chair, or kneels next to him, if he wants to feed her portions of the meal he's sampling." He glanced at her blood-laced wine. "You and I are not sampling human food. And I am here merely for your protection and diagnostics. Therefore, it made more sense to have our servants join us at the table and engage in conversation. Keep it more informal and relaxed."

"So this is the vampire version of eating dinner at home, in front of the TV?"

Brian inclined his head toward Gideon, acknowledging the sardonic question. "If you like. But there have been times, even when eating alone, that I have bade my servant perform at my direction as she would at a gathering. Test runs, to help her confidence." He turned his gaze back to Anwyn, a clear message there. "As well as for my own pleasure."

Brian shifted from absentminded genius professor to urbane and well-versed dinner guest with barely a grinding of gears. Since he was a born vampire, his father a Region Master, it shouldn't surprise her that he'd been trained to handle himself that way. Had Daegan imposed that directive about Brian not sharing servants because he didn't think her capable of the other right now? Or he didn't want to share her with anyone? Perhaps he was concerned about how Gideon would handle such a situation. She'd caught his sharp glance at the exchange. She knew Gideon wasn't going to participate in anything like that, because she could hear it in his head. *A cold day in hell before that will happen . . .*

It was no less than what she expected, but it still added to the heavy, cold weight in her lower belly. Every day she grew more dependent on him, the first man in her life she could say that about and not feel she'd betrayed herself. When he left . . .

By the time that happens, you'll be on your feet again, Anwyn. You'll have graduated, gotten your full-fledged bat wings and not need me in your head anymore.

How do you know?

Because I know you. And because I won't leave until that happens.

Was it something perverse in her that wanted to test that?

"What kind of things?" she asked Brian with not-so-casual interest. Crossing her forearms, she leaned forward, toying with the stem of her glass. Her nostrils flared, catching the scent of fresh blood as Debra cut her wrist with a tiny pearl-handled knife she'd had tucked in her bodice, let it flow into Brian's glass. He drank white wine, so the crimson exploded like a flower blooming, sparkling in the candlelight Debra had set in the center of the table.

Brian glanced toward his servant. She'd changed for dinner. While Anwyn expected it was still demure and casual by vampire standards, the short, sleeveless lavender dress hugged Debra's curves and gave her gray eyes a violet hue. Her hair was down, and the straight strands teased her fine cheekbones and lightly glossed lips.

As if visually recalling some of those "tests," Brian's gaze lingered on her as he spoke. "Simple things. Requiring that she strip naked and cook me human food, gourmet choices. Then lie on the table before me, with those samples placed on her body so I can use her as my table, my plate. Sometimes I bind her to a chair, with a vibrator inside her, and watch her writhe and beg to come while I drink her fresh blood from a glass and go over my notes for the day. If she's been a little too opinionated"—his eyes glinted as she turned back toward the table carrying the wine—"she kneels between my knees and holds my cock in her mouth as long as I demand. Not sucking or stimulating, merely holding it, feeling it grow harder until it fills her mouth and pushes into her throat."

Brian took the glass from his servant, his hand closing over hers. Debra was still, her eyes lowered, her lips pressed together, but Anwyn recognized the flush of arousal on her soft cheeks. She wasn't wearing a bra, because her nipples were points pressing against the fabric.

Gideon had put down his fork, sat back. Though he was trying to stay removed and wary from the turn in the conversation, Anwyn could tell the images Brian had painted were affecting him, as they would any male with alpha tendencies. Which her vampire hunter had in spades.

"That takes some self-discipline," she observed. "For both of you."

What Brian had described fired her own blood, ratcheted up her earlier yearning to be more demanding with Gideon again. But each time she thought about it, she remembered the way she'd lost control when she was overstimulated by the club environment. A Mistress's first responsibility was protecting her slave, and she was his worst danger. Vulnerability had crippled her confidence. Brian was here, yes, but she didn't trust him the way she trusted Daegan.

They said they needed readings. Gideon's voice, in her mind. *Why not handle two birds with one net, Mistress? Confidence and coitus?*

She didn't smile, because his mind-voice, which had some of the same sexy, deep cadence it had when spoken, ran chills and pleasure both up her spine. He knew. Of course he did. He was in her mind, but more than that, Gideon was always hyperintuitive when it came to her. He would have noticed her holding back.

You don't want me to do this. Not this way.

Yeah, I do. Because I miss the woman I met in the Queen's Chamber that first night. Almost as much as you do.

I don't want to hurt you.

You won't. Not that way. Just . . . I don't want him anywhere near me, all right? That's all I ask. On everything else, I'm all yours, Mistress.

This was why she needed to work harder to turn the thin screen between their minds into a solid wall when needed. He already knew what would heat her blood, arouse her Mistress instincts and put them in forward drive. She felt like a teenager whose driving instructor had just mashed down the gas pedal, taking them into a merge lane toward a busy interstate. Out of control, but a surge of exhilaration, knowing she could do this; she was just scared. She hated her own fear almost worse than anything else, but fear of what she might do to someone else was a harder animal to control.

Gideon rose from the table, collecting his dishes as well as Debra's, taking them into the kitchen. He dumped them in the sink and ran some water over them. Watching him do the domestic task, his hips shifting with the movement, head tilted down and shoulders flexing as he moved the dishes into the dishwasher, she made her decision.

"Gideon."

He straightened, turned, met her gaze. Whatever he saw told him she'd transitioned into that mode, because his firm mouth curved. "Mistress?"

He was calling her that more often now. To help her confidence, yes. If only for that, it would have irritated her, made her feel patronized. But in those dreamland drifts through his mind, she'd found he liked using the title, though like so many things, he couldn't define why, or admit it to himself when waking. Gideon's mind was divided between the lies he told himself to function while awake, and the truths that comforted him in his dreams.

She'd been the kind of Mistress who made a man face his truths, to bring them both the maximum pleasure that such brutal honesty could invoke. She could be that again.

"Leave the dishes for later. I want to give Lord Brian his readings. Go to the playroom, bring the strap-on with the six-inch phallus. The curved one that vibrates, and some lubricant."

He'd anticipated, or perhaps hoped, that it would be simple, Anwyn straddling him on the couch or chair, where he could close out everything but the vision of her riding him, the feel of her cunt clamped around him. The arch of her throat, those miles of hair tickling his bare thighs as she dropped her head back, her breasts straining upward, begging for the cup of his hands.

No part of my body begs, Gideon. It demands, and you beg for the right to give it what it wants. She arched a brow. *You wanted me to reclaim my confidence as your Mistress, right?*

A rueful, somber smile touched that tempting mouth, and he set aside the dish towel, giving her a look before moving toward the playroom. Anwyn concentrated, hard, brought that screen down, where thoughts and words, unless directed right at Gideon, were harder to discern, like parceling out chatter at a crowded mall. Looking toward Debra and Brian, she discovered the rules were not so different here than in the underground level of Atlantis.

When he'd released her hand, Debra had gone to a kneeling position next to Brian's thigh. He'd taken his wineglass from her, letting the silent interaction between Anwyn and Gideon play out while Debra assumed a common submissive position. Her hands were clasped behind her back, her knees spread in the short dress, making it ride high on her thighs. As Anwyn watched, Brian painted a drifting line of the blood-laced wine along the upper portion of her bosom, exposed by the low scoop neck of the dress.

Desire curled in Anwyn, seeing the tableau. She'd missed watching the games above, unable to spend time in her club during open hours. She could get the video feed, still did a lot of review of those tapes, but it wasn't the same as being a direct witness. With his vampire senses, Brian picked up on her response. Though he could send a command to Debra's mind, Anwyn realized he was offering her, a Mistress, something directly with his spoken words.

"Unzip your dress and let it fall to your waist. I want full access to your breasts."

Debra complied, and tugged the soft fabric over her aroused nipples, giving Brian a wider expanse of flesh to paint, increase that flush of arousal and the still tension of her body. Anwyn realized she could smell the response of each one of them. Debra's moistening sex, her own. Even Brian was hardening, such that he already had some fluid leak at the tip under his slacks. Heartbeats were quickening, Debra's breath becoming more shallow.

"Lord Brian, I'm on familiar and yet unfamiliar ground here." Anwyn straightened in the chair, met his gaze when it turned to her. He had such a level, calming expression, but now, in arousal, it had taken on that faint predatory gleam she realized that even a vampire scientist could possess. "I assume you would tell me if any step risks either of our servants?"

"I will. I assume you would tell me if anything we do risks your protector's displeasure?"

Anwyn smiled at the quirk at his mouth. Having been raised in Britain, Brian possessed that dry humor that struck at unexpected times and made the green eyes and sculpted face all the more appealing. She'd noticed he often pushed the dark blond, straight hair that fell over the high brow out of his eyes with muttered impatience when trying to look through a microscope. Despite his good looks, he didn't seem the vain type, so she'd wondered why he didn't cut it. Sliding a glance to Debra, noting her studying that very feature in his profile, she thought she maybe had her answer.

According to Daegan, Brian and Debra were supposedly a textbook example of the perfect Master-servant relationship. While there was an obvious deep bond there, Brian was clearly Debra's Master, in a way that even exceeded the definition of the 24/7 couples Anwyn had seen at the club. There was the same flavor, in terms of the sexual practices, but a different animal entirely in how it was manifested. Debra truly belonged to him. Anwyn didn't want to equate it with historic slavery or even indentured servitude—there was a willingness and devotion here that characterized neither of those situations—but the power Brian held over her, and her submission to him, were close kin to those states. And unlike the world in which her 24/7 couples lived, the vampire world did consider human servants property of the vampire who marked them. Debra seemed not only to understand, but to accept that.

She wondered if that was another reason Daegan had wanted them here. To remind her vividly of why Gideon couldn't be a permanent part of her life? Or to give Gideon an example to follow, a way to learn without dictating to him?

Daegan was mysterious, manipulative and arrogant. But he was also insightful, exceedingly clever and unmatched in his judgment of people. Seeing such a relationship was entirely too fascinating to her Mistress nature and the vampire blood in which it now churned. She kept telling herself to proceed cautiously in those waters. She had to proceed cautiously in all waters, because any type of volatility or passion could be taken way too far.

But still, as she heard Gideon returning, saliva gathered around her fangs, reacting to the surge of adrenaline through her chest, the tightening of her thighs and breasts. A simultaneous animal possessiveness and wave of lust washed over her as she turned to look at her servant.

He brought in the strap-on, carrying the sterilized sexual aid rolled up in his hand and low to his side, the way men carried things they didn't particularly want or know how to carry in a masculine way, like a woman's purse. When she reached for it, he gladly turned it over to her. Rather than rising to initiate something, however, she laid it on the table, in front of Debra. She shifted her gaze to Brian.

"I would like your servant to wear this, and take my servant from behind, while he is inside me. Would you permit her to do that, Lord Brian? Can you perform your readings that way, or do you need her direct assistance?"

Brian considered that, glanced toward Debra. Debra had lifted her gaze to Gideon, briefly, then cut back to her Master, awaiting his decision. Anwyn saw trepidation and curiosity simmering in the gray gaze. Debra had never done that to a man. And definitely not to a man like Gideon.

"Yes," Brian said at last. "I think that will work. Debra, remove all of your clothes, except your heels and stockings, and put on the harness." He glanced toward Anwyn. "Do you think the couch would be best?"

She nodded. If Debra wasn't involved, she would have chosen the easy chair, aligned with the sofa. She told herself it was a coincidence that it was Daegan's favorite chair. It was best suited for a larger man's frame, was all.

Brian got up to retrieve the sensors. She'd been aware of the turmoil in Gideon's mind, and now tilted her head back, studying him upside down, standing just behind her, arms crossed and thumbs hooked in his armpits.

"Gideon," she murmured. "Take off all your clothes as well."

His gaze flickered to Debra, already lifting her dress over her head. She was entirely naked under it, except for the thigh-high stockings Brian had mentioned that she wore with three-inch ankle-strap heels. She was also wearing a choker of steel links with a pendant. Anwyn realized it was a collar, something that Brian must have gotten for Debra, liking the symbolism of it. It was a romantic gesture, making her wonder anew what lay under the surface of the "textbook perfect" Master-servant relationship of these two.

Anwyn brought her attention back to Gideon, who hadn't yet started to undress. *Not afraid of two girls, are you?*

He narrowed his eyes at her. *I think you're obsessed with sticking things in my ass.*

I'll take a strap to your ass if you don't start undressing.

You and what army? But the devilish thought came with compliance as he unbuttoned the shirt he'd borrowed from Daegan's closet for their more formal dinner. He looked incredibly handsome in Armani, those vivid blue eyes even more compelling, the ends of his hair brushing the collar, but when he shrugged out of it, with a ripple of chest and biceps muscle, it was enough to make any woman take a breath. Anwyn rose, cognizant of Debra's gaze passing over those muscles, down to the waist and below, a moment before Anwyn shifted to block the view, deliberately bringing her gaze back to her.

"You've never done this before."

"No, ma'am. But I've had it done to me."

"All right." Anwyn unpinned her hair, let it tumble down her back until it caressed her hips. She shook it out, threading her fingers through it, and felt Gideon's hands pass over it, a quick tug. But when she glanced back at him he was unbuckling his belt, the picture of obedience. An illusion, she was sure. "Then you should know you ease in. Let him relax, and I'll help him get that way."

"I'll be fine," Gideon grumbled. Anwyn pivoted on her heel. With unerring direction, she closed her hand over his testicles in the slacks. They were a little snug, because though Gideon had a whipcord musculature she wanted to feed, it still had more Irish brawler bulk to it than Daegan's graceful physique.

"That's enough," she said softly, looking up at him. "It's time for you to listen, and be still, and obey your Mistress. Do you understand?"

There it was, that quiver in the muscles her senses were fine-tuned to detect. She'd been so gun-shy of doing this, but all of a sudden, she knew what she wanted and how she wanted it. She was demanding it from him. She wouldn't hurt him. Brian was here, and it was going to be okay. She could be the Mistress she'd been aching to be to him for the past few weeks.

His gaze held hers for a long moment; then he gave her a nod.

"All right, then. Unbutton my blouse, the first three buttons." She kept her hand on him through the slacks, kneading the organ that was lengthening, hardening there, indulging and amusing herself as Brian approached.

Gideon complied, his large fingers slipping the small pearlescent buttons. Brian was there with the sensors, but Gideon closed a hand on her slim wrist, drawing her attention. "Allow me?"

He'd done it before, knew where Brian needed them to go. She knew Gideon preferred to be the one touching her. It teased her mind, how she had a servant and a vampire who were equally territorial, in different ways. But she was of a mind to rub the fur of this predator the wrong way, drive up his reaction even more.

"Not this time," she murmured. "You just watch. Make sure he puts them in all the right places."

Temple, heart, throat, pulse points, back. Brian's touch was gentle, and though he didn't linger, Gideon's attention stayed locked on the movement of the scientist's hands. Over her breasts, down the back of her shirt where Brian's fingers slid along her shoulder blades to find the right point. Her throat. Gideon's gaze flared as she lifted her chin. It was the one place that Brian did linger, the vampire in him too strong to maintain his professionalism. It was just a slight caress along her carotid, but Gideon registered it. When his jaw tightened, she read the reason for his wariness. Sometimes older vampires took advantage of a fledgling. However, he held his silence, mainly because Brian's hands slipped away then, the task done.

The adhesive was strong, such that the sensors usually took skin when they were removed, unless they did it slowly. It caused more pain that way, but she could handle pain. She didn't want something like a dislodged sensor interfering with the next few moments.

In the past, wearing the tiny pads had diminished her shields, her self-confidence. It was a reminder that she was a victim, something sick and in need of care, protection. But she was in her element now and refused to be pulled from it. Gideon had continued to hold her wrist in that loose grasp as Brian did his task, but now she removed herself from her servant and indicated she wanted him to finish undressing. Turning on her heel, she saw Debra was adjusting the strap-on harness. The young woman bit her lip as the clitoral stimulator rubbed against her already aroused body. Brian was setting up his equipment, but she noticed his eyes kept cutting over to his servant. Everyone in the room was aroused, and that arousal was likely to get even more intense very shortly.

It reminded her of her dream, all the things her vampire senses gave her that she hadn't had before. The power and pleasure building in the room was a heated wave, and she closed her eyes, riding on it, the different scents, soft breaths, shifting of bodies. With the possible exception of Brian, everyone in the room was facing something they'd never done before. She'd certainly orchestrated acts like this before, but never as a vampire. The fear returned briefly, the flash of Gideon's bloodied skull, his glazing eyes. She did the exercise she often used before a session. Several deep breaths, held, then let out slowly, centering herself, making herself acutely aware of everything in the room. In fact, when she was in this mode, there was no Anwyn. She was the elemental directing events, no thought upon herself at all, simply guided by instinct, sensation and pleasure.

Aware of Gideon's attention and Debra's, waiting for further instruction, she reached under her skirt, wriggled out of her panties and let them fall. Stepped out of her heels and left those delicate female items in a pile as she moved to the roomy couch and lay down, propping her upper body on the array of cushions there. She eased the skirt up until it was high on her thighs, but would not reveal anything until he positioned himself between her legs. She would take him naked, while he would have only the sense of her under her clothes, in whatever way she allowed him to touch her.

Yet she knew there were times this was even more erotic to the male mind. Breasts cradled in lace, a half-unbuttoned blouse enhancing the cleavage, the crescent of the curves. A length of thigh, disappearing into dark fabric inches before the hip or buttock was revealed. Her bare feet pressed to the sofa cushions.

"Come here, Gideon." She stretched out a hand.

He was high and hard, his cock nearly brushing his belly. He hadn't looked toward Brian at all. In fact, his body had stayed at a canted angle to him, a defensive, belligerent posture. In his mind she saw his trepidation that she would push it, try to antagonize him in some way with Brian's presence, but she had no intention of doing that. Not this time.

He moved the several steps to her and she closed her hand on his forearm as he braced it on the sofa next to her hip. When he put his knee on the couch between hers, she gripped the other forearm, his hand now holding the top of the couch. The bite of her nails stopped his forward motion, a reminder. His thick lashes rose, revealing the dark blue eyes. "Ask me, Gideon."

"Let me inside you, Mistress."

"Say it the way you're thinking it."

"Let me fuck you." His lips were pressed together hard, his gaze locked on her so securely she knew it was a deliberate effort not to look toward Brian.

It's just us, angry man. You and me, and Debra. Brian will watch. That's all.

Gideon would react violently if Brian touched him, yet he had an overwhelming desire to please her. He was afraid she was going to let Brian do something to him, and he would have to disappoint her, refuse her, because he couldn't tolerate that. He was castigating himself for having limits, even as he knew he wouldn't budge on those limits. Another reminder to him that he wouldn't be her servant forever, because a vampire's servant couldn't have limits.

She read that swirl of thoughts, realized he was struggling with that cloud over their relationship, just as she was, but she decided she wouldn't allow that conflict to affect this moment. Laying her hands on his jaw, she brought his gaze to her face.

You cannot disappoint me in this, Gideon. Give yourself to me and Debra, and let your mind go. Simply be mine, and let me handle everything else. I promise Brian will not touch you.

He nodded, and she lifted up enough to brush her lips over his, holding his face steady so she controlled the movement. As she did, she angled her hips, brushed the edge of her gathered skirt against his cock. She could feel the heat of it emanating toward what it wanted most. Lying back on the couch again, she reached down, gripped him. His lips pressed together, those fine muscles quivering in reaction and barely leashed restraint that only drove her own desires higher. "Keep your hands on the couch where you have them," she commanded, watching his face tighten further as she levered his cock downward, fitted the head in the wet and welcoming gateway of her sex. Contracting her stomach muscles, she drew him in, lifting her hips to slide up his length, then back down again, her body rolling with the motion.

It drew his hungry gaze to her breasts, thrusting up against her blouse, the roll of her abdomen and the rock of her hips. She parted her lips, let out a sigh as his thick length filled her, creating unspeakable pleasure that only heightened his need to take over as he saw it in her face, felt it from her body. But though the leash of restraint was taut, he didn't try to yank it away. Not yet. And she wondered if he knew, intuitively, how that fired her own need to raging.

"Debra," she said. "Please join us."

Debra glanced at Brian. She'd moved to stand next to him, lubricating herself with the oil Gideon had left on the table. Brian was watching her glistening hands work the shaft. Now he picked up a towel, took each of her hands and wiped them clean. Reaching down, he caught two fingers in the top strap of the harness, tugged it, working the clit stimulator against her. Her lips parted, her hand closing over his biceps for balance.

"You heard the Mistress," the scientist said, low. "Do as she commands."

Debra nodded, moved toward Anwyn and Gideon. Anwyn knew that walking in a strap-on for the first time could be a very powerful experience, and she enjoyed seeing the pleasure and wonder cross Debra's face as she adjusted her pace accordingly.

Gideon had turned his head, but now Anwyn directed his eyes back down. "Keep your attention here." She placed her fingers at her collarbone, ran them down her sternum, into the folds of her shirt. "Don't look up until I say you can."

Do you want me to bark and roll over, too?

We might play fetch later, if you're very good. Curling her hand in his hair, she tugged, not gently. He held his position, enduring the discomfort, his blue eyes intently studying the rise of her breasts, the valley in between. He was a breast man, she knew, and he liked hers exceedingly well. He'd quickly learned her ability to read his mind could be turned against her, so that he showed her in painstaking detail how he would run his tongue down that valley, tease in between, scrape the pale skin with the rough shadow of his beard, move over to take the nipple deep, suckle her hard . . .

Her pussy contracted around his head, and his gaze flickered in triumph, his lips pressing together, for of course his thoughts stoked his own arousal.

Keep pushing, Gideon, and I'll have her change out that dildo for something much larger and thicker. Something far more like Daegan's cock.

His gaze snapped to hers. The recoil in his mind from such a threat was far more volatile and emotion-driven than his flat rejection of Brian or any other man touching him. But she doubted Gideon realized the significance of that difference in reaction, or what it told her.

Eyes back down, Gideon. If you want to please me. And so Brian can get his readings.

He hasn't gotten any for a near-death experience yet. But his gaze left hers, returned to her breasts.

Arching a brow, she ran a hand up his flank, nails digging in a little. *You don't seem to have any wooden stakes on you, vampire hunter. But impaling me on this would be quite a way to go.* She lifted her hips, taking him deep again, clamping her muscles so it was a slow, tight drag back down to the head that made him grimace, mutter a quiet oath.

She missed the razor tips she used to wear beneath her nails, but until she learned control over the seizures, they were a tiny pleasure she couldn't risk. She liked the way his body reacted when she left cuts on his flesh. He was particularly sensitive around the nipple area.

Debra had arrived behind him, and Anwyn glanced toward her, her gaze traveling over the woman's breasts, the slope of abdomen, the well-greased dildo bobbing gently between her legs. When she met Debra's gray eyes, the servant acknowledged her, then swept her gaze down, acknowledging her dominance. It was similar to working with Janet, Ella or Charlene, her Atlantis staff submissives, except this woman never had an end of shift. Her life was devoted to serving Brian, in whatever way necessary.

The type of slave almost impossible for a human Dominant to obtain in a civilized society. Feeling that familiar yearning return, she also remembered Daegan's words to her before he left. *I wanted you as my servant, but in truth, perhaps what drew me to you was that you were a vampire in every other way but blood.*

The desire to own someone down to the soul was a human sin, the desire of a god. She shied away from the thought, even as her vampire blood eagerly embraced it. Perhaps that was why the gods had given her Gideon temporarily. The humbling reminder that even a vampire couldn't always have what she wanted.

But she did have this moment. "Debra," she said, her voice low so it wouldn't break over the tiny storms of sensation emanating from that provocative joining point between her and Gideon. "Touch him in whatever manner you wish before you put that inside him. I want to see you enjoy him."

It was like giving a child free run of a candy store, she thought, watching Debra's gaze travel from Gideon's tense broad shoulders, down the length of spine to the rise of muscular buttocks, powerful thighs. He had one foot on the floor, so the spread of his legs would give her a nice view of the heavy testicle sac, a portion of his cock, before it disappeared into Anwyn where she still held the head in stasis, her tissues quivering around it, wanting more.

I can give you more, Mistress.

Shhh. Give Debra this. Remain still and prove that you're mine. At least right now.

A muscle twitched in his jaw at the poignant note she couldn't keep from her tone. But of course he didn't deny it. Then they didn't have to think at all, because Debra moved closer. Her slim hand cupped Gideon's shoulder, her fingers whispering over his hair, threading through and stroking the strands downward, so she straightened and pressed them against the upper edge of his shoulder blade. She did it again, surprising Anwyn with her interest in a less sexual caress at first. Perhaps the woman was reassuring him, understanding he was new to this. Or perhaps she was doing something she wasn't often permitted to do. At least not to the man Anwyn suspected she was imagining.

At length, though, she seemed to recall that, for all Anwyn's open invitation, there was a practical reason she was doing this, serving the needs of her Master and a Mistress. Letting her fingers drift down along his spine, that shallow valley, Debra fanned out over the ribs, curving around and whispering down his side, stopping above Anwyn's hands, low on his hips. A shudder ran through Gideon, a twitch, and a slight smile curved the servant's lips. "Ticklish," Debra murmured.

"A little." Gideon didn't change his focus, following Anwyn's direction, but there was an easing to his features at the small teasing exchange. It tightened the bond between the three of them, made Anwyn settle into it further as well. She was cognizant of Brian monitoring his machines, making his notes on his mini-laptop, but also of the way he was watching every minute physical and emotional exchange. She expected it was for more than data collection.

Debra turned her hand over, slid her knuckles over one buttock, down to the top of the thigh, and then across, to the testicles. When her hand closed over them, Anwyn knew it, from Gideon's mind and his reaction, his cock convulsing in her channel, his biceps hardening at the stimulation. Debra apparently had some very clever fingers, and Brian hadn't cleaned all the oil off them. Gideon's breath whistled through his teeth as she painted his rim, making his body jerk in tiny motions. Then down again, teasing the scrotum, another thorough fondling and kneading of the area that Anwyn knew from personal experience filled up the hand with a nice rounded weight. Then she reached under, and Anwyn felt the pressure as Debra wrapped her hand around his base.

"Would you like me to guide him deeper into you, Mistress?" she asked, her eyes focused and intent, mouth wet where she'd licked her lips. "Make him move in and out of you with the motion of my hand?"

"I'd like that, yes."

Debra tightened her grip, her other hand falling to rest on his buttock, applying pressure, giving him direction. Slow, guiding him in deep, at least until the ring of Debra's fingers pressed between them, and Anwyn felt the slim knuckles against her labia. Then Debra changed her direction and Gideon came out, just as gradually. Watching it, the struggle in his face to obey their direction, she knew he was going crazy caught between two sexually aroused women. The male need to rut was growing hard and fierce as the heat in his cock. It made Anwyn's own desires rise. Debra wasn't detached, but she was as controlled as a Mistress right now, holding her desires back, channeling them through what she was doing to Gideon.

On the fifth withdrawal, a groan escaped Gideon's lips, and his head fell a little lower, the hair on his brow brushing Anwyn's jaw. Tightening her fingers on his hips, she dug into the upper rise of those muscular buttocks.

"Don't you come, Gideon," she whispered. "That's for your Mistress to decide. The longer you hold it, the hotter you'll make me. Feel how wet my pussy is now?"

"I want to taste it," he muttered. "Love eating your pussy, Mistress. Sucking your tits. Fucking you, hard and long."

Oh yeah, he was headed into pure, primitive need and leaving everything civilized behind. "Five more times," she managed. "Then I want you inside him."

Debra gave a nod. Her hand had slipped from an innocuous pressure to a solid grip of his buttock, and when he gave a strangled oath, she knew the girl had slipped a thumb partially inside him, getting him ready, teasing him some more.

"Count it out for her, Gideon," Anwyn said, letting that ruthless edge into her voice that she knew caught his attention, and sliced him even sharper than her razor nails. "Or I'll make her start over."

"Five."

A muffled cough came from Brian, and even Debra was startled into a flash of a smile. Anwyn managed to suppress hers, but caught Gideon's hair in hard fingers, jerking his head back up so he was looking directly into her face. "Gideon. Count. From the beginning."

She cupped her breast with her other hand, the fingers teasing aside the cloth and pushing the bra down to reveal an aroused nipple that she began manipulating with her fingers before his avid gaze.

"Two," he growled, as Debra pulled him out for the second time. The muscles in his face strained, his lips peeling back, as he went back down into her. Anwyn tightened her own muscles, at a lower level, making sure she squeezed him tight.

"Fuck. Mistress. Three. Goddamn it."

"Don't curse at me, Gideon Green. Two more."

"Not . . . going to . . . make it."

"Yes, you are." She flicked her gaze at Debra. The woman understood, tightening her grip on him. A third mark had even greater strength, so she knew the constriction of her fingers would serve the same purpose as a cock harness. "Your seed is mine to command. You release it when I say."

"Four." His eyes couldn't leave her exposed breast now. His lips were parted, tongue making a quick swipe over them that felt as though he'd licked the hard nipple. She shuddered, and his eyes darkened. He was in her mind as she was in his now. No need for curtains during this, because the mutual desires and rough demands wrapped them together even more tightly. He knew what she wanted, what would give her the most pleasure, and she knew there would be no more jokes now, because at this level, pleasure was all he wanted to give her, past his fears or shields.

"Five."

Debra released him, maneuvering over his legs to kneel on the long couch behind him. She made a provocative and pretty picture in just her heels and stockings. Glancing at Anwyn to confirm she was still following her direction, the woman took the sleek black dildo in hand, and began to guide it into him.

Anal penetration was still something he resisted, such that she needed to hold the reins over him tight when it happened. This was the first time during these difficult weeks she'd had the courage to do that, and she'd only just broken him into it before she'd been turned. But his reaction to this, and the other things she knew, that he couldn't admit, told her it was time to start doing more of it. It broke him down, took his mind past everything, into pure, wild desire.

On stroke five, Debra had pulled him halfway out of Anwyn again, so now he was forced to stay in that position, waiting, powerful body shuddering as Debra worked against those tight muscles.

Anwyn took her hand from her breast and crept to his buttock, applying pressure. "Slow, Gideon. Push into me until you can't go farther, and then stop. Then suckle my breast."

He did, at a little swifter pace than Debra had managed, but she'd give him credit for not ramming home at this point. When he got there, he lowered his head. Unlike Debra, he didn't look for further confirmation, a chance she might change her mind.

"Oh . . ." Her breath caught in her throat as his clever lips closed over her nipple. A hot, wet, demanding mouth, pulling hard. Her angry baby. A strained smile touched her mind at the thought, but no other thought was maternal as she cupped the back of his neck. "Let her in, Gideon. Push outward and relax. I want her deep inside you. Surrender to my will. Let me give you everything."

That shudder again, his long fingers flexing. He'd moved one hand so it gripped her upper arm. She permitted it, knowing he needed an anchor, a connection between them. Debra made an approving murmur and Anwyn felt the sensation of it travel to her womb as Debra sank to the hilt in his ass, pressing her body against Gideon's bare back.

"Good. There you are." She reached up, stroked a hand over Debra's bare shoulder, then down to Gideon's rib cage. "Start fucking him, Debra. Ride him hard and take yourself to climax."

She pressed her lips to Gideon's temple as he nipped her and she gave a throaty moan. "As she does that, I'll come. Then you can come, Gideon. You can use me as hard as you want, pound into me like a battering ram."

She noted Debra glance at Brian, her eyes bright with desire, lips parted as she lifted her upper body to do as Anwyn bade. Brian met her gaze, nodded. Gave his permission for the climax. His green eyes were fierce with lust, and Anwyn knew she wouldn't be the only one used hard before this was over. She wouldn't be surprised if Brian called Debra over after and fucked her right there in that chair, hands cupped over that sweet round bottom, his gaze devouring the quiver of her full breasts as he pounded her down on him in a vulnerable straddle, making her keep her hands locked behind her so he had a Master's access to all of her, no control over her own motion or balance.

It was what she would do.

As Debra began to move, Gideon let out another strangled snarl against Anwyn's breast, renewed his suckling there with fierceness. *The other one, Gideon. It wants attention, too.*

He shifted his grip, yanked her shirt back on that side, so that the fabric tore, a button coming loose between their closely pressed bodies. He pushed the bra down and attacked that nipple, the animal taking over. The hand gripping her arm was bruising, but the other still held his weight mostly off her, so there was a part of Gideon still in there, taking care of her. As always. It swamped her, pushed her arousal up even higher, the emotional always capable of goading a woman's physical response ever closer to that shining edge of helpless pleasure. The point where everyone, Mistress or slave, gave up control in favor of that mind-numbing bliss.

She'd noted that Debra brought a singular focus and intensity to every task, and this was no different. She was being very thorough, trying different strokes, speeds, angles, impacts, probably cataloging Gideon's every response. Anwyn saw the colors of his mind go red and orange, a swirl of flame. He wasn't suckling in rhythm anymore, just nipping and licking at her nipple in a frenetic oral need, anything to distract him from a climax he wasn't going to be able to stop.

She'd punish him for it later, because she couldn't stop her own. Just the friction of him holding still inside her, while lashing her breast with ravenous desire, was enough. *Fuck me, Gideon. Let yourself go.*

He lifted his hips, countering Debra's weight and rhythm, and plunged downward. Hard, deep, pounding strokes, that snarl becoming a male cry of raging lust and release. Debra's moan joined him, evolving into a high, thin scream as his motion took over the pressure on the stimulator. Together, they brought Anwyn to that edge and took her over, so they jumped together into that delicious free fall. The powerful shock of Gideon's thrusts transformed her body into one long shudder of response that wrenched a cry from her own throat, one Gideon took into his as he covered her mouth in a needy, demanding kiss. He swallowed breath and sound together as they rocked to completion, turning in the flames of that red and orange field in his mind.

The power of it rolled over and through her, keeping her in its grip for longer than she anticipated. When at last it was done, an aftermath of relief and repleteness at once came in its wake. She'd taken command, taken control, just as she'd done a thousand times in the rooms above, and she hadn't hurt him. The shadow creatures had been nearly still throughout all this, not even their normal buzzing murmur able to rise above the sound of hearts pounding, desire surging and the thoughts of need and lust ricocheting between their two minds.

The very first night, Daegan had told her she could *choose* to let go of control, stay in command of who she was by acknowledging she needed their help, needed to rely on them. That she could trust them enough to allow herself that surrender. For wasn't that what she demanded of a submissive? What she wanted so deeply from Gideon? Not just for a moment, here or there, but fully, totally committed, as Debra obviously was to Brian?

As she came down, shuddering beneath Gideon, his hard muscles quivered against her, his mouth pressed to her temple. Debra's forehead was against his shoulder, both of them trying to keep their full weight off of her and yet catch their breath. It made her remember something else. Something that Gideon had said, about his brother and Lady Lyssa.

I've seen the relationship between a vampire and a servant, Anwyn. Between two of them who love each other. I'm not so sure that kind of ownership, the Dominance and submission, isn't a fluid thing that goes both ways over time.

He was wrong about it in practice, but in matters of the heart, she knew what he meant. He was her servant; he would submit to her sexually, with some resistance, more or less, depending on his mood. However, if he was rough or violent about his submission, it balanced, for when she surrendered to him, to help her through seizures, letting him into her mind, he was as gentle with her as if he'd been given the most precious of treasures to protect.

She put her hand on his skull, holding his head to the side of hers, and caught some of Debra's loose hair, pressing her lips to it in brief thanks, giving her the warmth of her eyes, since she was too wound up to smile. Debra nodded, but also, reading her cue, eased out of him and straightened, leaving it just the two of them, so Anwyn could wind her arms around him, hold him close.

Vaguely, she was aware of Debra dropping the strap-on to the side and going to Brian. His gaze slid over her naked body, lingering on the dainty ribbon at the tops of her stockings, the way the heels accentuated the tempting length of legs, the tilt of her ass. Her breasts were still rising and falling more rapidly with her climax, her lips parting at his regard. Placing his hand on her throat, he pulled her in to him as if he might take a kiss from her. Instead he paused just over her lips, holding her there. A tremor of need ran through her, her naked body almost but not quite touching his fully clothed one. He nodded after a weighted moment. "Go to the bedroom. I'll be there soon."

Lowering her gaze, she disappeared down the hall to the guest bedroom. Brian met Anwyn's gaze. "I'll sort this data out shortly. You can have your servant take off the sensors at your convenience. Thank you, Anwyn. I think Daegan's right. I think you'll get along quite well in our world. In fact, it's likely you might teach us a thing or two." A slight smile, and then he shut down the equipment and followed his servant, leaving her and Gideon alone.

Gideon lifted his upper body, running a thumb along her cheek. "Why don't I carry you to the bedroom, Mistress?"

Her limbs felt heavy, her mind a bit disoriented. "Is there another coming? Another seizure?"

"No. But I think that may have taken a lot out of you. You were stressing about it a lot. Afraid you might bite my head off or something, like a vampire praying mantis."

She pressed her lips together against a smile. "I'm never going to teach you proper respect, am I?"

"As I told you in the beginning, this is as good as it gets."

Anything better might kill me, Gideon. She put her mouth against his shoulder as he lifted her. She was in fact somewhat logy. "You were magnificent. We may have inspired Brian to fuck Debra within an inch of her life."

"He needs to reassert his claim, make sure her sticking a dildo up my ass hasn't made her forget she belongs to him."

"Do you think that's childish?"

"Not at all. Just the way we guys are." He slanted her a look. "You already knew that."

"That men are childish? Definitely."

"That what we did would make him react that way." He'd come into their bedroom and she was grateful to see the soft quilts and inviting pillows. Gideon put her feet on the ground, pulled back the cover, and then helped her ease in. She held on to his arm, pulling him in with her. *Stay with me until I fall asleep.*

As long as you need. He folded his arms over her chest as she turned her back to him, fitting herself to his planes and corners. "So why did you do that?"

"You know why, if you were listening in."

He shook his head. "Murky relationship-plotting stuff is a female foreign language, even direct from your head."

She bit his arm, gently, but enjoyed the way her fangs pressed into the flesh enough to take it deeper, find blood. He held her, didn't pull away or flinch at all as she enjoyed several drops, for pleasure, not hunger, and then traced the puncture wounds with her tongue, helping them close. "Daegan said they were the perfect Master-servant relationship, each one understanding how the relationship is supposed to work. I guess I see more there, simmering under the surface. I wanted to bring it to the top. Maybe for myself, more than them."

And maybe for Gideon as well, to remind him of what he'd said about his brother and his Mistress. She closed her eyes. She did herself no favors, making futile gestures like that. But Gideon's arms tightened around her. He said nothing for a while, and then, when she suspected he thought she was asleep, she heard his thought.

He'll be home soon, Anwyn. You won't have to worry so much about me then.

He was wrong, on both counts. Daegan wouldn't come home until she invited him . . . and meant it. And she'd have balance only when they were *both* with her in this bed.

Since Daegan had given her blood to serve as her surrogate sire, she could talk in his head and he in hers. However, as Daegan hadn't spoken in her mind since he'd left, she suspected he could be out of range. So she dialed his number on the cell and put on the earpiece so she could be hands free, tuck her cold fingers under her pillow. It was early afternoon, and she'd woken thinking of Daegan, what had happened last night. Gideon was on his afternoon run outside Atlantis, Brian was asleep, and of course Debra would probably be reworking the day's notes.

She'd thought about everything for quite a while before reaching for the phone. She didn't know what time it was there, but with a vampire, it didn't really matter. If it was heavy daylight, he'd sleep through the phone ringing. Otherwise, he'd be awake.

He answered on the second ring. *"Cher."*

She swallowed at everything that was in that one syllable. She didn't want inane chitchat, didn't want to circle around like a dazed moth uncertain of that flame. Not anymore. "I want you . . ."

To come home, to be with me, with us, even if I get angry again. But, remembering the night they'd met, she realized the words he'd said then covered it all for her, as they had for him. He'd just been waiting on her to come to the same conclusion. "I want you."

During the long pause, she closed her eyes. Imagining how close his mouth was to that phone, she had a crazy, adolescent desire to press her mouth to her own receiver, as if it would bring their lips together.

"Slide your hands down to your throat. Overlap them."

She turned to her back and did it, collaring herself with her fingers, and gasped at the immediate thought of it being his hand, holding her there as he often did, just enough pressure on the windpipe as he leaned down and sampled a breast, or nipped at the inside of her thigh, trailed his mouth over her navel and the quivering line of her upper abdomen.

"Now down over your breasts. Cup them, bring them together. Offer them to me. Arch your back. Don't touch your nipples."

It was hard not to do that, because she was itching to make a pass over them, imagine his mouth, his teeth, or the pinch of his fingers, but she did it, holding that position as the silence drew out. Was he touching his cock? Somehow she knew he wasn't, though she was sure he was hardening. This was about his Mastery of her, and all his focus was on it, such that she could feel his intensity even from this distance.

"Down your stomach now, to your pussy. Spread your legs. Are you naked?"

"Yes."

"You fucked Gideon before you went to sleep? His seed is still inside you, marking your thighs?"

"Yes."

"Next time, you tell him to clean you with his mouth. He shouldn't be leaving his Mistress messy like that."

Her breath whispered between her lips, curving in a soft smile. "Daegan."

"Cup your hands over your cunt. Seal in the heat, your desire. Let it feel the pressure of your palms. No fingers inside of yourself."

As she did, a gasp shuddered from her, her clit spasming. "Now." His voice had dropped even lower, and she heard it then, the note of the primitive male animal, the one he unleashed with her when he was at his most possessive and feral. Vampire. "Who do you belong to?"

"You," she whispered. "Come home, Daegan. Please. I need you." She swallowed, hard, and said what she'd never said to him. Never said to anyone in her entire adult life. "I love you. I hate you. I can't be without you."

"Will you still be angry with me?"

"Yes," she admitted. "But I can't get over it until you come back."

His chuckle shimmered over her like dark, erotic notes of music. "Spoken like the Mistress I know . . . and love."

Tears welled up in her eyes. "Daegan."

"More than life itself, *cher*. I will take your anger, your hatred, your love, and I will not fail you. I am yours, Anwyn Inara Naime. And I have been, since I walked into your club."

"Come home."

"I'm only a dream or two away." He paused. "How is Gideon doing?"

"Debra took him from behind tonight, while he was inside me. It was a new experience for him. Messed him up some, but he's out running it off."

"But Brian did not touch him. Or you."

Her body quivered under the cup of her hand at that tone, deadly and ferocious. "No. He didn't. Only to place the sensors on me. He touched my throat lightly when he did that, but nothing else. You were right about him, Daegan. He's a good man."

"He was Gideon's suggestion. It is Gideon who deserves the credit for his presence."

"Mmm. I didn't let him touch Gideon because Gideon doesn't desire men. I know what the vampire world is like, but whenever I have control over it, I'm not going to let a submissive . . . a servant of mine be forced to do something entirely against his nature just for my sake. He has no desire to be touched by a male. Not generally."

"Not generally."

She suppressed a smile. Gideon believed no male touch aroused him. He'd rationalized anything that had happened with Daegan as an ancillary symptom of his arousal for her.

She wasn't going to force the issue or the truth. She was saving that pleasure for the specific, very territorial male who *had* aroused Gideon, no matter how much Gideon tried to block it from his mind or bury it.

4

WOMEN. Once they knew when Daegan was coming home, Gideon wasn't surprised that his Mistress went into major to-do mode. The top three on the list were: she wanted Chantal to do her hair and toenails; she wanted to go with Gideon to pick Daegan up at the airport; and she wanted to drive.

The first part was easy enough. Pleased with her mood, and wanting to make sure she could hold on to it, he'd accompanied her upstairs, sat on the comfortable couch in the staff break room. With his booted feet crossed, long legs stretched out, he perused an entertainment magazine and listened to her talk to Chantal and some of the other "girls" during pre-opening. It was just girl chat, but for all they'd dealt with these past few weeks, he found it soothing and somewhat charming, though he never would have admitted that. Chantal did the hair and had Ella do the nails, since Ella also worked at a nail salon.

As he watched them and her mind was distracted, he mused over the challenges of the upcoming days. They'd be dropping Brian and Debra off at the airport the same night they picked up Daegan. Brian's work on the injection had improved to the point that for the past seven days her seizures had been low-level and easily predicted, between her vitals' monitoring and Gideon's perceptive senses. The restraints had been employed every time. In each case Gideon had had enough lead time to get her to a secluded environment, if she was no farther from one than her upper office. An added bonus was that the longer they spent together, the less vocal the nasty gremlins were. As long as their minds stayed closely interlocked. With Daegan back, it was just going to be a matter of continued practice and guarding against dangerous complacency.

Not much chance of that, though. For all the improvements, she still got antsy if Gideon got too far out of range. The flip side of the improvements was, when he was away from her, the gremlins were far more vocal, like trapped wild animals who'd been pent up in a cage. He'd started doing most of the necessary errands while she was sleeping, during the strongest hours of daylight, because if he left near evening, or worse, in the evening itself, the effort of keeping her reality separate from the nightmares they whispered in her brain, the images they delivered in front of her eyes, could exhaust her, as well as override Brian's serum.

He knew it could make her despair, and he ached for her. He and Brian both reminded her it hadn't been that long yet, such that they couldn't know how things would improve as time went on. Still, it was as if, as they got hold of the one thing they could manage, the one thing they couldn't was becoming stronger.

She was struggling with what every person who found their life significantly altered by a handicap faced. Depression, mood swings, intense flashes of anger. But he had to admire her grit as well. She worked through it, just as she had those first horrible seizures before they had the sire's blood. In between those bouts, she was humorous, determined, clever and always ready to use sex as an outlet for her frustration. He was happy to help.

She'd caught that thought, for she glanced over her shoulder at him, her eyes glittering with humor. *What are you reading?*

He lifted the magazine. Reading tabloid trash was something he'd done to pass the time as a vampire hunter, those brief pauses in safe places like grocery stores and newsstands. Truth, he'd gotten a bit hooked on it. It was mindless fantasy, no connection to his reality, and often had pictures of scantily clad starlets with augmented breasts. Most of the time they looked like they were ready to hurl themselves into a catfight.

She rolled her eyes at him, went back to talking to the women.

A lot of the staff had come through here to briefly hang out, talk to her, but this core group of women had stayed, surprising him at how close they were to his Mistress, who'd seemed so isolated to him up until now. James had expanded her alibi, said she was having some ongoing family issues that were limiting her working hours to brief visits during the pre-opening late-afternoon hours, while she handled most management tasks through her computer. He was impressed that they didn't pry, but they all managed to convey sympathy and support, with warmth and obvious affection for their boss. She needed that, and he could tell she enjoyed her time with them, though it was a little odd to see her having "girl time" with women she'd commanded to strip and oil down his body on his earlier visits to Atlantis. The Dommes who'd tried to break him were giggling and acting like any gaggle of women he might see out together at a Starbucks.

He wasn't oblivious to their speculative glances, or Janet's appealing smile, which made it clear, if he weren't involved with Anwyn, she'd be more than willing to keep him company.

Only if you want an appendage removed. With a dull steak knife.

Meow. Gideon gave her an arch look as Anwyn shot him a warning glance. *I'm all yours, sweet Mistress. Just nice to know I have options. She does have incredible tits. Not better than yours, of course . . .*

You do know I can read your mind? You better put down that shovel before the hole gets deep enough to put you in it.

He gave her another grin, returned to his reading, an article about a teary-eyed starlet who'd broken up with a top action-hero actor after a grueling six weeks of marriage. Against the cushion of female chatter, he realized he was almost relaxed. Knowing she was safe and everything was okay for now didn't happen often, these lulls. And not just with her. When he'd been on his own, he'd had one here or there, like when he'd visited aquariums or parks where he didn't have to be hyper-vigilant. But he'd always been alone there. He didn't feel alone now.

Of course, Daegan was coming back. That thought tightened up his gut, and he wasn't sure how he felt about it. Relieved, because Daegan could handle anything that came at her that might get past Gideon's guard? Or apprehensive and disappointed, because he'd sort of had her to himself for a month, no competition for her affection? The explanation didn't quite fit, because from the beginning, while he'd occasionally felt like that third wheel, he'd oddly never felt it necessary to challenge Daegan's claim. What went on between the three of them was different from that, as if he and Daegan fit the "apples and oranges" idiom, two different things she needed.

Or maybe he was just kidding himself, and Daegan's return just underscored the fact his days of truly being needed were numbered. Those gremlins quieted down when Daegan was in her mind as well, though not quite in the same way.

He was the understudy, whereas the main player was returning home tonight. Sourly, he turned the page, and wondered if he had room to criticize the teary starlet, since he might never reach six weeks with Anwyn . . . or any other woman.

~

"Okay, I said I wanted to do this. Demanded it. Now I'm scared to death. I feel like such a girl." She stared at the car keys in her hand. "Brian said this would be okay, right?"

"You are a girl, thank all the gods, and yes, he said it would be fine. He's dedicated his every waking moment to testing you like a lab rat, to the point you should have whiskers and a tail. He's 99.9 percent positive you are deep in the green zone for the next five to six hours. It's eleven o'clock at night. We're making a *very* brief stop to drop Debra and Brian at the main airport, and then we're going to go pick up Daegan at a private airstrip, where there will be few people. The risk is minimal. I have the restraints in the back. If we get a hint of something going south, we can get them on you and put you in the backseat until it passes. But unless you have an unexpected stressor, you should be fine."

"Should, minimal risk, less than a hundred percent positive. That's all I'm hearing. I should stay here. I'm going to bring on that stressor just thinking about it."

"Okay." Gideon shrugged, took the keys from her hand. "I'll go get him. And while I'm out, we'll stop at the Blue Room, your competition. Daegan and I will see if we can't find a Mistress with some balls. You know, you say I need a pretty firm hand, and since you're becoming a real chickenshit—"

The keys disappeared from his hand, and he let out a yelp as his testicles were given a sharp pinch by a hand that was gone as fast as it gripped him. She appeared at the driver's side, eyes shooting daggers at him. "Get in the car," she ground out.

Gideon grinned at her, a baring of teeth. "And she's back." He sobered, drew close, even though he knew he was risking further retaliation, temper still in her gaze. "You can trust Brian on this one. The past few days, he's been spot-on, right?"

Debra and Brian were already in the backseat of the car, waiting on Gideon and her to finish their conversation and join them. Brian had promised to see if there was any type of modified medication, similar to what human schizophrenics took, that he could develop for Anwyn to help with her gremlins, though no telling what side effects such a serum might have. Yet another way her life might change.

Gideon could tell she was trying to quell the resentment such thoughts brought, because she didn't want any of that disrupting her anticipation of Daegan's homecoming. There'd be enough things to disrupt that when he got here, since he knew the two of them still had some smoke to be cleared between them. He was in her mind, after all. But it was clear, she loved Daegan.

She'd told Daegan that, and Gideon had heard her recall the conversation more than once, much as he was trying his damndest not to listen in to her thoughts uninvited. Particularly when they ripped open his gut like a box cutter. Of course she loved Daegan. That was hardly a news flash, right? He'd known that the first time he'd watched them together. A woman could love only one man with that kind of heat and passion. Gideon was serving a different role for her, one that was valued differently. How could he want or demand the same thing from her, when they all knew he eventually had to leave? He should be glad she'd have someone to give all that.

He knew in her mind that she was getting really attached to Gideon and wanted him to stay, keep that balanced triangle. He wanted to absorb the happy fuzzies the thought gave him, but she knew as well as he did that she was going into a world he couldn't share. Eventually he was going to have to get off the train.

As he got into the passenger seat, Gideon watched her slide off her shoes and push them back under her seat with her heels, revealing her bare feet, the polished toenails with tiny flowers painted into the pedicure. She saw him looking. "So did Ella do as good a job as you could have done for me? You did say you know how to give a pedicure."

"Fair. I probably could have done better." He grunted, giving her a sidelong look. "I know how to paint inside the lines and everything."

"I'll bet." She smiled, glanced back at Brian and Debra, murmuring over some paperwork. "All set?"

Debra gave them a distracted smile. Brian didn't even register the comment, too immersed in whatever he was calculating on his mini-laptop. Anwyn gave Gideon an amused look and put the car in drive. They were in Daegan's roomy BMW, since he'd had it delivered back to Anwyn after he left, so they could use it as an extra vehicle if needed. She had to adjust the seat upward, a reminder of his long legs. Gideon fiddled with the buttons, found the seat warmer and started as the upholstery heated beneath him. "Why the hell would a vampire need a seat warmer?"

"It's possible for vampires to get cold. It just doesn't bother us as much. Plus, it feels good to humans." She looked back at Debra. "She's appreciating it. You don't like it?"

"I thought I'd pissed myself when my ass got warm."

She chuckled, checked the rearview mirror. "What are you two so intense about back there?"

"Brian thinks he may have figured out an improvement on another project he's been testing," Debra said absently. "Reverting a marking so a human is no longer a marked servant, no longer connected to the vampire."

Anwyn's fingers gripped the wheel as Gideon turned to look back at them. "Say what?"

Debra closed her mouth, apparently realizing too late the impact of such a statement on those in the front seat. Brian gave her a censorious glance, but suppressed a sigh. "I've been working on it for a while, because we've had instances where younger vampires rashly turn a servant against his or her will. Though it only works if the servant's bond is less than five years, there are other applications now, such as a vampire infected with the fatal Delilah virus who wishes to spare her or his servant. We haven't been able to test it," he added, "because in the two cases we've had of that, even with the bond being so young, the servant flatly refused to take the serum. They both wished to make the passage to the next life with the vampires who marked them.

"However, as far as the cases where a vampire turned a servant against his or her will and wished to undo that mistake, I tested it on several subjects recently. It worked well, but there were some unpleasant, but not fatal, side effects I've been trying to remedy. Nausea, headaches, et cetera." His brow furrowed, suggesting he was now conversing more with himself than with those in the car. "Those might be because of the interaction of the memory wipe with the chemical injection, two different mediums."

"Memory wipe?" Gideon prompted, before Brian could start his manic scribbling on the steno pad balanced on Debra's knee.

"Yes, the Council required that, because of course we have to limit human knowledge of our world. As you know, a servant who has seen so much of it can't be turned loose to risk sharing his or her knowledge. Even if he or she can be trusted for that, they could be used as a pawn of other vampires who want the knowledge of the particular Master or Mistress the servant served."

Anwyn still had that death grip on the wheel. Gideon cautiously touched her mind, found it almost unnaturally still. "Anwyn—"

"So if I reach the point I'm comfortable with the management of these seizures, you could reverse Gideon's marking. Free him from me when it's time for him to leave."

"I'm not going anywhere at the moment, sweetheart."

"Don't try to cushion this, Gideon," she snapped, then stopped, taking a breath. "If you look at that monitor, Brian, I swear I will stop this car and rip your arm off."

Brian's brows rose, but he still calmly checked the small hand monitor for the sensors he'd attached to her beneath her clothes. They'd discussed embedding them under the skin, but with the vampire penchant for healing, he didn't know how her body would handle that. Plus, once they established certain patterns, she—or her servant—could possibly become as accurate as the monitor.

"Hey." Gideon reached out, covered her hand on the wheel, brought her gaze to him. "Nothing's changed, Anwyn. I'm here for you as long as you need me. This just means when you're ready to be rid of me, you can really be rid of me. Though the memory thing is pointless—I already know most of the things they'd want wiped, and have for quite a while."

Plus, there was no way in hell anyone was giving him something that took away a single memory of Anwyn.

She pressed her lips together, and her fingers shifted beneath his, overlapping and tangling. "Yes, I suppose that's good news. My grocery bills have doubled since you moved in."

"That's not my fault. I haven't been making up the grocery list." His gaze roved deliberately over her. "Though I will point out, I'm eating for two."

While Gideon didn't do much cooking, Anwyn had started to do so. Apparently, it was something she'd used to do, but had gotten out of the habit with the demands of running Atlantis. As well as keeping company with a vampire who didn't really eat. She seemed to like cooking for Gideon, though, making him things to try, even swapping ideas with Debra, who also liked to cook. It created a familiar domestic respite in their typically unusual and volatile days. He knew Anwyn thought the knotted hardness of his body needed filling out, and he liked the look in her eyes when he ate for her. He hadn't gained much, not with how much he ran and worked out in Daegan's weapons room, but he'd made the lines of muscle more sleek, less knotty, and that pleased her.

They didn't say much for the next little bit. After a thoughtful pause, Brian and Debra had returned to their notes, tactfully avoiding further conversation on the subject. It didn't matter, since it was now out in the open, but Gideon was glad to see Anwyn was putting it aside for now, trying not to let it spoil the mood. She obviously really wanted to savor being out in the world, Daegan coming home, and Gideon at her side. It gratified him, to hear that he was part of the happiness equation tonight.

Anwyn gave him a sidewise smile, a tiny curl of her pretty lips, then slowed for a light. She lowered her window, perversely liking the warming seats on her delectable ass while she felt the cool air on her face, through her hair. Now she stretched her arm out the window, fanning out her fingers. Several times this week she'd taken the elevator to the roof apartment of Atlantis and sat out by the pool, staring up at the moon and stars, but she really hadn't experienced fresh air outside the property.

Gideon studied her profile, the firm chin and slim nose, the vibrant blue-green eyes that held so much. He knew the thoughts that moved behind them like ocean waves, liked being immersed in that flow, knowing no matter how happy or sad she was, it helped her for him to be there. He felt so connected to her this way. Even if he left, he wondered if he'd want that reversal of the marking, or if he'd prefer to carry this with him, so that when he was in range, he could have brief glimpses of the deep connection he'd shared with her, despite the abhorrent reason it had all happened.

"Look," she murmured. Gideon tuned in, followed her glance out the window and stilled at the sight of the butterfly that had landed in her palm. Its wings pumped slowly, just like the dream he'd seen in her mind a couple weeks ago. Then, like now, she brought her fingers slowly up, formed a loose cage around the tiny creature. When she opened them again, the butterfly continued to dry its wings for several pumps before it fluttered off.

"Like your dream," he murmured. It was a cool night, and though they were in the South, it wasn't the usual time of year for butterflies. He told himself not to get stupid, but it couldn't help but make him wonder. Was it all predestined, all he was doing with her? Was he meant to be with her, not just now, but more than now? That word hung on his tongue. *Forever.* Forever as a vampire's servant. Forever as Anwyn's.

But she wouldn't be his. It wasn't a two-way street, and that was what he knew kept hanging him up the most. That, and the knowledge that what they'd done with Brian and Debra had been tame next to the stories he'd heard. Anwyn had respected his wishes about Brian, but in mixed company, with more senior vampires, they'd test her by testing what she would do to her servant. She would need a servant absolutely willing to do and be everything she needed him to be, no matter his personal hang-ups. That wasn't him. Too many years, too many scars. Way too much history. He could handle someone like Brian, even Daegan, but he knew the types of vampires she would have to meet and play politics with. Vampires like those he'd killed.

On top of that, he'd become a servant to help her, not because he was one. If he had a woman, that woman was his, not someone who could share herself with whomever she liked. Call him a Neanderthal; that was the way it worked. The bitch of it was, he knew she was it, the one he wanted. There wouldn't be any more after her. Just more hookers, more brief hookups driven by loneliness and a need to get whatever drops of emotion he could out of the situation. He'd go mad with it.

No. No, he wouldn't. Because he would take every second he had with her now, burn it into his memory. Not just what she looked like on the outside, but the emotional terrain of her mind, every tear and smile, every quiet or crazy moment. He'd remember all of it, and use it like a monk's mantra to hold to a vow of loyalty to her.

Did she hear any of that? He wasn't sure he wanted her to hear it, and was glad when it appeared that she hadn't, her gaze on the city airport approaching ahead. Damn butterfly was just a fluke of nature, was all.

They entered the terminal drop-off area and brought Debra and Brian to their gate. Gideon got out of the car, helped Debra get their luggage to a sky cap. The equipment was being shipped by a special freight company on to Brian's next destination, so they carried only their clothes. They packed light. Debra turned to Gideon, smiled up at him. "I didn't know if I'd like you, but I do. You're a good man, Gideon. I hope never to see you again."

He blinked, not sure he'd heard her correctly, but she stepped closer, gave him a serious, straightforward look. "Don't talk yourself into being her servant for longer than you should. There's a lot of bad feeling among the servants toward you, particularly about what you did in South America at the Gathering. You won't be welcomed by them, and believe me, you really need the support of other servants when you get in groups. It can be harsh sometimes, the things that go on. You're tough, but you're not cut out to let yourself go the way you need to do to serve her fully."

"I know that."

She tapped his head. "This knows that." Her hand settled over his heart. "But this doesn't. Good luck."

"Why don't *you* have bad feelings toward me?"

"Maybe because Lord Brian and I aren't as integrated into that world. We're a bit of an oddity. And no one I deeply cared about was killed." She lifted on her toes, slid her arms around his shoulders, squeezed. "Plus, I care very much about your brother, and you look and act too damn much like him. Makes it hard for me to dislike you. You two are like knights from an ancient world, trying to live up to codes of chivalry long gone. Be careful, and be safe. I'd like to know you're alive out there. Teach martial arts, go get a job at Disneyland, whatever. Just get out of this as soon as you can, and stop being a vampire hunter. You already know it doesn't make sense anymore."

Letting him go, she turned away, joined Brian, leaving him surprised at what she'd noticed, for all that she appeared quiet and completely immersed in her work. But then, her Master was the same way, wasn't he? Both of them noticing far too damn much.

Having made his good-byes to Anwyn, Brian lifted his hand to Gideon, gave him a courteous nod, a proper good-bye from a vampire to a servant. "I'll keep Daegan informed about the status on Barnabus."

Gideon grunted. "If you need someone to go stake his black heart, you don't need to wait for Daegan. I'll be happy to do it."

Brian shook his head, a scientist's resignation with the unenlightened, which Gideon preferred to call academia-with-its-head-shoved-up-its-ass, but then the vampire nodded once more, gesturing to Debra to head with him into the terminal.

Getting back into the car, Gideon sat silently with Anwyn for a couple of moments, both of them following their progress. Brian's handsomeness and Debra's muted appeal were enough to turn heads toward them. Laying a hand on her lower back, Brian guided her past a group of outgoing passengers, rolling their carry-ons behind them.

"I'm going to miss them. Not necessarily because I wanted them to stay longer, though they were lovely houseguests, but because it feels like they were an important moment, something that has to move on, but still needs to be mourned."

"Yeah. Know that feeling." Gideon cleared his throat. "How about we head for the private airstrip, go pick up that bloodsucking boyfriend of yours?"

Anwyn nodded, not looking toward him. "Okay."

～

It was about midnight when they pulled up to the small airfield. "The only thing that's landed is a Gulfstream," Gideon noted.

"That's his." Anwyn gave a faint smile at his snort. "Well, he does a lot of traveling for his job."

"Being the Council's private assassin pays well."

She gave him a sidelong glance. "How have you funded your . . . missions?"

Gideon's jaw tightened. She didn't intend it, but perhaps because of how much he didn't want her to know, it flashed to the front of his mind, harsh and bright, so she couldn't overlook it. "You took money from your victims?" Her brow rose.

"They weren't victims," Gideon said shortly. "They were vampires. And it's not like I was using it to buy a fancy plane, or a car that heats my ass for me."

"That's true," she said neutrally. "Though I don't really know how Daegan got his money. I don't know if the Council pays him, or if it's just something that's expected of him. It's a pretty feudal society, from what I can tell."

"Yeah." Gideon focused on the airstrip. The pilot was talking to the controller, signing some paperwork.

Anwyn didn't see Daegan, though she was sure he'd notice their arrival. He was probably in the terminal. She ran a fingernail along the curve of the steering wheel.

"So how does it work? If you killed me, would you take my purse off my body, see if you could find bank account numbers or credit cards? Or would you go to my home before anyone knew I was gone, take valuables?"

"Anwyn, don't." He spoke through stiff lips. "I've made money other ways. The occasional protection job. And our parents left us pretty well set up. It was invested for us, divided equally. I just don't like to draw from that."

"Not when you can take from the vampires you kill."

He turned to look at her. "How about you answer a question for me? The last vamp I took murdered a twenty-four-year-old nurse behind the generator station at her hospital. He drained her dry. She had a fiancé, a life. They wanted kids, and she volunteered at a battered women's shelter. She also liked to go shag dancing on weekends and her favorite drink was a blackberry mojito. She had brown eyes as soft as velvet, and a great smile. What do you think she'd say about me lifting her murderer's wallet to fund my next kill, so someone else like her doesn't have to die? Think she'd be sitting there acting so damn self-righteous?"

The coldness in his eyes pierced her heart, because it matched the frost that covered his mind. But something else penetrated. Daegan had spoken of Gideon's last kill. *The night he came to you, he killed a vampire who didn't deserve his brand of justice.* Was this vampire Gideon had just described someone different? Someone Daegan didn't know about?

Gideon's gaze was still on her. At her thoughts, something flickered in his gaze, a realization that sent a shaft of alarm through his mind. Abruptly, his brain was flooded with the tabloid images from earlier in the day, random commercials, his interest in Gulfstreams, the fact he had an itch behind his knee . . . It was so instantaneous, she knew he'd been practicing it, ways to thwart her ability to read his mind, his own version of the curtain she practiced.

Daegan had said that, once fully marked, a servant couldn't escape a vampire, not if she was determined to plumb his mind all the way to the soul. She remembered there was a caution involved in that, one of the reasons fledglings didn't have servants, but her instinctive reaction didn't care for such caveats. That cold withdrawal sparked something inside her. The woman Anwyn would be nursing hurt, the Mistress some anger, but the vampire reacted in a much more aggressive way. In a heartbeat, she wanted to shove through that debris he was throwing up in front of her, toss it out of the way and rip away any shielding to find whatever it was he was hiding from her. Her blood wanted to prove he had no right to raise his voice to her, show him how vulnerable his mind was to whatever she desired to know.

The force of it frightened her, because this was no seizure, no fit of bloodlust. This was something integrating with what she was, an evolution into something else she seemed powerless to stop. Opening the car door, she shoved out of it, even though she was still in her bare feet. She strode a few feet away, blindly, trying to get a handle on the anger, find her humanity amid that demand. It was a close reflection of her own burning desire, taking her instincts as a Mistress and twisting them, tying her intestines into knots.

Bring him to his knees. Strip his mind, turn him inside out. The pulsing power in her mind told her she could unleash the power to do just that.

He'd gotten out of the car, was coming around toward her. She managed to shriek at him, although it was only in her mind.

Stay back, Gideon. Don't. I can't control it. I'll hurt you. Please . . . stay away. She didn't know exactly how; she just knew she would. Turning someone's mind inside out sounded high on the "not good" list. So focused on the physical danger she posed toward others, they really hadn't paid any attention to this one. But this was the first time Gideon had so decidedly defied her, shown he'd taken measures to wall her off from him, and every instinct as a predator wanted to take him down for it.

She tried to turn her focus elsewhere. When she'd been human, during a stressful day she'd do meditation exercises. Relax her muscles, one group at a time. Her mind laughed with bitter incredulity, daisies thrown on a gas fire.

She was alone on this one. Gideon could help her manage her seizures, but he couldn't help her manage this, her vampire instincts rising against her, trying to turn her into a monster. Not when those shadow voices were controlling the trigger and aim.

But I can.

Anwyn, he's here. Gideon's voice was a quiet echo in her mind as she turned toward that long-awaited voice. She was aware of the tinge of regret and pain in her servant's thought. A brief overwhelming sadness, laced with that loneliness that tore at her heart. But she couldn't respond to it right now. That fomenting blood held her attention, making her stay locked where she was. Until a pair of familiar hands closed on her arms, drew her from her kneeling position to her feet, up against his tall, strong body.

She'd wanted this homecoming to be perfect, not flavored by this, but Daegan didn't soothe or treat her as if she were broken. His mouth came down on hers, hot, firm and demanding, and that lethal demand pivoted away from destructive instinct, leaped for what she'd missed so intensely for nearly a month.

His scent, his strength, the feel of him. He let her hands go so she could stretch up against him, slide them through his short hair, lean full into him, enveloped by that familiar duster. The soft stuff of his slacks and linen shirt teased her skin with the hard muscles beneath, the steel of the weapons he carried. She moaned in his mouth as he pressed his firm cock against her abdomen, one hand lowering to cup her ass and the other curved around her neck under her hair, holding her to him, chest to thighs. He delved even deeper into her mouth, his tongue teasing her to mindless lust. His mind was in hers, giving her images of all the things he'd visualized doing with her, would do to her, driving everything else away.

Then, a gift like a bouquet of roses amid all the carnal images, she saw other things he'd been remembering about her, snapshots he'd pulled up to keep him company while in Europe. The tilt of her head, the way her mouth quirked when she was verbally sparring with him. How she brushed her hair at night, the way her nightgown lay against her breast and hip, the soft silk folding and straightening along those curves as her brush moved through the shining waves. Handling club business at her computer, her legs tucked up underneath her, chin in hand, her mug of tea at her elbow, her hair falling over one shoulder.

I've missed you so much, cher.

The volatile energy she'd been holding back from Gideon had become something else entirely. She'd been right. She needed them both, to feel this balance, this sense of being . . . home. It was a dangerous feeling, with so many things uncertain and unresolved, for all of them, but she didn't care. She'd take it for now.

Recognizing a fragrant scent, she realized then why the image of roses had come into her mind. When Daegan lifted his head, she looked down and saw he'd laid a full two dozen lush red roses on the ground before bringing her to her feet for the welcoming kiss. He retrieved them now, still holding her close with one arm, and gave them to her, so they were cradled between them.

"They are perhaps old-fashioned or cliché, but you are red roses to me. Exotic, classic, full of overwhelming passionate color and beauty."

"Charmer," she managed, stroking the petals, then looked up into his face. Now that the voices in her head had gone silent, she could really see him. The dark eyes and sculpted jaw, never a five-o'clock shadow, since vampires didn't have facial hair. That overwhelming presence, completely in control and in command of his surroundings . . . and of her heart.

He was a vampire, just as she was. She had no apologies to make to him, because he understood who and what she was, what she was becoming. In his eyes there was acceptance, anticipation. Pleasure.

She laid her head on his chest, hearing his heart beat. Then she closed her eyes to feel the strength of his arm, the brush of his coat against her side as Daegan shifted toward Gideon.

"Vampire hunter." The short greeting was warm, one man glad to see another, their typically minimalist-style communication.

Gideon grunted, noncommittal. "According to Brian, we should be calling you *Lord* Daegan."

"If you use that title, I'll be forced to remove your internal organs."

"I wouldn't dream of contributing to your already overinflated mythology."

Anwyn looked up to see Daegan's lips curve, a show of fang. "I've missed you as well, vampire hunter." He glanced down at Anwyn. "Though I believe I interrupted a disagreement."

She gave a harsh half chuckle. Yeah, a disagreement. She'd about peeled his brain like a grape.

But you didn't. It's all right, Mistress.

She turned to look at Gideon then. His eyes no longer held that terrible cold distance, but there was a careful reserve, as if something fragile hung in the air between them. Too concerned that the rage might return and take her over, she decided not to press it. Right now, she wanted to focus on Daegan, even though she was sure all three of them were aware that a pall had been cast over the homecoming, a pall she hadn't wanted there. But with a transition like hers, she'd better start assuming the best-laid plans might always have a wrench thrown in the works. It didn't make her feel any better about it, but it made her ready to move forward, leave it behind.

As if reading her mind—and she guessed he could—Gideon opened the driver's door. "I'll drive, so you two can talk in the back, if you'd like."

She took a step in that direction, then thought about the night she'd realized she couldn't allow Brian to use Debra to talk to her, relegate her to that level. She wasn't a coward. And she didn't let any man who served her, who submitted to her, get away with what Gideon had just done. She'd let it aggravate the vampire instincts, but Daegan had steadied and balanced her such that she could pull the Mistress to the fore-front.

"Gideon, what were you hiding from me? I'm not going to look in your mind, not if I can help it." She had to focus hard to put that curtain down, keep his thoughts to just white noise, but she could do it, as long as she spoke in simple sentences and didn't try to walk and chew gum at the same time. "I want you to tell me."

His gaze went to Daegan behind her, and she was surprised to see a look of deep regret cross the vampire hunter's face. "She didn't know why I killed Trey," he said to Daegan. "You didn't tell her about annual kills."

Daegan's muttered oath was enough to alarm her, but it did more than that. It was something they both were keeping from her. She rounded on him, accusation in her gaze.

"I thought we were done with lies."

"I've never lied to you, *cher.*"

She thought about screaming, but maybe men were incapable of considering premeditated omission lying. Sort of like the *I would have told you I fucked an entire cheerleading squad in your bed, but you never asked, did you? How did I know you'd want to know about that?*

Gideon made a short cough behind her, but she didn't turn, afraid of what she might do if it was a smothered laugh instead of a reaction to the cold air.

"What is an annual kill?"

Daegan hesitated. "Vampires must take a life once a year, Anwyn. The life of a decent human being, whose blood is not tainted by evil or a dissolute life. It's necessary, vital, to maintain our peak physical and mental stability. Without it, a vampire will start to lose that."

"You mean, I will . . ."

"It's not something you will need to deal with for many months. When you do, I'll help you, in whatever way is necessary." Daegan squeezed her hand. "Can we leave it as a subject for another time, *cher*? It will be there for us to discuss anytime."

Anwyn swallowed. *Yeah, what the hell. I guess we can put off the idea of me becoming a murderer for another day.*

Now she understood why Gideon had blocked her, the alarm that had disrupted his anger about his income sources. In his irritation, he hadn't thought about the path he was taking the conversation, until it was too late to cover the trail.

She had understood that there were bad vampires, just like there were bad people. Until Daegan had told her otherwise, she'd hoped Gideon's targets had been those that were closer to the monsters of the movies, than vampires like Daegan. Even when Daegan told her about the vampire Gideon killed right before coming to her, she'd comforted herself with the idea that Gideon was with her now. For the time being, he wouldn't be doing that.

But this made things different, didn't it? There was no vampire who hadn't done murder. Daegan . . . Holy Goddess, however many centuries old he was, that meant he'd taken . . . hundreds of innocent lives.

"It is necessary for our survival, Anwyn," Daegan said. "It's no different from what a wolf or lion must do to nourish itself. Only instead of making kills every several days, we only need to do it once a year."

She looked toward Gideon, understood a little better why that fortress existed inside him, a fortress that obviously rolled up its drawbridge against her when she hit the right button. If she could possibly come to grips with taking an innocent life, how on earth could Gideon reconcile himself to being a part of that, if he'd spent so much of his life trying to save the future annual kills of every vampire life he took?

"Take me home," she said to him. "You and Daegan can ride in the front."

5

WHEN they arrived at the apartment, Anwyn went to her bedroom, closed the door without a word to either one of them. Daegan shouldered his bag, took it down the hallway to his room. Looking between them, Gideon decided he'd take the opportunity while he was fairly certain Anwyn's mind would be shut to both of them, and followed Daegan.

The vampire had unzipped his garment bag. He hung a handful of clothes back up in his closet, expensive clothes that looked dry-cleaned and pressed, reminding Gideon of how they'd gotten to this uncomfortable moment. Jesus, he wished he hadn't let temper take him over. Of all the things for her to have to deal with. And tonight, of all nights.

Daegan pulled a pair of loaded nine-millimeters out of the bag, placed them in the top drawer of his dresser. "They won't delay her validation as a vampire to the next Gathering," he said without preamble. "They expect me to bring her back in two weeks. The time I spent on assignments in Europe for them was the only extension they would provide, and I drew those out as long as possible, to give Brian the maximum amount of time to help stabilize her."

Daegan hadn't turned on the light in the bedroom. The light was on in the bath, and the shadow thrown across his face made Gideon realize the vamp was a little paler than usual, such that he could see some stress lines around his mouth. It told him the past month had been no picnic for Daegan, either. "So there *is* something going on. Somebody on the Council is gunning for you, and they're using what should have been a straightforward kill to stick it to you."

"It's likely. They want to address that at the same time they do the validation. But she appears to be doing well. It's better to go ahead and get it done. The sooner she is validated, the safer she'll be within this world." Daegan sat down on the bed, began to remove his shoes.

"If someone wants to bring you on the carpet for Barnabus's kill, she could be in danger there."

"No. It won't be entirely easy for her there, but she is strong enough to handle herself, and I will be treated separately from her situation. Newly made vampires are viewed much as children, not yet culpable for the sins of their sires or associates. I'll be able to watch over her."

"We both will."

Daegan's head lifted, his dark eyes fastening on Gideon's. "You can't be serious. You do remember what happened the last time you attended a Council Gathering?"

"Well, I didn't have an official invitation then. I'll be better behaved. I won't bring explosives."

"Gideon—"

"I remember what you said before you left. If she loses it in front of the Council, they'll treat her like a deformed animal. They'll order you to execute her."

"And I told you I would never permit that, even if I had to take down every one of them." Daegan had started flicking open the buttons of his shirt, but now he stood, squaring off with Gideon. "You said from the very beginning you were not prepared to stand as her full servant like this, not among other vampires. Gideon, you would be in the very heart of it, for however long or short a time we are there. You will not survive that."

"Nice to know you care."

"It is not about you. Remember Morena Wilson?"

Gideon stiffened at the reminder of Trey's victim, the nurse killed behind the generator station. "You felt helpless when you learned of her death," Daegan continued. "That sense of helpessness was what sent you after Trey. You didn't think; you reacted."

"Fuck you."

"What will it do to Anwyn, her stability, if you are killed?"

"I know the vampire world pretty well myself. Seeing me as her servant, scraping and fetching and kissing her shoes, will get them off, way better than my death. They might knock me around a bit, but I can handle a rough time. I'll do that, if that's what's needed. I understand how important it is that she's accepted. Hell, Lyssa had to survive in the forest for months as a fugitive when they found out about her. Anwyn wouldn't survive that, not with her seizures. She'd be easy pickings."

"No, she wouldn't. But it will never come to that." Daegan pulled off a knife holster holding three blades and tossed it on the dresser, a sign of frustration and impatience that Gideon took as encouragement.

"If we can get her through this," he persisted, "she's pretty much home free. Then I'll step aside. But I won't walk away when she may be facing an execution squad. Yeah, you'll say you can handle it, but you can't be everywhere at once. I think you know it's going to take both of us to do it."

"I don't deny an extra mind and pair of hands would be useful. But you're still overlooking how it will affect her."

"If you're worried about how Anwyn would handle them picking on me, we can work that out. It's a risk either way, but the odds are better with me there than without me." Gideon stepped forward. "She *is* better. But, hell, if I so much as go to the grocery store, that crap in her mind comes out of the woodwork. I'm not in her mind now, but occasionally, I reach out, a formless feeling, no real invasiveness, just to keep them cowed down. It's something Brian showed me how to do.

"I'm not saying she's an invalid, not by any means. She can manage them on her own, but it's like having your head invaded by an army of vicious, asthmatic Darth Vaders. Yeah, you can be in her head, too, and you can probably keep them down, but are you going to fence with the Council over what happened with Barnabus, keep an eye on her, and handle the other hundred contingencies that could happen? Can you do it all?"

∾

Daegan studied him for a long moment. Though the vampire hunter obviously meant every word, and he knew the man had the courage to back it up—hell, he wasn't certain he'd ever met someone with such a foolish overabundance of courage, unless it was Anwyn—something was not quite right, something he couldn't quite place. It ticked uneasily in his gut. He'd seen a shadow of it in Gideon's face when he'd met them at the car, a sense of regret and odd . . . inevitability.

"Have you read the Harry Potter books, Gideon?"

Gideon was obviously braced for more arguments. At his startled look, Daegan gave him a tight smile. "Of course not. I expect you don't do much reading in your leisure time. In *Goblet of Fire*, Harry makes the very sportsmanlike decision to allow Cedric Diggory to grasp the Tri-Wizard Cup with him, the intention being that they would share the all-important tournament win. Harry's noble act results in him and Cedric being plunged into an evil place, and Cedric is killed. If Harry had been less noble, less fair-minded, Cedric would have lived. It is a very classic example of how noble intentions often lead to tragic results." He straightened, squared off with the hunter. "I have no desire to be Harry Potter."

"I doubt you have any noble intentions about anything." Gideon snorted.

"Probably true. I am painfully aware, however, that sometimes Fate has to play out her hand. If things go according to plan—a simple validation procedure, I am raked over the coals for making unauthorized kills—yes, Anwyn would be better off having you there, helping her maintain stability. But there will be considerable danger to you. Great danger. On top of that, we will need to weigh how it could play out if things don't go according to plan."

"What matters is her." Gideon set his jaw. "It's going to be sticky either way. You'll have to prove to me it's in her better interests for me to stay behind, or kill me. I don't think you'll do either one."

"Don't tempt me. I might choose the easier of the two." Daegan sighed. "I'll think on it. We'll need to talk to Anwyn. We must all be in accord on this."

"Agreed. But not tonight. And I want to be the one to tell her I'm coming with her." Though Gideon gave the vampire an even look, underscoring it, he couldn't help shifting, feeling the regret anew. "I wasn't intending to tell her like that. About the annual kill."

"She was going to find out soon enough. Perhaps it's best that she has time to digest it, before we have to travel."

"Yeah, but she wanted tonight to be different. She was trying to focus on your homecoming and put the rest on the back burners. She's been working her ass off these past few weeks, and she wanted to enjoy something." Gideon cleared his throat. "She really missed you."

Daegan swore softly, and returned to the dresser, emptying his pockets. The mirror's reflection showed the bed behind him, a reminder of many things shared there. It was good to be home, but it wasn't home until Anwyn truly welcomed him. He'd looked forward to that as well, but perhaps hadn't counted on it the way Anwyn had, knowing what lay between them.

"You told me once that you weren't used to relying on anyone, Gideon. I told you I was the same. I've never relied on anyone until her. It's easy enough for me to get what I want from a woman, but the night we met, she met my gaze, saw what I was, didn't flinch. Wasn't even really interested in that. She didn't have to give me anything, and I couldn't have made her give me anything. She's that kind of person. So when she did, it was her choice, her will, her desire. It made me trust her, believe in her and need her, in a way I've never needed anyone."

In Gideon's stillness, Daegan sensed his shock at the bald words, and wondered himself why he'd said them aloud. Spending long periods of time without any confidante, he thought he'd outgrown the need for one. But perhaps nothing had ever bothered him as much as this estrangement with the difficult woman he loved, what had happened to her, what he'd been powerless to stop.

He heard everything. It had amazed him to learn, early in his life, how little humans heard. Vampires heard more, but his hearing exceeded even theirs. If Anwyn let out a whispered sigh, even behind the closed door of her room, he could hear it. He heard the movement in the soundproofed playrooms above them. Knew there were insects and worms scratching and working their way along tunnels they'd made against the sunken foundation of this underground level.

So he heard Gideon move toward him. However, he was in for a surprise himself when the man's hand closed on his shoulder. He went still under the quick passing of a thumb over his collarbone, a rough grip that denied the hint of a caress. Then Gideon pulled back abruptly, leaving it hard to decipher the brief gesture. However, for some reason, the touch loosened things up in Daegan's chest. "Go see her. I'll hang out somewhere. She's in her room."

"I've told you before not to give me orders, vampire hunter."

"You don't care whether I live or die, except that it concerns Anwyn. Well, same goes. She needs you. And since I'm in a nurturing mood, I'll mention you look like you need blood. If you need to go coax a pint out of someone, we should be fine. She had her injection right before we came to get you, and she's good for a couple of hours yet. Plus, I have the restraints, and with advance warning, she'll put them on and I can handle her from there."

"I'll keep that in mind, Mom."

Gideon made a suitable hand gesture reflected in the mirror. Daegan glanced over his shoulder, flashed his fangs at him. The hunter gave him a sardonic grin in return, then left the room, leaving him to the unpacking and shower he'd planned.

Don't tempt me . . . The warning he'd issued to Gideon had several levels, but the hunter was as oblivious to them as he was to personal danger. Take Gideon Green to a Vampire Council meeting. *By the Holy Relics . . .* Of course, there would be some small pleasure in seeing the poker-faced Lord Uthe drop his jaw on the Council table. Shaking his head, Daegan started to move toward the showers, his hand on the hook to his trousers, but then he stopped. He really did need that shower. He'd executed one final vampire an hour before he'd gotten on the plane, and though he'd washed up in the sink, he still wanted the full cleansing effect. The vampire had been older and more aggressive, and had landed a lucky strike with a machete that had deprived Daegan of a quart of blood. He did need to feed, but he needed Anwyn more.

He'd told her he wouldn't search her mind without valid cause, but that didn't prevent him from using it as a direct communication link. *Anwyn, would you come take a shower with me?*

The night he'd forced her to make Gideon her full servant, mere days before he left her, he'd been beyond cruel to her. He'd savagely fucked her to rouse the predator in her, made her discard despair for fury. Afterward, he'd wanted to take her into a bath, sponge the evidence of his barbaric behavior off her thighs himself, hold her close, stroke her hair.

Instead, he'd been ruthless. This past month, he'd stayed away from her because it was best. But Gideon was right. Now he had the opportunity to show her the tenderness he'd had to withhold. Though, in truth, that might have to wait. He needed to take her roughly first, his body vibrating for her in a way that had almost spilled onto Gideon, when he'd come close enough to touch Daegan. Blood and physical needs were tied up in the emotional, all riding close to the surface.

At last she responded. *If I can stake you in your sleep afterward.*

It almost made him smile. So much for tenderness. *Would you like me to come get you?*

No response to that, but there was a faint sense of acknowledgment, positive or negative he didn't know. Leaving his room, he crossed over the shared living area, aware that Gideon was moving around the small reading room. Anwyn's door was cracked. Stepping in, he rapped on the boards, a simple courtesy, and gazed to the right, expecting her in the bathroom. He reached out with his mind and—

Stars exploded in his vision from whatever blunt object hit his head. He ducked the next blow, caught her around the waist and yanked the bat out of her hands, tossing it toward the bed, swearing audibly. But it was her swearing he heard in his mind.

You son of a bitch.

She was vibrating with full, glorious rage. The pathetic, weeping creature she'd so often been before he left wasn't anywhere to be seen, replaced by flashing eyes and a swirl of sable hair. She continued to swear at him in her mind, keeping the fight in silence. Obviously she didn't want Gideon privy to it, though her emotions were stormy enough he'd be surprised if Gideon wasn't picking up some of the fallout.

He shoved her up against the wall, keeping her arms pinned. Their bodies were intimately close, bare chest in his open shirt pressed to ripe breasts in lace, because she'd been changing. She was wearing a black demi-cup, one of his personal favorites with its propensity to be low enough to expose areola, particularly during this kind of struggle.

"Why the hell did you do that?" he demanded, low, overriding her mental diatribe. Blessed Virgin, he thought she might have cracked his skull, and wondered when she'd decided to keep a baseball bat in her room.

"Because I'm going to have to kill someone to live. Because I didn't ask for this. Because I wouldn't have changed anything about knowing you, even if I'd known this was going to happen, and I don't know what kind of person that makes me. Mostly because I'm tired of learning about things by accident, or having them sprung on me, because one or both of you doesn't think I'm ready to deal with it."

"Then let me bring Gideon in so you can hit him in the head, too."

She snarled at him, and the tiny needle points of her fangs glittered. Humor vanished, and he caught her chin. "I won't hesitate to do anything I feel necessary to protect you, to help you deal with this. You aren't invincible. You can't handle it all at once, Anwyn. We've made the best judgments possible. I told you from the beginning, for this to work you were going to have to relinquish some control to us, trust us with that much."

"What about the night you made me mark Gideon? The way you fucked me? You were pissed, and you were using your dick to make a point. That wasn't about trust and judgment."

"Yes, it was. You had no right to try to take your life. I had to break you out of your suicidal self-condemnation and deal with my anger at you at the same time. It suited both purposes."

She stared up at him. They held that locked battle of wills for several minutes. Daegan was acutely aware of the way her body felt, only that bra and her thin skirt between them, her bare foot pressed tensely on top of his.

"I want you to answer a question, and I want it to be the truth," she said between clenched teeth. "And don't you dare tell me you always give me the truth, or I swear I'll neuter you in your sleep."

Daegan pressed his lips together. If he smiled, he expected she'd react the same way. "Ask your question."

"We've been together five years, come this December. Do you remember back when you wanted me to be your servant, and I refused? You left me for six months."

He remembered, as much as he didn't want to recall that bleak period, or face the question he knew she was about to ask.

"When you came back," she continued, her voice strained, "you didn't ask me to be your servant anymore. You wouldn't even let me volunteer to do it. You never told me what changed. I want to know."

Bending his head, he pressed his nose into her hair, letting his eyes close briefly. She stayed still in his grasp, her body so close to his, her blood rushing through her veins, her scent in his nose. He could over-power her, seduce her into silence, take her to screaming orgasm, but the question would still be there, and her trust would be eroded further. He'd come home to something different between them. He could feel how much she wanted what he wanted, to touch her body, claim it anew, but only she could unlock her heart. To do that, he had to unlock his.

Lifting his head, he met her eyes. Over the past five years, he'd learned to give more of himself to her than he'd ever given to anyone, but there were places into which he still didn't invite her. He needed to start learning to handle that differently, not just because that was what she would ultimately demand, but it was what she needed. And he wasn't sure he could refuse her anything she truly needed.

"When I left, I had to come to grips with who and what you were at that time. Human, yes, but with a will very distinct from my own. Most vampires are attracted to humans who have an element of submission to them, *cher*. We sniff it out like bloodhounds, much the way nature brings together compatible creatures for mating. On the surface, and even in the deeper layers, you aren't that. When I touch you, you submit to me, but you don't do it as a natural submissive. You fight me; you challenge me; you do it on your own terms, as a Mistress. Much like your unique servant, there is something in you that allows your nature to surrender and submit, but only under specific circumstances, with one person. It makes you a very different animal. However, unlike Gideon, you could never have been my servant. Anwyn Inara Naime is a female Dominant. You would never view three marks as anything but a prison."

Sliding his other arm around her waist, he kept her pinned between the wall and his body. His cock was hard and insistent against the junc-ture of her thighs, making her lips part, but her fingers clutched his biceps, her eyes waiting, watching.

"There are things about each of us we can't change, things that no one can or should ask us to change." He spread his fingers over her right buttock, began to gather the skirt up, inch by inch, letting it climb her thighs. "That is what I realized. I realized that I would destroy what I loved about you by asking you to be what you couldn't be."

When her fingers dug into his biceps, as if to stop him, he shook his head, his dark eyes staying on hers as the skirt went up farther, exposing her to the cool air. "I will not be refused, *cher*. I've wanted you for too long, and you are mine, even if you try to deny it."

Her jaw firmed, and those nails pierced his flesh anyway. Glancing down, he saw his blood well up beneath her thumb, trickle over the curve of the muscle. "Brian told you that you could wear the razors under your nails again."

"Just the thumbs for now." Her eyes sparked. "I want you to promise me that you will tell me everything. Everything that's going to happen, everything that's happening now. Everything you know that will affect me. If you don't, I'll start scouring Gideon's mind like bakeware and you . . ."

His brow rose, waiting, and her lips firmed. "You're not impervious. I'll figure out some way to torment you, make your life hell."

"Oh, *cher*." Letting his touch ease on her buttock, becoming a fondling motion, he twined his other fingers in her loosened hair. She'd worn it down, because she knew he liked it loose. She'd worn his favorite lingerie, and her skin had a fragrant scent of lavender, also his favorite. "To do that, you only have to withhold your forgiveness from me." He slid a thumb over her cheek, acutely aware of how her lips trembled before she firmed them. "Do you have plans to forgive me for everything that still lies between us?"

"I've penciled in something for a couple of decades from now."

He'd been respecting her attempts to maintain a shield between them, weak and thin though it was right now, but he got a flash of mixed emotions, her desire for what he could give her now warring with pride and fear. She needed him too much for the former, was too brave to let the other hold sway.

Millimeter by millimeter, however, the tension eased from her, and then he was just holding her against the wall, her legs wound around his thighs. "Yes. I will shower with you," she said.

"Good." Taking a moment, he put his forehead against hers again. Tentatively, her fingers came up, outlined his jaw, the slope of his cheeks.

"Daegan." She spoke his name softly, and his eyes closed. In a quick movement, he lifted her in his arms, and carried her back through the main room. Gideon had stretched out in front of the TV. Feeling his gaze following them, Daegan headed for his spacious multi-jet shower. He wasn't a man who needed many comforts. However, having been bathed in blood so often, he was fond of a device that could wash away blood from so many angles, even the invisible blood of past struggles.

Gideon's lonely. Confused. Her sultry mind voice stroked his aroused nerves. *Wants to be with us, but doesn't know what that means.*

He's fine. We'll take care of him later. Daegan put her on her feet on the tile, steadied her as he turned on the water.

As her serious eyes studied his face, he unhooked her bra, slid it off her arms. He didn't allow her to undress, but handled it himself, wanting to touch her skin as he pushed the skirt over her hips, caught the panties and took care of them. When he straightened, she placed her hands on his chest, slid them upward. Like a bird spreading out wings, she fanned her fingers, taking them under the open shirt, sliding it off his shoulders. She curved her hands over the rounded muscle as it dropped to the ground. Her gaze devoured him.

"I still smell the remains of blood on you. Faint, but it's there. You look tired and pale. You need to feed."

"I need to fuck you more. Hard and deep. And I want your blood on my tongue as much as your cream."

The way her eyes flamed in response, the wave of increased arousal he inhaled from between her legs, told him it was going to take restraint to hold off on doing what he wanted to do so much. He wanted to draw it out, tease both of them with it.

Her gaze still on his, her hands lowered to his waistband. "You may open my trousers, *cher*," he said in a husky tone, "but you won't touch my cock. Not yet. I want you wet and begging for it."

"Afraid you might lose control and go off like a teenager?" Her lips curved but she obeyed, her nimble fingers slipping the hook and tugging down the zipper, incidental brushes of her knuckles only on the hard organ straining beneath.

"Behave," he warned. "Or I'll put you under the showerhead and let it force you to climax three or four times before I put myself inside you."

She wanted to taunt him. He heard her start the thought, *You won't last that long,* but then she pressed her lips together at the reaction in his gaze. She knew he'd do it, no matter his own desire. He'd given her the strike with the bat as her due, given her the answer to the question she needed for her heart, but he knew the difference between those things and her testing his dominance over her.

He'd held back through her anger, her nasty comments, because he'd needed time himself to know what was right and true. No matter what she was enduring, or the guilt he carried, the give-and-take between them was what they understood best. It was when they crossed blades, engaged in that delicate fencing, that they always found the way to the center of the complicated maze shielding each of their hearts. He was done holding back.

Shifting her naked body into the heated spray, he followed her there. Inside the comforting rush of water, he took up the soap. The spray pattered drops all over her, dampened her hair, the high breasts and tight nipples, sluicing down her belly. Considering that tempting view, he dropped to one knee. It surprised her, he could tell, as he began to wash her thighs. He followed the enticing limb up to the juncture between her legs. When he pressed the heel of his soapy hand to her labia, she bit her lip. Her fingers closed over his shoulders as she leaned back against the shower wall.

"It's all stupid games, isn't it?"

"What is, *cher*?"

"All those times I wanted something from you." Her voice was embellished by the water's whisper. "A word, a promise, things you couldn't give. So I kept myself at arm's length, not willing to give everything of myself because you wouldn't. It was stupid. Because all along you felt the same way."

"A promise unspoken is a promise never broken."

Her blue-green eyes flickered. "Like books of magic. Knowing a true name is power, which is why someone never speaks their true name. Unspoken makes it more powerful. More real."

Rather than interpret his statement as a reluctance to say what was in his heart, she'd understood. She knew him, knew his heart. He'd never really fooled her. She'd just needed him to have the faith in her to say the words. Though she hadn't yet completely forgiven or forgotten, it was something.

Rising, he cradled her face, staring down at her. With tenderness, he traced the bottom lip, touched the tiny lower fang, worked his way up to the longer upper canines, traced those as well. Her hand rested on his wrist, her body still, and he felt her attention like a magic of its own, closing around them both. Looking into her mind, he saw that there were so many things going on, orbiting around that center focus. Leaning in, he pressed his mouth to hers, realized how rarely they'd done this, a sweet, lingering, mouth-to-mouth, a barely touching. There was a slight tremble through her body, and maybe through his. A lot had happened these past few weeks; a lot had changed.

He'd lived in combat mode for a long time. A crisis was dealt with, handled, and then he moved on. He'd done it so well, he hadn't allowed himself much room to realize that, this time, more was needed, and not just for her. For him, as well. And maybe for another.

Her lashes lifted. He didn't know if she read it from him, as tightly closed as his mind always was, or if it simply moved in them both, a new synchronization to their thoughts and wishes that had perhaps always been there, but had been hampered by those shields and protections she'd referenced. Or what he was and what she hadn't been, until now.

I want him here, too. Does that make sense?

Yes, cher. *He's your servant.* But he knew it was more than that. While she didn't challenge it, her sensual lips curved, telling him she still wasn't fooled.

"Do you think he'll come if I call him?"

"I think so. Though keep in mind he's more terrier than retriever. Savagely loyal, but not always predictable."

"I think that's what we both like about him." Her tongue touched her lips, moistened them, and more beads of water rolled down the delicate architecture of her throat, caressing the firm, high tops of her breasts.

He'd waited long enough. In one effortless move, he had her up against the shower wall, gripping her thighs, and drove home. He knew her body so well he didn't have to hesitate. She moaned, startled at his sudden decision but welcoming it. Her slippery channel pulled him in, her body bucking up in his arms. She wrapped her own around his back, those razored nails sliding along his flesh, raking him and splattering his feet with crimson, the smell of his own blood.

Don't waste it, cher.

He'd felt her hunger. She had a moment of hesitation, remembering he needed to feed, but he had no patience for her coddling. He brought her mouth to his throat, cupping the back of her neck, fingers tangled hard in her hair. She read his need and answered it, puncturing him with those dainty fangs, making a sound in her throat as his blood rushed into her mouth. He surged back into her, holding her so close she was pressed flush to him, from groin to breast, as he hammered into her body. This first time, it wasn't about pleasure or climax. It was a deep-seated need being met, conveying how much he'd missed her, had wanted to be here, that brought her to an emotional pinnacle that overflowed in her mind, spilled over to his. More images than thoughts, but all of them were the things she'd wanted and missed so much while he was away.

Because of that, he was able to slow himself down enough to reach between them, stroke her, tease the stretched opening, caress her spread thighs, the tingling nerves there. When she dropped her head back against the tile, he caught her mouth, tasting his blood on her tongue.

He moved to her throat, but didn't bite, stroking the artery with his fangs as the hot water rained on them. He maintained a steady stroke, knowing her body so well, feeling every incremental shift up toward climax, the way her body was tightening on his, responding in kind, goading him higher. Her legs were locked over his hips, her vampire strength holding her easily on him, such that with the brace of the wall behind her he could curve his back, work his way down her sternum and issue the command in his mind.

Bring your breasts up to my mouth. Display them to me.

She didn't want to let go of him, but she did, cupping their weight and tilting them upward to increase the sensitivity of the nerves as his mouth closed over one. It took bravery for a woman to put her nipple in a vampire's mouth, but Anwyn had no fear when she surrendered her body to him.

"Oh." Her moans increased, her body undulating up against his. "Daegan. Come with me. Go over . . . together. Please."

Normally, he'd order her to come before him, but he didn't mind letting her have her way. He wanted to go over that cliff together. "Go, *cher*. I'm with you."

She renewed her efforts against him, and he drove her harder against the wall, straightening so that he braced one hand on the tile and kept the other cinched low and hard on her waist. Powerful thighs and buttocks flexed under her heels as he thrust into her, strong and sure, stroking those tissues, striking her deep inside, bringing her hot, slippery core to the flash point. His cock got impossibly harder, his balls drawing up. If Gideon came in right now, Daegan wouldn't care if the hunter staked him in the center of the back. He wasn't stopping, wasn't pulling back.

She cried out as his cock spasmed, jetting the first stream of hot seed into her. He felt the rippling of her clit, the clutch of her cunt, and he pushed harder, wanting to give her some pain amid the delightful pleasure, the flavoring he knew would take her soaring even higher.

"Daegan . . ." *I missed you missed you missed you . . . Oh God . . . Don't leave me don't ever leave me again . . .* Those shadow creatures didn't just cower back into the shadows. They were sent scuttling, disappearing down the tunnels and holes of her mind as the flash of climax detonated there. It was a fierce warrior's satisfaction to give her that, give her that moment of peace and pleasure, something that could be hers, if she trusted him to be in control.

The emotions such trust elicited made his heart ache. It was good to be home.

There were so many meanings to that handful of words, he was glad their aftermath didn't require speech. They leaned against the wall, Anwyn still held securely in his arms, holding him right back, hearts thundering and bodies still shuddering with those delicious aftershocks, her pussy rippling against his cock.

Have you ever had a home before me, Daegan?

He hadn't realized he'd opened his mind to give her that thought, but maybe he hadn't. Maybe she was so deeply in his heart, she knew what he was feeling. She had her head tilted back against the wall, but now she brought her chin down to gaze into his eyes.

"No, *cher.*" It was the simple truth. He'd never considered anyplace home, not until her, though he realized he'd never thought of it until she asked the question. "Not since I left my mother's home to go out on my own."

Her blue-green eyes softened and her hand lifted to cup his face. It was trembling, so he closed his own over her wrist, steadying her, still holding her securely about the waist. "No woman you've loved has ever given you a home?" she asked softly.

He stared down into her lovely face, wanting to press his lips to every cherished inch. Nuzzle her brow, tug her head back with that silky hair and touch his mouth to her throat, to the life-giving carotid. He knew at some point he'd piss her off. She'd do the same to him. He'd hurt her, make her laugh, cry, frustrated, annoyed, happy, content . . . It didn't matter. He wanted to be everything for her, every emotion, good or bad.

"I've never loved another woman, Anwyn. You're the first." *And the last.* He wasn't sure why he was so certain of that, but since he was seven hundred years old and she was his first love, he didn't think it was a wrong assumption.

The stunned amazement that crossed her face was a gift, one that he took with a kiss, another of those that lingered. As they held that way, she at last reached out with her mind. He followed that tendril, felt it touch Gideon, tug him to her. Slowly, Daegan let her down, sliding her off his now-semierect cock. He held her against the wall still, though, caged within his arms so he could indulge that desire to taste her neck beneath her ear, work his way to the collarbone.

He sensed when Gideon was standing in the bathroom doorway. Anwyn beckoned him forward. "Take off your clothes and come join us, Gideon."

The vampire hunter shifted. "You look like you're done. I can bring Daegan a towel if he'd like one."

When she slid her gaze toward him, Daegan noted the slight tightening of her lips at the evasion and felt that warning simmer to her blood, what he'd felt at the airport when Gideon had somehow thwarted her intent. She spoke calmly, but he could tell as well as Gideon that it was deceptive.

"Daegan needs blood. There's a reserve in the refrigerator, but I want to offer him the blood of my servant, hot and fresh from the source. He needs that, for his strength. I want you to allow him to drink from you while I bring you to climax with my hands, my body."

"No," Gideon said. While his response was quiet, his tone even, there was a leashed resolve that would detonate if she pushed it. "You already know I won't feed him, or any other vampire. Not ever. Only you."

"It doesn't matter, *cher,*" Daegan said, earning a surprised look from both of them. "I won't drink from your servant."

Gideon's reaction stirred that impulsive anger in her, and from the hunter's significant glance Daegan realized her demand wasn't unexpected. Gideon apparently had been dealing not only with the seizures and bloodlust, but the war between the Mistress, evaluating her slave's limits, and the reaction of the fledgling vampire, which believed everything was hers to take, struggling for the upper hand.

He shouldn't have been away so long. This was one side of the battle where his strength was specifically needed. *Do not push him,* cher. *He nearly died for you.*

You, who wouldn't let me shirk from being a vampire, wouldn't let me have a moment of panic, would cut him slack? She turned a gimlet eye on him. *Do you have a soft spot for him, Daegan?*

I am telling you that neither of us is your toy. That has never been the type of Mistress you are. Being a vampire will make you more demanding.

He came back to her then, touched her face to soften his next words. A hand shot out to knock his away, and he easily pinned it to the wall, continuing the cradling motion of her jaw without pause. *Power has always been the delicate brush you wield on a willing canvas, because you knew it was about consent. The Mistress in you craves that power enough to take it, if you let the vampire side have too much control. You know that about yourself. Don't let being a vampire take that from you. You will have a harder fight with that than most, but you will do it.*

When that blood shifted, uncertain, he hardened his feelings. *If you don't, you're less than I expected you to be. Don't do to him what Barnabus did to you. The Mistress knows the difference between rape and submission. So does the vampire, but the blood is hot and fresh in your veins. It takes time to settle it down.*

She shuddered, but he saw the red tide turn as she pushed it back. Even managed to give him a defiant look, but the one he knew, tinged with sexual challenge. *You might be the head alpha in this strange new arrangement, but don't get carried away with yourself.*

He suppressed a smile as she turned her gaze to Gideon, her blue-green eyes haunted.

"No apologies, remember?" Gideon said quietly, a towel for her already in hand. "It's been a stressful day."

"Yes. But I'll still apologize for that one. I could say I don't know what got into me, but of course, I do." She gave a half laugh, too close to a sob for Daegan's liking. "I guess I have a built-in excuse for being a heartless bitch, right?"

"Yeah, but don't take advantage of it too much." Gideon slid the towel over her shoulders as Daegan guided her out. He shut off the water, then pulled a towel off the rack as well.

"I'd like to go sit on the bed and talk about what happened at the Council," she said. Taking a deep breath, she glanced at them both. "There's something else I want to put out on the table. It's close to dawn now, but tomorrow night, I want to go out to dinner. The three of us."

Daegan looked toward Gideon. Before the man could give him a reading on whether or not it was advisable, Anwyn stomped on his foot, hard. Even though she was barefoot, her aim was enough to catch his attention. Her eyes flashed.

"Don't look toward my servant to decide what I can and can't do."

Daegan caught her chin, jerking it up, and was satisfied to see he'd caught *her* attention when those lovely blue-green eyes widened at the expression on his face. "Giving you my heart is not the same as snapping a collar on my testicles, *cher.* I've given you a great deal of latitude, to allow for what you are facing. Watch your tone and attitude, or I will prove to you, quite quickly, who wears the collar in our relationship."

Her eyes sparked, lips firming. He felt the temper simmering, deciding. This time it seemed goaded by Anwyn as well as her unstable mind, an improvement. He expected Gideon had learned to tell minute differences in her temperament from moment to moment, what was the result of her "gremlins" and what was her. It unfortunately underscored what the man had said in his room; his intimate knowledge of Anwyn's mind would be key to her success before the Council.

However, now the male had shifted forward a step. Daegan turned his gaze toward the hunter and read his body language easily enough. "Your Mistress will never come to any harm from my hands, Gideon. I swear that to you. But there are lines of etiquette, both in the vampire world she's entered, and the human world she still shares. You know it."

He glanced back down at the lovely, strong woman he knew hated not having control over the things happening inside of her. Now that he was back, and could help more directly, he'd given her another tool for dealing with it, whether she or Gideon realized it. The limits of Daegan's tolerance for bad behavior. Though she wouldn't appreciate the analogy, the gremlins in her mind, those voices that could rise up and take over her reality, as well as her fledgling bloodlust, were much like children, needing to learn boundaries from a parent. One day, he hoped that she would be that authority over them, but right now, every external source could help. He didn't mind being a formidable one. If he could, he'd hunt every one of the little demons out of her brain and skin them alive.

"At least for the immediate future," he noted, "you know you will be unique in our world. Your servant has far deeper and wider access to your mind than most vampires permit, because he is the one who can tell, better than the rest of us, what is you and what is the bad blood. The only time he gets confused is when it is tangled up with the odd balance of control and surrender developing between you, and the considerable emotional baggage he is carrying." He gave Gideon another look when the man scowled. "I will therefore look toward Gideon for that confirmation, not to demean you or relegate you to a lower status than your servant, but out of respect for you, and a desire to safeguard your well-being that overwhelms everything for me, even your pride."

He allowed his voice to soften, though his hand dropped to her throat, collaring it with a pressure that brought her gaze back to his. "Your pride is something I cherish as well, when it is a reflection of your deep self-confidence and inner strength. Not when it is a foolish worry that I think less of you for needing to depend on us more than you ever have. Can you not see how much we both cherish your trust? The trust of a Mistress isn't given lightly."

"What if I never learn control?"

"You've always been extraordinary, Anwyn," he responded. "Which makes me believe you will."

"I agree," Gideon offered. The vampire hunter met her gaze. "It's going to be a tough road, but you can't give up on yourself, Anwyn."

Remember our faith when you can't remember your own, cher.

~

Anwyn pressed her lips together. Perhaps the thing she hated most about the unstable vampire blood that Barnabus had inflicted upon her, as well as her transition, was that she could be turned into a dangerous, petulant child if thwarted. She hated not being able to stop her anger from surging forward into her mind, painting everything red. Though it was no fault of his own, Daegan had made it worse when he stepped back from her, leaving her cold against the tile, the water wet and unpleasant. When they'd both resisted her will, her mood had changed, becoming darker, uglier.

She'd wanted to taunt Gideon, ask him which he preferred; to let Daegan drink from him, or to fuck him. All she had to do was ask, and the answer would be there in his head. An answer she knew, even though he didn't want anyone to know that answer, even himself. Daegan was wrong. She would have been *worse* than Barnabus if she did that. How often would she have to ask their forgiveness for such things?

"I think we both told you a long time ago, until you get a handle on all this, you don't have to say you're sorry." Gideon came closer again, his jaw firm and resolute.

"Yes," she said quietly, pushing aside her shame that he'd heard that thought and hoping he hadn't heard all of it. "I do. Because it helps me remember how I should behave."

She realized it was another important role Daegan would play, because she would in fact capitulate to a chastisement from him, where she wouldn't from Gideon. Balance of power and all that. God, their world had become a crazy place, but there was a logic to all of it, as Daegan had implied. It was ironic, because a Mistress was as likely as a vampire to exploit a submissive's aversion to something, particularly if she thought it wasn't revulsion but suppressed desire that turned them away from a certain path.

A part of her was still shaking from Daegan's quick response, but her own wry humor chided her. *You said you wanted him to show his emotions more often.*

The vampire heard that, a surprised look crossing his devilishly handsome face, dispelling some of the shadows lingering between them.

She was still concerned about him needing blood. Maybe he would go out soon. Of course, Daegan Rei had been taking care of himself for a long time. It was pointless of her to worry over him.

Lifting her hand, she touched Daegan's forearm. Turning her hand over, she ran her knuckles up his arm, to the crook of the elbow. With her other hand, she reached out to Gideon. She noted he stayed a little behind her, using her as a buffer between them. When Daegan's eyes met the hunter's gaze, a faintly amused, taunting look in his expression, Gideon gave him his usual eat-shit-and-die look. The interaction between them helped steady her, made it much easier to regain her footing from these mini-episodes with the two of them working on her in a tag team.

"You haven't said, but from your face, I know we need to go to the Council. They didn't let me off on the validation requirement, did they?" At Daegan's nod, she drew a breath. "Okay, then. So I guess we need to reassess. We know I can't rely on my control as a sure thing. Not now, not a month from now. Maybe not ever."

She was proud the words came out smooth, steady, because inside they felt quarried out of her lower gut with a jackhammer. It might have been easier to say she had terminal cancer. It bolstered her, the way the two of them drew closer, closing ranks. Not reassuring her with empty platitudes, but making it clear they stood with her.

"We know if I get stressed, it will override the injections. We should figure out a system, practice drills as if we're expecting a fire at any time. That will help give me some confidence when we go to the Council. I can't . . ." She stopped, shook her head. "Let's move into the bedroom. I'd rather talk in there."

She led the way, sliding onto Daegan's bed, putting her back against the pillows and folding her legs under her. Letting Gideon keep her as a buffer, despite Daegan's amusement, she tugged her servant to a sitting position on the edge of the bed next to her, one leg crooked up to balance himself, while Daegan took his own seat on the opposite side, forming a loose triangle.

"I need to say something, not because you don't know it, can't already see it, but because I need to show you that I understand. I want to take charge of this, as much as possible. Not because I'm a control freak, but because in order for me to go down this path, I'm going to have to be holding the reins, to know that even when I'm out of control, that what's happening is what I've asked to have happen, as much as possible. All right?"

Gideon nodded, and she received a flicker of acknowledgment from Daegan. "We know there are voices in my head I can't control. We know I now have a vampire's needs and cravings, and apparently the dominance that's so strongly part of being a vampire has been amped up by those markers already existing in me." She made a face at Gideon's expression. "Don't make me slap you."

The grin that crossed his features freed more of the tension in her gut.

"We have two weeks, *cher*," Daegan put in. "We can practice, just as you say. Develop keywords, systems for how to react, test different ways of helping you keep control or manage stress. You have two minds at your disposal. You can use both of them to help your own." He passed a hand over her hair, easing the shadow that crossed her heart. "And remember, Gideon does know how to reach across your mind to mine, when yours is open. I can teach you to protect that conduit for him, so he can use it even when your mind is conscious but out of control. That should work, even if he's not in the same place as you are. He just has to be within a reasonable proximity to you."

So Gideon could be close, without being in the Council headquarters itself. That was reassuring, since she'd already been dreading the fact that Gideon couldn't be with them. She saw Daegan glance toward Gideon, an unfathomable look, but she'd investigate whatever testosterone-inspired meaning that had later. She had enough to think about right now without delving into Gideon's head or interpreting Daegan.

Daegan had shifted positions, parting the towel to show a lean and powerful thigh. She was already holding Gideon's hand, stroking his fingers, and now she ran her other hand along that expanse, which reinforced their connection, while stirring her nerves in a pleasant way. She needed the calming effect of both reactions, because her stomach was knotting. Daegan's words had reminded her how those shadow voices could make her a prisoner of her mind, helplessly watching from inside, like she had as she beat Gideon to death.

Memories like that, ambushes on who and what she'd been, chipped away at the foundation she was building, allowing those full-blown attacks in. Who was she kidding? It was going to take every ounce of her energy and focus to prepare and then hold it together for the Council visit. Her idea to go out to dinner tomorrow night was a bad one, indicative of how much she needed to work on her judgment. Her, in a restaurant? The things that could happen . . .

She couldn't overlook the fact she'd already be starting with a handicap when she traveled to Council headquarters. She'd have to go without Gideon. But he could stay somewhere nearby, where she could access the steadying influence of his mind, as Daegan had suggested. It wouldn't be the same as his physical presence, but it would be all right.

Yes, it was all going to be fine. She just needed more practice. She pushed aside the tired despair that tried to creep into her mind. Everything for the past month had been about learning to control this, and she longed for just one night of something different, something not these four walls. But she hadn't been trapped here for decades, only for a few weeks. She'd get by. It didn't matter that this transition had felt like decades, each day another ordeal of uncertainty and worry that she might accidentally kill someone.

As often as she'd had the affable desire to choke vendors or the occasionally difficult employee, who could have guessed what a stressor a true homicidal urge would be? Her humor fell flat, though, because it was truly awful, knowing what it felt like, the craving to snap the necks of her friends and coworkers with barely a thought. Inside her mind was a rabid cheering section, wanting her to do just that 24/7.

"Hey." Gideon put a hand on her bent knee. His concerned look told her that, even if he wasn't reading her mind, he was seeing her thoughts reflected on her face. "We'll get this worked out. Strategy is the stuff I'm good at. Much better than fixing your hair or helping you dress, like other servants probably do."

"If you occasionally brushed your own, you might be more aware of how it's done," Daegan observed. He mirrored Gideon's touch on her opposite knee, closing the circle between them.

"I can do a ponytail," Gideon defended himself. "Haven't tried pigtails, but if you're planning a Catholic schoolgirl fantasy, I'll do my best."

She closed her hand over his, her other over Daegan's, and lifted them both to press a cheek to either set of male knuckles. "I'm not sure what I did to deserve the two of you. And yes, I intended that to be interpreted both ways."

"Ouch," Gideon said mildly, but she heard Daegan's chuckle. Even though the walls felt closer and darker than ever, she tried to believe that they were right.

But she couldn't help wondering. Had the mythology about vampires and coffins come from the way it felt to be a vampire? Already dead and shut away from the world, long before the grave had ever been dug.

6

"WE need to take Anwyn out to dinner." Gideon pushed open Daegan's door with a knee as he thrust his knife into his back holster. "Before we leave."

Daegan was standing in front of his closet, dressing. The male was shrugging into a shirt, his jeans still open. "Oh. Sorry." Gideon glanced left quickly.

"Teach you to knock, vampire hunter. Do you usually blush in the locker room?"

"Piss off," Gideon mumbled.

"You want to look, Gideon. So look."

Instead, Gideon stared harder at the wall. "Just put your clothes on, will you? Stop flaunting it."

An irritating chuckle, but he heard the rustle of the shirt being buttoned, then zipping and buckling, though he could imagine in great detail the way all of it looked. Daegan tucking his shirt in, his hand sliding over his cock to position it, the smoothing down over the zipper, the tightening of the belt on the lean, muscular waist. Jesus, he couldn't keep his mind off of sex, with either one of them.

While he'd been more than eager to satisfy Anwyn's continuous desires in Daegan's absence, his return had ratcheted up all of their desires in an inexplicable way for the past few days. It had Gideon so wound up he had a compelling desire to go out and kill something just to relieve some of his tension, which was maybe why he'd felt the need to arm himself in the relative safety of the underground apartment. But there was no ignoring it. If it wasn't the soft fall of Anwyn's hair, her curvy body and that Mistress's way of getting his cock to rise on command, it was Daegan . . . being Daegan.

Reluctantly, he acknowledged Daegan's absence had given him a temporary reprieve from a variety of disturbing issues and realities. In a way, Gideon understood what had sparked Anwyn's temper with him in the shower on that first night of Daegan's return, when she'd wanted him to take Daegan's blood. It hadn't been so much about him letting Daegan drink, but about how Gideon viewed her. During that time when it was just the two of them, Gideon could focus on her as the victim, not the vampire she was becoming or even the Mistress she hadn't exercised as fully due to the circumstances. Daegan's presence underscored the vampire and dominant side of her. The moment he'd come back, she'd noticed the return of Gideon's wariness with her, something that hadn't been there, at least not as obviously, in the past several weeks. Part of it was him not trusting vampires, but part of it was something deeper, something he rebelled against even more violently.

When the three of them had been on Daegan's bed, ostensibly talking about Council matters, Gideon had been tense as a board, wondering how he'd deal with it if she tested that side of herself. In Daegan's absence, he'd told himself, a hundred times, if she played that game with him again, allowing the male vampire a few intimate touches, some seductive moves to get her juices going, he'd tell her flat out that wasn't his thing and back away from it.

Now he wasn't sure what he'd do, and that scared him to the bone. He'd rather face three vampires than deal with that.

Guys had a compulsive need for sex, right? They responded to it, whenever it happened. It explained why sailors at sea for a year or two would sodomize one another. Or some priests, obeying a centuries-old, now-irrelevant political mandate to remain chaste, started to see altar boys as *Penthouse* pinups. It didn't mean anything. But hell, he wasn't even like that, because he'd never had a glimmer of interest in guys until he got around Daegan and Anwyn. It was the way the two of them played off each other; that was all. In a sexual situation with them, his cock was going to respond to stimulation, whoever offered it, but it was Anwyn he wanted. That was that.

He ignored the fact his mental argument was getting old and thin. Especially when it was just him and Daegan in this room, and he was having a hard time keeping his eyes off the guy's body. Maybe it was something chemical about the third mark, and he just had to shut it down. He'd been good at shutting things down for a long time, right? This was some sick, twisted-shit side effect, no different from what Anwyn was fighting in herself. He could do it, too.

Damn it, that wasn't why he was here. Anwyn was occupied, working on her computer, so he had to deal with this, not his own baggage.

"We can't risk it," Daegan was saying. "It's too soon. It may be many months—"

"It may be never," he said, more brusquely than he intended. "She can't handle never, Daegan. That's why she went upstairs to the club, that day she had to give me the third mark. I still feel guilty as hell about it, but it was a sign. As intolerable as confinement is to her, she's handled it pretty damn well. Now we're going to go see the Council when she's barely adjusted to all this. We're going to have to test our preparedness, and I'd rather test it here than at the Council. We all know we're about to go into a situation that's going to be pretty high-risk, a lot of stress and tension. It will be able to trip her off faster, and knowing that is worrying her more and more. She needs a night to see what the good possibilities are, and that we'll be an effective safety net for her, so she can enjoy those possibilities. It will reassure her like nothing else."

"She tried that when she went up to visit her club."

"We weren't prepared then. She hadn't accepted it could happen anytime, or that she needs to depend on us to help deal with it. She has now."

Daegan gave him a narrow look. "If you want her fully prepared for the Council, it is past time to tell her you intend to walk into Council chambers with us, not just stay somewhere nearby. It's been nothing short of miraculous that she hasn't already figured it out. It will not be pleasant if she looks into your mind at an inopportune time and discovers that."

"She's been preoccupied and I'm good at not thinking about things I'd prefer to avoid."

"No argument there."

Gideon set his jaw. "I plan to tell her. Sometime after this dinner. Let her have something before she has to freak out over something else."

"We don't eat, Gideon."

"No, you don't. But you do like the taste of food. There's a food and wine fest in town, and tomorrow night, for an exorbitant all-for-charity cover charge, you can attend it." Gideon pulled the flyer from his back pocket, tossed the folded card onto the table between them. "A fancy black-tie thing where you get bite-sized pieces of a few different foods to sample, and a whole lot of wines. In addition to your cover charge, it's expected you'll buy a few bottles."

"Very ambitious for a man who carries his cash in the heel of his boot."

"Using your supersonic speed to spy on me?"

"Hardly. I have good hearing, and can hear the paper crackling in the sole." Daegan met his gaze. "For that matter, when you're in her shower by yourself, I can hear you jerking off. Your body aching for both the softness of a female body and the hardness of a male one. There's no reason to tear yourself in two, Gideon. We are both here."

"I'm only going to say this once," Gideon ground out, and he was pleased he sounded reasonably steady and menacing. "The pheromones you two put out are making me temporarily insane. It's not my thing. Not now, not ever. Like the blood-drinking thing. So get over yourself. Are you going to do this dinner thing or not?"

The flash in Daegan's eyes had Gideon tensing, knowing he'd pushed a little far. He was afraid that Daegan would try to prove him wrong. Other parts of him hoped he would. He hated those parts, enough that he'd consider amputating them if he didn't like using them for Anwyn so much.

"We will," Daegan said at last, with that steady, dark-eyed look that saw so much more than it should. "You should go tell her. Give her back her smile."

Gideon gave a curt nod, moved a couple of steps into the room, on surer ground. "I'll be your chauffeur, since you're looking at all the clothes I own."

"Then we'll find you some. James is close to your shoulder size and build, and he has a tuxedo for special events at the club. I'm sure Anwyn can convince him to part with it for one night, as long as you don't spill anything on it." As Gideon began to protest, the vampire shook his head, his voice firm. "I believe your judgment on Anwyn is sound. If this is something she needs, then we do it together. Otherwise, I will not consent to it."

"Consent? You think I came in here asking your permission?"

"Whether you did or not, you require it."

Gideon tightened his jaw. "Fine. I have one more thing to talk about; then I'll go."

"I'm all ears." Daegan's gaze gleamed, a reminder of what he'd just revealed about his hearing. Gideon forced himself not to grind his teeth.

"You're all bullshit, far as I'm concerned. You remember that night, a long time ago, when you told me to fire the crossbow at you?"

"I remember."

"You were showing off."

"Some, perhaps." Daegan shrugged, all unapologetic arrogance. "But I wanted to take care of any illusions that you could hurt me."

"Everybody can be hurt. Toe-to-toe, Hercules might not be able to stand up to you, but if someone plans carefully enough, a ten-year-old kid could. So when you get sent off on these assignments that take you away from her, don't get too confident, all right?"

Daegan considered him. "You are concerned for me."

"You mean a lot to Anwyn. And I've taken down too many cocky vampires."

A shiver of air, and Daegan was no longer at the closet. Gideon knew the male was at his back now, no more than an inch between them, but he chose not to turn, keeping his tone dismissive, with an effort. "That doesn't prove anything. As I said, planning."

"I think I mean something to you, vampire hunter." Daegan touched his arm, fingers curling over Gideon's biceps. Gideon shrugged him off, sliding away, except Daegan was now in front of him, arm braced, effectively caging him between the wall and the door. He stared into the vampire's dark eyes, tried not to get absorbed in the set of the firm mouth.

"Stop fucking with me," he snapped.

"Your concern is misplaced. I will be fine."

"Fine. When you get staked, I'll say I told you so." Gideon pushed off the wall and shoved at Daegan's arm, intending to leave the room.

Before he could complete the motion, Daegan had pushed him back against the door, Gideon's weight making it close with a resounding thud. The vampire had his hand beneath his throat, eyes and mouth so close to Gideon's that he couldn't think, though he automatically tried to break the hold, with no luck. Even when a run-of-the-mill vampire had a grip, a person was pretty much caught. With a vamp like Daegan, there was no "pretty much" to it.

"You have said I do not always have the attitude of a vampire. It doesn't mean I'm not one. As much as I respect your abilities, Gideon, I only take human defiance for so long. Particularly when your defiance is a poorly disguised mating challenge."

"Fuck off," Gideon managed through gritted teeth, but groaned as Daegan put his knee against his stiff cock, rubbed with devilish knowledge over his balls. But the harder thing to resist was the mouth that brushed over his.

"Kiss me back, Gideon. Devour my mouth the way you've been devouring me with your eyes ever since I returned. Show me your hunger. Show me how much *you* missed me."

It surged forth like fire, so that he almost knocked Daegan back a step. Gripping the collar of Daegan's shirt, Gideon slammed against his mouth, so violently that the vampire's fang cut his lip. Daegan's tongue curled around the blood, then met Gideon's, sliding, teasing, thrusting, a hard, openmouthed struggle and dance together. Daegan held him against the door, wouldn't let him move or take it any further than that kiss. His arousal built, his cock cramped in his jeans, and Gideon ached shamefully as his mind shot right to a moment that had happened before the vampire had left. Daegan and Anwyn holding him between them, Anwyn kissing him, Daegan's hand over his, on Gideon's cock, the two of them making him helpless to their desires . . .

Shame couldn't hold a candle to the explosive power of that memory. Gideon put everything into that kiss, his frustration and rage, his lust and need. He wanted to touch, but the only thing Daegan allowed was the hands on his shirt collar, clutching hard. The vampire gripped his head, his fingers in Gideon's hair, body pressed up against his, so Gideon could feel his hard cock pressed just to the right of his. He could rub against it if he could just move. "Let me move, damn you," he muttered against Daegan's mouth.

"No," came the maddening reply. "Put it all into the kiss, Gideon. Think about my tongue here, then think about it teasing your ass, getting you wet for me, then thrusting my cock in hard, making you groan. You crave the feel of it as you sink into Anwyn's slick heat. You need more than even an incomparable Mistress like Anwyn. You need a Mistress and a Master to be complete."

"No. No." But he couldn't stop kissing him, telling him with his lashing tongue and scraping teeth what he needed so badly.

"You know what Anwyn is doing?" Daegan whispered it, drawing back. "She has sensed our passion. She's leaning on the other side of this door, touching her neck, her breasts, sliding her hand down to stroke her pussy, her legs opening up, her beautiful ass braced on the door, just below where yours is."

Gideon sought her, and her mind opened like an orchid, rare, exotic, irresistible. He saw it, felt her desire flood his mind. Daegan shut up then, putting his full effort into the kiss, taking it over. Gideon was helpless to do anything but go along for the ride. Then Daegan went for an even more devastating tactic.

He slowed their movements, so their tongues were doing a slow, twisting, stroking fuck together. A thrust and dragging retreat by that agile, moist muscle, a nuzzle of the lips, a tease of a sharp fang. Like the turning of eddies in a lazy pond, beneath bright sunshine. Then, at long last, when Gideon was lying against the door, both more aroused and more lethargic than he'd ever been, Daegan pulled back a few inches, stared into his eyes silently as Anwyn's erratic breaths, her cries, filled their ears. She brought herself to completion, knowing they were listening, their bodies taut and hard against each other.

"Go see James about that tux," Daegan murmured at last. He pushed away from Gideon, gave him an even look. "And next time, vampire hunter, knock before you come into my room. You need my permission to enter, or I'll finish what I started here, to remind you of your manners."

∼

Gideon thought about blowing the whole thing off, disappearing until it was over. But he couldn't ignore how Anwyn's face had brightened like a new sun at the idea of an evening out. Or how she'd just as quickly needed absolute reassurance that they were both attending and everything would be fine. He couldn't ignore the obvious fact she was rebuilding her confidence on the basis of a tripod. Not a seesaw, with Daegan alone on one end. It made Gideon want to believe, too much, that he was a vital, irreplaceable corner of it.

It was getting harder to convince himself that he was merely a temp, and even harder to accept that whatever the hell he'd become, he wanted it to stay that way forever. Had it been only a month? Or had it started with that one night where he and Jacob had shared Lyssa, under her command, and every step since then had been a journey to Anwyn? And Daegan.

The hell with it. Here he was. He'd been relieved by James's unperturbed acceptance of the request for his tux as something perfectly normal. Now he stood, dressed up in a monkey suit, waiting in the living room. It occurred to him that he didn't really have his own room. When Anwyn didn't want him in her bed, he slept on the couch.

It didn't matter. He didn't need a damn bed.

No, you don't. You belong to me, Gideon. I don't want you to have your own room until you accept that. My bed is your bed, when I give you permission to use it.

An unexpected, silky threat and promise in her mind-voice, one that unfurled heat in his lower belly and an even stronger reaction in his chest. He, a person who'd resisted and scorned any form of authority all his life, reacted with hot need and deep pleasure every time she exerted a claim on him. It was too fucked-up.

He cleared his throat. *Shouldn't you be putting on makeup and curling your hair, doing girly stuff?*

I consider doing you girly stuff. Her sexy laugh, but then she put that curtain back in place again.

Daegan came out of his room then, wearing a tuxedo perfectly tailored for his perfect body and perfect face. Fucking perfect. Even from here, Gideon could tell how good he smelled, because of how the servant's mark heightened his senses. He'd been smelling that particular musk all day, thanks to that never-ending kiss while shoved against Daegan's door.

Yeah, he was totally fucked-up. Before he could figure out how to absent himself until Anwyn had joined them, he noticed the man's cuff links. Gideon raised a brow, recognizing the shape. "You're kidding, right?"

Daegan lifted one wrist to better display the tiny silver and diamond bats. "A gift from Anwyn, a couple of years ago. Her charming wit."

Fortunately, the door to her room slid open then. Typically female, she'd timed her entrance last, and it was well worth the wait. While Gideon wasn't surprised that she rendered him temporarily speechless, it was something to see Daegan's overwhelmed expression.

During the week, she wore some enticing and attractive outfits, determined not to slum around their apartment like some pathetic psych case—her own words—as well as to practice getting dressed without the benefit of a mirror. He remembered the very first night in Atlantis, how she'd come to him as a Mistress, pure sex in latex and lace. But this . . .

His soul rolled out in front of her, a coat he'd willingly throw over any mud hole to keep her from soiling her feet.

The dress was a teal sheath that glittered as she moved, a handful of tiny sparkle points like stars in the night sky. It clung from breast to midthigh and had no sleeves. She'd draped a transparent silver wrap over her arms. It picked up the topaz-and-diamond set at her throat. Her hair was twisted up on her head, all those little feminine tendrils artfully arranged on her slim neck.

Suddenly, he was greedy, wanting to jump forward in time to see her at the end of the night, when she'd let it tumble down. She'd step out of her elegant heels, accept his and Daegan's embrace as they worshipped her body with mouths and hands, bringing cries of pleasure from those wet, glossy lips. They were frosted a kiss-me deep rose and she'd sprinkled some kind of glitter dust across her breasts. A temporary tattoo of a blue-green fairy was high on one ankle, a further accent for her killer legs that her high heels made it impossible to ignore.

Of course Daegan was the first to recover. Crossing the floor, he lifted her hand to his mouth, giving her fingers a kiss that included a secret caress of his tongue between two of the digits. Gideon registered it because he saw her reaction to it in her mind.

He was so out of his league. He should be driving the car, or staying home to watch cable in a bathrobe, like a sitter waiting up for the parents to return.

"Oh my God, Gideon. Look at you."

Anwyn was so overwhelmed by the sight of her vampire hunter, she missed his reaction to her and Daegan entirely. For once he was smoothly shaven, the hard jaw clean and handsome. Despite Daegan's teasing, his hair had been brushed so it feathered over his forehead and lay gleaming on his broad shoulders. He looked as devastating in a tuxedo as only a handsome, rugged man could. His midnight blue eyes were gratifyingly riveted on her. She felt Daegan's amusement with the male, mixed with something else, something she herself was feeling. Moving to Gideon, she realized with a combination of joy and sweet sorrow why he was rooted to the spot. Reaching up to touch his face, she passed her thumb over his lips before he could speak.

"Daegan received a kiss from this mouth earlier today, but my servant didn't give me the same pleasure. I think you owe me that now."

She'd noted that he responded to the formally worded commands far better than he realized. They were a trigger, as if they made something deep in that chivalrous soul leap over his usual cynicism and self-deprecation. They were pushed aside, and he desired nothing more than to serve her every wish. Pressing against him, she slid her fingers up into that silky hair. Blissfully, that was all it took. When she took his mind out of the equation, things were far simpler for him.

His arms banded around her, bringing her even closer, so close she stepped out of one shoe and curled a bare foot around his calf as he cupped the base of her skull and kissed her deep and desperate, letting her feel the delicious desire race through every inch of his hard body. He was trying to be a gentleman, but his hands crept down, and at her sound of encouragement, he closed them over the thin, stretchy fabric to find she wore nothing beneath it. His cock leaped against her belly.

While Gideon gripped her buttocks, Daegan's fingers whispered over the bare skin revealed by the dress's low back. When he traced her spine, he dropped a kiss between her shoulder blades, making her shiver.

"Okay, enough." She pulled free, laughing. "You two *are* taking me to dinner. Keep that up and we won't leave this room. Really, I'm totally bored with both of you. I've had all the sex I can stand."

"Her mouth says one thing, but her body . . ." Daegan tried to dip under the short skirt and she spun away from him, grabbing hold of Gideon to thrust him in front of her.

"Protect me from this insatiable pervert, Gideon."

"What's he going to do, hit me with that enormous hard-on you've given him?" Daegan scoffed.

The banter loosened the tightness in Gideon's chest. It had been nearly a month of life-and-death situations, tears and denial, anger and unexpected rages, but this moment was perfect. They'd done the right thing. Maybe Anwyn wasn't the only one who'd needed this. Her light-heartedness was infectious.

Also, he'd helped make this happen. So maybe, at least for tonight, he *did* deserve to be here.

Her eyes laughed up at him as she traced a quick finger along his jaw, her mouth softening and getting serious at once. "Of course you do. You belong to me, Gideon. I want you here, and so does Daegan."

"It's too much trouble to slough him off. Like a wart, it's easier just to accept he's attached." Daegan offered her his right arm. "Are you ready, *cher*?"

Shifting to take Gideon's left arm, she smiled at them. "Yes. And thank you both for going with me."

"Actually, I've got several supermodels holding a table for me. I'm only hanging out with you two losers until I get there," Gideon mentioned. When Anwyn pinched him, he grunted. "Ow. That was entirely unnecessary."

"I should have pulled out the harness to keep you in line tonight," she threatened darkly. "One with a phallus that vibrates, so you'd worry more about coming during dessert than teasing me."

"Promises, promises, *cher*," Daegan said. "I wouldn't mind seeing you in one, so you would be deliciously wiggling and squirming. Perhaps each one of us could put a hand on your thigh under the table, tease your pussy while you ate—"

"I'm leaving," she decided, freeing her arms and skipping to the door. "You are not going to tempt me, Daegan Rei. Not tonight. Tonight I am going *out* to play. Coming, boys?"

Exchanging a glance, they moved to follow her. Daegan held the door for her, though when he gestured Gideon forward, the vampire hunter shook his head. "After you."

"Don't trust me at your back, vampire hunter, or did you want a chance to grab my ass?"

"I never trust anyone at my back. And was that a request?"

Anwyn turned in the hallway. Had Gideon actually just flirted with Daegan? Anticipation leaped in her own breast as Daegan's eyes intensified to flame, the sensual lips curving in a dangerous smile. "Better start getting used to having me at your back, Gideon. I intend to have you both tonight, and I will."

With that remarkable and tantalizing statement, he gave Gideon a shove, sending him out the door ahead of him.

7

I⊤ had been a long time since Gideon had participated in any group event that wasn't crashing a church barbecue or pancake breakfast to get a low-cost homemade meal. This high-dollar event was about as alien to him as the tux, but the food was good. Their private table was close to the stage, where a jazz band provided entertainment. Between sets, there were presentations about the food from the chefs who'd made it, or discussions of the vintages that were being poured. They were on the outer edge of the front row, so Gideon didn't feel hemmed in. He suspected Daegan liked the position for the same reason. In contrast, they chose seats on either side of Anwyn, protectively flanking her.

She'd slid out of her shoes and curled her feet beneath her, so she was now leaning toward Gideon. Daegan was rubbing her bare feet with idle fingers, moving in easy circles. Her hand lay on the chair arm, and when Gideon joined his hand to it, she sent a smile his way, her head cocked, listening to the jazz selection being played.

In this light, he could see the faint reddish hue of her irises beneath the normal color, but it was a trick of the light, not a warning of an attack. A couple of times in the car, she'd gotten tense, but he'd teased her out of it and Daegan had followed his cues to do the same. Now she was as relaxed as she'd seemed in a while. Still, mindful of the lessons learned and the system they'd agreed upon, he kept his antennae cued to her mind at all times, ready if that changed. Faithful as a diabetic, she also discreetly used the monitor Brian had given her to check her blood and temperature reading every fifteen minutes.

Daegan looked a little less pale. He'd gone out briefly at dusk, before they'd gotten dressed, and apparently found someone to take care of his breakfast. Anwyn had noticed, picking up the perfume of the woman from whom he'd taken blood. While she hadn't seemed particularly pleased about it, she hadn't said anything. Guy had to eat, after all. And it sure as hell wasn't going to be Gideon.

"So why don't you have a servant?" he asked Daegan, not wanting to go back to that sticky subject, in case Anwyn caught the stray thought.

Daegan shrugged. "The life I currently lead wouldn't work well with a constant companion. There's less liability in hunting alone."

Another thing they had in common. Great. A computer dating service would pair the two of them up in a heartbeat. "At least, I believed that to be the case," the vampire added, his serious gaze turning to Anwyn. Lifting her hand, he kissed her fingers. Anwyn brushed their tips against his jaw.

"You couldn't have predicted that. And I've forgiven you for it," she said softly.

"I have not." He nipped one of the fingers, but then shifted his glance to Gideon. "When I'm with Anwyn, she has been my primary blood source. When I am traveling, I get it where I can. Like today."

"You're not worried about the Delilah virus?" Gideon asked. The virus, genetically engineered by a splinter group of vampire hunters, had been spreading enough in recent years to create concern among the relatively small vampire population.

"I am immune to it," Daegan said, surprisingly. But before Gideon could pursue that, Anwyn broke in.

"And exactly who *was* breakfast this evening?" she asked sweetly, the tips of her fangs showing, a quick gleam.

Daegan wound his fingers in a lock of her hair, gave it a tug as his eyes warmed on her. "A woman in her fifties, very attractive. She was at the park, sitting on a bench that backs up to the wooded area, not actually a very safe place for her to be. She was reading a vampire romance novel and getting quite caught up in it. I helped her enjoy the fantasy for a few moments, and when she revived, she found herself on a bench in a more populated part of the park, with a very handsome fiftysomething park ranger asking if she was all right."

"Breakfast and matchmaking." Gideon gave a snort. "Don't believe him for a second, Anwyn. He took out his straw at the first hot blonde with big boobs that crossed his path."

Over Anwyn's chuckle, Daegan shot him a dark look. "More comments like that, vampire hunter, and your throat will look far more appetizing next time I need blood."

"Yeah, you and your army can try to take it, anytime." Gideon picked up the delicate wineglass by the bowl, hoping he wouldn't break it, and downed a couple of swallows. "You've had a servant before you worked for the Council, right? I mean, no vampire goes seven hundred years without one."

At Daegan's silence, Gideon's brow rose. "You're shitting me. You've never taken a servant. Ever?"

Anwyn looked between them. "I assume that's rare?"

"It's beyond rare. So it's more than the liability and hunting thing, isn't it?"

Daegan lifted a shoulder, returned his attention to the stage, clearly not caring to elaborate, but Gideon was remembering the conversation they'd had, soon after Anwyn's attack. *I'd rather have spent my whole life with no one, than have given her a moment of pain.* In that conversation, Daegan had as much as admitted he'd not given his heart to a lover in all his life. Nor had he ever chosen the closest bond a vampire could have with another, that with a servant. He'd wanted Anwyn as his servant, but had chosen to respect her wishes.

She was apparently his one and only. It was unsettling and entirely remarkable, not only for a vampire, but for anyone who lived a life long enough to yearn for companionship. No matter his antipathy toward the vampire species, Gideon knew that having a servant was more than just convenience or function. It was comfort. Like sitting down with family every night for dinner instead of strangers, having that sense of connection to another.

It was so remarkable, Gideon decided to respect Daegan's obvious desire not to pursue it more deeply. He gave an offhanded shrug. "Mind you, I'm not throwing any stones, not with the number of hookers I've chosen over an actual relationship. We've both chosen blood and sex over intimacy."

He wondered how an eHarmony profile application would write *that* one up.

"Probably for the same reasons," Anwyn observed in a saccharine tone.

"Yep." Gideon gave her a direct, intent look. "You weren't available."

He was rewarded by a softening of her expression, a mock sniff that pretended he wasn't off the hook, and a sensuous curve of those full lips.

"Well played, hunter." Daegan smiled as well, but there were shadows in his eyes as they both touched their glasses to Anwyn's. She gave them a look torn between pleasure and exasperation.

"I think it's a matter of maturity." Reaching out, she ran her finger and thumb over Gideon's lapel, caressing the man beneath the cloth, increasing his attention on her. "I've only had a servant for a little while, but it's a lot like having a full-time sub. There's a certain level of trust, an acknowledgment of a need for others, an interdependency that goes with having a human servant. You have to reconcile it with this vampire sense of superiority, much as a person rationalizes the desire of having a dog or cat. But it goes to the deeper connective need, and you have to be mature enough to realize and handle that."

"Woof," Gideon said, covering his surprise that she'd practically regurgitated his own thoughts. It earned a laugh from her, a short chuckle from Dagean.

However, when she focused on his face with that scrutiny he found discomfiting and welcome at once, he had to ask the question that had been floating in his head since they'd left.

"So why didn't you do what you threatened . . . with the harness? I know you like that kind of thing."

She shrugged. "Being a Mistress isn't so much about what I want as what you need, Gideon. That's what gives me pleasure. Teaching you to trust yourself as much as you trust me. Everything we do up to that point is just an appetizer."

The implication and threat of that stewed in his mind, boiling uneasily. She squeezed his arm. "I'm sorry I've been too preoccupied to devote the time to it I'd like."

"I'm not a damn client session," he muttered into his cup. "As I've said, you don't owe me anything. I'm here for you."

"We're here for each other." Seemingly unoffended, she plucked at his sleeve. "Like this. You helped make this happen, both of you, and it helps me. What's going to happen in the future is going to be bad, but I know as long as I can have moments like this, my pleasures won't change all that much. Maybe not even my worries, though they're a tad more intense and dramatic."

When he shrugged, self-conscious at her compliment, Anwyn cupped Gideon's face, her fingers tracing his jawline. "When you saw me and Daegan tonight, your first thought was you didn't belong with us. Didn't belong here, in a place like this." She frowned. "That's not your decision, Gideon. That's mine, and you fit perfectly."

Gideon lifted a shoulder, uncomfortable. "My brother's the civilized one. Took nearly a year's worth of training to know how to serve a vampire queen, but it was in him before that. He was playing Sir Galahad in the backyard when we were young, squiring around ladies, asking for their favors. Most days I don't even remember if I put on clean underwear, or any at all. I'm good at killing. That's about it."

"I see." Leaning forward, she met him eye to eye. He was vaguely aware of Daegan's attentiveness, their conversation taking a more intent turn. "What do you see in my mind, Gideon?"

Since the injections, she'd gotten better at using the curtain screen between them when she was calm. While he was glad for what it meant to her, it had given him a peculiar sense of loss. He knew it was a necessary thing for her, to learn that control. To learn what she did and didn't need. One day soon, the moments he could just reach into her mind would be a rare flower, offered only when she desired it.

She'd learned something new, though, because not only did her mind open to him; it pulled him in, as if he were in her arms. He saw her reaction to him back at the apartment, when he'd been standing in his tux, looking at her as if she was the most important thing in his world. From there, she turned the wheels of her mind back and he saw her in her bed during the late-afternoon hours. The way she'd woken several times, restless, but once she'd reached out with her mind and found where he and Daegan were, she'd been able to go back to sleep, reassured by their presence. She liked the way he and Daegan bantered, how it surrounded her and made her feel even more cocooned and protected. And now, in this present moment, as he held her one hand and Daegan the other, she felt content. More at peace, despite her unsettled mind, than she had at any other time in her life.

He raised his stunned gaze to her face. "As I said," she said softly, "surrender is something different for everyone. The problem is not whether or not I need you, or the feelings I'm willing to explore with you. The problem is your boundaries, your shields. You keep trying to run away before we can throw you out. You've belonged nowhere for so long, you believe that's the truth. The simple fact is you've been search-ing for your home all along. With us."

"You don't know that. You can't even predict that." Desperate, feel-ing like he was on quicksand, he went for the low blow of reminding her how precarious her state of mind was, how new this was to her, too new for any of them to make any kind of permanent decisions.

"That may be true." She nodded, though he hated himself for the frisson of hurt and doubt that crossed her features. "But before I be-came this, there was something between us. I wanted to explore it. Eventually, you will lose me, Gideon." His heart clutched, his hand tightening in reflex, but before he could respond, she continued. "Be-cause, in the end, we always lose everyone. Isn't that all the more reason to enjoy every moment, no matter how many days, years or decades it lasts?"

A waiter brought a new sample tray then, rescuing him from a reply. She and Daegan took their time, examining the choices critically. Dae-gan had already given her direction on how best to enjoy and yet not overindulge in the food they couldn't really digest.

As Gideon watched the two of them, their heads bent over the tray, he felt a warring of hope and despair in him. He was accustomed to the despair only, the dull throb of it. Always before, it had been made tolerable by action, violence. In suggesting this evening for Anwyn, he hadn't counted on how it would affect him, being in such normal sur-roundings, doing what people normally did on a special Saturday-night date. Or the anticipation and affection, companionship and laughter.

For a moment, he wasn't sure he could breathe, and he had a strange desire to bolt back to the shadows, run back to that empty existence he'd turned into his purpose. All because he wasn't sure he could handle the threat of happiness.

Her hand slid across the chair arm and closed on his wrist. She stroked the bones there, her fingers a caress he would have crawled through the desert to feel. Turning now, she brought a morsel to his mouth that looked like it had tomato and cheese on it. He opened for her, and she fed it to him, teasing him with her fingers on his lips as he tried to swallow it.

Anwyn . . .

Be still in heart, dear love / And give each beat to me. I will care for it / For I care for thee. She tilted her head, the rich brown of her hair catching the torchlight. *A simple poem from long ago. A child's lullaby.*

"I'm afraid to believe in this. And if I do, then what does that make me?" *The vampire hunter who finds a home with two vampires. It sounds like a bad sitcom idea, one that won't sell.*

His voice had cracked, and so he'd finished the thought in his mind, but he wondered if Anwyn shared it with Daegan. Because as her hand closed over his again, lacing with his fingers, Daegan's stretched out along the back of her chair and gave his sleeve a brief, absent stroke, the man's dark eyes finding his over Anwyn's intent face.

"It means the world is a strange, terrible and wonderful place," she murmured. "What did you think of that one? The bread?"

Gideon gave a harsh half laugh. "It's a microwave pizza bite, pretending to be fancy, overly priced food."

She snorted. "That's a gourmet red sauce and breaded, excellent gouda cheese."

"Red sauce, bread, cheese. Sounds like pizza to me."

"The world's most perfect food," Daegan commented, earning her exasperated look. The vampire leaned back in his chair, one ankle brought to the opposite knee, but the casual pose was deceptive. Gideon could tell he was keeping a constant surveillance on their surroundings, just as he was. Unfortunately, Anwyn could tell as well.

"Would the two of you stop scoping the area like you're expecting an invasion? No one is looking for me, no one knows who Daegan is, and do you really think someone with a vendetta against Gideon is going to look for him at a Gourmet Taste Fest? Only if they've never met him."

"Did she just insult me?" Gideon asked.

Daegan's lips quirked. "You yourself said you have no culture and class. She was simply supporting your opinion." However, his gaze sobered, the vampire sliding a knuckle across her fair cheek. "I have no intentions of ruining the evening for you, *cher*, but another lesson you must learn is that vampires sense one another. Like all territorial predators, they will check each other out to make sure the vampire is one they know, or one who is permitted in the territory. The Council knows I am bringing you to them, but, by necessity, the territory overlord knows nothing of you yet. If you were thought to be a loner without protection, others might take advantage."

"So you're both armed."

"To the teeth." Gideon gave her a disarming wink as he signaled to the waiter. "Do you have beer?"

"No, sir," the waiter said politely, though his expression held a mildly sardonic cast. "However, there is a convenience store four blocks from here with twenty-four-ounce Icehouse and prepackaged nachos."

"He'd be perfect target practice," Gideon noted as the waiter moved off. He narrowed his gaze at the laughing Anwyn and grinning Daegan.

"No sport in that," said the vampire. "You're lying to us, by the way. Or yourself. You *are* good at things other than killing." His gaze passed over Gideon's shoulders. "You played football in high school. Varsity."

"I can think of many things he's good at, other than killing." Anwyn gave him a heated lingering glance. Gideon tried to ignore the feeling that she'd closed her clever, smooth fingers on his cock and scowled at Daegan instead.

"Do you ever forget anything? Keys? Credit cards?"

"Was she beautiful?"

Anwyn's question, spoken now with quiet seriousness, brought his attention back to her. The fairy lights of the surrounding area gave a soft shine to her lips, her eyes. Her hand rested on his thigh, Daegan's arm still across the back of her chair, linking the three of them together amid the murmur of conversation, muted laughter, piano jazz.

"Yeah." He knew he shouldn't be surprised that their dinner conversation would possess a little more gravity than most, or that he'd feel oddly comfortable speaking the otherwise painful words about Laura, his dead high school sweetheart. "She was a kid, like me at the time. With blond hair, blue eyes, and a beautiful smile. It was wide-open, you know, taking everyone into it. She was a cheerleader, so we were the cliché, but she wasn't. She was down to earth, nice to everyone. She was my first sex, in the back of my old car."

He shrugged, stared down in his wine to recall words he'd rarely spoken, except maybe to Jacob, years ago. Before he'd walled himself off. "I was horny as any kid, but I was really gentle the whole time, you know?"

"I know. I'd expect nothing less of you," she responded, her voice laden with compassion. It didn't drive him back into himself, like it normally would. Maybe because he knew Anwyn was already there.

"Jesus, I was shaking. Scared I'd do something to hurt her. But she smiled so sweet when I finally got inside her, held my shoulders, and told me she'd never felt more complete. She was . . . When I finally cried about losing my parents, she was the one that held me. I told her I'd always take care of her, keep her safe, love her. And—"

"No, stop there." Anwyn's voice was so inexorably tender, he had to stop. Her hand tightened on his thigh. "The rest doesn't matter. What you just said, that's what matters to her."

He nodded, his jaw tightening. "Don't know why I said all that. Jesus, I—"

Anwyn put a hand to his face, and with the pad of her forefinger, she pressed on the corner of his eye, absorbing the tear that had gathered there, no matter how hard he'd fought it. As she did, Daegan made a gesture. The waiter came back to his shoulder.

"Yes, sir?" he said. His voice held an obsequiousness that told Gideon the fact he and Daegan both wore tuxedos couldn't disguise the truth. They were from two very different classes.

Daegan held up a folded bill, dropped it on the man's tray. "You have a fully stocked bar in the kitchen. Bring my friend a beer, now. Whenever he gets close to empty, I expect another to appear. Without the sarcasm."

Gideon thought the look in Daegan's eye was enough to send the waiter scampering to do his bidding, even without the C-note. Clearing his throat, he shrugged off the moment, gave Anwyn a forced comic look. "That's enough about me. It's way past time to include Daegan in our game of Twenty Questions."

It was the game they'd used early on to pass the time, right before or after her initial seizures. Not only had it helped her center herself, it had become a way to learn more about each other as well. Or defuse difficult moments, like this one. "You know he's got to have an embarrassing potty-training story in there somewhere over seven hundred freaking years."

"This is the thanks I get, after I secured you an endless supply of beer?"

"In this place? That will get me three, maybe. Two, if the waiter takes his twenty percent out." Gideon snorted, but when he shifted his legs, he managed to shove at Daegan's shiny dress shoe with his own, a grudging thanks.

"I think Gideon has an excellent idea." Anwyn took them past the awkward male bonding moment, thank God. Daegan appeared amused and faintly alarmed at her piercing regard. "You've told me why you work for the Council, but how did you end up working for them?"

Gideon wondered that anyone could resist her, the long lashes and straight, slim nose, that combination of imperious and completely female curiosity. Daegan confirmed it with the warm resignation that suffused his features. "My mother was on the Council."

"So that's how come you have the lordship title. You're a born vampire." Gideon had guessed as much, and he knew Anwyn was already aware of the keen disparity of rank between born and made vampires. "How come you don't want us to call you Lord Daegan? Not that I would, but I know it's not because you're all that egalitarian."

Daegan gave him a derisive look, but answered the question straight enough. "Everything about who and what I am is a Council secret. I had an unremarkable childhood, as vampires go, at least to outside appearances. However, I have certain abilities that set me apart. One is the speed. The other is my inability to be detected by another vampire. I don't carry that scent or aura."

"And your immunity to the Delilah virus." It was something that had impacted Lady Lyssa, arguably the most powerful vampire in their world, so that in itself was a curiosity. "Was your father your mother's human servant? It seems like most of the born vampires come from that vampire-servant pairing."

"No. My mother told me her encounter with my father was brief, and that he was not a part of her life. He is unaware of my existence, as far as I know." Daegan took a sip of his wine. "After the Territory Wars, a discreet, non-politic way was needed to eliminate vampires and others who threatened exposure of our kind. My mother proposed me for the role. I'd lived my life separate from the vampire world, so it made it easier." He glanced toward Gideon. "You're familiar with vampire tolerance for differences, I'm sure."

"Oh yeah." They'd tried to execute Lyssa when they found out about her Fey background, leading to the uneasy relationship the Council had with her and Jacob now.

"I'm indifferent to their politics and world. It was my mother I served, but since her death, the Council and I have not disagreed. I do not have a problem taking out unstable made vampires who are over-indulging their natural brutality. It is something worthwhile that must be done."

Gideon took a swallow of the beer the waiter had brought, putting it at his elbow with silent efficiency. He read Anwyn's tense expression easily enough, as did Daegan, for he covered her hand with his. "You do not have anything to worry about, *cher*. Though made vampires are not as highly regarded as born ones, they are accepted as part of the structure."

"Unless they have crazy, uncontrollable fits."

"Hey." Gideon drew her gaze to him. "We're out tonight, and you haven't foamed at the mouth once."

"Don't go weepy on me now, Mistress Anwyn." Daegan stroked a lock of her hair from her cheek. "I rely on your unflinching courage."

"You both suck," she said, giving a halfhearted chuckle. "A woman deserves a weak Victorian swooning moment now and then."

"We get past this Council meeting, and I promise you may whine when you need a new pair of shoes, or cry if your hair doesn't curl correctly. You can even ask Gideon to remove any spiders you find in the apartment."

"I think I'll just ask him to stake you in your sleep," she responded, teeth bared.

Gideon approved of Daegan's approach to lighten her load of worries. He only hoped he could bury his own trepidation below where Anwyn might stumble over it. He wasn't the world's most positive thinker, and yet, with her in his mind, he was going to have to become Mr. Freaking Rogers.

Anwyn snorted out a surprised laugh, and turned an amused eye to him. "I'm not really seeing you in pastel sweaters."

"You'd be surprised, *cher*. Every man can change. He can choose to lay down the sword and become something else."

As Anwyn turned her attention back to Daegan, Gideon furrowed his brow. "We're not talking about me anymore, are we?"

"Not everything is about you, vampire hunter." Daegan sent an arch look at Gideon's sneer, but then sobered again, put down his glass. "I've been giving it a bit of thought. This betrayal by the Council tells me it's possibly time for my role to end. Region Masters and territory lords can handle violations locally, no matter the politics. They can make application to the Council for the termination and handle it themselves. I will make sure you are acknowledged, that Gideon is accepted as your servant, and then I can tell I am done. I have served them long enough."

Gideon stared at him. "You're just going to walk away?"

Daegan kept his gaze on Anwyn's face. "The cost of my job has become far too dear. I nearly lost what mattered most to me. I do not work at their behest, but at my own."

Anwyn pressed her lips together, her eyes suddenly bright with emotion. "You said that just to play on my female side."

"*Cher*, you are all female. And I thank God for it." Daegan lifted a shoulder. "My mother is gone, an accident caused by the onset of Ennui. One of the few mind-diseases that can affect our kind," he added when Anwyn looked puzzled. "When a vampire has lived a certain amount of years, some are afflicted with a malaise, a severe apathy of sorts. She wandered outdoors too close to sunrise and wandered too far. Her mind was altered, thinking she was in her gardens, in darkness. Her servant tried to bring her back, and she wouldn't permit it. She kept telling him to let her smell the flowers. She became ash in a botanical park, which I think gave her some small measure of happiness. I was unfortunately on an assignment at the time.

"I will not be absent again when someone else I love needs me." He closed his hand over Anwyn's. "You deserve a life. Whether it's running your club or whatever you decide you wish to do, I am going to make certain you have it, sooner rather than later."

"Daegan," she murmured, obviously moved. Even Gideon couldn't doubt the sincerity and determination he saw in the male's expression. But Anwyn shook her head. "You can't. Think of all the vampires like Barnabus you've stopped. It's important."

"Yes, it is. But there will always be battles to be fought. If time is not taken to love and live, then it's easy to forget that there is more than blood and death in life." He flicked a quick glance at Gideon, making it clear the conversation might apply to more than one of them at the table, after all. "A vampire's life is long, Anwyn. I can take some time for this. Though I admit I do not intend to go quietly into the night until I determine who it is who betrayed me, and confront that loose end."

"Thank God. I was going to say you were a real pussy if you let that one slide." Gideon took another liberal swallow of the beer, appreciated the cold, bracing taste. It helped steady him. Being a witness to this significant turning point in Daegan and Anwyn's relationship gave him that out-in-the-cold feeling once more. But was it because he didn't belong, or because he was the one incapable of stepping back over the threshold?

Daegan gave him a narrow glance. "Of course, if I have to put up with your servant, I may already have lived too long."

"I'd be happy to help you with that."

"I'm sure." Daegan cocked his head. "How about you, vampire hunter? What do you need in order to stop? What will finally answer the blood-lust you carry?"

Gideon's brow creased anew. *Jesus, how did he do that?* "Psychoanalyzing me now?"

"No. But I am wondering if I might hold the key to the answer you won't give yourself."

With a jolt, Gideon realized Anwyn wasn't the only one on whom Daegan had planned to drop a bomb this evening. Only he felt an inexplicable urge to bolt, as if Daegan was about to throw that door wide-open, making it clear that only Gideon's will was keeping him out in the yard, off that threshold.

"The vampire who killed your Laura was one of my assignments, Gideon," Daegan said softly. "I executed him six months after he took her life."

∽

Everything stilled. He heard Anwyn's indrawn breath, but after that, nothing but a hushed silence. It was as if the musicians had stopped midchord and the breeze silenced its whisper. Even the lights dimmed. Everything in Gideon zeroed in on Daegan's face, the knowledge in his dark eyes.

"For her sake, and for yours, I wish I'd received those orders sooner."

When Gideon had faced the terrible truth that vampires existed, he'd had to swallow the bitter pill that he'd never know which one had taken Laura. So he'd resolved to kill them all. Somewhere, at some point, her murderer would fall. Yet her murderer had fallen a long time ago, at the hands of the male before him.

"Did he suffer?"

"Eli Wallace had impulse problems and an insatiable bloodlust. He was a slight male, almost effeminate-looking, and so he'd found it was easier to lure females to follow him. My job is about justice, not vengeance, so I can't give you the gift of his pain. But he is gone. I put him down like a rabid animal, quick and clean."

Gideon swallowed. Swallowed again. Daegan's gaze remained on his face, the male's eyes as always seeing too much. "So you see," he continued in that gentle tone, "the blood vengeance is paid."

Gideon barely registered the words. He couldn't put his mind around it, hadn't realized how much of Laura's unavenged death lay at the heart of what he considered himself to be. It was ludicrous. He knew he couldn't kill them all, and yet . . . He wanted to get up, walk away into the night, get a deep, deep breath of air, maybe suffocate himself with oxygen. Pointless.

"I didn't expect to have another purpose. I didn't . . . I couldn't even kill the person who killed her. She died, and I couldn't help her. You killed her murderer. You . . ." Gideon shook his head. "Jesus, I was right. You really don't need me. I'm a liability to you both, if anything."

When he started to get up, Daegan caught his lapel with an oath. As he dragged him back down, the vampire met him eye to eye, warrior to warrior. "Why are you determined to be fucking inconsequential?" he asked quietly.

"Daegan." Anwyn's soft voice made him ease off, though he uttered a second quiet curse. His fingers squeezed Gideon's neck, a rough caress, before he sat back.

Anwyn's hand found Gideon's, forming a knot of fingers locked beneath his aching breastbone. She cradled Gideon's face with her other hand, forcing him to look at her when he just wanted to go, bolt, run back to the shadows. Daegan's keen gaze told him that wasn't going to happen, but it was moot. He couldn't move when Anwyn was touching him like this.

"You keep trying to quantify your worth based on some physical measurement," she murmured. "What you can give me; how well you can protect me. How many vampires you've killed. You won't accept that letting yourself be loved is a gift as well, one of the most valuable. It's one I want you to give me above all others. It will be harder than all the rest, because you don't think you're worth loving."

He shook his head, tried to pull back, but she held on, stubborn. "Gideon, no. You won't withdraw from me. You think the world wasn't pulled out from under my feet a month ago? You and Daegan, you told me I have to deal with it. I'm not going to let you do anything less. Yes, everything about your life is changing. Join the club. Don't leave it. Don't leave me."

Her gaze became flint then, and those fingers dug in. "I'm going to give you a command. You *will* allow me to love you, in whatever manner, however deeply, I wish to do so. You will learn to surrender your heart to me, Gideon Green, and when you finally do that, you will understand your own worth."

"But I won't be here . . ."

"Time doesn't matter. That's another thing you need to learn. Whatever plans you have for the future, until then you'll put your trust in me, in a way you've never trusted anyone. Can you do that?"

She'd asked the question before, in a variety of ways, but not like this. There was broken glass in his chest. "I don't know." He closed his hands on her wrists. "Anwyn, I don't think I can give myself that. I don't think I can give myself anything."

"You're not giving it. I'm taking it." She stared at him, hard. "All right? Sit down now."

She eased him back into the chair with a firm hand, and then surprised him by sliding into his lap, bringing his arms around her so he cradled her there, feeling her soft body press against him, her arms wind around his neck as she laid her cheek on his shoulder.

"Don't think, Gideon. Just exist. Listen to the music, and the wind moving in the trees, and feel the connection between the three of us."

Daegan moved into the chair Anwyn had vacated, stretching an arm behind Gideon's chair. With shock, he realized they'd closed ranks to shelter him. To care for him. He wanted to be ashamed of his weakness, of this throbbing pain inside of him, but he couldn't breathe.

Laura was gone, and the blood debt was paid. Where did that leave him? Who and what was he now, if he wasn't sure he could be a vampire hunter?

"Shhh . . ." she murmured, and her lips were on his, coaxing them open, gently tangling with his tongue, catching an unexpected harsh sob. "Hold on to me, love. I'm yours. We're yours. We want you. You belong to us."

He knew it wasn't true, and even if it was, he couldn't be that forever. But for right now he was too overwhelmed to question or fight it. He needed the pressure of Daegan's hand on his back, his arm against his shoulders, the sheltering cant of his body. The curl of Anwyn's, like a beautiful pale seashell curved over his exposed wounds, keeping them safe from swooping predators.

In time, he got his thundering heart, the terrifying desire to break down, under control, and he just sat quietly under their touch. He could hate Daegan for telling him, but he saw the vampire hadn't realized the effect it would have on him, how it would taint their evening. There was some small satisfaction in seeing Daegan screw up for once.

But he wished it could have lasted forever, that brief, magical connection right before, undisturbed by any trauma or terror that might lie ahead, or truths too difficult to face. As he let the world spin around him, Gideon wondered what would happen when it righted itself. Would he walk away from the grave he'd haunted in his mind for more than a decade? Finally say good-bye?

But to who or what?

8

"WHY are you sent after vampires? What crimes can vampires commit, if they're allowed to kill up to twelve humans a year, including their annual kill?"

Over the next several nights, Anwyn continued to receive lessons from Daegan, as well as grill the vampire herself, on Council and vampire society. When she'd opened Atlantis, she'd learned the key to doing it successfully was to immerse herself in as much knowledge about how a club worked as possible, and then tailor it to her own personality. It was like making a dress. The fabric had to be there before the design could be cut. Understanding her need, and approving of it, Daegan patiently answered every question, as well as detailed the Council and the rules that governed the vampire world, a whole shadow society living beneath the radar of most humans.

Gideon remained quiet for much of it, and absented himself from their rooms for this or that reason on more than one occasion. Anwyn would have cornered him to draw him out, but she sensed he needed a few days' space. She even helped him, sending him on errands to the club levels or in town, and didn't remark on it when he stayed away far longer than needed to complete her lists. A couple of times, she touched his mind and found him sitting in a park, or a coffee shop, his thoughts whirling in a slow, confused spin, processing the things he knew, that he was becoming.

When in the apartment, he spent a lot of time in Daegan's weapons and workout room, testing his strength and endurance incessantly. She bit back any smartass observations about a vampire hunter honing his skills to kill vampires while caring for one, because Gideon's sense of humor was out of order for the moment.

When they'd returned from the wine and cheese event, Gideon's emotions had been in such a turmoil that, by unspoken accord, she'd brought him to her bed, taken him into her body in simple, sweet love-making, let him fall asleep that way. Daegan had come to her later, slid in behind her, and their hands had rested on him together, stroking his hair. When she woke at dusk, Gideon was gone and she and Daegan had been twined together alone.

She tried to not intrude into the deeper layers of Gideon's mind, simply reaching out on occasion, a subtle caress to let him know she was there. Tonight he'd come back from his errands with groceries for himself, some new clips for his guns. Now he was listening to their conversation about Daegan's assassinations as he cleaned and sharpened his knives.

He was sitting on the floor, his back against his sofa. He did his guns on one night of the week, knives on another. The crossbows and wooden weapons were checked and oiled on yet another. Usually the cleaning was a calming exercise for him, but tonight he appeared to be getting more agitated. Confirming it, he rose abruptly. "I'm going to go practice."

Daegan didn't comment on it, she was sure because he assumed Gideon was just impatient, listening to what he called the "farce" of vampire civility. She understood that she had to learn as much as she could about that world, but as Daegan shared his insights, there was an unfortunate side effect. Gideon, having to attend the same lessons, learned about a world he'd spent much of his life trying to destroy, a world into which he was now integrating himself solely for her benefit and protection. It meant that each day, he faced that fork in his soul that had been ripped there by circumstances.

Despite the power of that struggle, it was the fuse winding amid it, the one most likely to set off the full powder keg, that worried her the most. His fiercely deliberate, unacknowledged desire for Daegan kept growing, almost faster than his deep concerns about her attending the Council, and the temporal nature of their relationship when she embraced a vampire's life fully.

While cleaning the blade, Gideon had been drifting into some rather graphic images of her body twined with his. At first it had been memory only, remembering the night after their dinner. The sweet lovemaking, his mouth on her breast, her hand passing over his hair, the slick, easy penetration and tight clasp of her cunt around him, welcoming and holding him.

But as the memory spun into new imaginings, his hands performing the cleaning and sharpening by rote, he devised rougher, more demanding scenarios, things such as what they shared in the Queen's Chamber. It had distracted her enough to miss a couple points of Daegan's lecture. She'd wondered if Gideon was doing it on purpose, since she knew he could sense when she was in his mind, but he seemed trapped in his own head tonight, almost oblivious to her presence.

Her being in his mind wasn't a deep or intentional probe. It took so much effort to stay out of his head at this point, that he'd made it clear he was fine with her drifting in the upper layers if it was easier for her to focus on more important things, like controlling her bloodlust and the shadow voices in her head. They'd also found that her drifting in his head helped keep those voices quiet.

That was how she knew what had disturbed Gideon enough to send him to the weapons room. It wasn't what Daegan was saying, but how he was saying it. The sensual lift and drop of the syllables was what bothered Gideon. As he'd listened, the vampire had become a third member of the carnal triangle in her vampire hunter's mind. Touching them both, gripping, demanding . . . taking control of Gideon's responses as the three of them gave and received pleasure.

When Gideon recognized the turn of his personal fantasy, he'd snapped to his feet as if he'd been bitten, retreating to the weapons room to exorcise the unwanted but undeniable desire.

Though he was never easy in it, Gideon was far less resistant to her dominance when Daegan was absent. In his soul, Gideon was a strangely conservative creature. But below that, where his sexual self was laid bare, she knew he couldn't deny his fascination with the other male.

How he couldn't quite keep himself from looking at the vampire. It amused her, because nothing with a pulse could help appreciating Daegan's sexuality. She understood the vampire allure better now, because of how her staff had reacted to her before her bloodlust attack. But vampire allure or no, Daegan had something extra.

The mystery, the aura of unquestionable command, the hard body, beautiful cock and intriguing face, all sensual planes and shadows, dominated by the dark eyes and sinful mouth. She'd often wondered what he would look like with his hair long and silky, rather than cropped short the way he kept it for the work he did.

"At some point, the three of us need to cover servant etiquette. He'll need to observe it to avoid drawing more attention to him."

She tuned back in to Daegan. "But we won't be bringing him to the Council audience. He'll stay on the plane or somewhere farther away, where he can monitor my mind and give me the cues I need."

At Daegan's expression, she rose slowly. "He intends to go in there with us?"

"He does. I have not been able to dissuade him."

"It's not a matter of dissuading. He's not going."

"It will be dangerous for him, but he's resourceful—"

"Oh my God." She stared at him. "You've already agreed to this. Discussed it with him. I thought we'd agreed—"

"I did not break my promise to you, *cher*. It was his decision to share with you, not mine. He has waited too long, however, and I feel you need to know. To be prepared."

Letting Daegan get closer to her soul was another way to help her balance, like having Gideon in her mind or her in his, but at times like this it was a bittersweet pleasure. She'd wanted that closeness, and now doubted his heart far less, but residual anger could still flare when he made executive decisions like this one. "I may not know much about your world, but taking one of the most successful vampire hunters into Council headquarters seems like signing his death warrant."

"He'd be coming as your servant."

"And that will make it all okay? Can you guarantee he'll be safe the same way you've promised me that I will?"

"No, *cher*. But it's not my choice to make."

"Damn right it's not." She ignored the narrow warning glance he shot her way. "We'll call his brother and Lady Lyssa. Tell them what may happen. Surely the two of them will sit on him until we get back."

Daegan rose from the couch, his face getting that implacable set that made her want to simultaneously rage and despair. "They have a child, Anwyn. Vampire infants are rare and highly valued in our world. If the child has two parents, neither will leave him, nor bring him into a dangerous situation, until he is past the age where he could be taken and passed off as another vampire's child."

"Gideon wouldn't hurt his own nephew, and I won't be a danger to them. I won't even be close to him."

Daegan raised his brow. "You'd take away his free will, just like that?"

"To save his life? Absolutely. You told me almost the same thing, when I tried to take my life. Is it so different because I'm a female, under your protection?"

His lips twisted. "My double standard toward women is hardly a revelation."

"Why do any of us have to go? Why not just send them a fax or an e-mail? Videoconference, for heavens' sake. This is the technology age."

"Because the Council is very rigid on certain things. When a vampire is made or killed, they require a personal audience."

Anwyn was watching his face, and now bit her lip. "So if punishment must be meted out, it can be done swiftly."

"No harm is going to come to you there," he said immediately, his expression hardening. "If I thought there was *any* danger to you, I wouldn't take you, no matter their requirements."

"But risking Gideon is okay. God, he's right. You do think humans are expendable." She turned away, but he reached out, caught her wrist.

"I value Gideon. But anyone is expendable, when it comes to you. He agrees with me. He's doing this of his own free will."

"Neither of you has the right to make that choice." She resisted his grip, but he held on, giving her a level look.

"I make that kind of choice quite often, Anwyn. It doesn't mean I enjoy it. But you don't need to worry about what's going to happen. I'll handle whatever occurs at the Council."

Anwyn stared at him, yanked her hand back in an unexpected move. "You did *not* just suggest I shouldn't worry my pretty little head about it."

Daegan abruptly dropped, spinning back to his feet in a lithe move as a knife thumped into the wall behind him. Gideon leaned in the doorway, flipping his second blade in his hand. "Just making sure you're paying attention."

Anwyn turned her temper on him. "He shouldn't have to pay attention in his own home. What if you'd hit him with that?"

"He would have said 'ouch,' pulled it out, and promptly healed," Gideon observed mildly, though his eyes were far from casual. "I didn't use the crossbow or aim for the heart."

"Well, then, what am I worried about?" She cast an exasperated look at Daegan, who'd pulled the weapon out of her wall and sent it back to Gideon with a loose, twisting toss that the other male caught. He didn't look perturbed by Gideon's actions. But there was a tension to Gideon's body that showed he was perturbed about something.

"If it was my decision to tell her, you did a pretty good job of doing it yourself."

"Perhaps because it appeared you intended to tell her when we all got off the plane together in Berlin. Where the stress of such a revelation might send her into a seizure."

"I can't believe the two of you are actually talking about me like I'm not here." Anwyn stepped between the two men, interrupting the line of vision, and was incredibly irritated and amazed when Gideon merely shifted to reestablish it. The heat in the room was escalating, and while she was nursing her own anger, it didn't cloud the fact that something far more volatile was brewing.

"She's right." Gideon's eyes met Daegan's, a challenge. "You're the proverbial pot calling the kettle black. She deserves to know as much as possible about what to expect, even the things that will worry her, because knowing in advance will help her be prepared. If she thinks you're holding back on her, that's what will upset her."

"I expect you both to trust me on certain things," Daegan said stiffly.

"Sorry, Count Drac," Gideon said, eyes flashing. "Long as you have those fangs, I'm not going to be turning my back on you anytime soon."

Anwyn flinched, and Gideon glanced toward her. "You're different, Anwyn."

"Of course I am," she said flatly, but she knew his mind. She'd put her life into his hands more than once now. He didn't trust her to do that for him. Not now, maybe not ever. With her blood, how could she blame him? It still hurt.

The vampire hunter sheathed the other blade, took a couple of steps in the room. "In the past, you've been handling the Council alone. But we'll be with you. You're taking troops, and they should know the terrain, your strategy. I chose to hunt vampires alone, but when I went with others, I never John McClane'd it. Unless you're Bruce Willis, that gets people killed."

Anwyn bit back an oath as Daegan turned a puzzled expression toward her. "It's a character from an action movie, an antihero who always goes in and single-handedly saves the day," she said between gritted teeth.

Daegan pressed his lips together. "I am not that person. However, since you're so eager to be in the loop, we were just talking about Council etiquette. You'll need to observe certain inviolate courtesies while we're there, in order to stay as unobtrusive as possible. And before you start being your typical smartass self," he interjected at Gideon's scowl, "it's for Anwyn's protection, not your own. She needs you, for good or ill, and if you shoot your mouth off and disrespect the Council, they *will* kill you."

She'd asked for his bald honesty, but that hit her like a blow to the stomach. Daegan gave her a glance, his lips thinning, but turned back to Gideon. "They will not hesitate, give it a second thought, or feel a moment's remorse. You are a servant. In their eyes, you are property, subject to the will of your Mistress in all things. If she wanted to torture you to death, that would be no concern of theirs."

"Good to know," Anwyn said tightly. "In case I have the urge."

She wasn't done with this topic of Gideon going, not by a long shot. They were hoping to barrel right over her with their combined male intimidation routine, and she wasn't having it. However, she could set aside her own reaction for a moment, because the dangerous currents between them didn't bode well. She wondered if she needed to warn Daegan that Gideon might have other reasons for wanting to pick a fight.

"You follow three paces behind her at all times. Never beside her, never in front. You always address her as 'Mistress,' or 'ma'am.' Never meet a vampire's gaze directly unless he or she specifically commands it. Anything Anwyn tells you to do, you do it promptly. I know you give her pleasure with your resistance, but you need to shelve that kind of behavior at the Council." Gideon flushed, his eyes beginning to flash again, but Daegan pressed on. "Pretend to be what you are not. A well-trained, obedient servant. Perhaps they'll completely forget you were a vampire hunter, or be so impressed by Anwyn's skills at controlling you, they will focus on that instead."

"What if they threaten her?"

"Her protection is my job. Protecting your life so you can care for her, during and afterward, that is yours."

"What about you? Do I pretend to be your little dog on a leash as well?"

Daegan gave him a cool look. "You are Anwyn's servant, not mine. However, as I said, if *any* vampire commands you, you must obey. Anwyn has no rank among them, which means at the moment her servant is subject to serve their whims as well."

"Wait a minute." Anwyn broke in. "They can't—"

"There are certain boundaries." Daegan lifted a hand. "They won't threaten his life or subject him to prolonged torture, though they may challenge his tolerance for pain or other . . . inhibitions he may have." At Gideon's expression, Daegan gave him a straight stare. "Second thoughts, vampire hunter?"

"Gideon, you can't go if that's the scenario," Anwyn said emphatically. "There's no way I want you walking into that. No. Absolutely no."

"It's fine," Gideon said shortly.

"You already knew this," she realized. "Of course you did." And though Daegan had made his feelings clear, she felt anger at him anew as well, at the whole helpless situation. Well, fuck that. She wasn't helpless. "I'm calling your brother. He *will* keep you from going, baby or no baby. He can come down here and babysit you after we chain you in that cell in my dungeon. See how you like being caged up like a rabid animal with people treating you like you don't have a brain."

"Anwyn." Gideon stepped forward. He made the mistake of lifting a hand as if to touch her face. She slapped it away, but he caught her hand in one of those lightning-quick moves that reminded her of his training. She wrenched free, however, meeting his roused blue gaze with a furious one of her own. For the moment, she ignored Daegan. One ass-ripping at a time.

"If you can go down in some blaze of glory, defending me, that's okay? Even if it leaves me without a servant, alone?"

"I have no intention of getting killed, Anwyn," Gideon said, but his gaze said something different.

"I've had enough of this. Of your damn death wish, the one you've been carrying since the day you met me. If I don't get to kill myself, neither do you."

The jolt of reaction from Daegan startled her. The vampire's eyes darkened in shock, and his surprised anger filled her. She'd thought it was obvious, but she was deep in Gideon's mind, had studied different aspects of the man than Daegan had. Men didn't always see the things that the women who loved them did. Her servant was about to make it worse by confirming it, though.

"We both know I'm not a good long-term servant for you. If I can help get you through this part, then you'll be all right. You'll find someone. Hell, someone like James. Someone who knows how to serve. To submit."

Anwyn stepped forward. At her accusation, Gideon had retreated back to the doorway, his arms crossed, the knives holstered, thumbs hooked under his armpits, his body radiating tension. "Do you want to be my servant, Gideon?"

"I told you—"

"I know you feel an obligation to protect me. But when I've commanded you to your knees, or made you do things you didn't want to do, it felt like something you wanted, something you couldn't resist, didn't it? There's a craving in the pit of your stomach for more of it, even if you think you don't want it."

"You can read my mind," he said gruffly. "You already know."

"Yes, and no. I see all those thoughts in your mind, but I don't know which of them wins the struggle."

"Some days one side wins, some days the other."

"So it's still an ongoing war." She managed a stiff smile.

"Yeah." He straightened now. "But if you won't let me be at your side when you go into dangerous situations, the war will be over pretty quick. It's the one thing I'm good at, Anwyn. Don't deny me the right to protect you with all I have."

"Even if it gets you killed? I don't need to see your body cut down to know that you're willing to die for me. Except I don't think you're dying for me. You're dying for yourself, to prove something to that girl. To Laura."

He flinched, and she knew she'd hit a direct target. Good. She didn't mind confronting it head-on. In fact, as her anger built with the whole situation, with the idea of taking him to the Council like a fucking sac-rificial lamb, she understood what had fueled Daegan's rage the day she'd tried to burn herself alive behind the Dumpster. Karma could be a real bitch.

She closed the last space between her and Gideon, her breasts brushing his chest, her hands settling on his taut biceps. It was an inti-mate pose, but she knew her gaze was as unrelenting as solid ice. "Live for me or die for her, but you make up your damn mind before we leave. If you want her, then you clear out and go find the vampire that can grant your deepest wish. I'm sure Daegan can point you toward the nearest unwinnable, desperately heroic situation. You're *not* going to meet the Council with us. And that's final."

With that, she swept past him, headed for the corridor that would lead to the weapons room. For once, *she* needed to pound on something.

9

CAUGHT between annoyance and something worse, it took several moments before Gideon realized Daegan was still standing in the same place, regarding him with an expression almost as aggravating as Anwyn's opinion. Hell, why was *he* angry? He was the one who'd jumped the gun and let Anwyn know about him going before Gideon had figured out how best to tell her. If she was upset, Daegan was as much to blame as Gideon.

However, Gideon was getting a distinct vibe that Daegan was pissed at him for other reasons. The intent way the male was staring at him, in that manner that Gideon found damn hard to meet. It lifted his own hackles, making him itch to toss the other knife, test the vampire's reflexes.

With irritating perception, the vampire jerked his head toward the corridor where Anwyn had disappeared. "I've been working with her on her hand-to-hand, as you have. But earlier, before you came in, she said she'd like to see us fight each other, to observe the moves by those who know how to do them. I expect now would be as good a time as any to do that. Unless you prefer brooding over facing me on a mat."

Gideon bit back a snarl. "She's not being reasonable."

"Women have a tendency to look at things somewhat differently than we do. If you do get yourself killed, she will blame herself. I'll be left to deal with her anger and grief. But I suppose that matters little to you as well."

Gideon snorted, something ugly and bitter twisting the words out of him. "Save the martyred routine. It'd clear the playing field pretty good, wouldn't it?"

In that second, Gideon thought the vampire might start their sparring match right there. Daegan took a full, weighted second to reply, and when he did, his voice was flat. "We are not in competition, vampire hunter. Perhaps this is also as good a time as any to force you to face that."

God, he hated it when Daegan pulled the cryptic shit. He did want to brood. He also wanted to pound something, and though Daegan was likely to obliterate him, he might get in a few jabs of his own. So he gave a cocky shrug. "Fine. I guess I can go kick your ass if it will teach her anything."

"How magnanimous of you."

~

She was still angry when they joined her, but she was already sorting through those emotions to grip the cool rationality she knew would help her handle them both. Daegan and Gideon lived by almost the same code. Risking their own lives was acceptable, no matter how uneven the odds. It was something they actually respected in each other. Just as they were united in their desire to protect her.

She'd had Daegan and Gideon each teach her ways to fight better, because it didn't sit well with her to have them risk themselves on her behalf. Yes, they would always be more competent in that area than she was, because she wasn't a warrior. What they didn't seem to realize was she was as fiercely protective of the two of them as they were of her. If she was going to be part of a more violent world, she was going to learn to handle herself better. Maybe she'd shock the hell out of them and end up saving *their* asses one of these days.

She had her own arsenal of weapons, though, and knew the battleground where those weapons worked best. So by the time they arrived, she had—to all appearances—set aside their argument. She met Gideon's wary look with one that her alley cats had perfected, that aloof, mysterious expression that was neither invitation nor rejection. Neither forgiveness nor outright anger. He was intelligent enough to become even more concerned, but Daegan was already directing them onto the sparring mats.

Daegan had donned a pair of black drawstring *gi* pants and a dark tank that showed off the architecture of chest, shoulders and muscled arms. Gideon wore a similar pair of pants, borrowed from Daegan, and was likewise barefoot. Though she'd expected them to immediately start sparring, instead Daegan spent time with her first, doing their usual lesson, showing her offensive and defensive moves. Only this time Gideon was there, sitting on the sidelines and giving additional suggestions for her height and weight. In Daegan's absence, he'd also coached her, but this was the first time she'd had the pleasure of watching their different skills come together.

As they fell into what they knew so well, some of the tension she'd felt from Gideon eased. Interestingly, she detected more of it from Daegan, vibrating toward Gideon. Though she didn't have the same access to his mind she had to Gideon's, she understood the cause. Apparently Daegan felt far differently about Gideon risking himself for her protection than he did about Gideon wanting to get himself killed. *Males.*

At last, they squared off with each other, letting her take a seat on the sidelines to get her breath. As they went to work on each other, her volatile energy drifted in a sensual direction.

Lord, they were beautiful to watch. Daegan of course slowed his speed, and Gideon as well, so they could show her the maneuvers, stopping to verify she understood them. Once or twice they brought her into the middle to position her, demonstrate the proper way to turn, twist, flip, break, strong hands always making sure she was eased to the mat rather than flung there, despite her vampire resilience.

By the time they let her step out again, she was even more out of breath. Gideon's shirt was damp with sweat, but he didn't seem winded. "Can you show me some of those moves at a faster speed?" she asked. "I want to see what they look like in real time."

Daegan nodded, and he and Gideon faced each other again. Kicks, spins, dodges. Daegan moved swiftly enough, but she was impressed by how well Gideon choreographed with him. It was like watching two professional dancers, every move and countermove unconscious.

The flat of a palm slid along a leg, diverting its course. Two bodies came together, twisted like vines, smoothly breaking free, hands knowing just where to put pressure, grip, strike. A roll across the ground, a leg sweep, a quick grapple, an elbow into the side, and Gideon broke backward, taking them both down to the mat. Daegan was up and bringing down a leg to pin him, but Gideon caught the calf and twisted it, turning him away and then leaping back to his feet.

They didn't engage in the banter she'd expected. She was drawing her experience from action movies, the quintessential male bonding scenes. The two males she was watching had always used these skills to survive or kill. It was never a game for them.

Though she was mesmerized by the display of male virility, they disrupted her absorption on occasion by pointing out technique, giving her new information on the grips, other ways to break them, and the importance of balance.

"A vampire's balance is far better than a human's," Gideon said. "But if you catch him off guard, he's going to have a similar reaction. So if he has you in a chest lock"—he glanced at Daegan, and the vampire obliged, sliding his arm across Gideon's chest to grip him beneath the arm—"and you abruptly fall back against him, you can either break the hold or, if you're going for more debilitating, hook the ankle."

He demonstrated it, Daegan allowing the maneuver as Gideon flipped over him to pin his chest with a knee. There was a brief moment where he held him there, and Anwyn saw the men's eyes meet, the challenge in Gideon's, but then that moment was gone. Gideon shifted into a squat next to the man. He offered Daegan a hand up, the casual gesture at odds with tense shoulders. Daegan clasped his arm, but as he lifted his upper body, he startled both of them by curling a hand behind the vampire hunter's neck and yanking him down to his mouth.

Gideon stiffened, but he didn't pull away. Instead an involuntary noise came from his throat, as if he was fighting himself, the desire to stay greater than the desire to break away. Daegan changed the angle, delving deeper, coming up on his knees. Before Gideon could choose to withdraw, he'd shoved him so he landed on his back. In a heartbeat, Daegan was stretched out on him, one thigh pressed against Gideon's groin, his other arm bracing him just above Gideon. Though Daegan's broad shoulders shadowed the other man, Gideon's hand dug into his arm in a near-combative grip. For a second he didn't move, as if he'd been paralyzed.

Before Anwyn could absorb the sudden sexual charge saturating the atmosphere, Gideon broke the hold with an oath and a short, vicious jab to Daegan's mouth that drew blood. He flipped over and tried to make it to his feet, but the vampire had him pinned again, this time on his stomach, his knee in his lower back. Though he leaned down to whisper in Gideon's ear, Daegan was still clearly audible to her.

"You think I will tolerate suicide from you any more than I would from her, vampire hunter? You seek death when you cannot face life, when you cannot face who you are, what you are becoming. You've never been a coward, Gideon. Don't start now."

Bring me a set of restraints, Anwyn.

It startled her, but she covered her reaction, retrieving what he wanted from the playroom, a pair of padded yet extremely strong cuffs. When Gideon saw her, he started to struggle.

"No," he snarled. "Don't."

He was no match for Daegan in this position. The vampire yanked Gideon's hands up over his head and locked his wrists together. Then he hooked the restraints to a bolt in the floor that was used for the pulley weights in the room. Gideon continued to fight, but his arms were caught above his head, his body trapped on his stomach since Daegan was squatting on top of him, using Gideon's ass as a seat.

"You cannot run; you cannot deny yourself; you can only give in to me."

She shouldn't be surprised that Daegan had so clearly recognized what barbed conflict had been tearing Gideon up these past few days, and had chosen to address it in a combative way like this, male to male. However, Daegan was also angry. As she had been angry, realizing Gideon was determined that he was simply a way station for her, one that she might sacrifice without a second thought.

Daegan, this may be what his body wants, but it's tearing him apart. On something like this, you have to go easy.

He is strong, stubborn. And his need to come to grips with this is as vital and necessary as anything else we are facing. Time is too short. But she felt the mental pause, emotion struggling with the honor and integrity she knew ran so deep inside of him. So deep he had let her hate him to do what needed to be done, those long weeks of transition.

Help me, cher. *Make sure I don't push him too far.*

He was already pushing far beyond what Gideon believed he wanted. It took a very careful, very adept, Master or Mistress to get a slave to expand his boundaries like this without rupturing emotional scars into full, festering wounds. When their eyes met, she gave Daegan a slight nod.

"Son of a bitch. Let me go." Gideon spat it, pulled at the manacles in an impressive show of strength. He tried to buck Daegan off, but the vampire held firm. He flattened his palms on the flexing muscle as Gideon swore, then moved down to the waistband of the loose *gi* pants Gideon had borrowed. When Gideon bucked again, Daegan slid an arm under him, held his hips up to yank at the drawstring, bring the pants down to reveal the bare ass, strip them off his muscular legs.

"No. No. I don't want this."

Daegan reached beneath, closed his hand on Gideon's hard cock, so large and stiff it made Anwyn swallow. A throbbing ache started in her own sex, watching them.

"I can tell."

"It doesn't mean shit and you know it. I don't want this. Now, cut it the hell out."

He was panicking, his image of himself colliding with what his body wanted, his heart rate accelerating at the destruction of his identity, an identity that had been fragile for too long, explaining why he'd kept it behind such ironclad shields. But Daegan could tear away iron as if it were paper. Gideon needed her.

When she rose, Daegan held up a hand. Pure, cool command was in his gaze. It settled a different feeling over the room, one that even Gideon recognized, for he briefly stopped struggling, his eyes darting between them both.

"When I am inside him, you will take him, *cher.* This time, he will accept me first."

"Fuck you," Gideon snarled, though his hips could not help jerking, pushing into Daegan's sure grip around his cock.

"That's a privilege you haven't earned, servant." Daegan stood then, putting his foot on his back to hold him there. Loosening the drawstring on his own pants, he shoved them down, kicked them aside. Gideon squeezed his eyes shut, but in his mind, Anwyn saw it was because he was denying himself the temptation of looking.

You don't want to look at another guy's dick. You don't. That was what he was telling himself. But he did. Partly for self-preservation, a warrior's natural inclination to evaluate the size and force of the weapon that was going to be used against him. Partly for other reasons.

Daegan didn't yet want her physically near, but she understood how she could help. *Gideon, listen to me. You're being cruel to yourself, only because Daegan's touch is arousing you. You've told yourself that it's because we've been in sexual situations, the three of us, intense situations, and it's just overflow from how you feel toward me. But the truth is something far different. As long as you're afraid of it, you won't know the truth. This can take you a step closer to the truth, whatever it is. You have to trust us. Can you do that?"*

You can read my mind. Why the hell do you ask me anything?

You know why.

They were both naked to her appreciative gaze. Daegan sent her another mental command, and she returned with a lubricant. Daegan reached out, keeping her a few feet away from her servant as he took the items. He caressed her fingers, though, giving her a look that was part reassurance, part male predator.

When he turned back to Gideon, it was as if the dense energy gathering in the room had made everything slow down. As she folded her legs gracefully beneath her, seating herself close to them, Anwyn watched Daegan pour the lubricant over his hand. He thoroughly saturated it before he slid a palm over Gideon's left buttock. It left a glistening wide band of oil there, as he worked his way toward the tightly clenched seam. "Loosen up, Gideon, or this will be more painful than you want it to be."

"If you're going to fuck my ass, it's going to be agony no matter what. *Stop.*" It burst out of him as Daegan touched his rim with oil-slicked fingers. "Anwyn, Mistress . . . I don't want this."

She met his furious, panicked gaze as his head jerked toward her. *Your mind says you do, Gideon. All three of us know it.*

Pushing his face into the floor, blocking them both out, he gave a long, agonized growl of anguish that twisted her heart. She was a

Domme, she knew Daegan was right, but this was harder than she expected. Though her body was on fire, her pulse rate up, her pussy soaked, watching what was about to happen, she couldn't ignore the emotional battle going on in him.

Let me at least do the lubricant, Daegan. Soothe him with my touch.

No. There's a reason I do this, Anwyn. He might be asked to submit to worse in Berlin. If he can't handle this, then he'll know he can't go with you.

It stunned her enough to bring her up short. *Son of a bitch.* When the expletive came to mind automatically, she knew Gideon was influencing her language. Daegan gave her a significant glance, a bare nod.

He'd let her snarl at him, let her believe that he'd accepted Gideon's decision. And perhaps he had, but it didn't mean he didn't have a plan to test the hell out of it. One of these days, she was going to teach Daegan Rei to give her some inkling of his strategy before he implemented it.

Of course, even if she'd missed that, she wasn't thrown off enough to see that there was more going on here than a public service. She'd seen Daegan's anger and reaction to Gideon's challenge. As a vampire and Dominant both, she understood a predator's nature better. What was happening now made her see that duality in Daegan pretty damn clearly.

You want to be the first male to claim his ass. He'll be yours first, before any of them.

His dark eyes met hers again, and his sensual lips curled, showing a hint of fang. Then he turned his attention back to Gideon. He'd poured lubricant in the other palm and brought Gideon's hips off the ground to close it around Gideon's cock. As he slid his grip along it, the organ grew longer and thicker.

"No," Gideon whispered. His eyes were closed, and she saw fluid leak out of the tip of the organ, a convulsive shudder taking his powerful body.

Shifting to squat next to him, Daegan clasped a handful of Gideon's hair and pulled his head up. Gideon's eyes opened, and he tried to yank back, but Daegan's grip held him in place. The vampire hunter looked like he might spit at his captor, but then thought better of it. Daegan nodded, acknowledging the wisdom. In this position, Daegan's cock was almost under his chin. Gideon's gaze was almost tearing in his effort not to look at the fully erect organ brushing Daegan's belly, the weight of his testicles hanging beneath, the powerful thigh muscles that would help him thrust into Gideon's ass.

The knuckles of Daegan's other hand slid down Gideon's throat, caressing the taut windpipe, then lower, passing oily fingers over the trinity mark over his heart, earning a hard shudder. "You may not believe it," he murmured, "but the day will come, vampire hunter, when you will beg for my cock in your mouth. Anwyn will be fucking you from behind with one of her strap-ons, a clit stimulator bringing her to climax so you hear her cries, feel the spasm of her pussy vibrate through the rubber cock she'll have in your ass. All that will matter to you is our mutual pleasure. Whatever serves our pleasure will serve your own."

Anwyn drew in a breath, for it was the second time he'd acknowledged what she already suspected, that Gideon should belong to them both, serving a Master and Mistress. But first that last bastion had to fall, and it wasn't being fucked. It was letting a male vampire feed off him, subjugate him to his blood needs. That was what would shatter the last part of Gideon and the life he'd led, because male vampires had always been his target. It was a male vampire who'd killed Laura.

This was perilously close to shattering him now, and it worried her.

We will take care of your tough vampire hunter; never fear, cher. His soul may be fragile, but he is also stronger than you realize. Remember, when he first came to you, you thought he might need the hand of both a Master and Mistress, a male energy to confront his temper and anger and kick his ass when needed.

Releasing Gideon's hair, Daegean gave it an almost tender stroke, then moved behind him. Though Gideon's whole body tensed, Daegan slid his arm back under his abdomen, pulled his hips back up. He put his lips close to Gideon's ear again.

"If you're determined to stand at her back at the Council, you might have to deal with far worse than this. I'm throwing you that bone, a shield to imagine that's what this is about, no different from any other combat with an enemy. If it gets you through it, fine. But we'll both know that you respond to my cock, my mouth, in a way you've never responded to a male."

"Fucking . . . bastard."

"Fucking you, vampire hunter. Claiming your fine ass for my own." Using his other well-lubricated hand, he began to push into the opening Gideon couldn't deny him. A strangled noise came from Gideon. More pre-come oozed from his cock, making Anwyn lick her lips. She slid closer so Gideon could see her. Though her eyes were on what Daegan was doing, she could feel Gideon watching the arousal grow in her face. He was reluctantly drawn into it, his desire to give her pleasure overriding his denials. Which conversely spurred her own reaction.

"Is it easier for you to think of it that way, like a battle exercise?" she asked. "Rather than you learning to serve me the way I desire?"

"Maybe." His voice was strained, but the intensity of his gaze increased. She held on to that, keeping them both still by holding his eyes with hers. She wondered if it had been subconscious or more deliberate, the few times she'd tested Gideon with those different-sized phalluses in his delectable ass. She'd been preparing him all along for this, for Daegan to take him. And when Gideon's expression flickered with reluctant arousal, she knew she'd let him hear the musing, and it had given him a searing jolt of retroactive lust, confirming this was meant to happen. Was going to happen.

One finger slid in past the tight ring of muscles, and Gideon groaned again. "Oh yeah, he's as tight as you'd expect a virgin to be, *cher.*" Daegan was hard as iron himself, and she could sense how aroused he was. Being a vampire, she wasn't sure he would have stopped now even if she had told him that Gideon had been pushed too far. But Gideon's mind, though a tumultuous storm, was suffused with lust and dark, driving needs, his focus on what Daegan was doing.

A second finger worked in and Gideon gasped.

"Relax, vampire hunter," Daegan said in a rough, male croon. "You tighten up, it will burn like a son of a bitch. I intend to fuck you no matter what. You cannot stop me. Nothing you say or do will keep me from taking this ass, making it mine. And when I'm done, I'll be the one sliding my hand back in there with salve, easing the burn, making it better. You'll rely on me for all of it. I'll take care of you in a way no man has before."

Take away all choices, and certain slaves let go. Gideon's muscles trembled, rage crossing his face, but his body was jerking, humping air, responding to Daegan's erotic threat. Those words electrified his mind like lightning flashes, and Anwyn saw a jumble of memories. A father swimming in the waves, a young boy's fear of not being grown-up enough to take care of his brother, of never having any male he could trust enough to let go, to know he could let go and the whole world wouldn't fall apart.

Anwyn swallowed over the ache, let those images fill Daegan's mind, let him see what he was doing to the other male. Daegan's gaze flickered to her, a nod, his jaw flexing. Leaning over Gideon, he pressed his lips to his neck, spoke against him there.

"Trust me, Gideon. You want this, and so do I. It will be all right." He'd seated his cock at that lubricated opening. "It's going to stretch, a lot. You're going to feel like I'm splitting you, but let it slide all the way in. Let it in."

Anwyn knew she didn't need to breathe, but she was holding her breath again anyway as Daegan slowly, slowly eased into that passage, nuzzling Gideon's neck. Reaching beneath him, he pumped his slick hand up and down Gideon's organ, bringing back the surge of blood that trepidation had stolen away. "Let me in, and then you'll be able to fill Anwyn with your cock. Your Mistress is feeling generous, because you've given us this. Ah, God, you feel fucking good. Let me in deep. Take all of me, vampire hunter."

It took some time, some coaxing from both of them and concentration on Gideon's part, but then Daegan was in to the hilt. Gideon was gasping, his eyes watering, not with tears, but with the effort of holding him. Anwyn knew how it felt the first time. Even she, who'd been familiar with anal play, had been stretched hard the first time by Daegan's size. No amount of practice with poor substitutes could change that for Gideon, either. It was excruciating, but also a feeling of such connection and pleasure. She didn't see that in Gideon's reaction exactly, but there was some type of relief, a shadow of it, playing among his other roiling emotions.

"There you go." Daegan licked his neck, teased the skin, careful not to score him with his fangs. "Uncomfortable?"

"What, from that little thing?" Gideon coughed into the floor, his fists clenching in the restraints. "Didn't even notice it."

Daegan smiled against his flesh, withdrew slightly and pushed back in, earning a guttural cry from Gideon. "Then I'll make sure you remember it for days, servant." He glanced at Anwyn, and spoke aloud, though she knew he didn't need to do so. "You may come to him now, *cher.*"

She took her time, rising to her feet, knowing that Gideon was drinking in the way her thighs slid against each other as she dropped her clothing, piece by piece. Running her hands slowly down her bare body, she molded her breasts before she dropped to a squat right at his head, her splayed knees and open pussy just above him as he shifted his face to see her. She felt the heat of Daegan's regard as well, saw it translate into harder thrusts, a tighter hold on Gideon's cock with his long, male fingers.

"Don't you come, vampire hunter. Not until she and I have taken our pleasure."

"You better hope she comes last, then, because I'm not waiting on a damn thing for you." Gideon groaned as Daegan punctuated that defiant statement with a less gentle thrust. The vampire hunter couldn't help biting out a "Jesus Christ" that had Daegan baring his fangs. His bloodlust was close; Anwyn could see it in his eyes, but at her flicker of concern, he shook his head. He was fine; he could control it. She'd been afraid of her own, but right now, all was well, even the shadow voices muted in the face of this blast of heated desire surrounding her like a warm, welcome blanket.

She unhooked Gideon's manacles, making it clear she knew he wouldn't try to get away now, and they shifted him away from the weights.

"Lift him up, Daegan," she crooned, and the vampire shifted his hold from Gideon's abdomen to his chest, using that one arm to lift his upper body off the ground. Her fingers played along Gideon's forearms as they drew taut and she slid beneath his body, letting his arms settle back down on either side of her head. Aligning her hips, she was at the right angle as Daegan eased him back down so she was cradling Gideon's hips inside her legs. He tried to keep his head up, but she pressed it down to her shoulder, feeling his hot breath puff across her breast, making the bare nipple tighten further.

"Give yourself to us, Gideon," she whispered. "Feel me as I take you inside." With a sinuous writhe of her hips, she lifted up, seating his cock at her entrance. Daegan came down in a slow, slow thrust that let her take Gideon inside a bit at a time, milking him with her slick muscles.

"Fuck." Gideon pressed his face into her neck, biting, and bloodlust swirled up. But instead of freezing about it, she treated it the same way as she treated desire, the way she'd always channeled it to the point of eruption. To withhold it was to grow its power, the pleasure of the eventual release. Gideon was her servant, and his blood would be all the sweeter when his seed was spurting inside her, when Daegan was coming in his ass, the three of them moving together, Daegan's strength carrying all their movement.

As Gideon slid into her, the weight of his body blissfully upon her, a position of strength she'd never appreciated so much as at this moment, she wrapped one arm around Gideon's shoulders, her other hand reaching up to dig into Daegan's. His lips brushed over her fingers, fangs scraping her, and she made an erotic noise in the back of her throat. Her men. Her two men, linked together, linked with her. She let the thought fill her mind, gave it to them both, even though she knew they would meet it with different emotions. This was how she felt in this moment, so this was truth for her.

"Let Daegan's movements move you inside of me, Gideon," she murmured as he tried to thrust. "He will control all of it, and we'll ride his wave."

"Easy for you to say. You're not his surfboard." But his fingers flexed spasmodically against the floor. "God . . . it feels . . ." It felt good and terrible at once. Those destroyed shields might never be mended, but something else unthinkable might take their place. Daegan's cock, mouth and body somehow touched those raw wounds, licked them clean, offering comfort and undeniable desire while taking.

"I know. Your cock feels so good inside of me, and I can feel Daegan moving inside of you. You're both so irresistible, I could do this forever."

Looking up into Daegan's eyes, his bared fangs so close to Gideon's neck, she could feel how difficult it was to hold back, to not take the blood that was under his mouth. She had her hand on Gideon's shoulder and turned it now, offering her beating wrist pulse to Daegan.

When his fangs sank in, she arched with a cry, driving Gideon into her even more deeply. She lifted her hips, slamming harder against him, and Gideon's body became magnificently rigid all over, resisting the pull of the inevitable climax. However, when he'd taken one long, sweet draught, Daegan lifted his head and brought them to a halt.

He closed his hand around Gideon's throat, his thumb passing with loving attention over the thundering pulse, his other hand bracing them beside Anwyn's shoulder. "Move inside her, vampire hunter. Slide in, almost pull out, and then back in again. Go slow, and each time you come back out, your ass needs to take my cock in to the hilt. You go between us like that, while we remain still, as long as you can do it."

She knew Gideon wanted to rebel against Daegan's orders because of how much he wanted to obey. So she drew his attention by lying back again, her breasts tilted up to his hungry gaze. "Thrust into my pussy, Gideon. I want to feel you rub all along inside me."

He wet his lips, bracing his arms awkwardly, but then he withdrew a couple inches, slow, slower, watching her lips part and eyes darken with desire. As he did, he impaled himself on Daegan's cock, deeper, deeper. She could tell from the flex of Gideon's jaw. Then he was coming back to her, his face suffused with reaction to the two sensations. "Beautiful." Daegan murmured, voice unsteady as well. "Keep doing it until she comes."

The drag of Gideon's cock inside her was like fire. Normally she could hold out quite a while, but with the vampire transition, that hungry blood wanted only instant gratification, despite her training. She still managed to hold out long enough that Gideon was sweating anew, his eyes glazed, lips parted with his internal focus to hold back, his cock hard as steel. The ripple of the climax started low in her belly, telling her it was going to be a powerful one.

I want to see him come, Daegan. While I'm coming.

Then we go together.

Looking up, she could tell Daegan was indeed far beyond ready. At a nod, she let herself start over that tremulous edge, the gasping of her breath giving Gideon warning at the same time.

"Let go, Gideon. We both have you."

Because it was Daegan giving the order, he tried to hold out, but when the two of them climaxed simultaneously, there was nothing he could do. Gideon released, hard and hot, a hoarse cry close to a scream breaking from his lips at the dual stimulation. The power of that release, withheld so long, made his fingers dig into the floor, body bucking between Daegan's cock and her pussy, flesh and toned bodies meeting and withdrawing in a frenetic, hot and moist dance.

Curling her fingers in his hair, Anwyn bit down on his shoulder, drawing blood during that intense moment. Hot, sweet blood swirled into her mouth. At the same time she slid her arm, the one that Daegan had punctured, down Gideon's shoulder. Seeing the wound the male vampire had left, Gideon tried to lick it with erratic, frenetic care during the final spurts of his climax, soothing any perceived hurt. An involuntary reaction of course, but one that fired the two vampires further so Anwyn knew they easily could share him again and again. And why not? He did belong to her, this difficult, troubled man. Her eyes met Daegan's heavy-lidded, sexy ones.

Maybe to them both, no matter what the marks said.

~

As she lay flat on the floor, still gasping, but her body vibrating with delicious, spiraling energy at once, she looped her arms around them both, holding Gideon's neck and clasping Daegan's braced arm. "I want to lie in bed with you two," she said. "In Daegan's bed."

Though Gideon stiffened, she didn't withdraw the request. Daegan's bed was larger, better suited for the three of them. Plus, it was closer, and close was good. Daegan's expression needed no translation. Withdrawing, pushing off of Gideon's back, he rose and disappeared into the bathroom. She continued to lie on the floor, stroking Gideon. He kept his head on her chest, his arms leaden weights on either side of her.

"Okay?" she whispered, tugging on his hair.

"Not thinking right now."

She pressed a kiss to his brow. It surprised her when he tilted his head and met her mouth, teasing it with his tongue. At length, he pulled himself up so that he braced his weight on his elbows on either side of her head, his knees planted on the floor between her legs. He was still inside her, semisolid, inspiring her to squeeze him with her internal muscles, a slow milking that kept his gaze opaque, feral. Running her hands down his back, she cupped his ass, massaged the oil there, enjoying the slide over slick, heavy muscle.

"You could fuck me to death."

"I easily could. But then, I could have done that before I became a vampire." Managing a wicked smile, she traced his mouth with her fingers, tightened her legs over his thighs. Her bare feet brushed the sensitive area behind his knees. She smelled the musky odor of semen, both that trickling from her, and what Daegan had left behind when he pulled out. "Hurting?"

Gideon shrugged, but she saw it in his head. Though she knew the tissues were amazingly resilient and wouldn't even throb a half hour from now, right now they burned like acid. He had resisted enough to exacerbate the abrasion, so she knew he needed what Daegan was returning with now.

Gideon glanced toward him and blanched. "No way. I'm getting up."

"In a minute." Daegan squatted next to him, laid a restraining palm on his buttock. "Be still."

"What . . . Argh." Gideon tried to twist, but was unsuccessful as Daegan withdrew the large syringe, now empty. He'd positioned a basin beneath him to catch any excess fluid. "What the hell?"

"It's an herbal wash," she explained. "It makes it hurt less, almost immediately."

From the reluctant relief on Gideon's expression, she could tell it did. "Stop sticking things in my ass," he snapped halfheartedly. Daegan bent down, scored his ass cheek with a fang, earning an attempted kick. "Son of a—"

"You would do better to stop giving orders, servant. All it does is annoy me. And you've just seen what I do when annoyed."

"I'm her servant, not yours." Gideon gave him a withering glare. "It's way past time for you to grow up and get your own."

"Nope." Daegan rocked up to his heels and gave him an arch look. "They're too much work. A tremendous pain in the ass." He punctuated that with a slap on Gideon's that echoed in the chamber, caused another snarl. It left a delectable handprint on the cheek, one that lingered, despite the third-mark capacity for healing.

～

She knew Gideon was already worried he'd be in the center of the bed, but Anwyn was ready to give him a break and take that pleasurable position. She brought Gideon in behind her on the left side after he returned from her shower. Once Daegan had done his own cleaning, he slid in on the right. She'd seen in Gideon's mind the possibility of finding some underwear or any other type of clothing, but she made it clear she wanted them all to stay naked, so she could press every available inch of her soft skin up against their handsome, rougher flesh. Once he settled in, Gideon toyed with her hair, then brought his hand to rest on her thigh, brushing his knuckles along her hip. She didn't object.

If he belonged to both of us, she mused, *we could chain him here between us during the daylight hours. We might fondle and drink from him at will, leaving him hard and suffering until nightfall. By then he would be mad with lust, willing to do anything to please us.*

A tempting vision, cher, but he is your servant. His unwilling desire for me has no connection with a desire to become mine. As he himself said, his physical reaction to me does not mean anything. He is more servant than submissive, even to you.

She knew Daegan had felt a little differently in the heat of the moment, his own subconscious desires rising as strong and undeniable as his cock, but she didn't press it. It was hard to believe everything that had happened, the way the bonds between them had tightened in a mere handful of days.

Daegan had cocooned their thoughts, kept them from the male behind them, but it didn't really matter. A light touch told her that Gideon's mind was still in shock, reeling from his virgin encounter, being fucked for the first time by a man. She could sense a war developing, a conflict between shame and rage, something that would become ugly if she didn't defuse it. Too many things had been taken from Gideon; anything that suggested that same loss of control, the consequences it could bring, would dredge up ugly memories and feelings.

"More questions," she decided, ignoring their amusingly similar groans. "Fun ones, not instructive Council stuff." Shifting onto her back, she compelled the other two to do the same. Both men bent their knees, feet flat on the mattress, so she could put one foot on top of each of theirs, playing with their toes. "It's your turn, Daegan. Who was your first sex?"

"Or what," Gideon muttered.

The vampire snorted, turned his head to gaze at them both. "I'm sure I don't remember."

"You're lying. You can't lie for Twenty Questions. It's a rule. You'll burst into flame if you break it, swear to God."

"Oh, well, as long as your honesty isn't in question." Smiling at her solemn assertion, Daegan turned on his side, his gaze passing briefly over Gideon. He was staring at the ceiling hard enough to bore holes. "Like most born male vampires, it was my wet nurse, so to speak. Neela. She was second-marked, and with me into my teens. When the first tide of lust hit with the blood, I was suckling Neela's neck. Pretty straight-forward."

"All right, then, I amend the question. Who was the first sex you chose for yourself?"

"I'm not sure this game allows do-overs, if the question is worded incorrectly." Nevertheless, he turned his eyes upward, considered. "A noble's daughter named Jenna. She'd been thrown from a horse on a hunt. I helped tend her ankle, carried her to a hunting lodge. Unfortunately, it was close to feeding time, and she smelled so good . . ." He snuffled at Anwyn's throat like an animal, and she shoved at him, laughing. "I couldn't resist. Jenna had performed this stunt several times to get boys to take her off to this very same lodge, after all. With such unabashed sexuality, she should have been turned to a vampire."

"Did you?" This from Gideon, in a wooden voice.

"No." Daegan glanced his way. "Of course not. She eventually married very well to an older nobleman who traveled a great deal, and had a passel of children she adored. Probably with a variety of fathers. I think you would have liked her," he said to Anwyn. "Despite being a very repressive period for women, she lived life to the fullest. I regretted that as she aged I couldn't maintain our acquaintance. She didn't know I was a vampire."

"Well, that was horribly dull," Anwyn teased. "Though vaguely charming." She turned over then, facing Gideon, and slid into his arms, tracing his jawline. *I'm hungry again.*

He nodded, pulled her closer. As his hand cupped the back of her head, he tilted his throat up, his eyes closing. It was such a simple, generous offering, particularly when she could feel how his emotions were bludgeoning him, his heart hurting. It made her own heart contract. So she whispered her lips over his throat, kissing him gently now, stroking her hand down his broad shoulder, nuzzling the fine chest hair across his pectorals, tracing that crimson trinity mark.

*You take such good care of me, Gideon. You know that, right? You're
going to be all right. I'm here. We're here.*

The words weren't planned, but she answered the aching in his soul
with nurturing, at odds with her normal demands. But his personal
anguish, hidden so deep inside him it didn't even show in his face, was
old and ongoing, a dark, murky river that no one but her might have
ever beheld.

His arm tightened around her, his eyes not opening as she put her
fangs over the spot that still showed a faint impression from her last
feeding.

Will it become a permanent mark? She liked the idea. The third mark
had possessed a thrill of its own, but one she'd purposely inflicted would
have its own pleasures, a possessive need she well understood. For all
the submissives she'd mastered, she'd never had a slave fully give himself to her, all of it. It had always been contained within the club walls.
Though Gideon was far from reaching that point, something about the
way he offered himself to her now revived that wistful, adult-child
dream.

*In time, a permanent scar will remain at the places you bite, because
they are wounds marked so often with your own saliva. Wounds marked
with your own blood will also remain scars on him.*

As he answered her question, Daegan felt tenderness for them both.
He saw the thoughts in her mind, deduced Gideon's state of mind from
them. When Daegan spread her hair over her shoulders, caressing pale
skin, strands fell into Gideon's open palm. He held her close with the
one arm, but his wrist was loose as she drank deep, limp fingers brushing the small of her back.

Stroking Anwyn's sable locks, Daegan let the motion cross Gideon's
knuckles, a relaxed, inclusive caress. As he reversed direction to do it
again, Gideon's fingers unexpectedly curled around his wrist.

The blue eyes opened, looking over Anwyn's head at him. Daegan
held the gaze, allowing the restraint, wondering if Gideon had intended
it as a warning. His strong hand held Daegan's wrist as if he needed the
connection between them. Though there was confusion in Gideon's
expression, it was a book Daegan could read well enough.

If he'd fucked Gideon merely out of detached logic, his stated rationalization to acclimate Gideon to what he might face at the Council, then this moment might not be so significant. Even with the hot, raw desire they'd experienced, Gideon might have been merely pissed or rationalized it himself as he had in the past, just too many damn pheromones in the air.

But Daegan had led with his anger, made it clear he'd not taken kindly to what Anwyn had clearly seen for some time. He didn't know how he'd missed it, but then, he wasn't in the male's head.

Even so, he hadn't entirely expected the way Gideon responded, then or now. There was something deeper in his tormented gaze, something that affected Daegan unexpectedly. As he recognized it, he was the one who decided to pull away, but Gideon beat him to it. The man released him, closed his eyes. As Anwyn continued to drink, Gideon pulled her even closer, seeking a reassurance Daegan knew might elude him. The truth could be a bitch to outrun, and the truth was Gideon already wanted them both again.

Though the vampire hunter would get no comfort from knowing it, Daegan knew the feeling was entirely mutual.

10

ANWYN had told Gideon that Daegan was an incredibly light sleeper, to the point that if she so much as shifted a hand across a pillow when they lay together, he would wake. So she wasn't surprised to feel his attention as she slid out of the bed.

Before she'd become a vampire, every once in a while on one of her days off, if Daegan was traveling, she'd sleep in the top apartment, the one that had a full wall of windows overlooking the streets below. They were east-facing, so she could watch the sunrise. Since she worked late nights, it had been rare for her to leave the shades open so that newborn sunlight could kiss her awake, but she'd had the choice. She'd never realized the human compulsion to move to a window when in deep thought, as if looking out into a world bigger than oneself would help to balance the troubled waters of her thoughts, but she'd circled the room twice restlessly before she realized that was what she was seeking.

Daegan slid out of the bed, brought her his robe, a heavy terry cloth that came down to her calves, and slid on the drawstring *gi* pants he'd been wearing earlier. As he freed her hair from the collar, she looked up at his face, the planes she could see so clearly, even though the room was almost pitch-dark. A trio of candles burned on the dresser. She'd slept some herself, so she didn't know which of them had done that, but she suspected Gideon, who knew that she liked candlelight. He did the small things, because he thought he had nothing more significant to offer to her. Never realizing how large a part of her life he'd become in such a short time. A frighteningly large part.

"Come with me," Daegan murmured. He guided her out into the main room. Gideon had moved, of course, was sleeping on the couch. He'd tugged on a pair of worn boxers, frayed at the hem, and a hole or two along the thigh. She made a mental note to get him some new underwear, though she didn't mind him going without. Pausing at the couch, she touched his brow.

He knew her touch in his sleep, didn't react defensively. His eyes opened sleepily and she bent down, brushed his lips. "We're going up top a few minutes," she whispered. "Don't worry. Sleep."

He gazed at her, nodded, eyes drifting closed again, though his large hand curled around her wrist, held an extra moment. When Daegan loosened his grip so she could slide away, the vampire tousled the man's hair with brief affection. Gideon rolled over, grunting, and slapped the hand away, burrowing face-first into the sofa again.

Anwyn gave Daegan a smile and let herself be led to the elevator. "How did you know where we were going?" she whispered.

"Sometimes I dip a toe into your mind, so to speak." He gave her a sidelong glance as he pressed the top floor button. "Forgive me, *cher*."

"I think you already knew without doing that. You're just trying to make me believe you don't know me as well as you do."

"Hmm."

She leaned into him, enjoying the comfort of his solid body and his strong arm until the elevator reached the top level. Like her basement dwelling, it was coded for entry. The cleaning staff was taken up and supervised by James once a week, but of course she hadn't been up here since the night in the alley. The curtains were open, showing the panorama of the city, the jeweled lights a more dense reflection of the stars in the night sky. It was Sunday night, so Atlantis was quiet, no movement or vibrating music from the dance floor below.

She went to the sliding glass door in the living area and stepped out into her rooftop garden. It was mostly an artful assortment of potted plants and trees, garden statuary and benches, unique pieces she'd added now and then. There were three or four beds of perennials and some rosebushes. None was in bloom right now, but in summer they were rich colors of yellow and red. She sank down on a bench, gazed up at the stars. "I guess we should have invited Gideon to come up here with us. This is too beautiful a view to hoard all to ourselves." Just as she'd thought, the ability to breathe in fresh air, feel the enormity of the sky and earth revolving above and below her, helped free some of the tightness of her chest.

"But he's the one that's troubling you. You needed to come up here to think about him, talk about him. About him going to the Council."

"A know-it-all can be a very annoying thing." But she tempered the words with a sad smile as he straddled the bench behind her, letting her lean into the cradle of his body. She hooked her legs over one of his thighs, the other braced against her buttocks. "You remember that night before you left? You said no male had ever convinced me that I could rely on him to be there, no matter the circumstance. Except maybe James."

"I remember."

"James is widowed. Still as in love with his wife as the day they met. They were pure vanilla, the homemade, best kind. He visits her grave every week. Other than that, it's cable sports, workouts in the park with his dog, and his job here. He's one of those tough, no-nonsense males, made up of simple pleasures."

"A fortunate man, in some ways."

She nodded, pushing against his chest and accepting a boost over his leg to rise. Once there, she paced to the edge of the roof, leaned against the railing. "If things had been different for Gideon, I think he might have had that kind of life." She sighed, looked down at her hands. "The way you always described vampires and how they treated their servants, it was as if you were reading from an erotic novel, to arouse me and please us both. I never thought of the reality of it. I liked the way there was no choice given, that the servant followed the will of the Master or Mistress when he or she wanted the slave publicly displayed, shared, participating in sexual games. They were stories."

As he came to stand by her, she continued to stare out at the city. "That's going to be my reality, and the reality of being my servant. He can't do that. We both know it. I wouldn't ask him, let alone order him, to do it. He came to help me"—her throat thickened—"and I've pulled him under, into a world he despises. I've got to let him go. Before I completely lose who I was, the person who knows that truly forcing someone against their will is wrong."

"Letting him go is more complex than that, *cher*. Plus, it's not the real reason you're contemplating releasing him. It hurts you, the way he continues to distrust us, the way he feels about vampires. You are despairing that he'll ever change, that he'll always hate what you've become."

"God, couldn't you let me lie to myself once?"

"No more than you could allow Gideon to do so. It's not in those of our nature."

"We have to pick the flesh off the bones, take everything." Pivoting, she strode across the garden, her fists clenched. "I told you at the beginning I wanted to give Gideon as much privacy in his head as possible, and you seemed dubious about it, like a parent indulging a child who doesn't really understand the way the world is. But I wasn't ready to be that much of a vampire yet, at least when lust wasn't part of the equation."

She shook her head. She knew all about denial and reward, boundaries and consent. She'd wanted to stick with the human etiquette on those things, at the very least until she could get her own moral code integrated with her new self. But it seemed that, every day, the one was eroding before the force of the other.

"Daegan, when he resists, those voices, the blood, override everything else. They want me to push him to breaking, not the way a Mistress wants to push a submissive into his subspace, not a breakthrough. They want blood, failure, destruction. Is that what we did tonight, and we were just lucky it worked out okay? Is he right to hate and fear that part of me?"

"You didn't let them override you. You didn't push him so hard that you tore him to pieces. You, Anwyn, stayed in control. Guided me, so *we* didn't push him too hard. He's in new territory, he's bleeding from those old wounds, but it may help some of those wounds heal. Don't underestimate this man. There's far more there than you realize." He came to her, gripped her shoulders. "You've never been the type of woman to hide from the truth in yourself. Your predator's blood doesn't rule you. You do."

"Why are you so determined to let him kill himself?" she said, frustrated. "You'd forbid me to do anything that would endanger my life.

Hell, you'd use chains or whatever force necessary to keep me away from it, even if I cursed you down to your balls. Sexist bastard."

"It's more than that. Anwyn, the things we did for you were because you couldn't control your seizures and reactions. You were a danger to yourself and others, and you understood that. Gideon is a warrior at a crisis of faith. You force him away from what he feels he must do, you will castrate him, and there's nothing worse to a warrior than that."

"Sounds like macho drivel that will only get him killed." She swallowed. "He matters, Daegan. Don't let him do this. You tried to convince him tonight, and I appreciate that, but he passed the test. Now he'll be even more determined. Please, I'm begging you. You know I never beg you for anything. Help me keep him here, or at least on the plane. Keep him away from the Council."

Though regret suffused his features, Daegan shook his head. "Anwyn, I—"

"Fine, I'll do it myself. I'm stronger than he is, right? I'll wrestle him to the ground, strip him naked so he can't hide any weapons, chain him to a pole in the cargo area and tell the pilot to take him wherever he wants to go, as long as it's back to the mainland U.S. He's my servant; it's my decision."

"Anwyn—"

"This isn't about me. It's about him. You wanted to fuck him, because that's what we do, isn't it? We find their weaknesses, and they fascinate us. We have to exploit them, use them, because this blood is all about power and dominance. I've been a vampire for barely a blink, and I already feel that way. You didn't even really care about fucking him; you just wanted to do it because he didn't want you to do it, and you wanted to prove you could make him enjoy it. Just like I got off on watching, like some sick sexual predator . . ."

"It was not like that." Daegan's gaze narrowed. "And you know it."

"Don't tell me what it was like. I know it; I saw it. You're as evil as the rest of them. We have to embrace that evil. Why do we fight what we already know is part of us, in our blood?"

The shift was too quick, anger becoming something far different, and she clutched at his hands, swaying, fighting herself. *No, damn it. I don't want to do this now.*

He pulled her in close to him. "Don't let them take over, Anwyn. Breathe. Let me in your mind."

She wouldn't have been able to keep him out, but later she'd appreciate his courtesy. For now, he invaded like a calming force of wind. The shadow creatures, building in volume like a lynch mob, were thrown into chaos by the disruption. Her blood heated, and she felt her fangs elongating, but she was able to dig in her heels, refuse to let them have this moment. It was stress, and she could control it. Daegan was here. In fact, he'd folded her into his arms and taken them down to the ground in the way he did, where his body caged her with solid, heated flesh and comforted her at once.

It was a near thing. Sometimes it was inevitable, nothing she could stop, but tonight she gazed up at the stars, pressed her face into Daegan's bare chest, and held on to the tail end of her sanity while those voices muttered and her blood heated to boiling, making her shake and perspiration soak through the terry cloth. But the tide was turning back, a near miss. She swallowed, digging into his forearm.

She took a deep breath, tried to calm herself. "Gideon . . . tells me things, to keep me distracted. So, tell me . . . about Gideon. You followed him for almost a year. Tell me . . . things about him I don't know. Things that will help me know which way to go."

She'd never felt so incapable of making decisions, and yet such an urgency to make some before she destroyed his life, her future, and everything she'd built.

"He's given me a gift. I don't want . . . to abuse him."

"But it's okay to abuse me?" His tone was light, though his gaze remained fastened on her face, his hands both soothing and a restraint, if needed.

She let out a muffled snort, her body twitching but mind calming. "You need abuse . . . on occasion. Humility is a rare experience for you. So tell me more about him. What does the Council know . . . that I don't? Everything. Don't . . . pretty it up."

"Very well." His voice quiet, he stroked her back as he held her close. "In the past two years, he's killed a significant number of our kind, for a human hunter. With the exception of two, they fortunately were vampires who had racked up multiple violations of Council rules. His brother, Jacob, thank all the gods, figured out a way to channel Gideon's anger, and has been giving him the names of those who have crossed the line. Never speak that truth aloud, *cher*. I found that out through my own investigations and deductions. If the Council could prove Jacob had been doing that, it would not go well for him. Trust me when I tell you that Jacob Green and Lady Lyssa are the greatest friends to the survival of vampires, though not always to the Vampire Council.

"No vampire hunter has ever had the one-on-one kill rate Gideon Green has. You have seen our speed and strength. He succeeds because he is patient, methodical, and he figures out how to set up the vampire. He is also afraid of nothing. Not in the foolish way that would get him killed, but in the way that has kept him levelheaded in situations where plans went awry and he was caught. You have seen the scars."

She nodded, remembering the burns, the lash marks. "He's been caught twice," Daegan said. "In both cases, the vampire made a mistake, deciding to make him pay for his gall, rather than quickly dispatching him. In both instances, Gideon managed to escape and finish off the vampire who thought he could teach him a lesson."

Anwyn thought of her own burgeoning vampire strengths, the ones that had nearly killed Gideon, and those merely a whisper of the formidable powers that Daegan had demonstrated. "Oh my God," she murmured. "It's unreal. He should be dead."

"Thirteen times over. He is a remarkable man."

"Damn it, Daegan, they won't let that pass. They'll execute him."

"Gideon has a better grasp of a vampire's mind than I expected, but I don't know why that surprises me. A successful hunter does more than have the best weapons. He learns his enemy, inside and out. He believes the Council will be far more . . . gratified . . . seeing him subservient to a vampire."

She turned her gaze to him. "So they want to see him humiliated. Owned. A true slave. Like dragging kings through the streets of Rome behind a chariot, in chains."

"Possibly. It is hard to predict. Council politics can be a maze."

"Everything in me is screaming that this is a bad idea. Daegan, if they hurt him, if they try to take him from me, I won't be able to stop a seizure. I won't be able to stop myself from doing whatever bloody, terrible, violent thing I need to do to protect him."

Lifting her up and taking a seat on the bench, he drew her to sit next to him with his arm stretched out behind her, pressing against her shoulder blades. "What you will need to do to protect him will be what you do best. Be a Mistress. That is your greatest weapon to protect him and protect yourself. The world you're about to enter *is* Atlantis, one hundred times the intensity. There are no safe words, no rigidly enforced rules when it comes to the treatment of human servants except for those things that protect vampires and their society. What you have the power to do or protect is yours. But it is still the same world as Atlantis. You may not have my physical strength, *cher*, but I've seen you tear open shields twenty inches thick over a man's soul, and coax it to crawl to your hand. Like a wounded puppy who finally trusts a human to care for him. You use that sorceress's wisdom you have, and you'll be fine."

She wanted to believe him, didn't want his words to increase her worry, but they did. Daegan made a firm shushing noise in his throat, reminding her she couldn't get agitated, not right now. She had a legion of demon creatures in her head that they were trying to lull to sleep. The image of tiny horned gargoyles in cradles, rocking along the vine-like pathways of her neurons, came straight from his head, but she couldn't be amused. "Daegan . . ."

He put his hand on her face, stilling her. "Think of it this way. There are two scenarios if you force him to stay behind. First, that Fate outwits me, and some harm does come to you, but he wasn't there to try and help. Or Fate is kind, my sword is sharp enough, and no harm befalls you. Can you guess what happens after either one of those outcomes?"

She set her jaw, but couldn't refuse that direct gaze. "If I get hurt or killed, and he isn't allowed to be there, I'll become another Laura in his mind. That will end him. If I don't get hurt, then I obviously didn't need him, and he's as inconsequential as he believes himself to be."

"The soul is just as fragile as the body. Sometimes more."

"You wouldn't execute him if they ordered you to do it, would you?" She shifted to face him, her hands on either side of his neck.

Daegan gave her a steady look. "I would not simply do it at the Council's behest, no. Only if he leaves you and starts taking the lives of vampires like Trey again, those whose only crime in Gideon's mind is their annual kill to survive, or just being a vampire. I would have to intervene, Anwyn, as I would on behalf of any innocent."

She blew out a frustrated breath. "I want to get up, move."

"Easy, *cher*. Just another minute or two." Running his knuckles along her cheek, he fanned out his fingers to curve behind her skull, drew her head down to his shoulder. It coaxed her to slide her arms under his, fold herself close to him.

When a nearly silent sigh lifted his chest, Anwyn realized he was savoring it, assuaging the need to hold her, have her sink into his arms like this. She closed her eyes, inhaled him. *You really did miss me.*

Vain woman. But his mind-voice held only amusement, and when his fingers stroked her nape, teasing sensitive nerve endings, she let out a soft noise of contentment. *More than I know how to say, cher. I do not think I could have borne much more of your anger against me, and yet I am sure I deserve far more.*

He hesitated. "Because I have promised there will be no more lies between us, you need to understand something else. If Gideon accompanies us, once he is known to be your servant, you will not be able to let him go, ever. Not officially. Servants are not allowed to leave their Masters under Council law, because of the secrets they hold, and their connection to their Master or Mistress. Only his death would be acceptable."

"Brian implied something like that, though he didn't put it that baldly." She bit her lip. "So if Gideon survives the Council, when he gets ready to leave us, we'll need a cover for that."

"Yes, we will. Though may that day never come."

"Amen," she said quietly. "But we have to be prepared for it, Daegan. He thinks he can give me half of his heart and keep back the other half from the vampire side of me, but I can't live like that. After all we've been through, even for such a short time, I'm not seeing him relenting on that, even a little bit. If that doesn't change after the Council, I'll have to go ahead and cut him loose. The longer he stays . . . the harder it is for me to face losing him. And with this blood . . ." She pressed her lips together. "The more time passes, the more likely it is I'll refuse to let him go. He'd have to escape me, not leave."

"Let's cross this bridge first," he responded, though Anwyn knew it was an evasion, not a reassurance. She swallowed over the ache in her chest.

"Daegan, you promised you'd help me protect him. No matter Fate, or his being a testosterone-poisoned warrior, or my needs, how on earth does us taking him to the Council honor that promise?"

Daegan pressed his lips to her temple, spoke against it as his fingers curled against her upper arm, stroked. "The grim reality is that the Council knows about Trey. Knowing Gideon has become your servant may change their position on that. As I've told you before, you are the only thing that may save his life." He took a firmer grip on her. "Plus, it's a two-way street, *cher*. He does better when you're close to him, as you do with him. Taking care of you, that has become the most important thing in his life. He knows your being accepted into the vampire world will make things much easier for you. It gives him a purpose, keeps him by your side."

She mulled that over. "You said you could protect me, even if I had a full-blown attack in their chambers. Does that mean you have some kind of veto power over their actions?"

"Yes and no. I exist outside of the structure of the Vampire Council and the vampire world, for reasons I mentioned at our dinner the other night. Just trust me when I say they will not act against you without my consent." The dangerous note to his voice told her that his confidence in that had nothing to do with his diplomacy skills. Even as a shiver went up her spine, she didn't doubt him.

She tilted her head up to gaze at him. "You promised to protect me from Council execution. Promise me the same protection for Gideon. Swear it."

Gazing down at her a long moment, he nodded. "I swear it. Aside from your safety, nothing will be as important to me, Anwyn Inara Naime." He put a finger over her lips when she frowned. "He and I are in agreement on this. You come first to us both. You have to live with that. But if it eases your mind, I will also tell you that he must go because that is what Fate demands, not because it is what I want, Anwyn. I would prefer to keep him safely here as well."

She mulled that over. "Will you be going with me in front of the Council, or do I do that part alone?"

Daegan cupped the side of her face. "I should have said this to you, a long time ago. Whenever you need me, I will be at your side. And I will never, ever leave you. What I do may take me from your side for short periods, but I will always come back. Unless you yourself decide you no longer want me in your life." His gaze took on a gleam she knew well enough to feel it uncurl warm fingers in her belly, tug equally at her heart and lower. "But you will have to be very, very convincing in that argument, I warn you."

As he pressed his mouth to hers, desire unfurled, telling her they would soon be stretched out on the soft patch of planted grass a few feet away. While anticipation for that built, she held on to the reassurances he'd given her, and hoped that Fate would be kind. Though it might be challenging lightning to strike her down, she felt like the gods owed her a bit of a break. She'd willingly give that break to Gideon, if it could keep his ass safe to come back here. No matter what happened after that, even if she had to let him go, there would be some comfort in knowing that he walked somewhere in the world.

Carrying a major part of her heart.

11

"Yᴇs, I get it," Gideon responded impatiently, for what felt like the hundredth time. "If any vampire looks at me, I'm supposed to tuck my head down, wring my hands and say, 'Yes, Massa Boss.' Have I missed anything?"

Daegan threw him a speculative look over the *Wall Street Journal.* "You could just walk around on your knees the whole time, wearing a hair shirt on your back and nettles up your ass. That might be degrading enough."

"Would you two shut up? This is marvelous." Anwyn stretched out on the lounge seat, and sighed happily. "I think we should live on this plane."

"Yeah, it's easy to fight vampires when you have all the nifty toys, like a Gulfstream. You need real skill to take them down with your wits alone."

"Which is why I find myself amazed you're still alive. But then I remember there has always been special guardian angels for half-wits."

Anwyn rolled her eyes, hopped off the seat. Daegan emitted a mock growl as she crash-landed in his lap, crumpling his paper beneath her pretty ass, snugly encased in a dark skirt. "If you two boys don't behave, I'm going to spank you both and tell the stewardess not to give you any cookies."

"After that maneuver, I think you're the one who needs the spanking." In a quick twist, Daegan had her flipped, despite her shriek of outrage, and swatted her.

Seeing that generous bottom wobble under his smack made Gideon harden, even as their casual playfulness ruefully amused him. And hurt. He couldn't bring himself to be part of it.

There was too much going on with him, inside and out. Anwyn's internal demons had been planted in her. His were of his own making. Since the wine and cheese night's revelation about Laura, and the weapons room thing he really didn't know how to classify, he'd been carrying a darkness on his mind. He couldn't shake it. Anwyn wanted to talk him through it, but there was nothing to talk about. When she eased off, he expected it was because Daegan had convinced her it would be best to let him work it out. The vamp's accurate intuition rankled Gideon as well. Everything was making him cranky, but then, he'd warned them he was an unlivable bastard, right?

Gideon remembered the determined look in Anwyn's eyes, the grip of her hands during that intense moment on the mats. She'd ordered him as a Mistress to believe he was hers, not just in that moment, but forever, and he didn't know whether to be dismayed or consider it fucking hilarious, the way his heart had leaped at the idea, wanting to believe it like he was a gullible kid.

He wanted to tell himself she was lying, or that she didn't know what she was saying. After all, he'd been around long enough to know things usually lasted only as long as they were beneficial to everyone involved. How much he might be needing her . . . and possibly other things . . . was irrelevant to her future needs. And of course that wasn't the fucking point. They all knew he had his line in the sand. Though it seemed forces beyond his control kept dragging him over it, that was because he knew she really needed him right now, and he'd do things he wouldn't normally do to handle that. But in the long run, he couldn't be what she needed. They all knew it, and he was getting damn sick and tired of having to repeat it. To himself most of all.

The only sure thing was this meeting. Getting her through this, making sure she was okay. Whatever happened after that, happened. It was time to stop brooding over it. Jesus, there was a gorgeous woman flitting around the cabin in a playful, flirtatious mood and he was crazy about her. Why was he wasting time on the inevitable, instead of max-imizing every moment?

She'd struggled out of Daegan's grasp and was now stalking Gideon, where he sat slouched in his seat, eyes half-closed. She had to know he was alert and watching her, but she made the dash anyway at human speed. As she tried to leap upon him as she had Daegan, he rolled out of her way, making a few seconds' headway before she tackled him and they rolled to the plane floor, she laughing, and he with an armful of female. In a way too adorable to resist, she settled down on his chest with a contented feline sigh, as if ready for a nap.

"You seem in a good mood," he ventured.

"I've made an executive decision. I refuse to overinflate the situa-tion. If they're the all-powerful Council, how long will I really have to be around them? I wouldn't think this validation would take more than fifteen or twenty minutes, unless it's like some Catholic ritual that can take hours. And then anyone would go insane during it."

"Spoken like a true lapsed Catholic," Daegan said dryly.

Gideon thought it was amazing, how many people she could be. She had a playful side, a temptress face, and sometimes she acted like an outright girlfriend. Or friend. Then, in a heartbeat, she could become the cool, tantalizing Mistress or the scary, out-of-control vampire, call-ing up a wariness in him as well as a need to protect, watch out for her.

Much as he hated to admit it, Daegan had been right to let her know about Gideon's decision to join them for this, sooner rather than later. Despite Brian's injections, she'd had three seizures in the couple of days before they packed up to go to the Council. Getting it out of her system had probably helped. She'd tried in various ways to talk Gideon out of going, but maybe Daegan had asked her to ease up on that as well, be-cause she hadn't mentioned it in the last twenty-four hours. Good. Her failure to dissuade him just upset her more, and Gideon wasn't budging on it, especially knowing that she needed his physical presence to keep that blood and those voices under control.

"Sir, we're about three hours to landing." The pilot's voice came through the intercom. As Daegan acknowledged the information, Anwyn sighed, stretched and rose to her knees over Gideon. She gave him a seductive, I'll-fuck-your-brains-out-later smile he was sure was intended to fog his wits. Of course, it was possible it was a façade. She was getting better at smoke-screening her emotions, if not blocking him entirely. He wondered if she was burying her worries farther beneath the surface than he could reach to help reassure *him*.

The thought of her wasting time to protect his sensibilities made him scowl, but he admitted he was wound up about as tight as he could get right now. On top of his emotional shit storm and despite his determination to be here, he had a strong aversion to walking into the stronghold of some of the most powerful vampires in existence. He'd brought all of his weapons, including his flamethrower and a crate of incendiary grenades, but Daegan had made it clear he'd have to leave pretty much everything but a couple favorite knives on the plane. When he argued he would be helpless to defend Anwyn, Daegan of course reminded him sharply that was *his* job. Gideon was merely the meal on legs. Her anchor. Ballast.

Self-pity didn't sit well right now, so he took his seat again and frowned out the window, hating the gut-gripping anticipation. He wanted to go kill something. When things hurt or ached too badly, that always helped, at least temporarily.

"You look like a dour toad over there. Tell me one thing you *do* like about the Council." Anwyn settled back on her lounge, cocking a brow in his direction. "The power of positive thinking, you know."

"I'm positive they can't be trusted," he retorted mildly. Indulging himself and pleasing her, he tracked the way she folded her attractive legs on the cushions. It was simply impossible for a male mind not to imagine them bare and wrapped around his hips. She gave him a speculative look, moistening her lips.

"He's never actually met the Council. Not formally." Daegan's attention was back on his paper. "When he and his army of hunters tried to blow them up at the last Gathering, they didn't stop for introductions. Rather rude. It's a double-edged sword that I wasn't tracking you then," he added. "I could have alerted the Council of the plot against them before that group of vampires created such destruction. And maybe saved some of your far-too-gullible hunters."

Gideon shifted into a more combative stance in the chair and leveled a dagger look at the vampire. "Come to think about it, there is one thing I like about the Council. They don't whine or launch sentimental revenge raids when a human takes them out. They live by survival of the fittest. If a human can take you out, you didn't deserve to make it. I do appreciate that kind of misguided sense of superiority."

"I don't doubt that," Daegan observed. "Considering if they *did* have a sentimental desire for revenge, you'd have been hunted down and killed a dozen times over, in a variety of painful and creative ways."

"See? I *do* appreciate that. In a very positive way." Gideon gave him a gimlet eye. "I'd expect you to be happy about that as well, since you seem into the whole justice-versus-vengeance thing. How do you define the difference, Obi-Wan?"

Unexpectedly, Daegan didn't volley with a wiseass comment. Instead he set the paper aside and leaned forward, giving him a direct look, an even tone. "There is justice, and there is nature, Gideon. A being who kills another for sustenance, that is nature. A being who kills more than they need to kill, because of the pleasure of it, that is wrong. That is when justice or karma comes in. Justice is premeditated. Karma is Nature's way of handling it, because Nature always retaliates against excess, though not always in the time or fashion we wish." He considered Gideon with his shrewd look. "Sometimes a man may become the hand of justice through his vengeance, because of a wrongdoing against him or those he loves. That's a precarious decision for the soul, though. If vengeance is ruling the heart, it's best to let karma take care of the wrongdoer, even if you take the necessary steps to ensure the evil doesn't happen again."

"So when the Council sends you to lop off heads, I guess you go meditate on a mountain about it, or some shit like that."

"Something like that. I've told you before, I'm not their yard dog." Daegan lifted a brow, his dark eyes cooling, a warning. "It's more appropriate to think of me as a consultant."

Gideon snorted. "Really? I was thinking more of a Disney hero. Birds will be chirping on your shoulder in a few minutes. Or doing something else."

Daegan made a noncommittal noise, turned his attention to Anwyn. "You should feed before we land, *cher*. Would you like Gideon to mix his blood with your choice of wine? I know you like your white zinfandel."

"A vampire who doesn't go for red wine." Gideon cleared his throat, pushing off the unwelcome mood that Daegan had just set, instead going for the inexplicable anticipation and simple arousal that always came to him when she had to feed. There was an intimacy to it that Gideon liked, though he didn't care to admit it. "Didn't you tell her that was poor etiquette?"

Anwyn rose and moved back to Gideon, sliding easily into his lap. She slipped her hand into the open collar of his dress shirt, opening a button deftly to stroke the light mat of hair and muscles beneath. "I prefer to have my wine as dessert."

Gideon was caught by her blue-green eyes, penetrating and seeing so much. "We're going to be okay." She put a slim hand to his jaw. "Stop baiting him. Relax, and don't worry so much."

"Stop worrying about me," he responded, deciding not to comment on her other observation.

"Only if you'll stop worrying about me," she said.

Gideon glanced up at Daegan, who met his gaze briefly before turning his attention to pouring his own drink from the bar. "This is dangerous, Anwyn," Gideon said quietly. "I'm not scared of much, but I'm scared to death something is going to happen to you."

"I've nothing to fear. I'm with the two most dangerous males I know. Well, after James, that is. I'm pretty sure he could kick both your asses." At his snort, she leaned in, pressed her lips to his neck, letting him feel the teasing prick of her fangs. "You know, you never flinch," she breathed against his flesh. "Only that first time. You accept this, what I need from you."

He slid his arm around her back, providing her support as the scrape angled down into his cock. "Yeah."

"I'll make you a deal. If you decide to bolt, so will I. We can become fugitives together."

He closed his eyes, pressed his forehead against her shoulder. "Don't tempt me, Mistress." And he meant it fervently. "You need to be accepted into this world. I'm going to stand behind you, make sure that happens. Three paces back, eyes down, my lips kissing your ass, yada yada yada."

"Well, the last part sounds pleasant." But she suppressed a sigh. Gideon pushed her hair off her shoulder, gathering it in the small of her back to keep it out of her way as her fangs sank deep, and she began to feed. Trying to keep his mind off the arousal her bloodtaking always seemed perversely to stir, Gideon turned his gaze to Daegan. "So you've studiously avoided telling us which Council member you think sold you out. You might want to make us aware of that."

"It is my issue to address. But I wasn't deliberately withholding information. I'm fairly certain it was Lord Stephen or Lady Barbra. Perhaps both."

"Steve and Barb? Sounds like a couple who should be sipping cocktails in the suburbs."

"They are new Council members. Made vampires." At Gideon's raised brow, Daegan curled his lip. "Yes, I know. The older Council members thought it would be useful to have an advocacy position for *approved* made vampires."

"Strange, since the Council's about as autocratic as you can get. I thought they slapped a moratorium on making vampires after the revolt at the Gathering."

"They did. But they are trying to smooth things with the existing ones. Too few vampires overall to completely marginalize made vampires. Bedfellows, politics and all that."

Gideon considered that, tracing Anwyn's spine with his knuckles, but grimaced as she rubbed her soft ass against his thighs and groin, teasing him. When amusement crossed Daegan's gaze, he scowled. "Being the first made vamps to sit on Council, you'd think Steve and Barb would watch their ps and qs to make sure they keep the spot."

"Hmm. You might avoid calling them that when you meet them." Taking up his tumbler of whiskey, Daegan brought him a bottle of beer. Pulling up an ottoman, he sat on it, splaying his knees around one of Gideon's planted feet, and ran his hand down Anwyn's back, stroking her thick hair. As he did so, he brushed Gideon's hand. He'd been doing that more often, casual touches, as if the physical intimacy they shared meant something. Meant that he had the right to touch.

It wasn't outrightly sexual like what the vampire was doing to Anwyn now, running a finger along her neck as she swallowed Gideon's blood, or stealing a brief kiss along that slender column, such that his thigh pressed the outside of Gideon's. Still, it was an unsettling reminder of what was possible between them. Except to decide no way in hell was it ever happening again, Gideon hadn't even made peace with what had happened in the weapons room.

He didn't care how much his skin tingled after Daegan touched it, a different but no less provocative sensation than Anwyn's fingers, tunneling under the open collar of his new button-down shirt to tease his nipple. Dropping down, she stroked her nails over his abdomen, a scrape that had him shifting his hard cock against her hip and earning a murmur of approval.

Pulling back from her feeding, she pressed her lips to his throat, sealing the wound with a faint blood imprint from her mouth. Daegan slid an energy bar and protein drink toward Gideon's right hand to supplement the beer. "I'll get you a steak later."

"Thanks, Dad. I think I can handle finding my own meals."

"You'll need your energy. Don't let stubbornness keep you at less than your fighting best." Daegan's steady gaze told Gideon he meant it. "And remember, you don't address any Council member, let alone Steve and Barb, as anything less than 'my lady' or 'my lord,' and you don't speak to them at all unless he or she addresses you first. If you hold on to nothing else, remember that one. It is the one thing that may save your foolish life, which is important to Anwyn's well-being, if not your own."

Since being pissy would just upset Anwyn, Gideon swallowed his irritation along with the beer and plotted ways to get even with the vamp later for his high-handed tone and far too shrewd look.

Fortunately, Anwyn provided a distraction. When she slid off his lap, she had to straddle both Gideon's and Daegan's thighs to move past them. Daegan caught her hips, keeping her there as he cupped her buttocks. As Gideon watched at close range, the way those long fingers kneaded the rounded fullness of her ass, Daegan put his mouth between her breasts. He teased her there, a flick of his whiskey-flavored tongue in the low neckline of the silk blouse. "You wear these clothes just to taunt us."

"But unlike Gideon, you don't know how to mind your manners and ask for permission first. Hey." Anwyn turned a reproving glance on Gideon as he pulled his hand away. "I'm sure that wasn't a pinch, because if it was, I'd have to put my foot up your backside. I'm trying to build you up here. Make you sound reasonably housebroken."

"All they have to do is look at him to know that's a lie." Daegan rose and moved back to his own chair, bracing one foot on the footrest. It was his typically casual predator pose, but the sexual energy around him, the fact he knew the vampire had to be hard, made it difficult for Gideon not to look where he wanted to look. Holding Daegan's gaze was far more hazardous, though.

"All dangerous eyes," the vampire mused. "Strong jaw. Body never completely relaxed, hard as iron." His gaze flicked downward, lingered deliberately. "In more ways than one."

"Fuck. Off."

≈

Anwyn shifted her gaze between the two of them. Gideon's mind told her little, because when he became like this, everything was still, focused on whatever might happen in the next few seconds.

Daegan remained in his position, just as still and silent. She knew it was pre-battle nerves that had made Gideon lash out with real venom in his tone. Hell, since he'd boarded the plane he'd been as unpredictable in his moods as Anwyn on a bad day. He was clearly testing, and she knew Daegan wasn't likely to put up with it much longer. Gideon was purposely being immature and twisted, goading such a confrontation. From his mind, she knew he had no clue whether he was angling for the ass-kicking or something equally physical.

She'd been playing mediator-on-tenterhooks for most of the plane ride and it was dangerously adding to her anxiety. She'd heard Gideon's thought, knew she'd been doing a good job of keeping any trepidations she had under wraps, but these two were going to be her breaking point.

"You said Lord Stephen and Lady Barbra might have betrayed you," she said quickly. "Why, Daegan?"

He didn't remove his gaze from Gideon, unfortunately, but he did answer. "They were not part of the Territory Wars, and haven't faced the dangers that the others have. They don't understand that vampires who choose to ignore the rules risk harmful exposure of our kind to the human world. Being made vampires, they erroneously believe they should be loyal to all made vampires without discretion. So that they protect even those who commit vicious crimes, rather than advocating for the made vampires who do not. If they can undermine the strict position toward made vampires in a multitude of small ways, such as discrediting what I do, the Council may alter their stand on the matter."

"But if you step out and the Region Masters and overlords handle internal problems related to their vampires directly, it would cause more unease and power shifts within territories, allowing the problem vampires more latitude," Gideon pointed out.

Daegan lifted a shoulder. "Possibly. It would certainly slow down the swift retribution we implement now. Then again, Lord Stephen and Lady Barbra's motives could be more personal and less political. For all I know, before Stephen and Barbra were appointed, I may have been assigned to kill someone they considered a friend or preferred lover. While these two are not excessively clever, vampires are good at keeping their personal baggage under wraps." He shrugged. "Honestly, with vampires, it can always be a variety of motivators. They are not highly predictable in their grudges or politics."

Anwyn slid her hip next to Daegan's braced foot, putting a hand on his hard thigh. "I'd agree with the not very clever part. What did they think telling a crazy vampire where to find you, particularly one like Barnabus, would accomplish? Surely they didn't think he'd kill you."

"It was a limited risk. They didn't expect it to be tracked back to them, and if they killed me, so much the better."

"Yeah, that much may be true, but I don't think that was their primary motive." Gideon spoke up now, his hard eyes resting on Daegan. "What they did was force your hand, made you take Barnabus's life and the lives of his little band unsanctioned. No matter how justified, it means you've given Steve and Barb the opening to discuss whether you have too much autonomy, and cast suspicions on how powerful you are and how dangerous that makes you to them."

"The rest of the Council has known me a long time."

"They're vampires. Do you know how long it takes them to turn on one of their own? Lady Lyssa practically gave them her soul since the day the Council was founded. They turned on her in the space of one Council meeting, one piece of information. All it takes is a seed of doubt to be planted." Gideon scowled at Daegan's shuttered look. "Hell, humans are just as bad. People like to believe the worst about each other. Look at how they always scream government conspiracy, at the same time they talk about how completely incompetent the government is. Conspiracy by its nature suggests cleverness, discretion."

Anwyn nodded. "When it comes down to it, we're idiots. We're the Roman mob. We'd rather be thrown scraps of bread and shown a good gladiator fight than think for ourselves."

Daegan shook his head. "This isn't a mob. This is the Council. Gideon, I know your own shadow world, the vampire hunters, rejected you because they believed you had become too sympathetic to the other side, and were only killing vampires your brother sent you. Both of which were true. It does not mean that you can extrapolate their disloyalty to the Council."

Gideon's eyes narrowed. "Which one is it?"

Daegan lifted a brow. "Pardon me?"

"Which Council member was fucking your mother, and therefore still has you fooled into thinking you should trust these vipers?"

Anwyn knew she could move a lot faster now, but she had no chance of moving faster than Daegan. And Daegan in a temper could take Gideon through the side of the plane.

"Stop it," she snapped. "Both of you."

The syllables reverberated through the cabin, harshly enough she wondered if the pilot had felt the vibration. At least it brought their attention from each other to her. She was impressed herself by how intimidating she sounded.

"Gideon, it doesn't matter how much you insult him, how much anger you take out on him." She tried to calm her tone, cognizant of how they both went on alert whenever she showed the least bit of agitation. Which irritated her even more. "Nothing is going to change the fact we're vampires, and your loyalties are shifting. Nothing is going to change the fact you enjoyed being fucked by both of us. By *him*. Or that, in your heart as well as your cock, you know if you stay around the two of us, it will happen again."

She'd tapped the right buttons. He surged to his feet, his fists clenched as he loomed over her. "Stop fucking around in my head," he snarled.

Daegan tensed, but Anwyn spoke in his mind. *My servant, my problem. Do not interfere.*

His dark eyes flickered to her. *He's out of line with you,* cher. *If you don't set him back on his heels, I will take him down, no matter what kind of pain he is in.*

I can protect myself, and your feelings are as much the problem as his. It pisses you off that you told him about Laura, and he didn't react as you expected. You want to help him and you don't know how. You don't know what to do about how much you care about him. Neither does he.

She took advantage of his momentary surprise to square off with Gideon, rising from her seat in front of him so decisively he had to take a step back. "I don't need to be in your head to know what you're fighting. You'd face ten vampires without batting an eye, but when it comes to your own heart, your head, you're still that teenage boy. I can accept that you're immature emotionally, but you're not going to goad Daegan into a fight."

His lip curled but her eyes flashed a warning. "We're going into an uncertain situation, and I'm nervous enough as it is. Whatever baggage you have—either one of you—stow it until this trip is over." She tossed a meaningful glance at Daegan. "Or I swear I will kick both your asses. There are all sorts of ways to entertain yourselves on this plane. Movies, books . . . Hell, computer games. You two can beat the shit out of each other in World of Warcraft or Bug War, or whatever the hell you can do with your joysticks. Just quit. It's too small a space for this kind of bullshit."

She finished at a near shout, her hands on her hips. It actually felt good to vent some of her worry, rather than bottle it. At the flex in Gideon's jaw, the flash of frustrated anger in his gaze, she saw Daegan had nothing to worry about. Her vampire hunter wouldn't strike out at her. He was far too busy flagellating himself.

The thought she sent him now was considerably softer, a balm to her anger. *You think I'm past all of it? I still haven't faced what happened in that alley. Once this part is over, I'm going to need a month on my couch with old movies, chocolate ice cream and fuzzy slippers to come to terms with it. Hell, with everything that's happened and that I've lost. We don't have time to be fighting our personal demons. Not now. But we will. Later. Both of us.*

Gideon stared at her a long moment. When she saw a quiver at the corner of his lip, as if he'd been knocked off stride by the visual, she cocked her head. "Maybe I'll have an extra spoon," she murmured.

He picked up the magazine he'd been staring at blindly earlier.

He twisted it into a roll in his hands, reflecting his inner twistings and turnings. The anger had drained out of his face. "I don't really like chocolate ice cream. I've always preferred vanilla."

The warmth spread through her. He'd made that turn once again, away from his own darkness. She gave him an arch look. "Yeah, right. You keep telling yourself that."

"I'm sorry, Anwyn. I apologize. It's just pre-battle nerves, of a sort." He was charmingly formal, her rough vampire hunter. He even sent an awkward nod, almost like a courtier's bow, in Daegan's direction. It somewhat alarmed her, truth be told.

"It's tougher to go into a dangerous situation, knowing weapons aren't going to be an option," Daegan agreed quietly, his guard relaxing.

"And something that matters to me will be right in the middle." Gideon took a deep breath, met her eyes.

"Fifteen years ago, I was a kid. A kid thinking about junior varsity football and what a pain in the ass my little brother was. On one afternoon, that all ended. My parents died in a freak lightning strike. I can still feel the sand and sweat on my palms as I did CPR on my mom, not believing she was gone. Seeing Jacob's scared face, then him going into shock later."

"Gideon." It was Daegan who spoke, his voice kinder. Anwyn hadn't seen this coming, and so was rendered silent by the raw emotion in her servant's voice.

Gideon kept going, as if Daegan hadn't spoken, as if he was talking to some place deep inside himself, rather than to the two of them. "Several years later, I'm in high school. We ended up with my uncle and aunt, who love us, but you know, they aren't our parents, didn't ask for us. I'm playing ball, though, and Jacob seems to be doing okay. I meet this perfect girl. A girl who loves me, and believes I'm strong and capable. Her hero. I thought of us as engaged when I gave her my high school ring, even though everyone thought we were way too young for that. But for the first time in my life I think, Hey, maybe there was nothing else I could have done that day to help my parents.

"Then one night, a vampire takes my girl down in an alley, drains her, rips her open. She dies alone while I'm running off for help, when any fool could see it was over for her. What she needed was for me to stay, be there with her. She was begging me not to leave."

Anwyn closed her eyes, pain suffusing her face, but Gideon continued. "So I drop out of school, become a vampire hunter. For my twenty-first birthday, I staked my tenth vampire, my gift to myself." His gaze locked with Daegan's. "I mired myself in blood and rage, but there was still some part of me, some closely guarded part, that was still that kid. The kid who'd hung out at the dinner table with his parents, laughing and picking at each other. Hell, we played cards some nights, and Mom would cheat, shoving us cards under the table so we could beat Dad, but he'd always catch us, grab her and tickle her. We'd join in . . ."

He paused, his face getting such a strained look it was as if he were strapped to a rack, being tortured. "That guy who gave Laura his ring? The one who thought getting the chance to make love to her in the backseat, sweet and slow, was the closest thing to Heaven anyone could ever get? Maybe I thought that guy was still inside me, somewhere.

"But two nights ago, I found out that kid is completely gone. That I'm fucked-up in my head and dick over two people, and one of them happens to be a male vampire, one that represents a lot of what I'm supposed to be fighting. Yeah, I deal with it in an immature way, Anwyn, throwing out insults, hoping he'll get pissed off enough to tear off my head. Because it's a lot easier than dealing with this shit storm going on inside me. Jacob told me a while back that he doesn't even know who I am anymore. After that night with the three of us, I don't either."

He stopped, let the mangled magazine fall to the seat. Straightening, he looked at them both. "I'll just . . . I'm going to go take a nap for a couple of hours, make sure I'm fueled for this."

Abruptly, he slid past them, left the main cabin. When Anwyn moved to go after him, Daegan closed a hand on her wrist, though his own expression was troubled. "Let him go, *cher*. As you said, until this is over, we all will have to manage our own demons, in our own way. He will stand fast for you; never fear."

"That's what worries me." Anwyn reached out, a simple touch to Gideon's mind. *Do sleep, Gideon. And dream good dreams. It will be all right.*

She wondered if he realized that she had as urgent a compulsion to protect him as he did for her. When her gaze shifted back to Daegan, she knew that was another thing they had in common, another quality that bound the three of them together. Only time would tell if that triangle was made of Tinkertoys, easily broken apart, or a silver instrument that resonated with a beautiful tone on all three sides, no matter what struck it.

12

As he got out of the limo, holding the door for Anwyn, Gideon looked up at the castle looming against the night sky. He shook his head.

"What is it?" Anwyn asked, her fingers a light hook over his hand as she stepped out onto pavement.

"I just imagined sending my brother a postcard from here. 'Hey, hanging out with the Council this week. Wish you were here.' He'd shit a brick."

"If they have a gift shop in the creepy castle, we should definitely pick one up."

He gave her an amused look, one that lingered over her in a flattering way. She smiled up at him. "Do I meet inspection?"

He shrugged. "You don't look as pretty as me, but you clean up good." He caught her fingers before they could pinch his arm, and kissed them, a brush of warmth. Despite her banter, he felt her nervousness, but it was impossible to tell from the outside. She looked every inch the part she was going to play tonight.

They had changed on the plane. A Council audience was a formal one, even if, as Daegan explained, it was a completely private audience. So Anwyn wore a blue silk dress that clung to her curves and stopped just above her knees. She could have walked out of a silver screen decades ago, her hair perfectly coiffed and makeup in place, a pair of sexy, strappy pumps adorning her feet. By exactly following direction, Gideon had helped her with the hair and even had a go at applying her makeup. He'd won a few teasing laughs at his attempts. But the hand she laid on his shoulder now was cold.

"I'm sorry about this," he said on impulse. "All of it. I know I said it before, but . . ."

"It wasn't your doing, Gideon. The world can be a terrible place. I can be afraid of that, live my life cowering in the shadows, angry at everything that happened to me, or see if maybe a new path has been opened up to me."

"Was that one of those subtle hints aimed at me? I know how women like to twist words around and baffle the linear male brain."

"There you go, acting like it's all about you. Don't sass me, servant." She gave him a half smile. "I'm a terrifying vampire, you know."

"You're a terrifying woman. The vampire part is icing on the cake."

It was natural at that moment to slide an arm around her, but before he could, Daegan shouldered between them. As the vampire took her hand, he barely glanced at Gideon.

He says we're already being watched, Gideon. I'm sorry.

She was, but Gideon also saw how easily she fell into it, accepting a male servant following at her heels. He knew she was drawing on her experiences at Atlantis, but it still chafed. He put it away. There were more important things to him than his pride. For one thing, the more unobtrusive he was, the more time he'd have to examine and size up their surroundings. It was a strategic advantage.

They'd taken a Mercedes rental from the airstrip to the castle courtyard, and now that Daegan had dealt with the driver, they found themselves facing a lone individual standing in a stone archway. The thin man's sharp features were caught by flickering torchlight. A cool wind swept through the confined area.

"My lord." The man bowed. "I am Vincent, one of Lord Belizar's servants. The Council has instructed me to show you and the fledgling to your quarters. They will provide you an audience in thirty minutes, unless more time is necessary to recover from your travel."

"Thirty minutes is fine. In fact, we're adequately prepared now. I don't wish to linger here longer than necessary. The sooner we leave, the sooner the Council may resume its public business."

The tall male's features did not alter. "Some additional business is anticipated. Lord Belizar instructed us to have your quarters prepared for a twenty-four-hour stay."

"I will discuss that with Lord Belizar. Is there a problem with us proceeding to Council chambers now?"

"No, sir. The thirty minutes was for your convenience. If you will follow me."

Gideon missed the weight of his wrist gauntlets. Daegan had said a boot knife was permissible, but walking into this with nothing but a knife was one step above walking in naked. Of course, by coming to Council headquarters at all, he might as well have stapled "appetizer" on his forehead and "idiot" on his ass. To add insult to injury, his last memory would probably be Daegan's insufferable "I told you so" in his ears. There was a reason people weren't supposed to live to be seven hundred. They just got to be too damned annoying, knowing everything.

He kept his gaze on the two in front of him. Anwyn had her hand resting on Daegan's lifted one in that formal European-looking way. As they went down stone hallways illuminated with torchlight, even with their contemporary clothing, they looked the same as any lord and lady who might have passed this way centuries before. Gideon didn't see any signs of modern fixtures until they passed an open doorway. It led into an office with a computer and printer on the desk. The harried-looking assistant on the phone didn't even look up. It seemed out of place, a reverse glimpse of Wonderland. Old traditions, history and codes of behavior lay heavily over every square inch of the castle, making the air thicker. He suspected that was exactly why the Council preferred the Berlin location. Intimidating and institutional, it sent the right message. Unlikely to bend or change, it had settled formidably into its age.

The walls also whispered of old violence and blood. Where there were strong resonances from the past, his precognition sometimes worked in reverse, picking up visions of those times. Old battles and hatreds, pain and suffering that had happened here. It wasn't the Council's doing, but they didn't mind conducting their business on top of that environment.

He *really* didn't like it here.

Anwyn was holding up well, though, fully in charge of her faculties and with energy to spare. However, he kept himself attuned to her mind, just in case. He wanted to speak into it, make sure she was okay, but realized from Daegan's body language it would be best if they all behaved as expected, inside and out. Until it was absolutely necessary to do otherwise.

He'd gone into situations that he'd had a feeling from the beginning were not going to go well. Unfortunately, that meant his mind started to sift through possibilities, preparing for the worst.

Despite Daegan's insistence on Anwyn's need for a servant, his support for taking Gideon along, over Anwyn's protests, what did he know of the vampire's motives? He represented everything aloof, arrogant and secretive about vampires Gideon knew. Daegan loved Anwyn, that was easy enough to see, but he'd made it clear that didn't extend any protection to Gideon. If push came to shove, Daegan might use him as a bargaining chip to deal with the Council. Which, if it was for Anwyn's benefit, he'd do the same himself, but . . . Jesus, did he want the guy to betray him? Would that make things easier?

You can trust Daegan, Gideon. I'd stake my life on it. And I think you know it, too. Don't let your fear of this place mess up your mind. Remember our night at the wine and cheese festival, how it felt between the three of us.

I'm not afraid of this place. Hell, she was tuning in to his thoughts. Trying to reassure him like he was some kind of little kid. Fuck. He *really* missed his crossbows, though.

The doors to the Council chambers were suitably impressive, tall and oak, banded with black steel hinges that gave way soundlessly as the male servant slipped inside, bidding them wait. Before there was time to exchange a word, he was back, gesturing. "Lord Belizar says you may enter now."

The night he'd led an attack on the Vampire Gathering, Gideon hadn't actually seen the Council. When he found out it had been a trap, that they'd been used by the made vampires intending to overthrow the Council, he'd been involved in getting his guys out of there, and then distracted by helping Jacob. While he recognized them from file descriptions, it was beyond surreal to step inside the large chamber and see those assembled faces for the first time. With effort, Gideon remembered not to stare directly at them, as much as it chafed. Supercilious bastards.

Medieval-style chairs had been placed on an elevated wooden platform that formed a crescent shape around half the room. It clearly put the three of them in a petitioner's status, no chair offered. Unrelenting stone was beneath their feet.

"Lord Daegan." Belizar greeted them from his perch, centrally located to make it clear who headed the Council. Gideon identified Lord Uthe on his right, the councilor who'd been a particular friend to Jacob and Lyssa. There was no evidence of mercy now in his stern expression. It wasn't hard picking out "Steve and Barb." They were on the far end, clearly accorded the lowest status, but it was more than that that helped him recognize them. Whereas it was difficult to get born vampires to change their expressions, even if a poker was rammed up their asses, he picked up their simmering discontent and resentment of the current status quo under the mask of self-righteous indignation they both wore.

"During your recent visit, you informed the Council about recent events," Belizar continued. "We tabled several issues. Are you prepared to address them?"

"At the Council's pleasure, we are here to do just that."

Belizar nodded. "Begin by justifying your destruction of four made vampires without seeking our sanction first."

No preliminaries for this group. Gideon found himself appreciative of it. A pre-chat about weather or the latest bloodsucker gossip would have grated his nerves.

"I will be pleased to provide that explanation to the Council, but as I noted then, I feel you have a far more serious issue threatening your authority than four unstable fledglings. I spoke of it privately with you and Lord Uthe, and ask leave to discuss it with the full Council now." Daegan kept his attention locked on Belizar, waited for his nod before he swept his attention over the whole group. "That nest of vampires came looking for me. They sought me at a place I use as a sanctuary. Asked for me by my given name."

"So you chose to kill them all? For your carelessness at being discreet?" Lord Stephen raised a brow.

"Among our kind, my name has only ever been spoken inside this chamber." Daegan accorded him a cold glance that ran a shiver up even Gideon's back. *Dial it down, Daegan. You might not want to remind them you're the scariest thing in the room.* Of course, maybe Daegan didn't give a rat's ass. Grudgingly, Gideon knew it was one of the things he kind of liked about the male.

"I killed them all, because the lead vampire was a homeless schizophrenic whose mind was gone, and the others were teenage prostitutes he'd turned. Henry Barnabus also illegally turned Anwyn Inara Naime, this fledgling. He and his cohorts left her to die of madness from a lack of her sire's blood. Time was of the essence, as you know, so when I went to retrieve the blood, I destroyed the nest. It was efficient, for there was no doubt they had committed violations that have always resulted in a kill order."

"That never gives you the right to assume a kill is sanctioned without permission," Lady Helga said severely. "Lord Daegan, while you serve a valuable purpose to this Council, our decision to execute one of our own is always significant."

Helga was a conservative member of the Council, Gideon recalled, so not necessarily in Steve and Barb's camp, but a stickler for rules.

"I always take it as such," Daegan returned. "But as I said, time was very short. While I greatly respect this Council's authority, I thought I might be given some latitude because of the circumstances. The nest was a direct threat of exposure, and they might have scattered if I'd delayed."

"Mmm." Belizar gave a noncommittal noise. "We shall think on both of these things. But for the moment, present the fledgling to us, Lord Daegan."

Daegan's pause was minimal, but Gideon sensed his frustration, even if it didn't show. The male inclined his head, though, and offered his hand to Anwyn, drawing her forward. As always, the Mistress of Atlantis handled herself without flaw. She made a graceful bow to the Council members, but remained silent. Daegan had counseled her to say nothing unless addressed, just as he had Gideon.

"Anwyn is a business owner. Her Club Atlantis is an upscale fetish club, very prosperous. As you know, the Region Master and territory overlord are not yet aware of her presence, as I felt it more important to meet with you first on the matter of her validation and these other issues, but I expect they will welcome her addition in their territory."

Irritation curled in Gideon at the thorough appraisal of the other vampires, particularly the males. "A beautiful addition to Lord Walton's territory." That came from Lord Stewart, to the left of Belizar. "As a fledgling, she of course will serve the requisite period of transition in his household. A temporary manager can be installed in her club to handle its operations until that period is over."

"With respect," Daegan interjected, "I propose a less disruptive option for her club operations and for her. Anwyn has already provided me a sanctuary for some time in her home. It is well suited for a vampire's habitation, and I have assumed the role her sire should have during her transition."

"But if you continue to serve us, Lord Daegan, you cannot give her the guidance she needs. To our knowledge, you have never even taken a servant, let alone shepherded a fledgling. Your differences may make it . . . difficult for her to truly assimilate into our society."

Gideon saw the smallest finger on Daegan's left hand, held to his side, twitch. A bare movement, nothing anyone else would see, but he thought it was an indication that Stewart had struck a nerve. And despite his smooth, oh-so-helpful tone, Gideon had no doubt it was intended to do so.

"I've already established location and mind blood-links with her," Daegan said. "Almost all of my trips of late have been of short duration. Surely the services I have rendered will make it possible for me to have six months to stay close to her area, or continue such short trips."

"That seems unnecessary and unwise." Lord Stewart shook his head. "I strongly support her move to Lord Walton's home for the time necessary to oversee her transition and integration into vampire society. Her business will be an excellent source of income to compensate Lord Walton for his effort. He is a close friend of mine, and I will be pleased to visit periodically and monitor her progress."

Anwyn herself would be part of that compensation. That much was clear, sending a ripple of fire through Gideon's blood. However, he tried to hold steady, have faith in Anwyn's words. *Trust Daegan.*

Lady Barbra lifted a questioning brow. "Quite frankly, Lord Daegan, we are puzzled that Anwyn, as a human, was providing you such a haven without being marked as your servant."

Anwyn was unaware of the weighted politics behind such a query, but alarm bells went off in Gideon's mind. "The role I serve for Council isn't entirely servant-compatible. But Anwyn is a remarkable woman, as you can see for yourself. Our arrangement has existed for five years, where she provided me a clean blood source and a bed underground when I needed it. An arrangement that has never been compromised until someone leaked my name and location to the vampires who attacked her."

"We are not senile, Lord Daegan. You've already made it clear that you are accusing this Council." Lord Uthe spoke for the first time, his expression neutral. "That issue will be addressed."

"With respect, Lord Uthe, I am not accusing the Council. I am accusing the specific Council member or members responsible for the transgression. I do not know which of you felt that it was necessary to endanger the humans at Anwyn's club in this way, but if you no longer desired my services, you only needed to tell me so."

"You have been part of this fledgling's life for five years," Belizar noted. "A human life. How do you know that she did not let the name slip in a moment of carelessness?"

"Because I know." Daegan swept a cool look around the room. "It's not a point that requires debating. My only wish is to underscore that I serve this Council. If you feel someone is better suited for the role, or wish to handle it differently, you need only request I stand aside."

"And what would you do with yourself if that was the case, Lord Daegan?" Lord Welles spoke. Gideon recognized him from the red hair that spoke of an Irish heritage in his vampire parentage. "What territory would you suit, what Region? You can't move as a free agent, no more than she can. She must learn our ways, and Lord Walton can provide that."

Everything sounded so civilized, but the undercurrent was getting ugly. Gideon hadn't had a front-row seat to what had happened to Lyssa in Council chambers when they found out how her Fey blood made her different, but he'd seen the fallout that had made her a fugitive and almost cost Jacob his life. Daegan was useful to them as an assassin, but it was clear that, since his mother's death, somebody—or perhaps it was simply the Council's prejudices coming to the forefront without her meliorating influence—had been spreading poison, reminding them that since he was different, he wasn't one of them.

"I am more than capable of teaching her how to get along in our world, my lord." Daegan smiled, this time showing tips of fangs. As Gideon stood behind him and Anwyn, he experienced that cold ripple again. If the unease that joined the sensation were any indication, he wasn't the only one. "Let me make this clear. Anwyn Inara Naime belongs to me. No other vampire will be touching her without my consent, so unless someone wishes to challenge me on that matter, I will assume you have confidence in my abilities to ensure she is 'assimilated.' I have every desire for her to succeed in our world. Looking at her, I suspect none of you doubt her ability to do that."

Much like megalomaniac Third World dictators, vampires sometimes responded only to shows of strength. During the silent shifting of bodies, Stephen and Barbra appeared to be gauging the reaction of the older vampires, but otherwise Gideon couldn't tell what the response was. A lot of thoughts were being weighed behind those damned inscrutable expressions.

But if they were already weighing how much control they really had over Daegan, that threat couldn't have helped. Gideon remembered his warning to Daegan: *It's amazing how quickly people can turn on you.* He hoped Daegan remembered it as well.

"There is the matter of the tithe to Lord Walton." Lady Helga cleared her throat at last.

"That will be attended to, of course. Anwyn understands how the territory overlord and Region Master require such funds to benefit all vampires under their supervision."

But mostly to benefit the overlord and Region Master, and probably a kickback to the Council. Gideon wondered if Anwyn had known about this, and what she thought of others getting the benefit of her hard work. Of course, knowing how clever she was, he wouldn't be surprised if the profitability of Atlantis would drop a certain percentage on paper in order to allow for that loss. At the moment, Gideon expected she was more concerned about other things, as he was.

"Your desire to protect the well-being of a fledgling with such promise is unexpected. You appear quite devoted to her." This from Lady Carola. Gideon wondered if Carola had been a friend of Daegan's mother, because her speculative glance and relatively light tone had some of the prospective matchmaker to it, a brief respite in an otherwise tense atmosphere.

Daegan inclined his head. "She has been a friend to me. Truly dependable friends are a rare treasure." He glanced at Anwyn then, and Gideon saw it had a dual purpose, both to clearly cement that bond, and also to reassure her with the bald statement. "It is why I do not doubt her discretion. Though I am not responsible for betraying my location, Barnabus came looking for me. It made her a target, and I owe her a debt for her loyalty that being her sire will help to repay. Partially."

"Surely the Council makes the final decision on these matters. Unless he is a law unto himself?" Stephen threw down the gauntlet in a slightly shrill voice. Daegan turned his arctic gaze back to him.

"I think what I'm making clear is that I will not allow this female to be used as a pawn in your game to convince the Council I am overstepping my authority. If you feel that way, do me the honor of making your accusation plain. Anwyn has nothing to do with that issue."

Check and damn near mate. For a vampire that spent a great deal of time alone, Daegan had chosen his timing as perfectly as any diplomat. Stephen's expression froze, but Gideon saw amusement flash over the expressions of the three senior Council members. Lady Helga and Lord Stewart looked a little discomfited by the evenhanded parry. They were the ones on the fence, Gideon realized. Lady Barbra looked almost as out of sorts as Stephen, though she was covering it better.

"Enough on that for the moment, Lord Stephen. The execution of illegal, weak-stock vampires and the care for one fledgling are minor issues," Belizar noted. "We can take time later, in closed session, to discuss them and the more serious accusation Lord Daegan has raised. I wish to move on to the other matter. Her servant, Gideon Green."

Gideon stiffened, but Daegan merely lifted a brow. "My lord?"

"Oh, don't play obtuse." Belizar snorted with true Cossack disdain. "Surely you realize that this Council cannot blithely accept a notorious vampire hunter as a fledgling's servant and say nothing. Though we do appreciate Mr. Green not bringing any explosive materials to this meeting." He cast a look in Gideon's direction that was not amused at all.

Eyes down.

Daegan shot that arrow through Anwyn's mind, with urgent command behind it. Gideon reluctantly shifted his eyes away, but not down. He couldn't bring himself to do it, but it was more than that.

They're not going to buy me as a trained pet, he shot back. *That will make them more suspicious.*

Belizar grunted. "This human was already on your target list, Lord Daegan. You convinced us to push him further down in priorities when it became clear he'd altered his targets to vampires who were in serious violation of Council law." And though he didn't say it, his expression made it clear that it was no secret to anyone how Gideon had started to demonstrate such remarkable insight. Gideon noted he didn't say it out loud, though. While they were cautious about considering Lyssa and Jacob as allies, they weren't willing to make them outright enemies. If Gideon lived through this meeting, it would be an interesting tidbit to pass on to Jacob and Lyssa.

"However, his most recent kill was an executable offense. Trey had committed no violations of our code. He did not even exercise his right to take human life beyond the one necessary annual kill."

Exercise his right to take human life. Gideon forced his fists not to curl, tried to remain relaxed. He focused on Anwyn's intent profile, her remarkable self-possession in this incredibly high-pressure situation. *A third mark provides an anchor, strength when a vampire is wounded or weak.* Now he understood why Daegan had emphasized, over and over again, how much Anwyn's well-being relied on him staying calm. The vampire had anticipated Gideon being goaded. So, keeping that in mind, he absorbed his reaction to Belizar's words like a blow to the gut and stood firm. *Asshole.* It was probably a good thing that Daegan had threatened to gag him if he didn't swear to remain silent.

"Gideon made an error in judgment. Knowing his history and who Trey's last annual kill was, it was clear what happened. He came to Anwyn's club shortly after that, and when she was attacked, he was first on the scene, along with myself, to assist her. Despite his long-standing animosity to our kind, he assisted his brother in his transition, and he has been doing the same for Anwyn. He willingly became her servant, which says a great deal about his adaptability. She is now privy to his thoughts, able to delve into his soul, command it to her will. Gideon Green has effectively . . . neutralized himself. All for her benefit."

If the bastard had said *castrated*, Gideon might have had to punch him in the kidney. Though he was uncomfortably aware that Daegan had spoken only the truth, as long as he stayed at Anwyn's side. He could be her toy, anything she wanted. She hadn't acted that way yet—much—but it was possible with time. Vitriol stirred, though he tried to viciously shove it down. Not the time. *Focus on this moment. You lose it here, none of the rest matters.*

Still, his unease about this whole situation was gaining rapid ground. He suspected Daegan was picking up on it as well. Stephen and Barbra's agenda with respect to Daegan was apparently secondary to the rest of the Council, as well as Daegan's pointed accusation. While the first was vaguely reassuring, and the second indicated the rest of the Council knew he'd been sold out, it was obvious it was Gideon who interested them. And that wasn't reassuring at all.

He was accustomed to vampire indifference to humans. As a result, he would have anticipated having his throat slit right off the plane, his body disposed of in a Dumpster, before he expected his fate to be debated in front of the Council. Of course, as a human servant, he apparently had greater importance. More pomp and circumstance were required before they drove a metal pike through his heart.

Nevertheless, he'd expected something like this. He told himself that, made himself stay loose, calm. Neither he nor Anwyn nor Daegan had assumed he could just learn a few rules and "blend into the background" without remark or incident. It was why Anwyn had feared this. While Daegan had made the risks clear, Gideon had known this was the best choice. Of course, for the first time, he wondered if he'd been wrong. He'd been so concerned with protecting Anwyn, and so damn sure he understood the vampire mind, enough that even Daegan had agreed with taking the chance. But what if they did threaten to take his life, or worse, *took* his life? Could Anwyn hold on to her control? Why had Daegan allowed it, knowing it could come to this?

Jesus, had he really just wished Daegan had played the all-powerful vampire Master with him? *Stop thinking about this shit. She can hear your thoughts.* He could see the slight twitch of her shoulders, and felt that anxious buzz in his mind. *Anwyn, honey, stop listening. Close off my thoughts. It will be fine. You know it will be. I'm just running through strategies and variables.*

I won't let them harm you.

They're not going to. They're looking for leverage. Don't let them see you break. Hold it together, baby.

Her lashes flickered at the unexpectedly intimate endearment, and he wondered if he'd pay for that one later. He hoped so.

"Before the Council makes a decision about this, we intend to observe the fledgling's control over her unusual new servant. Tonight, you will join the Council for dinner, and we will see how things go. You should be aware the Council may decide that Gideon Green should be executed for the lives he has taken."

Gideon nearly bit through his tongue to hold back his obvious retort, but irritation was quickly replaced by alarm as Anwyn stepped forward. Daegan clamped down on her forearm. It was a brief clash of wills, but a very obvious one, her eyes flashing, mouth tightening against the strength of that grip. Daegan gave her a warning look that brooked no disobedience and turned his attention to the Council, watching them closely. "Gideon was brought here as her attendant. I didn't bring him here to be put on trial."

"We would feel far more certain of his being 'neutralized' if he was the servant of a much more powerful vampire. One such as yourself, who we assumed could be objective about the decision to execute a mere human."

Like Laura, or the countless others he'd been too late to save. Suddenly, Gideon felt stifled in the dim chamber, repulsed by this gathering of pretentious monsters. Everything he hated so much about vampires was displayed baldly before him. *We live or die at their behest. We're nothing to them. That is, until I stake one of them. Then the last thing he sees is that a fucking inferior human took him out.*

Gideon, hold fast.

A shudder ran through Anwyn, snapping Gideon back from the red haze of unexpected fury. Oh, Jesus. He hoped her reaction was because

Daegan had used her mind with brutal quickness to channel the sharp admonition, not because she'd personally felt attacked by his feelings, the rising tide of old wounds.

"I have full confidence in Anwyn's abilities," Daegan said mildly, as if there wasn't an escalating sense of combustion sparking off their threesome. "After all, as a practicing Mistress, she's probably more adept at bringing a difficult male to his knees than anyone in this room."

He flashed his teeth, a humorless smile, but the comment won an easing among the older Council males and amused Carola. "Plus, as you know, two vampires don't usually mark the same servant."

"Circumstances might suggest this is one of those unusual times. Are you refusing, Lord Daegan? It seems you have a particular soft spot for this hunter. As well as this fledgling." Belizar's silver gaze was piercing and sharp.

"I have respect for his value. Which, no offense intended, the Council might be missing. This is a human who has had more success than any other in taking out vampires. He has willingly allowed himself to become Anwyn's servant. I can't imagine a better servant to help her adapt to and understand our world. If she rises in our ranks, as I think you can see is inevitable, her choice of servant will only add to that stature."

It must be nice, having a silver tongue and a deadly way with a blade, Gideon thought darkly. It was beyond *Twilight Zone*, to be standing in a room where his fate was being discussed as if he weren't there. Or rather, because he had no right to speak, his opinion irrelevant. Shades of Charlton Heston and *Planet of the Apes*. But he'd gotten a grip on himself. Daegan was right. There was so much going on beneath the surface here, his best use was standing strong behind Anwyn, trusting Daegan to handle the situation. It was an unusual role for him, and Gideon wasn't sure how he felt about it. But then Anwyn gave him a minor heart attack.

"My lord." She spoke up unexpectedly, putting her hand over Daegan's on her arm. When she sent a shy, uncertain smile toward the Council members, the torchlight glittered off her blue-green eyes. As she shifted, the fit of her dress made it clear there was nothing under it, but in a classy, subtle way guaranteed to torture the male imagination. "Lord Daegan is being very protective of me at his own expense. At the risk of incurring his displeasure and yours, I wish to explain. The vampires who turned me . . ." Her gaze shifted to the left of Belizar's head. "They took turns on me. All of them, during it."

At the ripple of response, she pressed her lips together. Gideon could sense a curious stillness in her brain, as if she'd shut off her true feelings to get through this moment. She hadn't spoken directly of her rape, even to the two of them. Only in the madness of her seizures. "Gideon and Lord Daegan came to my rescue. He could of course override me at any time and decide to mark my servant, merely share him with me. But I think he wants me to feel I have some choices, to give me time to adjust to my new circumstances. I would beg you . . ." She paused, letting the words linger on her parted lips. "Please don't judge Lord Daegan harshly for such kindness. I certainly do not wish the Council to be concerned about my choice of servant."

Belizar studied her, a brow lifted. "Prettily spoken, fledgling. I can understand Lord Daegan's regard for you, though I'm sure he also explained you shouldn't be speaking in this chamber unless directly asked to do so."

Anwyn bowed her head. "My apologies, my lord."

Belizar made another of his vague Russian noises, but Gideon wasn't sure if it was disapproval, or like a lecherous grandfather putting on a stern ruse. "We will have dinner tonight, as we discussed, and we'll see what we will see."

He turned his attention to Daegan. "At the very least, you should be prepared for this Council to require your full marking upon him before you leave. Now that we understand her circumstances—something you should have told us—I believe a majority of us will agree it is reasonable for you to be in charge of her transition and mentoring. We are not unaware of the fragile state of a fledgling's mind, particularly one who was turned in such a heinous manner. But that simply underscores the fact that Gideon Green cannot be reined in by a mere infant to our ways. He has far too much of a history to give us that confidence."

Daegan's expression took on a hint of steel. "So the choice is I mark him or you kill him?"

"Unless the Council decides to execute him, regardless." Belizar's flintlike gaze matched Daegan's. "I expect a lot will depend on tonight, yes? We will dine at ten o'clock. Council adjourned."

~

Their quarters had all the trappings necessary to reassure the ego of a visiting born vampire. It was of little consequence to the three of them, though. An awkward silence descended as soon as the door closed after Vincent.

Gideon decided he might as well break it. "So . . . I've never been to Berlin. Want to go catch some tourist attractions before they decide to spear me with a butter knife at dinner?"

Daegan gave him a dark look, but Anwyn dissipated the weak attempt at humor. Moving a step forward, she stumbled, nearly twisting her ankle in her elegant heels.

As one, they were with her, guiding her to the nearest chair. Gideon went to his knees to chafe her cold fingers between his, while Daegan slid a hip onto the chair arm, stroking her hair. "I was right," she said, staring into Gideon's face. "I should have called your brother. He would have come and done whatever was necessary to keep you from following us."

"It does not matter," Daegan said brusquely. "They're not going to carry out their sentence."

"You think it's a power play, to negotiate some kind of leverage," Gideon guessed. "Or they're just enjoying the chance to play with me, like I expected."

"I don't know," the vampire responded. "But it doesn't matter. They can make all the demands they wish, but they have no true power over me."

"Yeah. If they and all their minions attack, you can fight them off. I get that. But what about with Anwyn in the middle? It only takes a second to stake a vampire."

"Aren't you worried about yourself, Gideon?" Anwyn freed her hands, rubbed them in frustration over her own face. "What if—"

"It wouldn't matter, Anwyn; you know that. Something kills you, we both die. That's part of the link."

"That's supposed to reassure me? I don't like this place, or them." Standing up, she moved away from them both, but turned to look at Daegan. "And I understand about the tithe, but it's so . . ."

"Feudal?" Gideon supplied helpfully. "If you're looking for that group to go all free-market capitalist, don't hold your breath. That's a pure oligarchy in there."

"There are overlords and Region Masters who abuse their tithes. But many use them for what they are intended," Daegan assured her. "To protect and enhance the lives of all the vampires in their district. It is a closely connected, interdependent network."

"But one that hasn't ever included you," Anwyn observed. "Why do they hate you?"

Daegan looked startled they'd noticed it, which surprised Gideon, because it had been just as obvious to him. So he supplied the answer for her. "Whatever's different, whatever they can't defend themselves against, they fear. Unlike humans, they don't give a rat's ass about pretending to be fair-minded or tolerant. He can melt in the shadows and never be seen again. He could kill off the entire vampire population, one by one, and they'd never have a chance against him. He's not just an assassin. He's a ghost, just like they call him."

Something in Daegan's dark eyes made him reluctant to continue in the same frank manner, but he knew the reminder was needed. "They'll turn on you if Steve and Barb plant enough seeds. You can already see it happening. You said it yourself. Your mother's gone. You've done a lot of cleanup; they've passed more stringent rules about making vampires, et cetera. Now they feel more comfortable testing you, seeing if you'll prove their fears right, that you'll try to take over their narrow little psycho world."

"For a loner, you know a great deal about politics, vampire hunter."

"Some of the same shit happens in vampire hunting cells. Hell, anytime more than two human beings get together in the same room. There were times I thought what I was fighting alongside might be as bad as what I was fighting against." Gideon smiled grimly, but brought Anwyn back to the chair between them, squeezed her still-too-cold hands. "Feeling better, honey?"

"As opposed to what?" She sighed. Sliding her feet out of her shoes, she braced the stockinged soles on Gideon's bent knee and leaned into Daegan's side. "How is it that you two, when you combine forces, always make me feel things will be okay, even when everything tells me things are going to hell in a handbasket?"

"We're good bullshitters," Gideon offered.

"But I can read your mind."

Daegan pressed a kiss to the top of her head. "It's because he and I are united in one resolve. Nothing is going to harm you, ever again, no matter what we have to do."

"Then make sure you both stay okay." She put a hand on his face, one on Gideon's, linking them to her. "You can't protect me from everything, but if I know you two will be there, no matter what happens to me, I'll be okay. I mean that for tonight, too. You've told me about vampire dinners." Her gaze lifted to Daegan. "Tonight they become reality. I know I'm the low man on the totem pole, so it's possible"—she bit her lip, firmed her voice, though they both heard the quaver—"they might want to test me with some of their games."

"No, dearest. They'll test your servant, and your command of him." Daegan cast a faintly apologetic look at Gideon for using him as the sacrificial lamb to reassure her, though Gideon knew it was only the truth. "This is the Council, Anwyn. While there are power games that go on within territories that might demand shows of sexual and physical submission by younger vampires, the Council typically doesn't dirty their hands with that. They will test Gideon's obedience to you, however." Daegan met Gideon's eyes. "And they can be ruthless."

"Then we should leave now," Anwyn said.

"It was my original intention. But they have made it clear they will oppose that. How stringently, I do not know. Gideon, if you think you cannot handle what may happen tonight, then now is the time to tell me. I can send you back to the plane, and have you flown out of here."

"What will happen to you and Anwyn?"

"We will be fine. Their ire will be toward me. Anwyn is a fledgling in the company of a stronger vampire. The responsibility is mine."

"But you've applied to be her guardian of sorts. That will ruin that chance."

"I tire of repeating this to you both." Daegan said with an edge. "I do not need their approval for any of my actions."

"Being ostracized by this group can be about as bad as a physical attack, particularly for Anwyn. That's why you brought her here, to get validated, right?" Gideon glanced toward Anwyn. "I can handle this. I *will* handle this. I've faced death and torture." He forced himself to hold her gaze, though his tongue had difficulty with the words. "If some Council member wants me to suck his dick or have every one of them take me in the ass to prove I'm subservient enough for them, then I'll do it. It's one night out of my life. It's my choice, which was a hell of a lot more than you got, right? And hell, as Daegan said, that night in the weapons room was about preparing me for this, right? I passed that test; I'll pass this one." Rising to his feet, his hands sliding from Anwyn's, he nodded. "I'm going to go take a shower. Probably the first of a hundred tonight."

She could tell he hadn't liked comparing that night to this, the only comfort Anwyn took from his words. She watched him disappear into the bathroom area and looked up at Daegan. "If that's what happens, he'll do it, but it will break something in him." *It will break something in me.*

Daegan cupped her face, his fingers sliding along her cheek. "Nothing can break you, *cher*."

You'd be surprised. A trembling fear grew in her belly a little more every day, telling her what she'd told Gideon earlier. Once she got past the drama of being initiated in the vampire world, she'd be in for some major post-traumatic effects from the alley and everything that had happened since.

Daegan bent, pressed his forehead to hers. "Oh, *cher*."

"I survived. I'll be fine. But he . . . It's not fair, Daegan."

"He loves you, Anwyn. I don't know if he loves *you*, or the idea of having a woman to protect with everything he is, but in this moment it is all the same. Love is vital, not fair. Fair doesn't really matter."

"I think I love him as well." She managed a half smile. "Both the idea and the actual man."

Daegan nodded, unsurprised. "I saw it in your eyes when you let him lay down upon you in the Queen's Bedchamber. It took me months before you could relax when I did that. It took him minutes."

Though he displayed no hurt about that, Anwyn understood his emotions a little better than that. "It took him minutes *because* it took you months," she said truthfully. "What took me so long to see in your eyes, I didn't forget, not once I learned what it looked like. I saw it in his, recognized it. If I'd trusted that feeling sooner, maybe I would have become your servant, and then all of this would have been different."

Daegan shook his head. "You are no servant, Anwyn." When her lips curved, he chuckled. "I know. Neither is he. You've acquired the most terrible servant possible."

"No. I've acquired the best."

Her vampire's eyes darkened in fierce agreement, his mouth firming. "Then tonight, focus all you are on helping him. He will think he can shut it all out, everything they do to him. He will believe if he goes on autopilot, he will be all right. Vampires are the cruelest, most clever Dominants imaginable. They can take away the deepest anesthetic of the soul, hold it above a human head and laugh as he struggles for it. As a result, he will need the sanctuary of *your* soul—the soul of the best Dominant I know—to survive tonight."

13

Go numb. Just as Daegan predicted, that was what Gideon had decided would be his best strategy. She could hear it in his mind when he came out of the shower at last. She hated to knock him out of his false calm so quickly, but she'd been thinking. Presentation, drama . . . the impact of appearance. These were all parts of her skills, and she was keenly aware they would be useful tonight. Looking through the extra wardrobe items she'd brought also gave her something to do other than go insane at the idea that she was about to lead him into the same kind of alley she'd experienced, only he'd be fully aware of what could happen there as he walked into it.

Once she had him dressed, he stood in front of the mirror, scowling at himself. "I look like one of the Village People."

Anwyn rolled her eyes. "Shut up or I'll put my foot up your backside."

"That might prepare it for tonight," he jested, a brittle note to his voice.

Impulsively, she slid her arms around his chest from behind, putting her cheek against his shoulder. "Gideon, I hate this. I hate it so much. But no matter what happens, I'll be with you. If things get too difficult, you come into my mind, you hear me? You talk to me, cry out to me, whatever you need to do to get through it alive. That's what matters most to me. That we're all headed out together on that plane as soon as possible."

He clasped her hand, his grip almost bruising. "Don't worry. I can handle the dinner. These clothes, on the other hand . . ."

Knowing about vampire "dinners," Daegan had encouraged her to include such garments in their suitcases as a precaution. As a result, before they left, she'd made a short foray with Daegan to the fetish store that Atlantis had on its premises. The fetish fashionista that ran it assured her the newest line of men's pants, made with a cunning combination of latex and spandex, would mold a slave's body in a way that would make her order him to wear them seven days a week. Looking at Gideon now, she had to agree.

She'd been familiar with all the store's offerings, but had found herself looking at them with a new eye. She'd considered the Cocoon, a suit that encapsulated the slave from head to toe, trapping his arms and legs inside a tight latex mesh, with zippers at the crotch, mouth, nipples and buttocks. Of course, since Gideon was chafing at one pair of tight pants, she knew it was good she'd left that one in the store. For now. She'd use that at a later time, when his only source of anxiety was what she might demand of him, not a phalanx of vampires.

It was good to be thinking of the future, thinking of her club, of having him serve her. A life beyond all this. She couldn't afford to get upset about the rest, the thought that Gideon was being despicably sacrificed for her preservation.

When he turned self-consciously at her command, she forced herself to concentrate on this moment. This man. At least her vampire and female libidos didn't have any problem changing focus. In fact, they responded vehemently to the display. The pants fit like a second skin, shiny, sleek and black, molding the curvature of the buttocks, the groin area so that the cock and balls made a tempting and very eye-catching package. It took a very fit man to pull off something that defined every muscle group so distinctly, and he did it—in spades. She'd kept his upper body bare, wanting the Council to see the impressive musculature and scars, reminding them of his capabilities. The trinity mark would remind them of what he'd decided to do with them instead.

His carefully crafted appearance was intended to make a psychological impact on the Council. So, too, was the last item in her hands, but that wasn't why she'd purchased it. She'd bought it because of its psychological impact on *her*. Ostensibly, she could tell herself it had to do with this "performance," but she wasn't in the habit of lying to herself. The price she'd paid for it had been far more significant than what she'd pay for a simple showpiece. When Daegan had watched her charge her store account for it, by his silence she knew he understood.

"You know, when you get worried, sometimes you still drop that screen between our minds, the one that keeps your thoughts and gremlins down to a dull roar, like a dinner crowd at a nice restaurant." Gideon sat down on the ottoman. He'd been sitting there earlier so she could use charcoal to embellish his third mark. She'd made the scarlet teardrops stand out more dramatically. He seemed surprised the pants gave easily, since they looked so tight, but she knew the fabric combination gave him almost full flexibility.

"Yes. I'm still working on that."

"Hmm." Gideon slid off the ottoman, dropped to one knee before her, making her throat thicken. It put his head on a level just above her waist, at her breasts, and while his gaze flickered there, it was to her face he went.

"You know, a lady used to give a knight a favor, telling him that whatever he did, it was in her honor. I think this is kind of similar, in a way. Don't you?" His gaze moved to the collar in her hands.

"Does it help you to think of it that way?"

"Maybe. Am I right?"

"It's a part of it. But you're wrong. Not about that, but about your brother being the only knight in the family." It gave her poignant pleasure to touch his hair, brush a fallen lock back over his brow. "He might be Sir Galahad, but I think you're gruff Sir Kay. No less noble or brave, merely rough at the edges."

He seemed charmingly taken aback by that, but she looked down at the object in her hand. "Gideon, I don't really think in terms of boyfriends, or lovers. I've never wanted a husband. That's not who I am. When you walked into Atlantis, I looked at every inch of your powerful body, the wariness in your eyes, the danger you carry with you, the pain and nobility, the intelligence and resourcefulness. You know what I thought?"

She knew he was capable of delivering a smartass comment at the most inappropriate times, but this time he didn't. He waited for her to answer her own question, gazing up at her with those serious blue eyes.

"That's *my* slave. Mine."

His mind tumbled that over, but didn't outright reject it. "So that's what this collar says. No matter what happens tonight, you're mine. They won't take that away from me, from us. Even though they might have something to prove, you still belong to me. Your pleasure is my property. I won't see it abused." She gripped the collar, and felt the power of it vibrate up her fingertips. "I asked you to trust me, before I became this. Will you trust me to be your Mistress tonight, Gideon? Everything after that, we'll negotiate. Vampire or not, I go in there as a Mistress. Will you go in as my slave?"

"Yes." Seeing and feeling the core of her resolve, so strong it rippled over his skin like erotic heat, Gideon spoke from his heart. "Anwyn or Mistress, they're the same to me. I can't claim to understand what I want or need most days, but the answer to that one is clear enough in my head. I'm yours. Whenever you need me, however you need me."

Within limits. But she knew his limits, didn't she? When she put the collar on his throat, sliding the buckle into place, her fingers lingering, Gideon felt the emotion well up inside her. It was like a divine energy, a strong magic that held him still beneath her hands, as if he was part of a sacred ritual in truth. Fleetingly, he wondered if this might be what marriage felt like, that commitment to forever. What he might have felt sooner, if they'd had more time to do the third marking the way he'd heard it was supposed to be done.

The collar was definitely for a male slave, a wide three-inch strap with prongs worked into it so there was a warning prick of steel all the way around the top and bottom edges. Two long lengths of chain ran from the front steel loop, and fastened to two matching cuffs she tightened over his wrists. She closed her hand on those two lengths of chain where they met at that collar loop and followed them down, drawing his hands together until they rested on his knee and he felt the pull against his throat. Her gaze was molten, a blue-green sea under a hot sun, so that his skin burned beneath it. Latex didn't have as much give as it first seemed, for his cock swelled painfully, pushing its limits. His body responded to that collar in a primal way, and he couldn't control it. The collar was the sign of her ownership, his fealty to her. Whom he served.

His own fervency made him uncomfortable. Better able to handle his physical reaction than his incomprehensible emotional one, he let his gaze pass over her. She'd prepared herself as well. She'd put a sleek corset over a black bodysuit. There was a brace of topaz at her throat, one additional sparkling pin to dress her hair. A loose braided belt, studded with silver metal pieces, embellished the corset, low on her hips. Thigh-high boots with her trademark stiletto heels inspired a sudden desire to put his mouth on them, a peculiar feeling he hadn't experienced before.

"My ankle, Gideon," she said softly. "The material is very soft. I'll feel your mouth through it."

He bent, not caring about the extreme subservient position as he brought his lips to the creased ankle of those sexy-as-hell boots encasing sexy-as-hell legs. She shifted, putting the other boot on the curve of his bare back, holding him in the clamshell position as she adjusted a lacing, the point of the heel digging into his flesh. Catching his hair, she brought his head up, his mouth mere inches from her pussy. His nostrils flared so he could almost taste the scent through the thin fabric, saliva gathering on his tongue. "Smell that arousal? That's all for you, Gideon. Be good tonight and you might get some of that."

"I expect I might get more if I'm bad." He tossed his head back against her hold, gave her a shit-eating grin. She bared her fangs at him.

"I'll be happy to beat him if you'd like to watch," Daegan offered, now standing in the doorway to his room.

Before they could respond to that, there was a knock on the door and an envelope slid beneath it. Glancing at Anwyn, Daegan retrieved it, looked at the addressee and extended it to her. "Apparently the Council has before-dinner instructions for you."

Anwyn took it, turned it over in her hands and opened it. From where he now stood, Gideon could see only several lines of writing, but her mouth tightened in a hard line, matched by a sharp, vicious anger that electrified her mind and sent her shadows stirring with blood-thirsty eagerness. Daegan stepped closer and Gideon became instantly more alert. "What is it, Anwyn?"

"Damn it." She closed her eyes, shook her head, fighting for calm. She handed it to Daegan. As he read it, his brow creased.

"They want me to dress in women's underwear," Gideon guessed, hoping they'd tell him before he had to snatch it from them or pluck it out of Anwyn's head.

"Nothing so dire," the vampire said, though there was a spark of angry fire in his gaze as he glanced at him. "They want Anwyn to mark you in some way before we arrive. Something that will have some pain and blood associated with it, so they can see that you stood for it."

"Why not once we get there?" she asked. "Wouldn't they want to see me do it?"

"This is just an appetizer, Anwyn," Daegan said quietly.

Her expression hardened. "Bastards," she said with quiet viciousness. "Gideon—"

"Your belt," Gideon nodded to it, meeting her gaze. "It's a whip, isn't it? It'll do as well as anything. They like floggings. Jacob told me."

When she said nothing, her eyes stormy, he cocked his head. "You get aroused at the thought of flogging me. You like pain, Mistress."

"Just because I can't keep you out of my head when I get upset is no reason to take advantage of it," she snapped. "And I like pain if it takes the submissive in the proper direction. You don't do it just to torture a person."

"I don't suspect you will be." Conscious of Daegan's regard, trying not to think about the indecent fit of his clothes, Gideon took a step forward. Deliberately, he let his gaze wander over her, just a shade on the insolent side. "The thought of it makes you hot. You're already creaming the nonexistent thong you're wearing under those fuck-me pants."

She narrowed her gaze. "You think baiting me will make me accept this?"

"That's my hope." He forced heat and challenge into his expression. Whether it was the overabundance of nerves and emotion in the room, or anger, it wasn't really feigned. He took another step, deliberately using his greater height and weight to intimidate her. "One of the things you like about me is that I'm tough to tame. That we could go three hundred years together and I'd never be your pet."

Anwyn unclipped the whip, let it slither off her hips in a practiced sensual move that made Gideon's cock harden even further. Was it possible for a dick to suffocate? Jesus, it was painful. And pleasurable at once. He was glad he hadn't had to walk more than a couple of steps.

"Turn around," she ordered. "Put your hands on your head, fingers laced. You'll stand without a wall. If you fall to a knee, I'll make it worse, twice the number of strikes."

"You need to mark him with your blood, Anwyn," Daegan interjected, his voice neutral. "Otherwise the strikes will heal. They want whatever you do to leave a permanent scar."

That was bad enough, but when Gideon obeyed her, turning away, Anwyn's gaze fell on those old lash marks, the ones that had been left by one of the vampires who'd captured him. The vamp had tortured him until he bit into the wood of the beam he'd been restrained against and his nose had bled. She knew, because she'd seen the images when he came out of nightmares.

The thoughts were too strong to mask from her servant. His voice came into her head, steady. *When you stripe me, they'll be gone. The scars will belong to you, like the rest of me.*

Overcome, she shot a glance back at Daegan, her gaze full of helpless fury. He held her gaze, understanding but implacable. *It proves your strength to them. And don't you dare ask his permission to do it. You know the kind of Mistress you are.*

That they need me to be? Her lip curled.

No. That he needs you to be. He's an untamed tiger, cher. *You know it. No matter your distaste, you know he's responding to this. He requires a firm hand to balance the gentle. Break him down to build him up. You've done it before.*

No one mattered this much before.

So do it better than you've ever done it before.

Anwyn tossed her head in defiant answer, but turned her burning gaze back to Gideon. God, she wanted to hate herself for it, but she felt it as he'd known she would, the surge of that pleasurable power, looking at him waiting for her, the skintight outline of his ass the pants provided, every thigh muscle delineated.

Open the pants so they'll drop lower on his hips. I don't want him to take his hands from his head.

Giving orders to me, cher?

She closed her eyes at that silky, dangerous tone. *I'm angry. What if I am?*

There are always consequences.

Fine. She pushed back the flush of desire. The heat in front of and behind her could wrap her up in a passionate storm that would take her beyond the genuinely horrible nature of what she was doing.

Daegan moved past her, his fingertips grazing her ass, a promise, and then he circled in front of Gideon.

"He's going to open your trousers, Gideon. That's all."

"He is your servant, *cher*. You owe him no explanations. He simply obeys."

Daegan was in front of Gideon, and the two males' gazes had met. She didn't know what thoughts might exist in Daegan's mind, and at the moment, she didn't trust herself to be in Gideon's, so she let whatever unspoken communication had just passed between them stay between them.

Daegan's deft fingers slid across Gideon's waist, to his hip, where the nearly invisible zipper rested between the overlapping seams. Daegan worked it down about six inches, did the same to the matching fastener on the other side, and the pants loosened, dropping to the rise of the ass, revealing that pleasurable curve of lower back. Daegan's fingers trailed across his flesh, gripping the hips briefly before withdrawing.

Gideon stayed in place, quivering, giving her a beautiful display of bare male muscle from nape to buttock. Stepping forward now, she pushed two links of the chain running from his wrists into the clip at the back of the collar so his hands were forced to stay at his neck. He hadn't anticipated that, but she ignored his reaction and stepped back, measuring out the proper range for the short whip's strike. Daegan returned to her.

"When you're done, we can use one of my knives to drain your blood over his wounds. It will burn, but if you've done your job, it will burn in a way that will keep him hard."

Anwyn nodded. Gideon stood there, that faint tremble still happening, a reaction she recognized, because all the muscles in her lower abdomen drew tight. This meant so much to her; how could she let the Council use it? Make it into something so . . . despicable.

It's still willing submission. Gideon's voice in her head, stroking her nerves. *We aren't letting them take that away from us.*

"Losing courage, honey?" He changed tactics, the taunt in his voice obvious. "Maybe Daegan should do it, since he's not a girl."

Whzzt pop. She was well practiced with most types of whips. The strike slapped his shoulder where and as hard as she intended, the metal pieces leaving a tiny pattern of bites. Typically she built up a tolerance for pain with lighter strikes leading to heavier ones, but in this case, she went for first blood. Gideon drew in a breath, swearing through it. But she clearly felt the afterburn, the slow fire leaping to full flame in his groin.

"That's Mistress to you, Gideon. You don't call me 'honey,' 'baby,' 'sweetheart' or anything else without my permission. Ever. And you better clamp down on that swearing tongue of yours, or I'll gag you with a bar of soap and a strap."

It took hold of her, the Mistress she was and the vampire she'd become, that sense of absolute control, of connection to the male who was her servant, following the intuition she'd always had. She'd lost confidence in it these past couple of weeks, but now she wondered why. She didn't need to ask him what he needed. She already knew it, with or without the mind reading.

She gave him some of the lighter stripes now, building sensation as she interspersed the harder strikes, this one crossing over the first, and crossing over the older ones, despite the hitch in her heart.

The scars will belong to you, like the rest of me.

Damn right. His muscles knotted, bunched, pure, raw male beauty, withstanding the pain with courage and savagery both. Two more stripes and his mind was in turmoil, caught between pain and the expected unreasoning anger, rising to the top along with that glorious mix of mindless lust that would sweep it all away.

When she reached eight bloody stripes, and got a nod from Daegan that it was enough, she sauntered around in front of him. Any trepidation she'd had disappeared at the rampaging size of her slave's cock. She might like administering pain, but, for her at least, he liked taking it.

Daegan had taken a seat on the settee, within Gideon's peripheral vision, and she saw the vampire had an aesthetic appreciation for it as well, though his gaze was stroking over her formfitting bodysuit, his desire obviously growing, the heat of it filling the room.

"Anwyn—" Gideon's voice was hoarse.

"Mistress," she corrected. "You fuck it up once more, I will truly gag you. You'll wear it for the rest of the night. Eyes down."

Even though she desperately loved the look in those sparking blue eyes, the confusion and rage, the lust and yearning need, she knew his concentration needed to be internal.

Sliding up against him, she threaded her arms behind him, pushed his loosened pants down farther, revealing his ass for Daegan's pleasure as well as her own. Using her thighs, she smeared the pre-come gathered at the slit of his cock over the broad head, and heard Gideon's breath catch, his broad chest rising and falling with the provocation and the throbbing strikes on his back. "I'm going to mark your ass the same way. Then I'll put blood on those stripes, so you'll always remember your Mistress's touch with a whip, her way of getting you to pay attention."

Gideon bent, mouth darting down to catch hers, an insolent lash of his tongue over her teeth. He caught one of her fangs, giving her another taste of his blood. She pushed him back, hard enough he fell. With his arms bound against his neck, he might have fallen, but she'd counted on Daegan's speed.

He caught the male, lowered him to the floor, flipping him over on his stomach at her mental direction. Gideon grunted as the position mashed his engorged cock between the carpet and his belly. Before he could start struggling, Anwyn took the whip to his ass, enjoying the flex and shudder. It created a stimulating friction that had him dry-humping the floor despite himself. Daegan stayed crouched over him, his hand on the back of Gideon's neck, fingers curving over his clasped hands.

Anwyn took a seat on Gideon's thighs then, and offered her wrist to Daegan. With a nod, he drew his blade, cut her skin, and then held her forearm in his grip, turning it to drip along the first of the cuts. When Gideon made a strangled noise, she smelled the burning of the acid reaction. Her arm tensed.

Keep going, cher. *It is what the Council wants to see. But more important, I think it is what you* both *want.*

Daegan was as aroused as the two of them were. The Council

couldn't touch this, she realized. They couldn't force what wasn't already there.

She marked the other stripes, then did the same to those on his ass. Gideon's upper body was sweaty with the pain, but she knew from his open mind that the greatest sense of discomfort was the hard bar of iron trapped beneath him. She leaned down, blew on the cuts like a gentle mother, but then licked the areas of unmarked skin between them. Turning her body around, she moved back until her knees were braced high on his shoulders, enjoying her lithe flexibility, and put her hand between his thighs. Pushing them as far apart as his pants around his knees would allow, she licked his testicles, catching the sac in her teeth, tugging lightly, before she moved her mouth elsewhere.

Gideon gave a strangled cry as she parted his buttocks and teased his rim with her mouth, playing with the nerve-rich entry point. When she sent a thought to Daegan, the vampire reached into the overnight bag she'd left in a chair outside of Gideon's line of vision and gave her the other things she wanted. She manipulated her tongue in that sensitive area, making him buck and groan, a moment before she eased a tube inside, letting a flow of lubricant go down into that channel.

"No," Gideon said emphatically.

"Gag him," she said softly, and Daegan complied, taking a dildo from the bag shaped like a short, thick phallus. She expected the vampire would take visceral pleasure in forcing the cocklike object into Gideon's mouth, stretching it and pushing the hard rubber to the back so it would tickle his throat, making him feel even more vulnerable.

She would get Gideon to let go, make him think of nothing tonight but pleasing her, whatever she commanded of him. She couldn't get trapped in sentiment about his past life. This was their "now," and he belonged to her.

Gideon tried to bite Daegan, cursed him fluently, but Daegan deftly caught his thumb in the corner of his mouth and shoved the dildo in, strapping it around his head to hold it fast. Then Anwyn took the well-lubricated phallus, one that was twice the size of what she'd put into him before, and slowly began to ease it in. It was smaller than Daegan, so she knew he could take it. Slow, ease, ease, ease, and she teased his balls with her fingertips, stroked the base of his cock, felt him tremble. A strangled, frantic curse against the gag, a sudden jerk, and she knew he hadn't been able to hold back his climax. She used his mindless bucking to seat the dildo all the way in. Impossibly, it made her want him more, the unconscious way he pushed back, encouraging her to fuck him vigorously even as she seated it. Daegan's eyes were fastened on the movement of the phallus, the heaving of Gideon's flanks, telling her he wanted to be where that dildo was now. Not surprising to her, Gideon was imagining the same thing, hard as he was trying to banish that thought from his mind.

"There. Shhh . . ." As he came down, panting, his breath rasping around the gag, she soothed, running a hand down his tense back. "This is the way it needs to be, Gideon." *Whatever happens tonight, I'll have been there first. What they do won't mean anything. It can't touch you. You're mine.*

But they'd strip his pride, his dignity. It didn't matter how she changed his perspective with the tool of lust; she knew the truth, and it made her deeply, terribly angry. They would rape him, violate him, punish him for having been arrogant enough to believe he could hunt vampires. For succeeding at it. She closed her hand into a fist on the small of his back. He would take it, because he loved her. And maybe because he didn't think he deserved any better, because he was still punishing himself for never being enough, for being a failure when all he'd ever done was fight and protect the innocent and those he loved.

She found the idea intolerable. "Gideon, I want you to listen to me." Changing tactics, she squatted at his head, yanked his chin so he was forced to look into her face, despite the humiliation of the gag stretching his mouth. His eyes were so tortured and angry, his climax still gripping him. It only fueled the fierceness of her voice. "If Laura were here today, and if she had the heart you say she did, she would tell you that you did your very, very best. Anything any woman could ever ask of the man who loved her. She would be so angry at you for holding on to this guilt, denying yourself love, life . . . value."

His gaze steadied at her fervent conviction, and she was aware of Daegan's regard as well.

"You fight me when I do things like this to you, because you hate the fact that you let go when I push you hard enough. I push you into a place where it's not about anything but pleasing me, getting lost in the pleasure of being mine. You think you have to fight because it's your nature. And it is." She allowed herself a soft smile, running her fingers through his hair. "But this isn't about that kind of fighting. You don't want me to think I can push you around all the time, and I know that. But your overwhelming desire to give yourself to a Mistress, that's in your heart. I feel it."

He shook his head, but before she thought she'd failed, his voice came into her head. *Not to a Mistress . . . Plenty of clubs, plenty of places. Only to you. Only serve you.*

His expression was filled with old pain and new, but a yearning so strong, she couldn't help but respond to it. She slid the gag free but bade him remain silent with fingers to his lips. Bending down, she pressed her mouth to his left eye, held there, conveying all the tenderness she had for him. Daegan touched her hair and in her peripheral vision she saw him grip Gideon's shoulder. He was moved as well, telling her Daegan was in her mind, hearing Gideon's words to her.

"Then do this for me," she whispered. "I've put marks on you with my own hands." Her fingers slid across one of the welts, and he shivered at the pain. "You bear my third mark." Now she passed under his shoulder, finding the deep crimson scar high on his pectoral. "Tonight, I want you to do what a submissive does. Release everything, know that everything you do is for my pleasure and your own. Only you and I exist in that room. The Council is no more significant than this whip, that gag, or the lovely cross we have in our playroom at home. They're props, Gideon. They're not what's real, and I want you to remember you have every right to be proud and strong and defiant. Because you belong to me. And because every damn one of those bastards knows you can take down a vampire."

Unfortunately that's why his life is in danger. A quiet reminder from Daegan. She lifted her gaze, let them both hear her savage retort.

And it's what burns their asses to the bone, knowing he could do it to any one of them. Fuck them all.

Gideon closed his eyes then, nodded his head once, his shoulders releasing tension as if he'd let go of a burden. Whether or not she could keep him from picking it up again would depend a lot on what happened tonight and going forward, but Anwyn realized she'd just released a burden of her own. Barnabus had turned her into a vampire, but she'd always been in control of her destiny. For the first time she accepted and believed that all that had changed was she was now a *vampire* Mistress. All Henry Barnabus had done was give rocket fuel to the skills she already possessed in full measure.

Maybe she'd always have the voices, the occasional nightmare, or carry deep-seated fears from what had happened to her in that alley, but tonight was a reminder that she'd sworn never to let fear run her life. She'd made that oath long before that alley. Back in childhood, a memory she'd partially shared with Gideon during the early days of her transition. Closing her eyes, she willed the thought away. Tonight was not about that either.

What was important was now. When the nightmares came, Gideon would be there. He was hers.

She looked up again, met Daegan's eyes. Reaching out a hand, he touched her cheek. *I as well,* cher. *We will both keep your nightmares away.*

14

S HE'D taken great pleasure in cleaning Gideon up and tucking him into his trousers. She'd strapped a codpiece over the sleek latex shell, a handsome silver accessory with linked chains on the hips that matched the collar and wrist chains. It gave the outfit a medieval look with the polished calf boots she'd put with it. She left the dildo in his ass, so that when she and Daegan helped him up, he was moving stiffly. His cock had been impressively semierect before she cupped the codpiece over it, gaining another spark of fire from those blue eyes at her teasing fingers.

Once she was done with that, she used a linen handkerchief to clean the saliva around his mouth from the gag. His hands were still tethered behind his head, and she ran her hands over his biceps, down his chest, enjoying all of him while he watched her, saying nothing but simply feeling.

Moving in, she slid her arms around him, traced the firm meat of his buttocks, and then smiled as Daegan slid an arm around her waist from behind, pressing his body to hers, so he and Gideon had her sandwiched between them. Daegan was also impressively large, and she toyed with the idea of asking him to fuck her while she held on to Gideon, making him her anchor point, making him suffer, imagining how long he would have to wait for her willing pussy.

No time, regretfully. The knock on the door came, the servant's call to dinner. Gideon's gaze dropped, however, as Daegan's hands molded over her breasts, flicking her nipples so even through the corset they beaded up, hard. When she arched her neck, Daegan gave her a quick bite, scoring the skin but not breaking through.

"Let's go," he said. "You might want to give him back the use of his arms, *cher*."

When she did, releasing the tether, Gideon brought his arms down around her, over top of Daegan's, so they had her in a pair of interlocking rings. "Don't take any unnecessary risks tonight," her servant said, giving her a hard, searching look. "I'm glad you're in a kick-ass mood, but be careful. Mistress."

It sent a thrill through her, because he said it with full knowledge that she'd made calling her that a requirement. He could have ignored it, now that the moment had passed, but he hadn't. He'd embraced it for himself as well as for her.

"You're both being far too serious." She tilted her head to see Daegan giving her the same protective frown. "This is like Saturday night in Atlantis, corralling CEOs and high-powered lawyers, making them beg for their mommies."

Ducking beneath their hold, she went toward the door as the servant knocked again, looking for acknowledgment. "Are you two coming with me, or am I going to have to entertain the Council by myself?"

She opened the door, met Vincent's eyes, and then it hit her.

No warning, full force, as if those shadow creatures had been planning an ambush all evening. It drove her to her knees. The nausea clamped her stomach in a painful vise. Before she could stop herself, she'd expelled what looked like a gallon of blood, splattering the servant's immaculate trouser legs.

Her mind was seized, pulled away, kicking and screaming. Barnabus's insanity took the forefront, contorting her mouth with his dire rants. She wished she couldn't hear them in her mind, a stark echo of how the words tore from her throat in harsh screams. *Another demon. Bathe it in blood. Then we can always find it. Death and dying, that's our way.*

God, like a singsong nursery rhyme. Stupid, pointless gibberish. She was on the floor, a broken chair beside her where it had toppled when she grabbed it. But that was just a vague impression, because the room was swallowed by darkness. She was in her mind, surrounded by those shadow creatures. They'd never been like this. So much larger, a physical presence grabbing her limbs, her throat, their heated breath in her face. Fangs dripping, fingers clutching, like the alley. She screamed for help, no shame.

Daegan, Gideon. They'd promised to protect her. Where were they?

Was it possible for her to conjure them so they landed fully formed onto her brainpan? Gideon was suddenly there, shoving through the dark, fearsome bodies, scooping her up. She heard Daegan's snarl, even more frightening than all those creatures combined. But another one grabbed her away from Gideon, filthy hands and fetid breath. It was going to tumble her into an abyss from which there would be no return. She could see it, a hole in her mind so deep and dark it would be a living death. It was where Henry Barnabus had cowered in his childhood closet, his own personal hell.

"Gideon," she cried.

He spun, wrapping his arms around her waist, heedless of the demons beating on his shoulders and back. He refused to let her go, even to defend himself. Instead, he tried to cover her with as much of his body as he could.

"Daegan," he bellowed.

What came out of the darkness toward them was what she imagined the Grim Reaper must look like. His eyes flashed bloodred as he loosed something silver and wicked from his hand, a blade that sliced through the air toward the creature still trying to drag her from Gideon's grip. The blade severed the creature's throat, inches from her face. It fell away, tumbling into that darkness, but she was falling, too. She'd been too close to the edge.

Gideon was holding her, though, and he didn't let go. As they fell together, his whisper was in her mind, his body sure and unafraid under her frightened grasp.

You'll never be alone. I won't leave you alone. Not now, not ever. And wherever we fall, Daegan will find us.

~

Fucking A, it was a good thing Anwyn had encouraged them to play computer games on the plane, because the idea had sparked to the forefront of Gideon's mind when she went down. The darkness rose up in her mind in a way it never had before, like an invading army, and he'd reacted on instinct. Plunging into her mind, fighting those shadows as if they were flesh-and-blood enemies, had been a split-second decision, as abrupt as her seizure, and motivated solely by his gut. Thank the indifferent gods, it had taken Daegan less than a second to catch on and join him.

Now, moments later, he emerged from the astounding experience of putting his mind fully into hers. He'd seen those shadow creatures up close and personal. Freakishly, they'd *seen* him, recognized him as an enemy. Unfortunately, Gideon had no time to marvel at it.

Daegan turned her over to him, now that it was down to shakes and quivers rather than hard convulsions. As reluctantly impressed as Gideon was by many of the vampire's skills, his ability in this moment to appear unperturbed bordered on loaves-and-fishes miraculous. Gideon was still dumbfounded by the fact there wasn't a mark on either of them, though he'd felt the fists and teeth of those shadow creatures as if he'd been under attack by wolves.

Daegan turned his attention to the flustered servant, who'd been firing questions throughout as to what he could do. Of course, all he'd seen was the two of them on the floor with her, Daegan containing her stronger movements, Gideon with both hands on her head, trying to hold that connection. The servant didn't realize they'd been off playing World of Warcraft in her brain.

"She's fine. Just part of her transition. Before long, she'll be good as new." Daegan kept his expression aloof, that fuck-off-I'm-a-vampire-and-you're-a-lowly-human frosty politeness. "Please tell the Council we'll be there in a half hour. I apologize for the delay."

"Very good, my lord. Are you . . . are you sure I can't get anything for you?"

"No. Her servant will take care of cleaning up."

Gideon didn't mind being treated like a janitor. Neither of them wanted to give anyone an excuse to pry around their rooms.

"Fuck, we had no warning of that one at all," Gideon hissed as the door closed behind the servant.

"Yes, we did. I was careless," Daegan said grimly. "We both were. She's just too damn good at internalizing stress. I should have known from how she was acting on the plane, like she was going to a fucking cocktail party. I should have warned you to stay at a deeper level of her mind. Those damned things in her brain knew. The very absence of them was a warning to us."

He was right. He'd thought it himself on the plane. It made Gideon just as pissed off for overlooking what now seemed obvious. But, like Daegan, he knew there was no time for guilt. "I think she threw up her last three meals. Is she going to need more blood?"

"It works differently for vampires. She absorbed the nutrients, which is what she needed. She'll be a little weak, but she should be all right. We'll get her cleaned up." He glanced at Gideon's pants. "At least you were wearing latex. Easy enough to wipe clean."

"Yeah, I'm Teflon." A muscle in his jaw twitched, but Daegan laid a hand on his shoulder.

"You did well, Gideon."

They both regarded the woman in his arms. "I've never seen or felt anything like that," Gideon murmured. "Does that . . . Is it getting worse, or is it like the darkest-before-the-dawn shit?"

"Do you want an opinion from the floor?"

Anwyn spoke the question in a hoarse voice. As she raised her lashes, they were wet from tears, the stress of her vomiting. Daegan stroked the moisture from the corners of her eyes as Gideon held her upper body. "You'll be fine. Nothing has changed from a moment ago."

"Putting me down is no longer an option," she said, as if he hadn't spoken. "Gideon's life is dependent on mine. You'll have to treat me like Barnabus, lock me away in a cage—"

"Anwyn." Gideon tightened his arms around her, drew her gaze. "You never need to worry about that. It's not going to happen, but if you couldn't get better, we'd go together. It would be that simple. I wouldn't let you suffer just so I could live."

"I thought I'd made this very clear." Daegan's hands were gentle on her face, but the expression he gave them both was implacable. "No one is dying; no one is being executed; no one is going to sacrifice themselves in an act of pointless nobility. We are going to get through this. It is going to be difficult and terrible at times, but we are going to do it. As soon as the two of you can accept it and stop having these morbid fantasies, the better. Gideon, get her cleaned up, and yourself as well. I'm going to go change my shirt. We leave this room in twenty minutes."

Rising, he strode into the next bedroom. Gideon lifted a brow. "You'd think he was the one with something stuck up his ass. Which, by the way, means I should get extra credit for what I just did. I could feel that thing the whole time."

Anwyn tried for a smile, but instead laid her hand on Gideon's face. "That was amazing, what you both did. How did you know that would even work?"

"The usual. Good old intuition and dumb luck." He lifted his shoulder. "When I'm not tracking vampires, I have to do something. Arcades are great places for anonymity, and practicing hand-to-eye coordination. Your quip about computer games helped me remember it faster." He stroked her hair from her face. "You need to stop holding it in, Mistress. Don't internalize the stress. Those bastards feed on it like candy."

Anwyn shook her head. It was the only way she could do it. She wouldn't accept that control was an illusion. Perhaps they'd wrest it periodically from her hands, but she wouldn't hand it over to them without a fight. She drew in a deep breath. Though it felt beyond the realm of possibility at this moment, she knew they were right. She couldn't let this shake her confidence. Not tonight. She had to reclaim the feeling she'd had before she opened the door. Daegan was right to be irritable with her.

Gideon grunted. "You know, for a smart lady, you've still got a blind eye when it comes to him."

"What do you mean?" As she struggled to her feet, Gideon helping her, she tried not to look at that puddle of blood she'd left soaking the stone floor and what was likely a very expensive Persian rug. "I'm sorry."

"You should be. I provide you perfectly good meals, and you go wasting them." He cupped her face, pressing an unexpected kiss to her forehead. "Don't be stupid. Mistress."

She curled her hand over his thick wrist, tangling the chains, using the support to steady herself. "What did you mean about Daegan?"

"He has no family, no close friends. It's obvious even the vampires don't fully claim him. Just you. You're his family, Anwyn."

"Not just me," she said. "You've got one of those blind sides yourself, Gideon."

"Yeah, he and I are best girlfriends." He snorted. "If it wasn't for you, we'd probably have killed each other by now."

She arched a brow, even as he firmly guided her into a chair, probably because he could tell her knees were shaking. "He knew you before I did," she said. "Maybe he made a connection to you long before you were ever introduced formally. He told *us* to stop dwelling on dying. Not just me. Since you die if I die, it would seem redundant and unnecessary to tell us both, right? Unless he values both of us."

"Or he could be shaken up and wasn't thinking straight. He can get insecure too, you know." At her dubious look, he snorted. "Regardless, loving and doting big brother just left me with you and this blood to clean up, and wants us ready in twenty minutes. If he values me any more highly, I may stick this broken chair leg up his uppity backside."

Anwyn began to rise to help him, but her servant made it clear she was going to sit on a chair while he did everything else. Bringing a cloth, he cleaned her up first. Fortunately, projectile vomiting like Linda Blair meant she hadn't gotten enough on her to warrant changing. Gideon then cleaned the floor as only an impatient man could, with a haphazard use of the good bath towels that made her wonder what curses the cleaning staff would be heaping on him. But it was better than dwelling on what else the night would bring.

Particularly when it was off to such a promising start.

~

The chandelier was a waterfall of glass shards brought to shimmering life by the low-toned bulbs hidden somewhere among their curtain. Gideon expected it was probably worth as much as the college education he'd refused, despite the football scholarship he'd been offered.

Somehow, the idea of hanging out in dorms, drinking beer and indulging in the starry-eyed academic idealism that the world could be changed if you wished hard enough, like Dorothy in Kansas, didn't sound as appealing once your girlfriend had been ripped open like a downed deer. The people who said you didn't dream in color were full of shit. He hated the recurring nightmare where Laura's pastel yellow dress glowed like neon mustard, the arterial blood like graffiti paint.

He guessed he should have expected his immediate surroundings would plunge him into those kinds of memories, but with effort, he tried to bring his mind back into the present.

The dining table was probably twenty-five feet long, with the Council members, Daegan and Anwyn placed at generously spaced intervals. He deliberately kept his attention away from the centerpiece as the waitstaff brought out appetizers and small portions of gourmet meals in several courses. The vampires would savor those morsels through smell, sight, and discerning bites before sending the bulk of it back to the kitchen. It would probably be enjoyed by the serving class of the castle, like him. Maybe Daegan or Anwyn could ask for a doggie bag. Particularly if his stomach started growling.

Vampires.

The one bright spot so far, with some reservations, was that the Council had invited Lord Brian to join them. In their flurry of preparations, Gideon had forgotten Brian had returned to his main laboratory and research facility in the Berlin compound by now. What made him uneasy was that Brian wasn't high enough on the totem pole to be invited to a Council private dinner, unless there was a specific reason for him to be there. It was likely that Vincent had reported on the incident with Anwyn earlier and they wanted their resident pet scientist to observe her.

While predicting a vampire's loyalties was never foolproof, it wasn't likely that Brian had told the Council about his time with them earlier, since that had been a favor to Lady Lyssa, one Brian had agreed to keep discreet. His behavior confirmed it, because he greeted Daegan and Anwyn as if it were their first meeting. It made Gideon like the scientist even more, but he wasn't going to bank on it too heavily. If the Council requested an evaluation of Anwyn, he knew the man would be honest with them on what he found, no way around it. In truth, the fanged geek was probably itching to have her come to the lab so he could track how his serum was doing on her.

Of course, despite the vampire propensity for hiding emotions, Brian couldn't completely disguise the brief flash of utter shock that went through his green eyes when he saw Gideon attending Anwyn as her servant within the Council walls.

Yeah, you and me both, buddy. It's a weird world.

Debra was with him, of course. Compared to the fetish wear and more seductive fashion statements worn by the other servants, positioned along the wall behind their Masters' or Mistresses' chairs, Debra was classic sensuality. She wore a formfitting deep crimson sheath and heels, simple jewelry and a ribbon choker that dangled a bloodred stone. Her blond hair was piled up. Though she looked pretty, Gideon had the sense she'd thrown the outfit together after a long day in the lab. He wanted to smile at her, but knew they had to pretend not to know each other. She gave him a cool, polite nod, which was actually far better than the vibes he was getting elsewhere in the room.

Just as she'd warned him, the scrutiny of the other servants was decidedly unfriendly, a "you have no business here" message, loud and clear. While vampires didn't hold a grudge about his acts of sabotage against their kind, apparently servants did. Servants bonded closely with other servants, an exclusive little trade union, and a lot of servants had died during the attack on Mason's estate.

He'd never understood servants. Even now, he'd chosen the path he had because Anwyn, a victimized human, needed him, not because a vampire had asked for his loyalty. Turn ownership of your soul over to a creature who already saw your species as inferior, who would consider you their property once those marks were in place? Crazy. And yet most servants who entered a vampire's service willingly seemed to embrace it.

He understood that Jacob and Lyssa loved each other, even though it was an oddly intense, brutal sort of devotion. But most vampires weren't Lyssa, who'd been willing to die for her servant. So he still didn't get it.

Think of knights and their liege lord or lady. Or both.

Cute. His attention returned to Anwyn at her murmur in his mind. Her profile was enticing, the sweet rise of her breasts over the corset as she responded to something Lord Uthe said, a smile playing on her lips. It distracted him from the irritating soreness of his back, kept him from twitching over it. He wouldn't give the bastards that satisfaction. Plus, if she could handle this without flinching, so could he. When she turned her face toward him on occasion, he could tell her smile didn't reach her eyes. A large part of what she did at her club had to be performance, but there he'd sensed her full heart was in it. She wanted to be anywhere but here, but she was doing a good job at portraying herself otherwise. He didn't think anyone other than he or Daegan could tell, except maybe Brian. For all that the scientist tended to immerse himself in his research to the point that Debra had to be his communications liaison, he didn't miss much that was important. He probably knew Anwyn's emotional fluctuations as well as they did.

Anwyn had also taken Gideon's warning to heart, not expending any energy on keeping the curtain of her mind drawn between them tonight. Fortunately, he was getting better at sifting through multiple sources of information in his head.

She was pouring all her effort into holding it together in this environment, as well as giving him the maximum ability to recognize another seizure coming upon her. They'd devised several different ways to handle that, but none of them had anticipated the Council trapping them into a formal dinner where she was the center of attention. What they could do in this situation, he wasn't sure, but he hastened to add in his mind that he would be resourceful enough to come up with something. He was sure Daegan was staying just as close to her gray matter.

Her lips curved, a faintly rueful gesture as she tossed him a surreptitious glance. *It sucks, knowing I can hear "I haven't a fucking clue what I'll do," right?*

Yeah, but that's the way I handle most crises in my life. I'm still here to talk about them.

Her gaze sparkled with a trace of humor. *Noted, and reassured. Thank you. I notice you haven't been appreciating the table centerpiece.*

Sex slaves surrounded by spring foliage is so last year. Martha Stewart's mag says so.

He heard her laughter in his head, was warmed by it and the ever-so-slight easing of her tense shoulders, before she turned her attention back to the conversation. He'd need to give her a massage tonight, take out some of those kinks. He could do that passably well. He hadn't ever had any training, just somehow knew where the knots were, and how to untie them. And touching her was no hardship, ever.

Brian had been placed across the table from Anwyn. Daegan was seated at one end, Belizar at the other, Anwyn to Daegan's right. Gideon of course was against the wall behind his Mistress's chair. He'd covered every inch of the terrain, but now, against his will, his eyes were tugged back to that centerpiece she'd teased him about.

Just beneath the impressive chandelier, two males were on display. He assumed they were servants who belonged specifically to Council members, because Barbra and Carola had no one standing at attention behind them. The men had been oiled down so every muscle gleamed. They were manacled flush to each other, one's chest against the shoulder blades of the other, hips nested together so intimately it was clear that the blond guy in back had impaled the redhead's ass. The bands of steel holding the arms to one another allowed the slight difference necessary to compensate for the width of their bodies, but if one of them moved his arm, they'd both be moving it.

Of course, they weren't moving much of anything, because they were locked on a rotating dais. A steel pole rose from it with a short, horizontal, wood platform for the man in back to lean against. Of course he was strapped to it, because that platform had been fitted with a dildo so his ass was impaled as well. Their arms had been drawn together forward and low, so their two sets of hands encircled the erect genitalia of the man in front. The blond in back clasped the cock at the base while the redhead cupped his own balls.

The guy in back had been instructed to pump into his companion's ass and ride the phallus up his own backside in slow, methodical rhythm with the classical music filtering into the room. He'd been commanded to follow the beat, no matter how agitated either one became, so the Council was treated to what Gideon assumed they'd feel was an artistic display of smoothly flexing buttock and thigh muscles. As well as the rise and fall of broad chests as their arousals waxed and waned.

They both wore condoms, which was good since they'd already come once or twice during the second and third courses. While the vampires noted it with flashes of lust or approval, they continued on with their conversations as if it was no more exceptional than seeing the waitstaff move in and out of the room.

Fortunately, there was female eye candy. As he'd noted from entering the room—acute observer that he was—all of the female servants in the room, other than Debra, were dressed in ways that would have made a porn movie look tame. Lord Stephen had explained his servant was being punished for an unmentioned transgression, so she was as naked as the men, except she wore a chastity belt fitted with a clit and anal stimulator. Breast and nipple clamps had her already ample breasts distended with the constriction. She also wore a full neck collar that allowed her head no mobility, and a ball gag almost too large to get past her teeth had been shoved in to stretch her jaw muscles hard.

She was rasping around that gag because Stephen had control of the pace and power of the stimulator. She never came, but at different times she was excruciatingly close. Then he would dial her back again. Gideon noted the males in the room couldn't help responding to her agony. He was one of them, though he was uneasy with the distress in her eyes. Jacob had told him what this could be like, but Jesus, seeing it firsthand . . . he felt like he was in the middle of a macabre circus. Despite his offhand banter with Anwyn, his pulse was up, his cock was hard and his hands were sweating. Which was what he was sure these bastards wanted to see.

"Lord Stephen," Anwyn said unexpectedly. "Would you mind if I had my servant wipe your servant's chin? I think she's becoming a bit of an eyesore for those of us eating our dinner."

"Drooling on the carpet *is* considered bad manners," Helga mentioned wryly. Her tone suggested Stephen's decision to punish his servant so severely at the table, when it wasn't a planned part of the central entertainment, was improper etiquette. She sent an approving look toward Anwyn, as if she appreciated her subtle objection.

"Of course," Stephen said, though agreeable was the last thing Gideon read in his voice. "Whatever will give you ladies more comfort and pleasure. In fact, he can remove the gag. Tell him to push her to her knees and use his cock to remind her what her tongue is for. Or do you have to *ask* the vampire hunter to do such things for you? A 'pretty please,' perhaps, to coax him to do your bidding? Beg him to eat your sweet cunt?"

Gideon's blood went to boil, but Anwyn's laughter checked his desire to use a dinner fork to teach Stephen manners. He did note that several Council members were less than pleased with his vulgarity. Apparently, as Daegan had said, such bald sexual behavior toward another vampire wasn't encouraged in a private Council gathering.

"Do you think I'm so easily baited, Lord Stephen? A new vampire I may be, but I've been dealing with pushy males for a very long time. I've spent time with Lord Daegan, after all." She tossed Daegan a provocative smile and leaned back in her chair, crossing her shapely legs so the dress inched up. Daegan acknowledged her barb with an indulgent nod, but Gideon noticed his eyes didn't leave Lord Stephen, unwisely oblivious to his regard.

The women responded with appreciative chuckles, though Barbra was not one of these. She smiled because the others did, but it was tight, unfriendly. "Are you refusing to entertain us with your servant, Anwyn?" she asked. "For all his exploits, your vampire hunter is expected to have far larger balls than most. I for one am curious to see."

Gideon, Daegan said to tell you Stephen's servant is pleased to be punished by her lord this way. She's very aroused and not being tortured against her will.

I know how servants work. He managed, barely, to keep the contemptuous sneer off his mouth. At the flicker of hurt from Anwyn, he cursed his stupidity.

Yes. Her response came slowly. *But can you work the same way?*

I told you I can. Issue your order, Mistress. Let's get done whatever bullshit they want to prove.

I like it when you call me Mistress.

He remarkably liked using it, but he decided he wouldn't admit that to her. At least not directly. He'd rather let her fish for that one than throw it right in the boat. Her lips curved, a softer smile that told him he was forgiven.

Then she met Lady Barbra's gaze. "I am not refusing you at all, my lady. I'm simply new to your ways. You must forgive me if I am not as quick to respond to your games . . . or rather, entertainments."

When Barbra's eyes narrowed, Anwyn's brow lifted, as if in innocent question. "And of course," she added, "I'm never averse to showing off his gifts. Gideon?"

He moved forward. She'd lifted her hand toward her shoulder, toward him, though she didn't turn her head, clearly expecting he would be there. Following impulse, when he reached her, he bent so his lips touched the cup of her open palm. He left his hands out of it, not touching her or grasping the wrist, just offering that teasing homage, tickling her lifeline with the tip of his tongue so her fingers curled slightly. He inhaled her perfume, the scent of her hair, and it steadied him. "Yes, Mistress."

"Please go relieve Lord Stephen's servant of her gag in the manner he described."

He would shut his mind down and do this. He could do it. He'd had to do a lot of things as a vampire hunter, and keeping a poker face was one of them. Inclining his head, despite the turmoil of his feelings, Gideon turned toward Stephen's servant. She was a beautiful woman, exotic and long limbed, with red hair that swept around her face and shoulders like tongues of flame. Her eyes were a rich dark brown, an animal's liquid deep color that gave her Fey-like face a fragility that pricked his dispassion.

He reminded himself she served Stephen, probably helped with his kills. Her Master was the guy who'd likely sold out Daegan, who wanted to see him dead. She was part of that.

It both helped and hindered that this servant's eyes were consumed with particular venom when they shifted to him.

"You might be interested to know that Alanna's twin brother was a servant as well. To Lady Theresa, who died in the bomb blast at the Gathering." Lord Stephen offered the information with satisfaction. "Their bodies were found together, of course. Maybe you'd like an oral bit to protect your servant's overblown assets, Anwyn. Alanna has very sharp teeth."

Shit.

"Gideon knows how to handle himself around angry females exceedingly well. I am not concerned." When Stephen curled his lip, the tips of his fangs showing, Anwyn gave him an indifferent look.

Great. With a slight bow for permission, just as Daegan had showed him, only the vampire's movement had been much smoother, Gideon took a piece of chocolate off the silver tray next to Anwyn's plate. He also borrowed her cloth napkin. When he reached Alanna, trying to walk normally despite the dildo, he thought if she could have spat at him, she would have. He was conscious of every eye in the room, some murmurs over the stripes he revealed on his back. The dried blood itched but had been left uncleaned at Daegan's suggestion, for more dramatic impact. As he unbuckled Alanna's ball gag, he slid the slick orb from her mouth. Using the napkin, he caught the saliva that came with it and dried the rest from around her lips and chin. He hesitated over the cleft of her breasts, where more saliva had dripped, but at a glance at Anwyn, receiving her nod, he rubbed it off, trying not to linger. Despite what he'd been sent there to do, he didn't want to take excessive advantage of the situation. Servants might be willing and ready to do whatever their masters ordered, but he didn't like the idea of touching any woman without clear consent. And this one clearly hated him.

Still, after he did that, he brought the piece of chocolate to her lips, knowing from his earlier gag that the rubber left a nasty aftertaste. While there was a flicker of surprise in Alanna's eyes at his courtesy, the flash in her gaze warned him. When he put the chocolate on her tongue, she snapped down, just as he expected.

One of the vampire hunters he'd known had a dog named Evel, who would bite anything that aggravated him—which was pretty much everyone. When he tried to bite Gideon's hand one day, Gideon had deterred him from doing it again by doing what he did now. Though he did it in a bit gentler fashion, since a fragile woman's jaw was a little different from the machine grip of a Rottweiler's, he jammed his closed hand toward the back of her throat.

Expecting him to pull back, she hadn't been prepared to lock her jaw against a forward thrust. It wrenched her mouth wide-open, hitting her gag reflex.

"You won't bite me," he growled. "You'll behave and do as you're told, or you'll learn worse tricks I have than this. Settle down to business and we'll be done in no time. I'm not any happier about it than you are. Okay?"

It took some coughing, gagging, some outraged strangled snarls from the back of her straining throat, but eventually her jaw relaxed and he removed his fingers. She gasped for breath, staring at him with hatred and uncertainty both. He was cognizant of some audience appreciation of his tactics, but he wasn't interested in their approval. He focused instead on his connection to Anwyn, held that silken cord of awareness, already wanting to climb out of this moment and be back beside her.

Gripping Alanna's shoulder, he pushed her, not ungently, to her knees. He focused on the wall when he opened the tight latex pants and freed his cock. At least his ass was still covered, concealing the dildo shoved into it. He couldn't say he'd accepted Anwyn doing it to him with good grace, but it had been reluctantly pleasurable. Now it grated, suddenly a symbol of what this group wanted to do to him, how they would humiliate him.

Gideon, no. Nothing has changed. It's only you, me and Daegan here. Just focus on that.

Then who's this pathetic creature being forced to suck off the dick of her brother's murderer?

Gritting his teeth, not waiting for an answer, he fed the head of his cock into Alanna's mouth. He did it slowly but inexorably, keeping one hand on her face. He was ready to jam his thumb in the hinge of her jaw if needed, but she eventually opened, took him deep.

"Don't move your mouth, Alanna," Stephen said abruptly. He tossed his next comment Anwyn's way. "I like the look of this. More torment for them both. It gives us something else pleasurable to look at. Push those pants down to your knees, servant. They're hampering the view."

"Absolutely," Helga murmured, to amused chuckles around the table.

He knew what Daegan had said, but it would be a cold day in Hell when he did anything that asshole ordered. If he'd set up Daegan, he was also responsible for Anwyn's attack.

Gideon, do as he says. Anwyn's voice in his head, urgent.

Damn it. This was his choice, for her. With a rough jerk, he shoved the pants down his thighs, wishing he could go deaf rather than hear their salacious reactions to the additional stripes there, as well as the dildo's wide base spreading his ass cheeks. He knew his balls had to be visible from his spread leg position. Alanna's breath was hot on him, her tongue moist on the underside, and of course he couldn't help getting harder. Maybe that was good, because it kept at bay the horrified incredulity he was actually doing what he was doing, and exposing himself this way in front of a group he'd give away his soul to stake.

He'd pushed his cock only halfway into Alanna's mouth, since he was a lot for a woman to take. Lady Carola made a satisfied comment about his diameter. Darkly, he wondered if she was going to send someone over with a tape measure. He'd happily strangle them with it.

Lord Uthe brought up something about the quality of the cheese they were eating and suddenly they were discussing which country had the best reputation for cheese production. Gideon might have been astounded, but his shock meter had overloaded and blown a gasket three courses ago. Just your typical vampire dinner.

He could steel himself to handle all that, blank his mind enough to get through it, but what he couldn't ignore were Alanna's hot, hitching breaths on his cock, silent sobs. Or the tears running down her cheeks. It didn't matter that she was another brainwashed human servant to the damned vampires; he didn't treat women like this, force himself on them when they wanted nothing to do with him. He wasn't supposed to have an enormous erection, or be fighting his desire to thrust, rough and fast, into that wet mouth. Damn third-mark made it impossible not to be aroused, but what was making him hotter and harder had nothing to do with that, not really. It was something far more disturbing.

Her fists had clenched in frustration at her sides and he wanted to do the same with his own. Looking down, he saw her feet were bare. Since the other women servants wore shoes, he assumed it was a further punishment, no emotional or physical armor. That was what vampires were all about, weren't they? Stripping their servants down to a shivering soul. The vulnerable pink soles, the round heels, made him wish he could be anywhere else. *Jacob, how did you do this? How do you do this?*

Hang in there, Gideon. Anwyn again. *Focus on my mind. You're doing fine.*

Don't worry about me. I'm all right.

I know you are. You are a brave, good man. When we get through with this, I will personally hold your head while you throw up.

He closed his eyes, his throat tightening. Yeah, he hated this. But the trigger factor here wasn't the physical stimulation. It was that Anwyn had commanded it. That was what had him thick as a steel beam, stretching Alanna's jaw. The aphrodisiac was doing this at a Mistress's demand. No. *His* Mistress's demand.

A pause, where he felt his acknowledgment of it hit Anwyn. Her internal reaction made him want to groan in need. But she kept her mind voice steady, cool. *You understand why that is. It's in your unconscious, but every day it comes closer to your subconscious. It's why you can do this now. It's why you sought me to begin with.*

He wanted to keep his eyes closed, but that made the sensation that much more acute. Taking advantage of the fact that the vampires were still involved in their inane small talk, he laid his hand on Alanna's hair. Curling his fingers around the shell of her ear, he grazed the side of her throat where he could feel her swallowing back the sobs.

"I'm sorry," he murmured.

"Torrence," Lord Stewart spoke then. "With Lady Helga's permission, I'd like to add to Lord Stephen's little sculpture. Let's see how the vampire hunter endures being staked himself. Go replace that dildo with your ample attributes."

Fuck. Helga's servant, Torrence, was a mountain. When Helga nodded, the man wasted no time, unbuckling the kilt he wore and draping it over the back of her chair, his eyes alight with vicious anticipation. Great. Gideon figured he'd probably blown up one of his family members, too. So much for Hell being an after-death experience.

Torrence bent over Helga, much as Gideon had touched base with Anwyn first. She stroked a hand up his chest, cradling his jaw with affection. Her favorite pet grizzly. As he moved away, she leaned back against the kilt, watching him.

So did Gideon, because when Torrence emerged from the cover of the table, rounding the corner around Lord Belizar, he revealed an organ the size of a fucking tree branch. However, it wasn't that which put Gideon's mind into full refusal mode. He knew he should be able to do it, that it was just putting Tab A in Slot B, and a whole fucking heap of pain, but as Anwyn knew, it was a hell of a lot more than that. It wasn't sex Barnabus had been after. It had been humiliation, subjugation, torture . . . It was different, so different, from what he'd allowed Anwyn to do to him in the bathing chamber and every day since, no matter how compelled he felt at times.

The barbaric anticipation in the room was suffocating. This was only the beginning. It was a test to see what he'd endure, for their obscene curiosity as well as punishment. They intended to see his blood tonight, one way or another. He'd known it, thought he'd been prepared for it, but the reality was different from the plan, right?

He shouldn't be thinking these thoughts, should be able to close it all down. Probably for the first time since he'd been marked by her, he wished with every cell of his body that he could keep Anwyn out of his mind. He didn't want her in there when this happened. He couldn't even look toward her, afraid of what he'd see, or not see. He was starting to get the shakes, deep in his abdomen and spreading out to his chest. In a few minutes he was going to shame himself by letting it get to his limbs. Then he'd go ballistic and tear Torrence's head off. He just couldn't do this.

Anwyn had tried so hard to keep him from coming to Berlin. Better than anyone, even himself, she knew this wall existed in him, a wall he couldn't push past. Yeah, Daegan had broken through further than expected, and so had she, but they'd made it past the castle walls, not into the inner bailey that guarded those really essential things, the ones that made him who he was. He was going to fail her because of what he couldn't give up there. He'd fail her, as he'd always failed the people he loved most.

Lord Welles had a quirt lying by his plate. He was toying with it, his eyes lingering on Gideon's shoulders and ass with unmistakable intent. Maybe that was the follow-up, to fuck him until his internal organs bled and then open up his flesh on the outside. *Bring it on.* What was the big deal, after all? He couldn't be killed by such minor things.

"Lord Stewart, I don't believe you asked my permission to use my servant this way." Anwyn's voice was strained, making Gideon curse his weak mind anew.

"I don't have to do so, Anwyn." Stewart's voice was cool. "Until you achieve a certain rank, higher-ranking vampires may engage your servant in whatever games they desire. Because you don't know the etiquette, I am going to assume your question was ignorance, not disrespect. Seasoning a new servant is a very valuable exercise, so sit back and observe. If you do in fact get the right to keep him, it will help you prepare for interacting with other vampires. He is a valuable distraction for gaining power in the ranks of your territory. As Lord Daegan pointed out, it is not every day a vampire calls a vampire hunter to heel."

It's all right, Anwyn. Gideon viciously pushed everything else away, including his rising certainty that he was going to grab the nearest steak knife and fight his way out of the room. *Maybe it's tit for tat. Those hookers I told you about, that I had before I met you...I used some of them pretty hard. And I killed this girl's brother, even if he did make the wrong choice of friends.*

Shut up, Gideon.

~

Anwyn kept her face still, but her mind was far from placid, hearing everything going on in the rising tornado of his mind. He wasn't going to be able to do this—truth, she'd been impressed with his ability to handle Alanna. Her fierce vampire hunter had difficulty looking at female slaves being flogged for their own pleasure in Atlantis.

But what made this intolerable to her was how he thought it was his defeat, not a reflection on the very wrongness of what was going on in this room.

There was a line between compelling someone's surrender for a fight they *wanted* to lose, and knocking them to their knees, forcing them to give up a fight that was everything of who they were, right down to the core. Gideon thought he was about to lose control, but he didn't realize she was perilously close to the same. It had nothing to do with those shadow voices or Barnabus's blood. It had to do with her blood, and for once that vampire blood was brewing because of what she knew a Mistress was supposed to be.

Neither Gideon nor Daegan relaxed in the company of vampires, probably because they were both far too aware of these kinds of excesses. They were a lot like the cops she'd seen come through Atlantis. The ones checking for violations as well as the ones who came in as clients. Never trusting, because in their experience, there was no one deserving of trust. So far Gideon had surrendered his trust to her, a couple of brief, precious times. Gifts. Doing that was so new to him, making him so vulnerable. She valued his trust and she couldn't bear to see it stomped upon like garbage, his will held hostage to her well-being. Closing her hands on her chair arms, she began to rise.

"This is not happening," Daegan said.

The pleasant chatter that had started up again after Lord Stewart's well-meaning instruction to Anwyn stilled. All eyes moved to the end of the table. Daegan had been quiet for most of the meal, watching, listening. Few of the Council members engaged him in conversation, except Lord Brian. Daegan rose now, gave a half bow to Lord Belizar.

"Most vampires who value their servants know that they must be trained and brought along like a prize Thoroughbred colt. You don't push too hard or too fast, or you ruin all his potential."

"If he is not strong enough to handle such games, then she needs to know quickly she needs a different servant." Belizar shrugged. "I personally feel she might do better with one of the trained servants who are part of the Inheritance, like Alanna. Those who've been raised under Council guardianship as a first-mark, with the intent of graduating to a third-mark when an appropriate vampire is assigned to them."

"The mettle and strength of made vampires must be tested. She must earn her way, learn to get along." This was added by Lord Uthe, though his expression remained dispassionate. "You have not been part of such rituals, Lord Daegan. It is understandably difficult to see the first few times, but it has good purpose."

Daegan nodded. "While I appreciate both of the lords' great wisdom, I am familiar with some things. This is not about testing the command of a made vampire or the mettle of her unusual servant. Whether or not you decide to execute him, death isn't good enough. You wanted to torture him tonight, humiliate and damage him for the gall of what he has accomplished, what he is. A true warrior, down to the bone."

~

Gideon didn't dare look up, holding on to his control with both mental hands, but he was hypercognizant of Daegan's eyes upon him, not just the mixed regard of Alanna and Torrence, in front of and behind him.

"You accord honor to one who has killed so many of us?" Stephen's voice was pitched with outrage, but Daegan moved his attention to Belizar and Uthe.

"Everyone in this room recognizes our dominance over humans, except perhaps Anwyn, who is new to our kind. However, we also recognize their finer attributes. This human won my respect, because he is a soldier, dedicated to his belief. It is hard for those who have not known the sacrifices and trials that occur in our line of work, in the Territory Wars and other conflicts, to truly understand the cost of taking lives beyond what is necessary for our immediate survival, or defense of those in imminent danger."

Gideon had to admit there was something else he liked about the arrogant male, aside from the fact he didn't let diplomacy turn him into a doormat. Daegan had just reminded the older Council members of their superiority in experience, an ego stroke that couldn't hurt the situation.

"I do not acknowledge him as an equal, but he is a warrior, and I respect him for that. We are too few to be guided by our petty vengeances. We live by survival of the fittest. A hunter like Gideon Green keeps us away from dangerous complacency. Do not force this issue. If you have no use of him motivated by pleasure and entertainment, then let us move on to others."

"You know this is our way." Lord Welles spoke, though his countenance was thoughtful.

"I disagree, for the reasons I just explained. But I can tell you for certain, it's not my way." Daegan met his gaze, his dark eyes becoming even more opaque.

"No, it wouldn't be, would it?" Lord Stephen broke in with a sneer. "Not a half-breed with an unknown father. Vampire blood is not what governs your actions."

Anwyn drew in a breath. Gideon's head snapped up despite himself, a flood of unexpected outrage filling him on Daegan's behalf. Even the Council appeared somewhat taken aback by Stephen's ire. But before Lord Uthe could speak, Daegan did.

"No," he said in a neutral tone. "The Council reigns my actions. By my choice, because I believe in checks and balances to ensure proper behavior."

A full moment's silence held the assembled as Stephen's face flushed with anger. Check and mate again, Gideon thought, trying not to tense as Torrence's breath brushed his nape. The behemoth was a step closer than he was a moment ago and it took everything Gideon had not to visibly tighten up his ass, like a walnut refusing to be cracked.

"Well said." Lord Uthe raised his cup. "Gods, is it too much to have one dinner among ourselves that doesn't involve political carping? Lord Stephen, save your strategic manipulations for the Council chamber, and let us enjoy our meal. I for one am content with the current arrangement." He glanced toward the table centerpiece. "Though I admit to enjoying our past female creations more, we were catering to the ladies tonight."

Unexpectedly, he gave Anwyn a cordial nod, a feral glint that might have been grim humor in the depths of his eyes. Then he gestured with his cup toward Carola, Helga and Barbra, generally including them in his comment.

Belizar cocked his head, considering his right-hand Council member, then shrugged, glancing back at Daegan. "Have you fucked him?"

"Pardon me?"

"I said, have you fucked the vampire hunter?"

Gideon thought it was like watching a tennis match, seeing the Council members' chins bounce back and forth to follow the conversations. Yet the question raised a disturbing memory in his mind that distracted him from that. Daegan's hot breath on his neck. The strong grip of his hands, the startlingly erotic invasion of the vampire's cock. The way his own had jumped at the penetration, the possession, even as Gideon sunk deep into Anwyn's wet heat.

"Yes." Daegan glanced at Gideon, then back at Belizar.

There was a murmur around the table; then Belizar cocked his head, his expressive silver eyes locked with Daegan's. "Pushed him to his knees, made him take you down his throat?"

"No."

"Hmm. One is easier, you know." The Russian toyed with his wineglass, waved away a servant when she came forward to refill it. "Seems you have managed to shame us just a bit, Lord Daegan. Not an easy task. Lord Uthe tells me we should avoid hasty decisions, but perhaps there is a middle ground to resolve this matter."

"I am listening, my lord."

Belizar nodded, then threw his gaze out to the Council. "With apologies to Lord Uthe for suggesting business at supper"—he shot Uthe an arch look—"here is what I propose. As we agreed, it will help our deliberations about executing the hunter if we have proof that he is well under the command of Lord Daegan, as well as clearly submissive to Miss Naime. While she's marked him with some lovely stripes, I propose thirty-six additional lashes with a bullwhip of our choosing. A blood strike for every vampire life he's taken. That we've verified."

He shot Gideon a speculative look that Gideon caught in his peripheral vision, because he was staring a hole in Alanna's forehead. Her eyes glittered with satisfaction. Apparently, she had no objections to him being whipped. "During that flogging," Belizar continued, "he takes you down the throat, Lord Daegan, here in front of us. If, for some reason, you are averse to his mouth on your cock, we will settle for you marking him fully right now, at this dinner."

Before he returned his gaze to Daegan, Belizar waited until he'd received answering nods from around the table, though Stephen's looked somewhat reluctant. "I know what kind of man this Gideon Green is. If he will go on his knees, suck you to completion and swallow every drop, we at least know he will capitulate to you, which will reassure us you have control over him. It will not guarantee our decision, but it may sway it considerably."

Or they may be just fucking with us, Gideon thought darkly.

"So another ultimatum. I take his blood, or he takes my cock?" Daegan's tone was flat, unexpressive.

"We do not often give a petitioner more than one choice." The warning was clear in Belizar's face. Daegan's expression did not change, as if such a threat meant little to him.

"Choose." Belizar's voice hardened, the Council head obviously picking up on it. "Or defy this Council. Lord Stephen, tell your servant to withdraw."

She'd been on her knees awhile, so it was instinctive courtesy that had Gideon helping Alanna to her feet, a hand beneath her elbow. She gripped his forearm necessarily, but let go immediately and didn't look at him. Backing up to the wall, she took her place behind her Master.

Anwyn's voice slid through his mind. *I don't exactly know what this means, but Daegan said, "Head or gut?"*

Despite all the feelings coiled like a noose around his throat and cock, chest and soul, that volley surprisingly loosened it. Somewhat. He felt like he was merely choking, instead of about to fall through a gallows door to have his neck snapped. He wasn't afraid of being flogged, but he knew enough about being hit with a bullwhip to know what thirty-six lashes could do. He didn't want to shame either one of them. When he felt the wrench in her heart at his thought, he lifted his head, met her gaze with a reassuring spark of fire in his own.

He's been watching Bruce Willis. The Last Boy Scout.

He's always been able to surprise me. A pause. *Gideon?*

I don't want him biting me. And I won't drink his blood. You know that.

He shifted, met Daegan's eyes. The vampire gave him a slight nod.

"Get on your knees, vampire hunter."

Up until that moment, Anwyn had been spiraling back into the alley, to places where all choices were yanked away, obliterated by blood and barbarity, where tenderness and love were cruel jokes, unbearable mockeries of the way the world really should be. Though the blood and brutality were not aimed at her, it was no different, when she felt charged with protecting Gideon. If anything, she knew it was worse, being forced to stand to the side and watch it be done to him, rather than experiencing it for herself.

She was a Mistress, yes. In fact, she'd considered herself quite a formidable Dominatrix, but in this world, she was coming straight from the kiddie pool to the deep end. For once the call of the shadow voices was desperately seductive, a way to escape this, but that in itself made her fight. She wouldn't run. She'd never again run from someone who needed her.

Then Daegan spoke that soft, velvet command, and suddenly the world righted itself. He took control back for all of them.

Gideon had lifted his head, his hair brushing the broad bare shoulders, the midnight blue eyes riveting in their intensity. When he looked toward Daegan, the charge of energy between the two male bodies brought a hush to the room.

It was then she saw clearly what Daegan had seen from the beginning with Gideon, what even the more perceptive of the Council had to see. No matter what barriers separated them, Daegan Rei and Gideon Green held the same warrior code, the same inviolate integrity and inner strength, no matter how battered Gideon's shields had become. It put every one of the vampires in this room to shame, to her way of thinking.

She had another revelation as well. One that was more private, but no less shocking. Somewhere along the way, Daegan's tracking of Gideon had turned into an active pursuit of the hunter. An emotional pursuit, beyond the call of lust. Whether it was admiration or kinship, or something else, Daegan desired him, wanted him as his servant as well. Not as a humiliation, like the Council might suspect, but because that was the closest bond a vampire could make with another. He wanted to be Gideon's Master as much as she wanted to be his Mistress, because for both of them, it was the deepest offer of body, heart and soul they had. She felt it like a current, connecting the two of them.

Even Gideon, whose emotions were always such a tangled jumble, such that he followed an erratic course of instinct and self-denial to jump from moment to moment, allowed desire and hunger, savage need, to cross his expression. For the both of them.

Anwyn.

She let her mind be a conduit, so that Daegan could hear Gideon's thoughts, linking the three of them. *Yes, love?*

It was the first time she'd ever used an endearment with Gideon, with anyone, and his mouth tightened. No one would know from the tough-guy expression what vulnerability existed in that powerhouse body.

I've never done this. Can you walk me through it, so I do it right?

Just do it the way you'd like it done to yourself, vampire hunter. Daegan's dark eyes sparked, and Gideon's cock jumped in reaction. Anwyn felt like she was standing between two flames.

You're going to need that big mouth of yours, because I intend to ram myself down your throat. Daegan's mind-voice made it a taunting challenge, so that Anwyn actually almost smiled. It was just the three of them. The rest didn't matter.

Big talk. But Gideon swallowed. He didn't quite seem to know where to go from there, but Anwyn reminded him. *Daegan ordered you onto your knees, love.*

Come to me, vampire hunter.

Daegan hadn't moved, waiting, which somehow made the moment more charged. Gideon hitched up his pants to allow him to walk, the loose hold making the waistline caress the appealing line of hip and buttock musculature as he moved around Torrence. He gave Helga's servant a menacing glance, which suggested if Torrence lifted so much as a finger to stop him, he'd lose the digit. But when Gideon passed behind Anwyn, she let her fingers trail along his side, pleased when his hand briefly gripped hers, caressing.

As he reached Daegan, Gideon stopped, hesitated.

Gaze down, Gideon. Don't look me in the eye.

That jaw flexed again, a quiver running through the powerful back. Daegan placed a hand on his shoulder, gripping lean sinew and bone, and exerted downward pressure. Anwyn found she wasn't the only one holding her breath as Gideon's knees bent, taking him down into a kneeling position. The pants slid lower, giving her the upper rise of his ass, and without being told, he pushed them all the way down, revealing the dildo still firmly in place.

A slight bow from Daegan toward Brian. "Lord Brian, would your servant mind removing that so it doesn't impede Miss Naime's efforts?"

Brian glanced up at Debra, gave her a nod. The woman moved from the wall, keeping her eyes down, but Anwyn noted her hands were gentle as she balanced on her heels in a squat and removed the dildo, wrapping it in a towel provided by one of the waitstaff and laying it by Anwyn's chair. Gideon had shuddered slightly at the removal, and Anwyn felt the way it stroked him inside, the arousal that was still there despite the rising tension. She'd also noticed how Debra had managed a stroke of the cheek with her fingertips. She was fairly certain it was a reassurance rather than a sexual indiscretion, and wished she could give Gideon a similar reassurance right now.

"Put your palms flat on your knees, Gideon," Daegan instructed, still in that silky tone. "You'll do it all with your mouth."

Anwyn started as a servant touched her arm. Turning, she saw Belizar's full servant, Lena, extending a coiled bullwhip. The size and thickness brought an instant denial surging to the forefront. Her lips parted.

"If you prefer to watch, we can allow Torrence to do the honors," Lady Carola said smoothly. "He's very skilled."

"As a Mistress, I expect Anwyn is a fair hand with a whip." Uthe met her gaze across the table. "Can you draw blood with a bullwhip? Be accurate enough to administer thirty-six lashes to a kneeling man's back and buttocks while he's servicing Lord Daegan? Draw blood every time?"

"And not hit Lord Daegan," Lord Welles added, a smile crossing his face that was anything but pleasant. "I'm sure he would not take kindly to that."

Since she still had not moved to take the whip, Belizar cocked his head. "Torrence was obviously looking forward to fucking your servant. I'm sure he'll reflect that in his accuracy and strength."

So it was a test of them both, making sure she didn't think she'd gotten away with any defiance on her part. Anwyn closed her hand on the whip. "I am more than capable, Lord Belizar. If the whip is properly formed and maintained."

"Feel free to test it, fledgling."

While Daegan waited, Gideon at his feet, his hand resting on her servant's shoulder to keep his head down, she rose. Meeting Daegan's gaze, she shook out the six-foot whip. Looking over the belly's taper, she tested the balance of the braided length, as well as the weight of the handle. It was well made, as Belizar had indicated. The west end of the dining room where she and Daegan had been sitting was open space, as if intended for performances, so she moved back the right number of steps to take a few practice swings. A straight overhand, a flick, a coachman and a volley helped familiarize herself further with the single tail, the energy the body of the whip delivered to the popper. It was similar to the many she'd used at the club. The amazing difference was that she could actually see the popper snap, something impossible for the human eye to follow, since the resounding crack of a bullwhip came from the fact its speed broke the sound barrier, when thrown properly.

When she noted Stephen watching her with a sardonic sneer to his lips, and heard his mutter to Barbra, "She's more likely to take out the Van Gogh on the opposite wall than stripe his back," she executed a graceful overhead. The whip snaked out and took out Stephen's wineglass, lifting it from the table and sending it spinning into the wall, well clear of the Van Gogh or any other artwork. The glass shattered, spreading wine over the stone like a bloodstain. Before anyone had time to react, the whip was back at her side.

"More than adequate, Lord Belizar," she said, with a cool smile, caressing the handle. "Thank you. My apologies, Lord Stephen. You seemed concerned about my servant's welfare, and I wanted to assure you of my expertise."

She could tell she'd successfully impressed the Council members with her unexpected maneuver, and the fact that Stephen hadn't been spattered with even a drop avoided any accusation of disrespect. Daegan gave her an inscrutable look, but she suspected he was applauding her effort. Gideon, his head still ostensibly bowed, had practically high-fived her in her head, which would have amused her under normal circumstances. Unfortunately, it didn't buffer what she was about to do to him with that lethal strap.

Serving staff quickly moved in to clean up the mess as she turned back to her two males. She could feel the anticipation building after her little performance. Seeing that bare back, already marked with her stripes, given reluctantly but in conjunction with pleasure, she felt torn between rage and her own despicable anticipation.

You know you like giving pain with pleasure, Mistress. Gideon's words from earlier.

Damning all of these monsters, including the one inside herself, she stepped forward, slid her arm around Gideon's chest. Bending so she could press her cheek to his, she let her hair fall to curtain them both. *They want me to make it hurt, to punish you. Can we refuse?*

No. It was simultaneous, from both Daegan and Gideon.

She closed her eyes. *I hate this. This isn't what it's about, Gideon. Not what it's supposed to be.*

His hand came up, gripped her wrist. *Then make it what it's supposed to be. I don't fear any pain at your hands, Anwyn. A weird part of me . . . Well, you already know, right?*

She nodded, gave him an additional squeeze, and then paced back, locking gazes with Daegan. The vampire didn't have to do this, didn't want to do this any more than she did. She knew that with a clarity that made it hard to breathe. He was doing this for her, to ensure she was accepted by this world, and so Gideon's life wasn't taken. Over the past month, for the past five years, he'd been part of her life, the best and the worst, and he'd refused to give up on her or the love he wanted from her.

She didn't know what foolishness had ever made her doubt his love for her, just because he wouldn't say the words. On that same note, she knew she'd never doubt Gideon's love for her, either. No matter he hadn't quite sorted out his feelings, he was trusting her implicitly, the most important step toward unconditional love. When the day came that he couldn't be part of this world, she'd accept and know it wasn't because his love for her wasn't great enough. Some scars in a man's heart could never heal, no matter how much he, or she, wished they could.

Tying it all together, Daegan spoke in her mind. *You can do this, cher. All three of us can. Just breathe, and know that we love you.*

Gideon gave a faint nod, though he kept his gaze on the floor. His broad shoulders rose and fell, slow breaths. He was preparing himself. That slight acknowledgment was a simple declaration, a reassurance that undermined the foundation of this horrible moment.

They were different from everyone else here. She wanted to give both of them what they gave her. She was done setting conditions of her own, except the conditions Gideon needed from her as Mistress, and those that she and Daegan embraced for that glorious push-pull relationship they had. It was a miracle, all three sides of their trinity. Even if it couldn't be forever, it didn't make it less miraculous, less valuable.

Meeting Daegan's gaze once more, she saw his burning response to her thoughts and nodded. *Let's do this.*

Daegan had worn a jacket, slacks and a silk shirt, so now he shrugged out of the coat, putting it into the ready hands of a waitstaff person. He unbuttoned his shirt in a carelessly sensual way, then opened his trousers. He kept them on his waist, of course, so the Council was not granted the vulnerable look at his bare ass they'd require of a servant. When he freed his cock, Anwyn let herself indulge the moment, the pleasure of watching it stretch out long and hard toward Gideon's taut mouth, and know no other lusting mind at this table had the right to touch it, tease it, the way she did . . . and had so often.

Don't distract me, cher. Daegan's warning made her want to smile. Mostly because she knew it might be a while before she'd feel like smiling again.

"Take me deep," Daegan murmured, moving his hand to Gideon's hair. Sliding his fingers through the clean, thick strands, he cupped the back of the man's skull. Anwyn was in Gideon's mind when he tasted the first salty flavor of the broad head, let it move between his parted lips. Then Daegan pushed all the way in, a rough, urgent move, as if he didn't care to hold back his desire anymore. At that moment, Anwyn landed the first strike.

～

She'd had the occasional client who wanted his flesh split open. Even at her club, they limited that to three strikes. She'd had only one who made it to that number. The reality of it was far different from the imagining. It could require stitches, leave permanent scars. She didn't encourage it. She wanted her club to be a haven for those who used pain as an avenue to a complete bonding between Dominant and submissive, not to feed a destructive pain addiction.

The heart rate accelerated under extreme pain, and adrenaline kicked in. When the pain grew too intense, and there was no safe word, as now, the mind would go into fight or flight mode. There would be struggling panic, or rage. She expected at least the latter from Gideon, which made it more impressive to see him hold his position. The Council was visibly amazed that she hadn't chosen to bind him, because staying still would be almost impossible as the pain got worse. She knew Daegan would help with that, though.

The third mark helped Gideon's resilience considerably, but she knew beyond all of that, it was his heartbreaking stubbornness that kept his body jerking but his knees still. A slight noise came from the back of his throat on strike eight. Daegan pushed him deep onto him, and Gideon bucked, this time for another reason.

Swallow, love. Concentrate on relaxing your throat. He's a lot to take at once. Relax the muscles in the back. Let your saliva gather to lubricate him. Suck your cheeks in as he pulls out and pushes in. The suction increases the pleasure. And use your tongue. Then she struck again, the whip leaving a red, angry stripe across the broad back, the shoulders that had borne so much.

Gideon knew what a cock felt like, knew that sense of steel under liquid silk of a blood-filled erection. The way the tip would pearl with pre-come, indicated by the musky taste on his tongue now. Daegan had large balls, of course. At another time, when he didn't feel like a flamethrower was being used on his back, he would have been tempted to cup and squeeze them. The random thought would have horrified him, but for the overwhelming pain which kept him from embarrassing himself in such a crazy way. That, and Daegan's order to keep his palms on his knees, which gave Anwyn a clear strike field.

On the eleventh strike, it started to get crazy. Crazier, really. Pain, rebellion, pleasure, need. It all started to roll together, like a snowball, though this one had jagged glass that stuck out like people's feet and hands in the cartoons when they rolled down a hill.

Perversely, though, the pain helped. It wiped everything out of his mind. What he was doing to another male, what the Council was watching and would decide to do next, any worry about this being too much for Anwyn, possibly triggering another attack.

The Council had done them all a favor, bringing the mind-wiping pain into it for him. They were linked together in one focus. Anwyn kept up that quiet murmur of encouragement, reassurance, even as Daegan flavored it with the sexy male commands to suck him harder. *Fuck, your mouth feels good, vampire hunter.*

How he could be getting harder during this was one of those fucking twisted vampire-servant things. He groaned, a half scream, as the next strike landed and fire erupted anew. Holy Christ, it hurt. It hurt like all the lonely moments when he'd crouched in dark places, soaked to the ankles in blood. It hurt like it did when the adrenaline drained away, leaving him standing over a body to be burned, an area to be cleaned up. It hurt like all the hard, dirty mattresses he'd slept on alone.

Thwack.

He didn't know where the emotional shit was coming from, so he sucked harder, focused on the physical, because that was damned baffling and amazing at once. His mindless cock was straining. Was his lust simple, bestial reaction to doing something that most males enjoyed so much themselves? Or was it deeper than that? Was he actually getting stiff from doing this to Daegan? Being on his knees, taking the vampire's cock, tasting him, giving him pleasure, making him shudder as he handled him as roughly as he'd want it done to himself? Slickly sliding up and down, teasing him with a tongue that seemed to have a mind and direction of its own, flicking at the vein beneath the broad head, then down, following that thick ridge, sucking hard on the whole thing like a favorite damn treat.

And he was doing it while experiencing some of the worst pain he'd ever felt. Fuck, he was having to imagine his knees nailed into the ground to keep from bolting. His whole body was shaking, and his gut was turning over.

Thwack. Thwack. Thwack.

He strangled on the cry, unable to stop himself. The blood was running down his back, over the dried blood from earlier. The pain and irritation were beyond description, just a white inferno. His hands clenched on his thighs. Holy Christ. What number were they on?

Let go, love. Just let it go. It doesn't matter.

He locked the Council out of his mind. He deserved suffering, but the pain of this lash could make him free. It would creep into his battered heart and soul, make him let go, take him to a place where he'd just feel what Daegan and Anwyn were doing to him forever. But oh, how it hurt. There was nothing but them, but it was all pain, and pleasure, never one without the other.

Daegan reached down then, gripped Gideon's fists and lifted them so Gideon's hands were clasped over Daegan's hips, digging into him with hard fingers, an anchor. Daegan kept his hands manacled on Gideon's wrists, so when the next lash landed, and Gideon reflexively jerked back, he was held fast, Daegan making him a prisoner. It just made him hotter, harder.

He was still pumping him with his mouth, but he was in full, hellfire agony, and didn't know how much longer he could keep it up. *Thwack. Thwack.* She was striping over existing wounds now. He didn't want to scream, would bite down on his tongue if Daegan's cock wasn't there, and fortunately for the vampire he had enough of a brain not to do that. He dug his fingers hard into his thigh muscles, bruising. He wouldn't scream, not in front of those assholes, whatever they were thinking.

You scream if you must, Gideon. Anwyn's sensual tone, her Mistress's voice. *You are ours, and this is what we desire. You are serving us, giving us pleasure with your pain.*

He realized he'd divided his focus solely between Dagean's cock and Anwyn's lashing. Perhaps because of the weird contrast to what was happening, he was drawing peace from the familiar smell of Daegan's clothes, the cologne he'd used tonight. Muscular buttocks flexed just beyond the range of his fingertips as Daegan fucked his mouth.

I should have shoved my dick in here a long time ago, vampire hunter. I just never realized how effective it would be for shutting you up and getting you to focus on more important things.

Gideon managed to clumsily score him with his teeth, hard enough to earn a grunt. Daegan's hand shifted to give his hair a sharp, warning tug, but he thought he heard the vampire's feral chuckle, and a muttered, "Careful. Payback is hell."

It was going to be okay. Daegan was ragging his ass. He was going to survive this. He was. A clear image arrived in his brain, compliments of Anwyn. Gideon, stretched out and tied on a rough wooden wheel like a medieval torture device, turned upside down so Daegan could close his mouth over him without the subservience of being on his knees. It made Gideon still the slave, Daegan tormenting him, holding him helpless and upside down, sucking and sucking until he was so close to coming . . .

Thwack. The wet meat of loosened skin slapped against open wounds.

He did scream this time, and the pulsation against Daegan's cock made the organ jump. Daegan's hand convulsed as well. *That's it. Scream, vampire hunter. Vibrate against my cock, so I can shoot come down your throat. That is what a servant does. Serves his Master and Mistress's will, no matter what he is enduring.*

Gideon thought he might black out or vomit, but he did neither. Drawing on the determination that had gotten him through a couple decades of hell, he pushed past the pain, heard the voices of Anwyn and Daegan's encouragement in his mind as he worked himself up and down that organ, pushing back into the lash. Somewhere along the way, screams turned into animal growls, snarls of rage, defiance and rutting pleasure. He became all beast, red-eyed and ready to kill, to fuck, to do anything but break.

Daegan's grip on his wrists was iron, while Anwyn decorated him with a crisscrossing of stripes on his ass and back that dripped blood onto his thighs, running down inside his pants.

Come for me, you bastard. Give me every drop.

You do not order me to do anything, Gideon. Tell me what you want.

I want you to come. But I'm not begging for it.

One day, you will.

With a matching growl, Daegan released, holding Gideon's hair in a hard grip to shove himself to the back of his throat, shooting hot seed there as Anwyn landed the last five strokes in hot, hard, bloody succession. Gideon howled, even as he furiously worked to keep Daegan's jetting come going down his throat. He was dying, except he knew no one ever seemed to die of agonizing pain. Another of God's constant stream of ironies.

You're done, Gideon. You did it.

Exhausted satisfaction swept in among the wreckage. He'd done it. He'd given them both what they wanted, hadn't failed. Was a part of them.

No, that didn't make any sense. Fuzzily he recalled this had been a test for the Council, not something he was doing for Daegan and Anwyn.

It doesn't matter. It's all the same. And you never fail us, love. Never.

Daegan was slowly withdrawing, and Gideon couldn't help himself. He cleaned it as it left his mouth, nuzzling it, giving it a sharp bite that won another of those sexy warning noises. He tried for a sneer to tell the vamp what he could do with his warnings, but he couldn't seem to find the energy to curl up the corners of his lips. He should have been falling down. Instead, embarrassingly enough, he was leaning into Daegan, his head against his hip. Crazy world that it was, Daegan stroked his hair, that manly tousle, sensual affection. He hadn't failed.

You've never failed, Gideon. Daegan shifted, and Anwyn took his place, letting him lean into her soft abdomen, his head below her breasts. Perfect. The male musk and enticing hardness of Daegan replaced by female perfume and soft flesh. The best of both worlds, as long as both worlds were named Daegan and Anwyn. God, his brain was turning into a sentimental mush. He'd never hurt so much in his life.

Then he felt two things. The first was Daegan, behind him now. At the first touch of the male vamp's lips, he shuddered, somehow wondering if he should object. He'd said he didn't want Daegan marking him, drinking from him, but this was different, right? His tongue sliding along those welts, gathering the blood, licking it away, soothing, using the blood-clotting agents in his tongue. Anwyn brought her wrist under his nose and Gideon smelled that rich burgundy of her blood, a vein opened for him.

Drink, Gideon. It will take away the pain, and you'll heal more quickly.

She pressed it to his mouth, and it was easier not to resist, to simply seal his mouth over it and drink. It tasted so much different than he'd expected blood to taste. It tasted like her, the best chocolate and whipped-cream dessert, flavored with exotic female sex.

Daegan's sensual firm mouth, following each welt, tasting his blood, made him tremble with pain and desire at once. God, he was hard as nails. If anyone touched him right now, he'd go off like a geyser, despite the fact he hurt like he'd been hit by a truck. Jesus. Those third marks were something else. He should be half-dead, or all the way dead, not even thinking of his cock. Instead, he wanted to plow into Anwyn's sweet, slick cunt, feel her arms wrap around him. He'd maybe even be okay with Daegan there. Gideon could sink between her legs, and then maybe Daegan would guide himself into Gideon, so they were locked together and Gideon was between them, full and complete, the center of everything they needed. Like the weapons room, except maybe he wouldn't fight so much this time. See where surrender took him.

But that was just more pain-crazed talk, wasn't it? He'd lost his mind. It floated away from him like a child's balloon on the wind. He lay down and watched it drift ever higher, until he couldn't see it anymore.

～

Daegan rose at length, his slacks refastened and belt buckled. Gideon was slumped against Anwyn, unconscious, his arms still wrapped around her waist and hips, his large body partly leaning against Daegan's leg now. Putting his hand on Gideon's shoulder, Daegan experienced a tender and dangerous protectiveness toward the man that he'd felt only toward one other, and he was clasping her shoulder with his other hand, a united front.

He'd done many things in his life, experienced horrors and wonders great and small, but he wasn't sure he'd ever felt such an explosive mix of emotion as he carried within him now. Putting a mask over it was perhaps one of the hardest things he'd ever done, but he did it.

"Did that prove what you needed proving, Lord Belizar?" He hoped his tone accurately conveyed that if it wasn't, the Russian wouldn't be keeping all of his appendages.

Belizar leaned back in his chair, looking sated with the aftermath. In fact, there was a fairly weighted silence in the room. The servant Alanna looked stunned and pale. Drained in some odd way.

"Indeed," Lord Belizar murmured. "I think you and the fledgling have provided us a more intense entertainment than we have experienced in some time. Far more emotional than I expected between ones with such a short history together."

Daegan knew it wasn't always the amount of time that formed bonds, but the circumstances. He inclined his head, though. "Then, if that is all, I will take them back to our quarters to recuperate. I expect to take my leave tomorrow night, unless there are other matters to address."

"You expect?" Lady Barbra rallied enough to send him a sharp look. "You may request to be excused, Lord Daegan, but you never presume to expect anything of us."

"I believe I was addressing Lord Belizar," Daegan said shortly, making it clear how much authority he gave her. While he hadn't held much doubt, the moment he'd met their gazes, he'd known Stephen and Barbra had been responsible for Barnabus. Like Gideon, he understood that meant they were responsible for Anwyn as well. For that alone, they'd earned a death sentence, and as soon as he could figure out how to administer it so it didn't endanger Anwyn and Gideon, he'd carry it out.

"Though I do concur with Lady Barbra's admonishment," Belizar said, in a reassuringly mild tone, "I will allow for the fact that, if you have amazed and depleted us, you have likely depleted your limited diplomacy skills as well. Go to your quarters, Lord Daegan. I will send word as to the Council's pleasure regarding you and your charges before dawn."

16

WHEN Gideon surfaced, it was to a gentle hand on his brow and cool cloths on his back and buttocks. He was facedown on a bed and bare-assed naked. When he tested movement, he found he could move far more easily than he expected. Reaching back, he found one of the deeper stripes along his rib cage was already a pink strip of healed skin.

"The blessing and curse of being a third-marked servant. They can beat the hell out of you, torture you all they want, and after a day or two, they could do it all over again, your skin completely unmarked."

"Not entirely," he murmured, finding her hand, whispering over her stroking fingers. "My Mistress gave me some permanent ones. You did good, Anwyn. They're the jerks, not you."

She paused, adjusting the packs on his back, though he thought the whisper of her fingers felt even better over his flanks than the ice.

"Let me amend that," she said. "You'll be fine in a day except for your brain damage. That's inoperable because no surgical saw is strong enough to cut through your thick skull."

"Nice." Gideon cracked his eyes open at last to see her lovely face. "Hi there."

Her eyes crinkled, though he saw the strain around her mouth, in the blue-green depths. "Hey yourself. I can probably remove the towels if you want to sit up." She stroked his brow again. "Gideon, I'm so sorry."

"Not your doing, Mistress. I'm just grateful you remembered you have a vampire's strength before you started swinging that thing, else you might have had to reassemble my ribs like bowling pins." With a cautious groan, he pushed himself up, giving Anwyn time to move the packs. Except for an initial moment of light-headedness, he was remarkably himself. "Wow. I feel like a superhero. How did I get here?" He gave her a sidelong glance. "Please don't tell me that you carried me. Flesh-ripping pain I can handle; being carried by a girl will require ritual suicide."

"Worse than that. Daegan did." She gave him a mock grimace. "And though you weren't carried by a girl, you were carried like a girl. He cradled you in his arms as gently as a mother. It was very touching. And impressive, considering how big you are."

"Christ. Tell him next time to just drag me by one boot heel."

"Letting your head thump, thump, thump down the stairs?"

"Well, you said that couldn't hurt anything, right?"

Anwyn put a hand on the side of his face, her gaze sobering. "I *am* sorry."

"Sorry for having to do it, or sorry for the fact you kind of enjoyed it?" He kept his gaze level with hers, no condemnation in the simple truth. She cocked her head, stroking her knuckles through the hair at his temples, teasing the light scattering of silver strands, and passed her thumb over his lips.

"I was immersed in your thoughts there at the end," she murmured. "Though I've always known the relationship between pain and surrender, pleasure and release, there is something about what I am now that has made testing those boundaries that much keener. I felt how you let go to me, and to Daegan, and for a moment, despite how horrible it all was, it was . . ."

"Perfect." He finished it for her, lifted a shoulder. "Whatever it is that you have in you, combined with what was before, found an answer somewhere inside me. Don't know how to deal with it, how to talk about it. Hell, really don't want to talk about it. Would rather just leave it there, you know. It happened, and that's that."

He was right. On the surface, the horror of it should have sent her straight into a seizure, watching his flesh slice open at her hand, the blood running down his back. Yet somehow, somewhere along the way, she'd let go of that as well, her consciousness and Daegan's twining around the chaos of Gideon's pain-wracked brain. A thought had come to the top of that spiral, from her servant's mind. Something his brother, Jacob, had apparently said. *The true meaning of utter trust and surrender, Gideon. Being stripped so bare that a Mistress could walk the avenue straight into the darkest room of a man's heart, and he would want her there. Need her there.*

"It happened, and that's that." He'd repeated it. She knew it was far more complex than that, yet she found his way of summarizing it uniquely him, and therefore appropriate.

"You've never been very verbal." She watched him lace their fingers together, bring her knuckles to his lips.

"No, I'm not. Mistress."

It flickered in her heart like a warmed flame, made her fingers tighten on his. His lashes fell against the proud cheekbones as he pressed his mouth harder to her flesh, holding it there.

"Well," she said, somewhat unsteadily, "I've had one good thought, sitting here with you. As long as the two of us are connected to a super-secret agent like Daegan, it's not likely we'll often be required to be part of the vampire social scene."

"Supersecret agent." He gave a muffled snort against her hand. "I guess there might be one perk to hanging around with the arrogant bastard. Now all we have to do is get out of here alive to enjoy it."

"True enough." She spent several more precious moments stroking his face, the line of his shoulder; then he lifted his head.

"I seem to be wearing nothing, so maybe I should put some clothes on. If you have no objections."

"I have plenty, but given the circumstances, I'm going to wait until we're home to start imposing the no-clothing-except-when-I-allow it rule."

He couldn't tell if she was serious, God help him. He decided to leave that alone as well and rose to go to the closet. "Where's Daegan?"

"One of the Council servants came and got him about two hours ago. You've been out awhile. I'm not sure what it was about. He told me not to worry, that no matter what, we leave here when he gets back." She nodded toward her laptop, open on a desk. "I've been working on some billing issues and logging messages to James and Madelyn, though I have to go up top for them to go through. For some reason, stone walls don't lend themselves to good Wi-Fi reception." She attempted a grim smile. "I really do need to get back. We have an annual VIP reunion coming up, and it's always our busiest weekend. I need to be there."

At his look, she lifted a shoulder. "Insane, isn't it? Daily life goes on despite this kind of thing."

He grunted, a noncommittal acknowledgment. But when she rubbed her arms, he saw an ink mark and gestured. "Did you get yourself with a pen?"

She glanced down at it. "No. I was asked to accompany Lord Brian to his lab so he could take some tests. This was a needle marker."

"Ah, hell. It was because of what Vincent saw, wasn't it?"

She nodded. "Daegan said I shouldn't be concerned about it. But then, he says that about everything, doesn't he?"

Gideon gave a gruff snort at that, and she managed a half smile. "I don't know what will come of it, but at least it wasn't that difficult. It was actually pleasant to see him again. It was private there, so we didn't have to pretend we'd never met."

Though Anwyn wouldn't say the conversation had been entirely comfortable.

~

Still shaken from the dinner, Anwyn had gratefully received the injection Brian had prepared for her, which he said also included a vampire version of a sedative.

"I can tell you need it," he said gently when she at first balked. "It has no sluggish side effects. It won't dull your wits. I know Gideon is still unconscious, because you get a particularly strained look to your face when you're having to manage the gremlins by yourself."

"After that dinner, how can you tell the difference between that and your standard nervous breakdown?" She gave a harsh chuckle. "Daegan can help, but they're intimidated by his presence in my head. They cower, but they're sullen and angry about it, testing. With Gideon, they calm, lie down like birds in the grass. I haven't quite figured out why."

"It's likely a mixing of their psychology with yours. When you're agitated, Gideon calms you because he is your servant, not a threat to your dominance."

Her lips twisted. "Early on, Daegan said something similar. He always has to be right."

"Well, he's about seven hundred years old, I believe. There's a theory, not entirely proven, that there's a connection between time and the accumulation of wisdom."

She slanted him an amused glance. "Did you know that Gideon went out and found me a stuffed toy from that old movie *Gremlins*?" She'd put it on her night table. Sometimes, when he got up to get a shower or otherwise had to leave her, she'd wake to find he'd placed the plush creature in her arms, like a protective totem.

"It doesn't surprise me." He sat down on a stool, his slacks pulling attractively at a length of thigh as he braced a hand on it and leaned forward, studying the slide of her blood. He'd also taken some saliva and a skin swab. His forehead creased, but the firm line of his mouth was approval.

"Good. The serum is helping, isn't it?"

"Yes, it has been. You're right—it's only extreme stress that knocks it off-kilter. And Daegan and Gideon both think I need to figure out ways to release stress, rather than trying to block it."

"Wise idea. But I'll keep working with the injection serums to see if I can't help with it as well."

For the first time, Anwyn was calm enough to notice something amiss. "Where's Debra?"

"In the hallway." Brian straightened, made a few notes on a small laptop at his elbow. "With vampire hearing being so acute, I wanted to ensure you could speak freely. She'll warn us if there's anyone lurking about."

"Hmm." Anwyn studied him. "I'm surprised you had this injection ready."

He shrugged. "I told you I'd keep working on it, refining it. It's unfortunate that you had a seizure here, but it may become a blessing. Vampire events like these will be far less stressful if you don't have to worry about concealing your seizures to protect yourself. In my report, I intend to suggest, with a great deal of truth, that your unique situation could hold answers to other medical challenges we face." He gave her a direct look. "My opinion does not carry much weight on many things, but it does on the science. It may make them far more tolerant of your existence, and once you're out of sight, safely under Daegan's care, you'll be mostly forgotten as they pursue higher-priority objectives."

She drew deep breaths as she felt the injection work with those rattled nerves, the snarling whispers in her head. Brian's warmth and reassurance were a godsend, but also puzzling. She wasn't the cynic that Gideon or Daegan could be, but Brian was an ambitious, eighty-year-old vampire. And she was too protective of Gideon and Daegan to keep from asking.

"You've helped us so much, so please don't be offended, but I can't imagine your favor to Lyssa extends to you risking your backing by the Council."

"You'd be surprised," Brian said dryly. "Plus, the favor is a two-way street. There's no harm in having the friendship of the Queen of the Far East Clan and her mate. Or that of a vampire assassin." He gave her a look that came the closest she'd seen to mischief, somber in tone though it was. "The second-most powerful vampire, Lord Mason, also owes me a significant favor. Having that triumvirate—Daegan, Lyssa and Mason—interested in my well-being can only be a good thing, if my work here runs afoul of the Council. I do support their governance, but I'm not blind to their weaknesses, or how they could hurt my species."

At her look, Brian inclined his head. "Many scientists will lie to you, Anwyn. Tell you that science isn't political. The truth is that vampires and humans both are intensely political by nature. Politics is the concern with the balance of power, and there is no living creature that can claim exemption from that, because those interactions and relationships are how we survive. Much of science, ironically, has been about denying our connection to Nature and how important it is to stay balanced with it, but I won't block myself from any possibilities. That's because I have one objective. To help my species survive."

She'd been told that eighty years was young to vampires, but seeing the sudden intensity in Brian's gaze, she thought that he might be maturing at an accelerated rate. With his intriguing mix of distracted professor and Machiavellian awareness of his actions and the actions of those around him, she suspected far more tangled issues than medical cures were being worked upon in Brian's agile brain. Because he was a vampire, she knew that could be highly amoral ground. He would bear watching. At the moment, he was a friend, but she was a close observer herself, and the way Daegan interacted with all vampires, even one like Brian, whom he claimed to trust, told her there was an unpredictability to them that shouldn't be underestimated.

It was as if the entire world she inhabited had become like her most volatile dungeon sessions, where the senses had to be on high alert, always ready for anything.

"There are so few of us, Anwyn," Brian continued, more quietly. "While it may not seem that way, that's because you're part of our world now. We're cloistered together because we're so interdependent. But at last count, there are no more than five thousand vampires in the world. That is why, as feudal and barbaric as it may seem, the Council built the Region and overlord system to keep everyone working closely together, something not entirely easy for those of a predatory nature. We're more like cheetahs, who hunt and live alone, than wolf packs. Lady Lyssa had a remarkable, chilling ability to understand what structure would ensure our survival and progress. She allowed room for both compassion and cruelty, the art of war as well as the art of velvet-over-steel diplomacy.

"To keep my eye on that ball, I must stay clear of the politics. Which, ironically, means I must stay very cognizant of where all the interweaving threads are. It's like negotiating a laser beam security system around a large diamond."

"So it's like that adage, isn't it? The best person to lead is the one who doesn't want to be the leader." She gave him the teasing prod without a smile, but he shook his head.

"A true leader does want to lead, because he or she believes the goal is important. The more appropriate adage is that a person takes a leadership role, not because he or she wants to be important, but because the job itself is important."

She sighed, put her head down into her hands, drew another deep, shuddering breath. "I don't think I've ever done anything that horrible . . . or astounding, in all my life. And Gideon . . . I don't know what to say to him. I'm learning how to be a Mistress in this world, and though Daegan said I'm uniquely suited to it, this is different."

"Hmm." Brian cut and transferred several lines of powder into a waiting beaker. "You know, I remember having a conversation with

Gideon one of the times you were unconscious, after a seizure. I told him I wasn't concerned about how he would handle helping you within the boundaries of your apartment. I was worried how he would handle the vampire world. He told me, in that charmingly brusque manner of his, that you'd get another servant for that. That he was just here to patch you through your transition." Brian gave her a sidelong glance. "He also informed me he didn't give a shit about my rule spouting on 'letting a servant go.' He said that Daegan, or I, or even one of the Council, could kill him—or try—but no one was locking him into anything. Do you know what I found interesting about that?"

"What?" She felt the dull pain she always did at that side of Gideon, that stubborn wall he refused to break down. She could get around it in myriad ways to the soul beyond it, but it was always temporary, and the wall held firm, no obvious door or window through it.

"I found it very interesting that he didn't say anything about what would happen if *you* wanted to lock him into it."

She lifted her head, met Brian's eyes. "You think I'd force him to that?"

"I think it would be easier for him to do what he truly wants if you did. I think he will spend the next three hundred years with you, Anwyn, always claiming he'll only hang around 'as long as you need him.' A caught bird who just needs the illusion of the open door."

"That may be true," she said. "But if he does that, he'll never know the pleasure and happiness of true surrender. He'll never get past his wounds and heal." She pressed her lips together. "And, selfishly, I'm not that kind of Mistress. I won't be able to tolerate him standing, straddling a threshold, for much longer. I've never wanted a male to surrender to me the way I want him to do it. He'll do it in temporary fits and starts, but it's not the same as him stepping all the way across. We both know it.

"My need for his total surrender may be the vampire blood, or the way I've always been, just waiting for the right guy. In that case, his timing sucks or is a great coincidence." A tight smile touched her lips. "Regardless, soon I'll want all or nothing, and I think he knows that. We had one night, one session, before this all happened. He's seen the Mistress in me come forward in various ways since then, but his responses have been buffered by a different perception."

"He rationalizes his responses as helping you cope, rescuing the damsel, not truly surrendering as your servant."

She cocked a brow at him. "You're a little scary, you know that?"

When Brian had been staying with her, she'd occasionally been able to surprise a rare smile out of him, one that was uncalculated and genuine. He was attractive, as all vampires were, but the curving of his lips emphasized his unique, handsome appeal, and gave her a glimpse of the younger, less regimented side of Brian. One that she saw sometimes in his interactions with his servant and probably explained why Debra was more attached to him than the girl thought was wise for her heart. Brian wasn't the only observant one.

His usual serious mien settled back in place. "Your ultimatum, whenever you feel it's appropriate to deliver it, may be what he needs. That's more your area of expertise than his. However, as far as your discomfort with what occurred tonight, I can tell you that whenever it involves your well-being, there is nothing he will not do for you.

"During our month together, he did a wide variety of things I never expected to see a hard-core vampire hunter do, particularly this man. I admit it was all I could do to keep my eyes from bugging out of my head when I saw him behind your chair tonight. Then there were the things he did to keep you from despairing when I was treating you. Your seizures, the aftermath—you only truly tolerate Gideon's or Daegan's hands upon you. No matter how gentle I tried to be, you'd become so violent at my touch we had to abandon that in favor of getting you restrained as quickly as possible."

"The problem isn't what he'll do for me. It's what he'll give himself."

Brian nodded. "That's my hypothesis as well. Though I'll leave the testing to you." Giving her a sedate wink, he made another note on his laptop. "Given the fact you already knew all this, why does tonight disturb you so much?"

"I hope that's a clinical question, because I would think that's obvious," she responded dryly. "Yes, he's been everything I need right now. But he's my third-marked servant. I can read everything in his mind, down to his soul. Gideon never wanted to be any vampire's servant. There's far too much water under that bridge. How many vampires has he killed? How much carnage has he seen of those who take their full quota or exceed it? Or even one innocent, annual kill he was too late to save? I think he loves me," she admitted, aware of Brian lifting his brows. "Or rather, he loves Anwyn, the residual human woman that lies within this new form. But he can't accept the rest."

"Do you think he has a choice?"

"As long as I say he does." She gave a tight smile. "That's the vampire talking, right? I may give up every other aspect of my humanity, but that was the core of who I was, Brian. Everything I did in those rooms as a Mistress, I knew was consensual. It was what the man who submitted to my touch wanted, even if he couldn't bring himself to say it. I knew that with Gideon, too, the night he came to me. Now I truly have full access to his mind, and I don't have to be guided by instinct alone; I can't fool myself about what he is or isn't. If I give him that ultimatum, and I will, he'll walk." A tight smile crossed her face. "No matter what rules you or Daegan 'spouts' about allowing a servant to walk away, I'll let him. And have to hope he'll come back."

"Hmm." Lord Brian sat back, crossed his legs. He pushed the laptop aside, instead picking up a steno pad to jot some handwritten notes. Anwyn had noticed that Debra kept a healthy stack of them, because the scientist's mind was constantly figuring some random problem, the way someone else might do crossword puzzles as they multitasked. He seemed to prefer an organic connection with paper and pencil.

"Did you know one of the most difficult variables in scientific inquiry is subjectivity?" he asked, sketching something out that looked like a chemical formula. "Many scientists consider it a plague they go out of their way to avoid, such that they actually incorporate it unconsciously. For instance, the fear of anthropomorphizing animal behavior out of sentiment means we often dismiss out of hand the ways species are obviously similar to us in how they feel pain, express emotions and needs, leading to horrific cruelty. When they do things like that, scientists ignore a basic truth. That all life is connected, and there *are* similar motivations between many species. Including vampires and humans.

"Your fear of becoming something that takes choices away from him can cloud your judgment. Yes, he wants nothing to do with our world. No, he may not be suitable servant material. But that's only one side of the scale. If his love for you exceeds his aversion of our world, if his ability to accept our world is greater than his ability to give you up, then that changes things for him. I was there in that room tonight. I know you felt what the Council required was horrible. But I also saw a chance for a knight to prove his worthiness to his chosen lady . . . and lord"—his gaze flicked up, quick and intense—"and as such, he embraced it, lost himself in it. That's the sign of a true servant, some of the best ones I've met. Including his brother."

Anwyn had felt it, seen it, as well, but he was right. She was so afraid of what she was becoming, she couldn't fully accept it as truth. But hearing it from Brian, she knew he was right.

"If he did love you enough to truly become your full servant, despite what you feel inside of him, his feelings toward our world . . ."

She bit her lip. "No matter his love, I'd know I was destroying his soul a little bit every day."

"But perhaps his love will protect his soul. Perhaps you would need to trust that. Perhaps you would have to believe in his choice, accept his gift."

"Ignore what's in his mind."

"Accept that humans are more than what they seem, at face or thought value." Lord Brian shrugged. "Think of behaviors you may have, entirely at odds with what you believe about yourself. Humans only use a small percentage of their brains, and we don't use much more. That means a great deal of it is uncharted territory, and I expect much of that has to do with the true needs of the soul, which they spend a great deal of time denying. One of the things pleasant about vampires is that there are many things we don't deny ourselves. We accept what is rightfully intended to be ours."

"That's incredibly egotistical."

"Yet it's incredibly straightforward. We don't waste a lot of time agonizing. And it's amazing how often it works out exactly as it should." He gave her an absent smile, still looking down at the pad. "I know you're making faces at me."

"Can't prove it."

He chuckled. "You obviously had siblings."

"Yes. I did."

He lifted his gaze, met hers. After a moment, he gave her a nod. "I'm sorry for your loss, however it happened. It doesn't change the fact that our lives don't always go the way *we* intended. But sometimes the path we end up following was meant to be. Human obsession with sacrifice can be a not-so-good thing sometimes. Desires also have the ability to be God's road map to show us which direction to go."

At her ironic and curious look, he lifted a shoulder. "The best scientists firmly believe in a Divine Principle. There's entirely too much order and well-timed chaos in this universe to be otherwise."

Anwyn cocked her head. "Did that balanced perspective come from your human mother, your vampire father, or neither?"

He looked momentarily surprised at the intimate question, but before she could think she'd offended him, he gave her a light smile. Fishing a pewter disk out of his pocket, he handed it over.

The etching was small, words circling around a tiny heart. *Death's wisdom is finding, at the end, that you think only of those you loved, and why you didn't love them more. Love is the only true force that endures.*

"When I turned twenty, she gave me that. I think she was trying to tell me something, more about servants than vampires. We are not a sentimental species, and my blood is more aligned with my father's than hers. But it is an unwise scientist who discounts wisdom when he hears it, merely because he doesn't yet fully understand or see it manifested in his life. Don't close yourself off to that."

When she returned the disk to him, he rose. In a blink, his manner changed, transforming from thought-provoking companion to the vampire who had seniority over her. The tone of his voice now reminded her of the pecking order of vampires, and what they could demand from those weaker than themselves.

"All that said, don't ever forget that trying to turn away from your fated path can have some extremely unpleasant consequences, especially in the vampire world. If you believe you are facing two evils, be sure you are choosing the lesser of the two. For both of your sakes."

Gideon had pulled on jeans and threaded in a belt. He was buckling it, watching her. She'd turned her back to him, presumably to study something on the computer, but he sensed it was more than that. He saw flashes of the conversation she'd had with Brian, but she was putting some effort into screening it, so he respected that, choosing a different tactic.

"Did Brian have any preliminary findings?"

"The serum's working as well as to be expected. He's still working on strengthening it for stressors. He said he'd give Belizar a truthful assessment of my current status, so I don't know what will come of it." As she propped her chin in her hand, a wave of sable hair spilled down her right shoulder, but it couldn't mask the strain in her face. "Daegan said not to worry, so I've decided I won't. There. Easy as that. I've never wanted to be home more in my entire life."

Sliding his hip onto her desk, he bent to press his forehead to hers. She allowed it, closing her eyes, and he cupped the back of her skull, holding there a soothing moment. "You're a remarkable woman, Anwyn," he murmured. "Do you know how fucking amazing you've been through all of this? I've seen battle-hardened warriors who couldn't handle what you've handled these past couple weeks. I think you should schedule some time to fall apart in the near future. You deserve that."

She pulled away, rising. The anger in her expression startled him, but he saw it wasn't directed at him, but at herself. "No. I don't deserve to fall apart, Gideon."

"Why not? You didn't ask for any of this, Anwyn. What makes you think you have to be more superhuman than anyone else?"

"Well, there's the pot calling the kettle black again. You and Daegan just trade the honor back and forth." The tension in her body became more pronounced. "I wasn't just flogged half to death."

"Stop. Please." He rose, biting back a sigh as she merely detoured, did a lap around the couch. He could feel it in her, the worries she was juggling like the proverbial hot potatoes, afraid of dropping one, holding tight even as they burned her fingers. He marked her track around the room and this time when she made the circle, he successfully made the intercept, catching both hands.

"Hey." Fortunately, when she tried to shove away, evade him, she forgot she could use vampire skills to do it. Catching her waist, he turned them so they tumbled into a deep chair, her across his lap. He gathered her into him with unyielding arms.

"I'm not a baby. Stop it."

"I know that. Hey, I do. Relax." When she glared at him, he cupped the side of her face. "You're the scariest thing I've ever met. But I still think of you as my baby. Just as Daegan does. No denying it, even if you kick our asses over it." He teased her lips with a finger until she gave him an irritated look and snapped at him. Then the fight went out of her and she had her arms around him, holding him so tightly he thought he might have heard his ribs creak. He didn't mind, holding her back the same way.

"I was afraid of losing it in there," she murmured. "So afraid, because if I lost it, I knew I might lose you. I hated it."

"For a moment or two, I think all three of us were ready to open a can of hurt on that group of losers. We would have all gone down together. Shhh . . ." He pressed his head down on hers, twisted his hands so her hair curled around his wrists, both holding her fast and making her feel he'd attached himself to her, a silken tether. He was starting to know how this particular Mistress worked, how she reacted to the reminder of her slave's devotion and nearness.

"You think you've got me all figured out."

"I'll never do that, but I'm picking up clues. Why don't you think you're deserving, Anwyn? What's going on with that?"

"It doesn't matter, Gideon. Just let it drop."

"Everything about you matters."

It made her mouth soften, but her fingers were clamped together, her body tense, as she leaned back in his arms, lifted her face to look up at him. Unfortunately, that little shift inappropriately woke another part of his body, the one that had been revved up in high gear during the dinner but not allowed to release. It woke to full, impressive life against her soft buttocks. He winced. "Sorry."

"No apologies needed. I might have a use for that." She gave him a feline smile, but he pushed the lust that infused his brain aside and tried to focus on the point at hand.

"We're not talking about me. Whatever this is about, does Daegan know?"

"No. Well. I guess he could find out now, if he wanted to do so." She sighed. "Fine. I guess withholding it turns it into this big dramatic moment, and I don't deserve that, either. Plus, it was a long time ago."

But her muscles refused to relax. He caressed her back, squeezed her. "Please tell me."

She closed her eyes. "You remember, a while back, I told you my aunt and uncle took us in, like yours did. But my uncle . . . you know."

"Yeah." His fingers flexed on her, a reassurance and protective anger at once.

"I had a younger sister. Beatrice. I called her Trice." She shifted, rubbed a palm over the side of her face as if something was irritating her there. "I don't want to draw this out. Long story short, as I told you, my uncle was a sleazebag who liked young girls, preferably those who'd just hit puberty. I was thirteen and didn't quite understand what he wanted until one night when my aunt was gone. He pinned me down, tearing at my clothes. Trice hit him with a bat. I was so frightened, I ran."

"Good." Gideon relaxed his fingers from the fists that wanted to smash into the uncle's face, but then he saw her expression. She shoved out of his lap, moved away, her fingers raking through her hair. This time he let her go, sensing her need for space.

"No, it wasn't. I *ran*. My uncle was enraged, aroused, and he had something to prove. He raped my little sister. She was *nine*. Nowhere near puberty. She'd just started envying the fact I could wear a bra and she couldn't yet. Liked using my makeup, trying on my clothes, imagining how she'd look in them eventually." Her voice broke, but then she got it under control by dropping to a lower octave. It made her sound more savage. Her fingers were claws, digging into her biceps as she wrapped her arms around herself. "She fought him. She was brave where I wasn't, my nine-year-old sister, and though he raped her, she kept fighting him. He hit her in the face, over and over, to get her to submit. He broke her neck, and she died."

"Oh, son of a bitch. Anwyn." He rose, wanting to hold her again, but she shook her head, looked at him with such glassy-eyed vehemence he knew she was shoving back tears, an emotion she also didn't think she deserved.

"I *ran*, Gideon. When I did, I discovered there is nothing as horrible, not in the entire world, as failing someone when they truly need you. There's no pain or fear that matches that, even if you think so at the time. Right?"

As their gazes held, he remembered a girl in a yellow dress soaked with blood, who'd begged him not to leave her, but he had. She'd died alone among the stink of fear and monsters lingering in the shadows. Coming back to that, and to her still body, had chilled him in the marrow of his bones, such that he wasn't sure they'd ever know warmth again. "Yeah," he said.

"So what happened to me in that alley, I hated it. It was horrible. This . . . inability to control what's happening to my body, that's almost unbearable. But I would endure it all over again, every day. Hell, I'd let Fate magnify it ten times, if I could turn back time, go back to that moment and not run. To take what she did, so she'd still be alive. Which means I *can* endure all of this. And I will."

She straightened, looking fierce and endearing to him at once in her strength and fragility. It broke his heart when she tightened her jaw and extended a hand, lacing her fingers in a knot with his that held, a shared bond. "I'll not only endure it; I will continue to live my life and be everything I want to be, because that's the gift my sister gave me. Daegan is right. To even indulge for a moment the idea of giving up, taking my life or just dying . . . I abhor that this can make me feel that way most of all." She gazed at their clasped hands. "But one thing a Domme knows is that you can't control everything you think or despair. You can only do your best to get past it. To keep getting past it, and live in the moment every day. That's what I remember when anything gets too awful. To live in the moment if it's good, or remember that it's *only* a moment if it's bad."

"Okay," he said quietly. "But you need to get past this idea that you don't deserve it, that somehow your sister hates you for what you did." He saw that in her mind, too strong and illuminated to ignore, though she gave him a reproachful look for the breach of privacy. He pressed forward, though. "People, at the root of it, they just . . . When it comes down to pain, it's different."

He rubbed a hand over his face, realizing generalities weren't going to cut it. "There was this one vamp I killed. It was one of those that Daegan mentioned before, where it was self-defense on my part, and he had a female servant." He swallowed, the memory still a tough one, but this was for Anwyn's comfort, not his. "Sometimes it takes two or three minutes for the servant to die after the vamp does. I ended up staying with her, holding her hand until she passed, lying on his chest."

He lifted his gaze to hers. "I'm supposed to hate her for the fact she chose to be the servant of a guy who did unspeakable things, but when she looked at him, she didn't see that. It didn't mean she was right, or less blind, but when she needed a hand to hold while dying, because she was afraid, I couldn't deny her that. And in that moment, she didn't seem to mind her last comfort came from her killer. Things are always more complicated, and less complicated, than we think they are. Wherever your sister is, she loves you, and she's hoping like hell you're happy, because she knows you deserve it. I don't have to know anything else about her to know that. Because I know she loved you. There's just no way she didn't."

Tears filled her eyes. Her chin firmed again, holding them in, the fragility and strength warring against each other so fiercely. He knew she needed that battle, so he let her have it, though he suffered watching it. She didn't move for long moments, and he didn't disturb her, merely holding that connection as she found that balance she needed between the horror of her memories and the volatility of their present, and how she would rise above both. He would give her whatever strength she needed to do both, and so was content to stand there as long as she needed him to do so.

Her gaze lifted to him, her eyes telling him she heard his thoughts. She had a personal struggle about that as well, thoughts he wasn't sure he wanted to hear. But as her lips parted to speak what he was trying to avoid reading, they heard the sound of footsteps in the corridor.

Both of their heads turned immediately toward the door. Anwyn slanted Gideon a smile, the shadows of her past lingering but obviously already being drawn back into the corners of her mind, where he knew she'd bury them even deeper than her gremlins could find. "Look at the two of us. We both perked up like a pair of spaniels, didn't we?"

"If it's all the same to you, I'd prefer to be a more masculine breed."

"How about an ox?" she asked sweetly, and then fended off his pinch with an indignant swat as Daegan came through the door.

"I see being flogged half to death hasn't taught him any more respect," he remarked.

Gideon didn't bother to retort, more concerned about what he saw in Daegan's face, the taut lines around his sensual mouth. His dark hair was spiked, as if he'd been raking it. Anwyn went to him, rising on her toes to smooth down the strands.

"What's going on?" she asked.

"As we thought, Brian was at the dinner because of what Vincent witnessed. Belizar demanded a full report from him after he met with you."

Gideon's eyes narrowed. "Did he tell Belizar about his time with us before?"

"No." Daegan shook his head. "Brian confined his report to the present. He made it clear the condition was manageable, as long as Anwyn had my continued supervision as sire. He smoothly noted he already had some ongoing research, some injections that he thought would keep her functioning quite well. Unfortunately, the Council tends to turn information to their own objectives."

"We met their tests, and it pissed them off. They want somebody to suffer, to feel like they still hold the upper hand." Gideon saw the truth in Daegan's gaze as Anwyn let out a creative and very unladylike curse.

"Us torturing Gideon in front of them wasn't enough suffering? Are these people all psychopaths?"

"A servant suffering isn't really suffering," Gideon said shortly, so Daegan wouldn't have to say it. Calm readiness descended on his body, as if it already knew a fight was ahead. "So what's the bullet?"

Daegan swept his gaze over them both. "Lord Uthe pointed out that someone with this type of uncontrollable affliction would be an automatic addition to my termination list."

Gideon scowled. "They're not touching her."

"That was also my reaction."

You know what needs to be done, and you are refusing to do it. Lord Belizar had said it in such a perfectly reasonable voice, and Daegan had reasonably noted he would disembowel anyone who thought about hurting her. Gideon's assessment was correct. They wouldn't be happy until they'd had him do something against all his principles, to prove his loyalty to them. Which meant they were in danger of losing it forever.

"So what do we do now?"

"I leave."

"What?" They spoke in unison. Gideon straightened while Anwyn's brow creased.

"What the hell are you talking about?" he demanded.

"After I refused to allow a discussion of Anwyn's termination, Belizar ordered me to perform a task while they deliberate. There's a rogue nest, fifty miles above Berlin. They've been preying on small towns. Reliable sources have provided their location for the next several days. This group is much like Barnabus," he reassured them. "They're made vampires, loose cannons, easy enough for me to dispatch. But taking care of a housekeeping matter in the Council's backyard will prove useful to their state of mind."

"You're not this stupid." Gideon stepped forward, anger in every line of his body. "Belizar's getting you out of the way to take care of Anwyn and me while you're gone."

Daegan shook his head again. "This is no longer about the two of you. It is clear to them that you both belong to me, so it is about my loyalty to the Council. And I do not go based on my trust in Belizar. I trust Uthe. I flatly refused to go on the assignment until I had you safely returned home. However, Belizar insists on more discussion of Anwyn's seizures, given our track record with other made vampires with erratic behaviors. Uthe gave me his personal guarantee of your safety until I return, and he will post Brian here as a round-the-clock watch on you." He inclined his head to Gideon. "I trust Uthe's word. He is the one who loved my mother."

Gideon paused. "So what I said . . ."

"There was an element of truth to it, though I still take exception to the phrasing. However, as I'm sure your brother has told you, of all the Council members, Uthe holds the most honor and integrity." A grim smile touched Daegan's mouth. "Once, a long, long time ago, Uthe was a Templar. He's never left those principles behind. He also mentioned if I show my trust in the Council by leaving you in their hands while doing this, it's likely the older members will be sufficiently mollified to confirm my guardianship of Anwyn, with frequent reports on her status."

"We should just leave," Anwyn said. "I hate all of them. I don't care about their approval. I'll take the consequences of that."

Daegan laid his hands on her tense shoulders, commanding her attention. "This is a new world for you, *cher*, and I know it is hard for you to understand. As I said from the beginning, I will not abandon the idea of your being accepted in this world, and the security that will bring you, until I have no other choice. Gideon, for all he abhors vampires, knows I speak the truth, for it is in his expression even now. He knows I am right."

Confirming Gideon's reluctant nod didn't make the words easier for Anwyn to hear. "I still don't care."

"Then you must trust us that it is important that you *do* care, even when you don't wish to do so."

"I don't like this," Gideon said. "It feels wrong."

Daegan considered him. "You think I am being misled, that he will allow harm to come to either of you?"

Gideon frowned. "No . . . What feels wrong is the nest of vampires. It's a trick, isn't it?"

"Perhaps more of a test than a trick." Daegan shrugged. "Uthe is sending me a message. They wanted to see if I'd trust their word, that you will remain safe while I'm gone, or if I'd defy them and take you home before performing their will. My loyalty appears to be the primary issue for them. The intel on the group is sound, though. I was seeking them when I was here before, but I ran out of time. Belizar told me he was expecting, or rather hoping, for information on them while I was here this time."

Gideon frowned. "There could be more of them than you expect. You might need reinforcement."

"I will be fine. Your job is to care for Anwyn." His tone final, in that way that raised Gideon's hackles, Daegan turned his gaze to Anwyn. A slight smile appeared on his serious mouth. "As I said, my loyalty is the issue. I think the rest is mostly show, because even the ones who suggested exterminating you are quite taken with you. If this is a trick to test my loyalty and abilities, and I take care of it, then I agree with Uthe. They will be more open to a different solution and accepting our proposal for your care and Gideon's continued service to you."

Daegan slanted Gideon a glance. "They are also intrigued by you, and what you seem to have become under her . . . thumb. You were right. Seeing you as her servant is more intriguing to them than your death. Vampires despise boredom above all other things."

"I'm thrilled to entertain them." But Gideon's gut still made unpleasant grumblings as Daegan drew Anwyn to him, his fingers tangling in her loose hair.

Though he always noticed the appeal of Anwyn's body, Gideon

wasn't sure why his attention became even more pronounced when Daegan's hands were outlining those curves. Regardless, his brainless cock didn't seem to realize now was not the time to whine about the backlog of unreleased need.

"You believe you'll be safe if I tell you it's true?" the vampire asked her. "You won't worry?"

"I'll worry about you." Anwyn laid her hands against his chest, inside the open collar of his shirt. "I always have, every time you've left me."

"There is nothing to fear. When I get back, we will take care of this. As I have said"—his gaze took on a steely glint—"it matters not what the Council decides. You will be safe."

"And Gideon?"

"Who? Oh, yes, him, too. Maybe." Daegan was quick enough to evade her head slap, but caught her wrists and brought her to him for a long, thorough kiss, running his hands down her back to palm her ass. Gideon wasn't sure which way to look, so chose to watch, caught in the unexpected trance of the voyeur, watching Daegan slide a hand up to her breast, kneading it so the curve expanded provocatively in the opening of her silk blouse, and her skin flushed, her nipple becoming obviously aroused under his manipulation.

"I wish I had time to give you pleasure, *cher*, but perhaps this sorry servant of yours can finish what I started, keep you occupied until my return."

"Or perhaps he'll do such a good job I'll have no need of you in my bed at all." She tossed her head, and then managed a short laugh as Daegan caught her hair in a less gentle hand and branded her with a harder kiss that stole away all smiles and laughter, left her gasping and Gideon aching from the raw sexuality of it, his cock tight against his jeans.

"We'll see about that when I return. For now, *cher*, I need you to promise me something. Try not to listen to your servant's mind while I take him outside and talk to him a moment."

"Is it something you think I can't handle?" Her blue-green gaze narrowed.

"No. You can handle anything. But I think there is some information that shouldn't be known to you, but should be to him. If you need it, it will be yours, but I think it will help protect you in certain ways. Plausible deniability. You understand?"

She nodded, though she looked confused and vaguely dissatisfied. He kissed her hands, backed away. "I will see you in a day or so, *cher*. All will be well."

Gideon arched a brow. As he followed Daegan out and shut the door, they moved down the hallway until they were out of her fledgling-vampire hearing range. "What kind of bullshit was that?"

"The kind that will keep her alive." Daegan turned to face him, all traces of humor gone. "Despite your display of . . . loyalty, apparently the question of your fate is still undecided. Some still want you dead, even if Anwyn is allowed to live."

"Son of a bitch." Gideon shook his head, but now he understood. If Anwyn had thought he was still in danger . . .

"You are safe until my return, just as she is," Daegan said. "They know the impact on a vampire when her servant is abruptly terminated. I've convinced them that Anwyn would need me here to support her if that is the decision they make. Her well-being will give them pause where yours will not. It, and Uthe's guarantee, will keep them from acting prematurely. However, if anything happens to me—"

"Whoa. You said this was going to be an easy mop-up."

"Yes, it is. But we both know there's more to it than it seems. Even if it's not, every fight can go wrong. If that is the case, tell Anwyn to appeal to Uthe's protection. Tell him my last wish is that he honor my mother's memory by protecting the woman to whom I gave my heart. Let her keep the servant best able to care for her in my absence."

Though the words were spoken in a businesslike, brusque manner, Gideon was taken aback by them, the directness of Daegan's gaze. He cleared his throat. "So if I'm just as safe, why didn't you tell me this in front of her?"

"Because we both know she is far more fragile than she will acknowledge. She is nearing the end of her patience with this Council, and that would be the final straw. You understand why it is important for her to be accepted before we leave. She does not." Daegan lifted a shoulder. "If the time comes that she needs to know everything, you will know when and how to tell her."

Gideon digested that. "You asked me if I felt you were being misled. You were willing to trust my judgment over Uthe's loyalty."

"I have a great deal of faith in your precognition, Gideon. Don't let it go to your head, though. You're still dumb as a post on most other things."

Daegan put a hand on his shoulder, forestalling a retort. "As long as you tuck these thoughts in your mind somewhere and don't dwell on them, she won't see them. She hasn't mastered mind manipulation as well as all that yet. As before, Lord Brian will be useful if she has a seizure and you need a vampire's strength to help contain her."

Gideon still didn't like any of this. He agreed with Anwyn. He'd never wanted to be out of a place more, and Atlantis was looking as close to a home as he'd had in a long time. But he sighed, curled his lip in a half snarl. "Get your ass back here as fast as you can, then. Any other reassurance you want me to give her?"

Daegan nodded. Quick as a striking snake, he caught Gideon behind the neck, giving him a hard, thorough kiss, as thorough as the one he'd given Anwyn. When he let him go, Gideon was appalled to find he was clutching the male's waist beneath his duster, feeling the metal of his sheathed sword, the weapons he wore. His throbbing cock was pressed hard against Daegan's thigh in insistent need. Daegan pushed him back gently, but with pleasure in his gaze.

"If I wanted to be a cruel Master, I would order you and Anwyn not to take your pleasure with each other until my return. But I think you've suffered enough for one day. I'll enjoy arousing you twice as much when this is over."

Tangling his fingers in Gideon's hair to give it a hard tug, he offered one more sexy smile, a flash of fang, and then was gone.

~

If he'd had any intention of doing as Daegan had suggested, finishing with Anwyn what the vampire had started, it was halted by the immediate arrival of Lord Brian. The scientist wanted to run a few more tests and question Anwyn further on her current state, to fill in more blanks for the Council. After a couple hours of that, Gideon left them talking and prowled the suite restlessly.

Yeah, he couldn't settle down in a castle full of vampires. But that wasn't it. Those rare instances he'd ignored his gut, it had always been a mistake. Sometimes he'd very nearly not lived to regret it. Something was wrong with the whole setup.

He looked at Anwyn again. While he always worried for her, nothing raised his hackles, not even Brian's proximity. Daegan's belief in Uthe's and Brian's trustworthiness was apparently sound, because his internal concern compass showed no flags when it pointed toward her. And while Gideon didn't like keeping Anwyn out of the loop, Daegan had been right. Gideon understood a great deal about the myriad contradictions of the vampire world that she didn't yet. He and Anwyn weren't a threat to the Council. Their fate had everything to do with Daegan and the power games the Council was playing with him.

However, as he turned his thoughts to Daegan, chills ran through his lower belly. Danger was headed his way, not theirs. And Daegan thought he was goddamned invincible.

When a quiet knock came on the door, Gideon already had his weapon out. He kept the knife at the small of his back as he went to answer. Lord Brian rose, drawing Anwyn behind him with firm courtesy. It upgraded him a notch in Gideon's estimation. The vampire's face made it clear that if there was a threat, despite Uthe's assurances and Brian's service to the Council, the young vamp was ready to fight.

Gideon opened the door. His suspicions ratcheted up tenfold at the sight of Stephen's servant, Alanna.

"Let me in, quickly." She was already moving across the threshold. Gideon allowed it, mainly because she wasn't wearing much to hide a weapon, a diaphanous creation that would have made her more at home in an Arabian Nights tale than a drafty Berlin castle. Still, he grasped her arm, controlling her movement into the room as he closed the door. "Don't touch me," she said sharply. "I'm not armed, and I only have a few moments to tell you this."

He ignored her request, but his touch did ease when she seemed willing to stay standing in the same place, far from Anwyn. Of course, logically, Anwyn had the strength to snap a human servant in half. "Here to deliver a message for your Master?"

"No." Her color was pale, her eyes feverish, making Gideon even more uneasy. When he worked with cells of vampire hunters, some had carried that kind of expression. They'd usually just lost someone they loved, and that fuck-it-all look made it almost a certainty they wouldn't come home from the next fight. Because that was the way they wanted it.

"Lord Stephen has deceived the Council. He is sending Daegan Rei into a trap."

Anwyn stepped forward then, heedless of Lord Brian's hand on her arm. "Tell us what you mean," she said sharply.

"Lord Daegan was told this was a disorganized, weak group of made vampires. That group actually left Lord Stephen's territory some weeks ago. Instead, Daegan Rei has been sent to the stronghold of a vampire called Xavier."

"Xavier?" Brian's brow creased. "He has no stronghold. He's one of the lower-ranked vampires of Stephen's former overlord territory. Last I heard, he was living quietly in the North."

"No." Alanna shook her head. "That is what Stephen wanted the Council to believe. Xavier has only gained in strength. Stephen allowed him to recruit and organize a military-trained force of vampires."

"To what end?" Brian demanded.

While Gideon knew Lord Brian had seniority here, and the ear of the Council, he silently hoped he'd get past the politics and find out more about Daegan, before he or Anwyn—especially Anwyn—blew a gasket.

"I won't speak to Lord Stephen's motives. Those are obvious enough." Alanna turned her gaze to Gideon, surprisingly. "Xavier is a well-educated man who prefers to act as a mercenary. He and his vampire force own and operate out of a fetish club called the Coffin. I don't know his ultimate plans, but Stephen has allowed him to act as if it is his territory within a territory, so to speak, in return for the favors Xavier's vampires do for Stephen—"

"Son of a bitch." The missing motive fell into place at last. Gideon gritted his teeth. "Barnabus was a test run, to see how Daegan operates. Stephen wants Xavier to take out Daegan."

"Yes. Because Daegan terminated Ella Maher. Stephen did not know until he came onto the Council how she died, when he learned of Council's use of Daegan Rei. Ella Maher was a lover of Stephen's. They were close, as close as my Master comes to affection. He wants the Council to cease using Lord Daegan for assassination of made vampires, but he also wants personal vengeance."

Damn if Daegan hadn't been right about that as well. *I may have been assigned to kill someone they considered a friend or a preferred lover . . .* "How does Barbra figure into this?"

"She supports Lord Stephen's objectives for made vampires, though she is unaware of his personal vendetta."

"So Xavier knows Daegan is coming." That came from Anwyn.

"Yes. He has had time to prepare, and has a force of fifteen combat-trained vampires." Alanna reflexively took a step back toward the door as Anwyn moved forward, her expression forbidding. Brian put a quelling hand on Anwyn's shoulder, but Gideon didn't know if she felt it. Of course, he was having difficulty reining back his own reaction.

"But Lord Stephen is beginning to fear Xavier's strength," Alanna continued. "Xavier is being less respectful. Stephen did not foresee the long-term result of his actions. If he gives Xavier up to the Council for accumulating a private army, he will reveal his own wrongdoing. Xavier knows Stephen holds no power over him."

"So while Stephen assumes Daegan will be killed, he also hopes he'll kill a big enough group of Xavier's vampires in the process so that Stephen can control Xavier's base once more." Gideon's lip curled.

"I must go now," Alanna said shortly. "You do what you will with this."

Gideon grasped her arm again. "We need more information."

"You have all that I have time to give you. My Master will demand to know where I've been when I return to his quarters." As she gazed up at him, reality dawned. Gideon's gut tightened.

"You're Stephen's full servant. He'll know what you've done."

"Yes."

"We can protect you." Gideon had no clue how he could do that, but the way she stood there, quiet and brave, with thin, pale arms and the eyes of a wounded doe, made it impossible for him to say anything else. But the look she gave him told him she'd already accepted whatever outcome came from this.

"No, you can't." Her gaze shifted to Lord Brian now. "I do not betray my Master lightly. At one time, I believed he cared for me. Then he denied me the right to go to my brother's funeral. He had another engagement, a dinner in France. Twelve vampires. Despite my grief, or perhaps because of it, he had me fully participate in that dinner, giving me to all twelve of them. And to their servants. It went on for three days. I realized later it was to test my loyalty to him over my love for my brother."

Lord Brian's gaze flickered, but he said nothing, nothing on his face indicating whether or not he condemned or held compassion for the woman.

At his lack of response, her face went even more wooden and she looked toward Gideon again. "A servant serves, because she believes she is vital to the heart and soul of her Master. I was an Inherited servant, so I did not expect or ask for anything except an unconditional sense of value. Stephen does not have a heart or soul. Good-bye."

"Wait." Gideon stopped her once more at the doorway, his mind still sifting through possibilities, ways they could keep her from Stephen's retribution. "Why did you help us? I was responsible for your brother's death."

Those liquid brown eyes reached deep inside of him, squeezing his jaded heart. "Because you told me you were sorry," she said simply. "And you meant it. It was the first time anyone acknowledged my grief. In your eyes, I saw you understood, truly, what it was to lose one you loved. I may hate that you were the instrument that took him from me, but in the world we live in, I know genuine feelings from false. And I have now seen the monstrous side of them that causes you to take their lives. Do not worry about me, Gideon Green. I do not want or need your help. The end will be a blessing for me. Go save your Master. Good-bye."

Shrugging off Gideon's hand, she slipped out the door. Brian came to Gideon's side, Anwyn with him. Anwyn's eyes were angry, worried, searching. "Anything?" Gideon asked.

She shook her head. "I'm calling to him. He said it was fifty miles away. Maybe I'm not strong enough yet, but he can hear my mind from that distance. If I was worried or afraid, calling to him, he would hear. He would answer, Gideon. Oh God . . ."

She pulled away before he could touch her, reassure her. "No, he's fine," she told them both, told herself. "He's so fast. He's the best at what he does."

Gideon remembered what he'd told Daegan, what was pounding in his head now. *Everybody can be hurt. Toe-to-toe, Hercules might not be able to stand up to you, but if someone plans carefully enough, a ten-year-*

old kid could. He was glad Anwyn appeared occupied with her own reassurances to herself, giving him time to push his damaging thoughts aside.

"We have to get to my lab," Brian said. "Once Stephen knows what she did, he will anticipate my reporting this to the Council. He'll go there to do damage control before he tries to contact Xavier. It will never occur to him that you two will try to leave the castle and help Daegan. And I fear he will need your help. If we are lucky, the Council will not think to call you from your rooms for this discussion, and it may be quite a while before they realize you have left the castle."

Apparently Brian had already anticipated what he and Anwyn were going to do, and Gideon appreciated his intuition. A look of warrior fierceness crossed Anwyn's expression before she pivoted and disappeared into the bedroom. She must have moved with the speed of a vampire, because the two men had only a handful of seconds to be impatient before she returned, carrying her overnight bag.

"Things we'll need," she said shortly. Brian nodded, opening the door and investigating the passage before he waved them out. "We must move swiftly."

"Why don't we go to the Council as well?" Anwyn asked, hurrying alongside him, Gideon covering their rear.

"Because you are a fledgling and Gideon is a vampire hunter," Brian said. "They won't believe either of you over two Council members. If you have no proof, your life is forfeit for an accusation brought against them. I will handle the Council until you return. While my account will be secondhand, it will give them pause, buy you time. They will believe Daegan, if he can get back here with proof."

"What about Alanna?" Gideon asked.

"She is correct. Stephen will execute her as soon as he knows. There is no leniency for a servant betraying her Master. If she is lucky, he will be in a hurry and make it quick."

Gideon and Anwyn came to a stop together, but Brian gripped their arms and propelled them on. "There is nothing you can do for her. Not and save Daegan as well. She chose her path, and she does not seek rescue. If you looked in her eyes, you could tell she is already dead. She was groomed and raised to be a servant. If she betrays her Master, no other will want her, and she has no desire for purpose beyond that. Her heart and spirit are broken. She did this for her brother, a final act. If there is anything to be done for her, Gideon, I swear I will try to intervene. But you must choose. You can only save one of them."

Christ. Gideon forced down his helpless rage, the vision of what might be done to the woman. "Why are we headed to your lab?"

"You need something that will help you overcome fifteen military-trained vampires. Debra, my servant, is preparing what you need. I've sent her instructions already."

"You keep incendiary rounds in your lab?" Gideon queried.

Brian gave him a wry look. "I'm sure you already have that on your private plane. I have something far more useful."

True to his word, when Brian entered the lab, Debra was already packaging three vials for transport. She had a backpack of other materials put together, which included directions to Xavier's club, the Coffin. Gideon wondered if she'd ever considered throwing in her hat with the vampire hunters, because they could have used her efficiency.

Anwyn gave him a quelling look at that thought, but in several seconds they were both paying close attention as Brian gave them further instructions on how to use the vials. He barely acknowledged his servant as he took the items from her hands and turned them over to Gideon, showing he knew who would handle battle strategy. For exit strategy, he turned his attention to them both.

"There's an underground passage from my lab, the beauty of old castles," he said. "It'll bring you out about a quarter mile on the service road. Steal a car and get to the Coffin as soon as you can. This time of night, you shouldn't be stopped. When you get there, Anwyn can tell them she's visiting the Council to be processed as a new vampire, and she was told there was entertainment to be found at Xavier's club. I'll include a note in the pack to ensure she is accepted, so they know she does have the protection of this castle."

Brian put a hand on Anwyn's shoulder, drawing her gaze up. "Xavier is not a loose cannon. Not exactly. He was made during World War Two, and believes Hitler should have won. Which is ironic, considering Xavier is not a populist; he embraces the vampire world's brutal definition of order based on aristocrats. He is dangerous and merciless."

Pausing, the scientist considered her from head to toe, a critical survey. "However, from my brief encounters with him, I remember he enjoys beauty. Deeply."

"She shouldn't go in there except as a last resort."

Anwyn turned to Gideon, but Brian spoke first. His tone, while mild, was implacable, his eyes sharp. "She's your Mistress, Gideon, not the other way around. I doubt she'll give you much choice. Plus, it will take both of you to get him out. I would prefer to go with you, but as I said, my voice will be needed to hold the Council's decision for a time.

"This is going to be very much a case of trial by combat." His gaze shifted between the two of them. "If you return alive, that will say much in your favor. If you do not return, then Stephen's claim will be believed, because his will be the only firsthand account heard. Xavier's role will be too easy to conceal."

"Why are they so determined to believe this asshole?" Gideon demanded.

"He and Barbra were chosen to fill the made vampire positions after a severe selection process. There was a strong reaction from many conservative vampires, those who felt that they would ruin the Council's judgment. The Council is determined not to be perceived as having made a mistake. As you heard from Alanna, it is possible Stephen intended initially to practice his role as intended, advocating for made vampires, but his desire for vengeance overrode the possible good he could have done."

"If you say so. I think that asshole was always a little weasel. Hate to say it, but I agree with the conservative vampires."

"The idea was not misguided." Brian glanced toward Anwyn. "I have met many worthy made vampires. Change is just slow in our world. Unfortunately, Stephen and Barbra already have over half of the Council doubting Daegan's loyalties. His behavior here, his defense of the two of you, has not helped."

"So why don't they just let him resign?" Anwyn snapped. Her gaze flicked to Debra as she hastily brought Brian the castle letterhead, on which she'd already written out the note for him to sign.

Brian shook his head at the same time as Gideon. "Doesn't work that way, Mistress," Gideon said softly, meeting her gaze. "He's too powerful."

Anwyn locked her jaw, looked as if she might say something else.

Then a look of panic crossed her face, a peculiarly internal, concentrated look. Her gaze shot up to Gideon's. "No," she hissed, her eyes flushing to crimson.

Damn it. Of course, it had to happen at the most inconvenient moment, though he didn't blame her for that. With Daegan being in danger on top of everything else, it was a wonder she hadn't broken down in the hallway. And he'd been focused on this, not in her mind. He fucking needed to learn to multitask better.

He leaped to her side, but Anwyn's hands clamped down on his with bruising force. "Restraints . . . in pack. Knock me out, Gideon," she rasped, struggling past those shadow voices. Her face contorted, fangs lengthening. "There's no time. Don't you dare leave me behind or I swear to the heavens . . . you'd better stake me. If I wake . . . here . . . I will take the skin off your—"

Gideon tried to pull her out of the way, but Brian was too swift. He hit her with a metal pipe that looked as if it had come from under a sink. Gideon caught her in his arms as she immediately dropped, though her body continued to twitch, obscenely like maggots feasting on an unresponsive corpse. Debra was already pulling the restraints out of the tote and bringing them over.

"Goddamn it," Gideon swore. "That wasn't necessary."

Though he knew it was. Brian's objectivity had enabled him to make the decision far more swiftly than Gideon. It didn't sit any better on his mind, though, to see the woman he loved struck so brutally.

"I know where to hit, and how hard, to temporarily knock out a vampire. It requires a vampire's strength at the precise point. When she awakens, you might mention that to her. It could be useful where you're going. She's right," Brian added in an urgent tone. "She must go with you. I don't know how Stephen will twist this, but he could dispel the protection that your Master imposed for you both before he left."

"He's not my Master," Gideon said. Lifting Anwyn in a fireman's carry, he kept one hand free to use a weapon. "Give me the tote bag and show me the passage we need to take." He gave Brian a measuring look. "You know, you're far less of a science geek than I expected."

"You need to learn not to look a vampire directly in the eye before one teaches you better manners," Brian returned. He glanced at Anwyn, regret crossing his features. "She is truly exceptional. Tell her to use that as a weapon as well. Don't hold her back, Gideon. Go swiftly now. I will let it be known where you have gone, and why, at the appropriate time, to ensure the Council will watch Stephen until your return and prevent him from contacting Xavier. If they do as I suspect, they will not allow him outside contact until you return . . . or this is resolved. They will wait to see the outcome."

"Trial by combat," Gideon echoed, and the vampire scientist nodded. "I'll go with them."

The men both turned. Debra had been busy during their exchange, shedding her lab coat and gathering purse and keys. "I can get your car, my lord, and meet them at the passage entrance. It will save time."

"You will not," Brian said. Debra, unaffected by his stern expression, touched his arm.

"Until she wakes, he'll need help. Someone to drive while he watches over her. When he gets there, an extra scout on the outside will be vital. She's formidable, but they're both new to our ways. At least from the inside view," she amended, glancing at Gideon. Then she brought her attention back to her scowling Master. "I can be useful," she insisted.

"Once she's up, she'll hold her own," Brian said, but Debra shook her head.

"I won't put myself in direct harm, my lord, but I can help him and Miss Naime. You both know it." Her gaze shifted between them. "It's the right thing to do, and we can't shirk that because you might have to train a new lab assistant."

A muscle twitched in Brian's jaw, and he drew her aside. "You think that is all your value to me?" While his hand on her elbow was their only contact, Gideon felt the pulse of a connection far stronger than that. However, the tick of seconds was as loud as cannon report in his mind. A couple more and he was going, whether they'd resolved it or not. That sense of urgency for Daegan was only getting more severe, starting to cramp in his gut. He hoped Anwyn woke soon, because he wanted her to keep trying that phone call to the vampire's mind, see if she could get him to answer. Daegan also couldn't use the conduit across her mind to Gideon when she was unconscious.

"I am a servant, my lord," Debra said. "I never assume my worth is greater than what it is. Let me continue to prove my value to you. Lord

Stephen and Lady Barbra are weakening the Council. You know it as I do. We can show that to the rest of them."

A wealth of furious thoughts apparently passed between the two of them then. Masters and servants. Tools or more than tools? It seemed to vary from servant to servant. Gideon didn't fear that Anwyn would ever think of him as Stephen did Alanna, but Brian was closer to the "norm" for vampires and servants.

He knew his time with Anwyn was limited, but what if, before that hourglass ran out, the day came when Anwyn did view him with the same absolute sense of possession most vampires had for their servants, that he was her property? How would he reconcile his feelings toward her then, feelings that would no longer be appropriate to who and what she was? Or what she thought of him? Worse, what if he found his view of his own role had changed, and he *accepted* that? Embraced it, even? Fucking craziness.

Nothing was ever simple, was it? Or maybe it was so simple it was hard to face it.

And why the hell was he wasting time soul-searching about it right now? He opened his mouth to tell them to move their asses, etiquette be damned, but Brian beat him to it.

"Go, then," Brian said. When Debra nodded and turned, his arm shot out, bringing her back against him. She let out a short gasp as his fangs pricked her neck, just enough to render her still and quivering against him. His arm stayed locked across her chest, fingers curled under the shirt at her waist, teasing bare skin. "You come back without a scratch, or I shall be very displeased with you."

"Yes, my lord," she responded. She lifted her head to look at him, her lips inadvertently brushing his jawline. He let her go with an oath, but it seemed to Gideon he had difficulty turning back to the two of them after his servant slipped out.

"Good luck," he said.

"I'll watch after them both," Gideon said. "It's tough to find a good lab assistant."

Brian gave him a sharp look. "Your clever tongue may get your throat ripped out before it's all over, human." But as he held the door open, he paused, stared into the darkness of the passage. "She will be

an asset to you. She is exceedingly intelligent, as brave as she is beautiful. Perhaps too brave."

Gideon nodded. "You might think of telling her that when we get
back."

Because whatever a vampire-servant relationship was or wasn't,
Gideon knew sure as hell that no one should be treated as Alanna had
been treated. A heart freely given wasn't a disposable item.

It was a treasure beyond price.

17

Daegan swam through Anwyn's consciousness. *Invincible.* From the first time she'd met his gaze across her club, it had been the one word that applied to him, no matter the circumstances. She hadn't realized how much she'd learned to count on that, how much of her strength she'd built upon the idea that something in this world could withstand anything. Maybe that was why she'd pushed him away, time and again, just to see him come back. She'd wanted to see if his heart was as invincible as the rest of him, willing to take any level of rejection and keep right on coming. And he had. Nothing could stop him.

But now in her dreams, there was a roar of rage, his own, broken by an explosion of blood, pain, nothingness.

"*Daegan.*" She surged out of her dreams, only to find herself bound. "Gideon."

"I'm here." His hand was on her brow. She was in the back of a roomy sedan, a car blanket tucked around her for warmth. When she tried to sit up, she met the restraints, holding her arms and legs fast.

"Take this off."

"Easy." His hands were already busy, doing just that. Then his touch was on her back and waist, steadying her as she struggled to a seated position. Thank the heavens she hadn't thrown up on herself this time, a small blessing. Maybe she should have someone knock her out more often when seizures occurred. She could save dry-cleaning bills.

"The bag I brought. Is it—"

"Right here in the front seat, no worries."

She nodded, taking a deep breath. It was night, but no longer early night. Her vampire senses told her it was around midnight.

"He's in trouble, Gideon. He doesn't open his mind to me unless he means to do it. Yet, just now, he was under attack and couldn't control it. *Daegan* couldn't control it. In pain . . . I think they knocked him unconscious . . ." Her voice trailed off. "Oh my God, what if he's dead?"

"You would know," came a firm female voice from the front. "He shares blood with you, right?"

Anwyn focused on Debra, driving with both hands prudently on the wheel, her hair a neat plait down her back. "Yes."

"If he was killed, you'd know at that second. Much as a vampire knows when her servant is killed. It's a feeling that can't be mistaken for anything else."

Anwyn's gaze flickered to Gideon. She didn't want to dwell on either option. He *was* alive. She wouldn't accept anything else. "If they were strong enough to do that, Gideon, we have to get more help—"

"We're it," he said grimly, and filled her in on all she'd missed in Brian's lab.

What had Daegan told her? That the vampire world was a more intense version of Atlantis, and that he was certain she was better prepared to handle it than most new vampires. She'd wanted more time to get used to that idea, but Daegan didn't have that kind of time. And she wasn't alone.

Straightening her spine, she tightened her chin and met Gideon's midnight blue eyes. In the shadows of the car, he looked lean and dangerous, long leg stretched out beneath Debra's seat, the other bent to give her something to brace against. She was sure he was armed to the teeth, and wondered if they'd had time to stop at the plane for his guns and crossbows.

"It was on the way," he confirmed with a flash of teeth. That was fine. She trusted him in her head fully right now.

"I brought clothes, so we can fit into a club environment," she said.

"I'll ask for a tour behind the scenes. I'm fairly certain I can get us close enough to the owner to use the weapon Brian gave us."

"I didn't want you to go in there. Not if there was any way to avoid it."

"I know." When the moonlight filtered through the window, she knew he saw the lingering trace of red in her eyes. She could feel the bloodlust simmering through her, the heated whispers of her shadow gremlins, but tonight she would use their savage madness, their absence of fear. She would take control and turn them into her weapon. "I'll never run again, Gideon. You know why. Plus, Brian was right." She reached out, caressing him, not an absent touch, but a deliberate, firm stroke, a reminder. "I am your Mistress. We do this together, because that's the way I want it to be. And," she added in a quieter tone, "as the more experienced strategist, you already know it's the best way. Right?"

He gave a reluctant nod. "No use lying." Then he gave her a look she knew well enough to be reassured by it. "Of course, if you're going to dress me up in something embarrassing, I'd rather leave Daegan to die. He's not worth abject humiliation."

Anwyn's lips twitched, but then he put his hand to her face, fingers stroking her temple, the line of her cheek. As their gazes met, she knew it was a dangerous moment, acknowledging how badly tonight could go, what they might lose. But his voice stayed firm, even, steadying her. "You still feel a little wiped out. We've got about another half hour on the road before we'll stop and get ready. Why don't you lie back down and build up your reserve? Take some of my blood, if you need it."

Though her stomach wasn't yet settled enough to feed, his reasoning about the rest was sound. She complied, putting her head on his bent knee as his hand fell naturally to stroking her hair. Touching his belt, she found the scabbard for one of the daggers hidden at his lower back and traced it. They were silent a few moments, but she knew his mind was in the same place as hers.

"Can you still . . . feel him?"

"No. Nothing. But he's not dead, just like Debra said." She closed her eyes, but not to sleep. She tightened her fingers on his knee. "Gideon . . ."

"We'll get him out of there. Once we do, we won't let him live it down. That alone is worth the risk. Maybe even the humiliating costumes."

She nodded, feeling his resolve despite his typical male refusal to speak of danger, death . . . pain. The humor was the veteran fighter in him, instinctively soothing her nerves, helping her to relax. How many young vampire hunters had he helped this way?

Best thing is not to think about it a lot, Anwyn. We'll go over our strategy right before. It's not going to be overly complicated, and we're going to have to think on our feet, because things will likely change moment by moment. We're both good at that. Think about this as a night at your club. The way you wander through it for your own enjoyment, taking in all the new and unexpected things, but not missing a single detail, because you own *the fucking place.*

His insight was uncanny, as usual. When she'd been human, she'd done such a transformation every night she stepped onto the floor of Atlantis. Leaving behind the Anwyn that read books, drank tea and played with alley cats, she became Mistress Anwyn, every thought and movement aligned with the sexual energy of the club she'd built. Rubbing her cheek against his thigh, she closed her eyes to immerse herself in the images, the provocative scent of heat and arousal, lights and music. Voices raised in sultry laughter or pleasurable cries of aroused pain, just like her dreams. She let it all unfurl in her lower abdomen to compete with the nerves. If she could fool her mind into thinking it was going to a new fetish club for her own pleasure and challenge, not to rescue the male she needed more than she needed blood . . .

"I liked the two men manacled together at dinner."

"Yeah, I pretty much got that."

She looked up, also liking the way the moonlight highlighted the hard planes of his face, the determined eyes. He would be hell on wheels tonight. She might be crazy, but seeing it, she wasn't afraid. Whatever happened, they would be fighting, fighting together. She could accept that.

He met her expression then. He was concerned about protecting her, but he also believed in her strengths. That meant something to her. Still, if she might be dead in a few hours . . .

You're still resisting your attraction to Daegan.

Gideon grunted. "Vampires are enough of a pain in the ass as it is.

Don't need to make it a reality." Then he shook his head. *You're better at explaining things. I'm too busy avoiding thinking about it to analyze it.*

She smiled then. *Gideon, I love you.*

A wealth of meanings was attached to the words, the new and un-tried, as well as the deep and always. It was that thing that had drawn them together from the first and might continue to hold them together, no matter how things evolved. When the words hit his consciousness, she felt his mind surround them like a protective detail, not certain how to handle the impact of such a missile. He caught her wrist when she reached to touch his face, his eyes deepening in color.

I had a different idea of a table centerpiece tonight. Want to hear what it was?

He cleared his throat. "I'm sure I don't, as much as I'm sure you're going to tell me anyway."

"Mmm." Turning on her side, she ran her other hand up his thigh, all the way to his inseam, raking her nails across the denim-covered curve of his testicles. "I'd have the other man bound behind you like that, only he wouldn't be inside you. I'd just manacle you flush so you'd feel how hard he is, his cock compressed against your ass. He'd be get-ting fucked from behind, by Daegan." Satisfaction speared through her at the jump in his cock, the contraction of testicles beneath her thumb.

The movements, the grunts, would stir your possessiveness for Dae-gan. Your ass would clench with a need you don't want to acknowledge as you hear Daegan's rasping breath. "By the time Daegan came, you'd want that other male gone from between you, want only Daegan behind you." Her fingers teased him. "When Daegan finally released you, he'd hook two fingers under your collar, the collar I put on you. He'd yank you onto your knees, bend down to kiss you. Something would break loose inside you so that Daegan would have to take you rough, pin you to the ground. You'd fight him, of course. In order to give yourself free-dom to touch and taste, to feel, you need to fight, to strike out first. To tell him he's yours and you don't share what's yours. It's your way."

Gideon tugged her hair at her knowing chuckle. "Don't be smug. It's unattractive."

"Not according to what I'm feeling beneath my cheek." She rubbed him there as he scowled.

"Jesus, do vampires *ever* stop thinking of sex?"

"No," Debra supplied helpfully from the driver's seat. "And they make it damn hard for us to stop thinking about it as well."

~

Gideon found it immensely difficult to place anyone in the path of danger, male or female. Hell, it was why he'd worked solo for so long now. But being in the company of a woman, and in this case, two women, made him wish he had some of Brian's ability to knock a vampire senseless. Even if he'd had that ability, though, he knew Anwyn was right. It was going to take the both of them. Once they'd pulled off into a quiet copse of woods to change, they discussed their plans. Debra was going to drop them at the club and wait in the car until a predetermined point of time. At dawn, when the club closed, she'd leave, return to Brian for help or further instruction. Otherwise, hopefully she might be their getaway car, as she already knew several safe places they could go to ground for daylight.

Despite his trepidation, Gideon felt renewed admiration for his vampire Mistress when Anwyn calmly instructed Debra to pull right up to the curb next to valet parking. Appropriately, he got out first to hand her out of the vehicle. It also gave him time to assess the area.

The two working the entrance were vampires. The moment her scent was detectible from the car door, they went on alert, their eyes trained on that opening in a way that went beyond their casual perusal of the other oblivious human attendees filtering in.

Daegan would have known in the first few seconds that this club didn't house a reckless group of bloodsuckers, but if he thought they were killing people in the local towns or choosing marks from this club—and that part might be true, the numbers disguised by Stephen for Council reports—Daegan would have proceeded with his assignment.

While the vampire had a strong, and mostly justified, opinion of his superiority, Gideon knew he wasn't rash. But they'd known he was coming, had time to plan. Just as Gideon feared, they'd set a trap for him, something Daegan hadn't expected, and it had worked. Plus, the vampire had an additional distraction this time. He'd done this to smooth the way to save Anwyn's life, preserve her status with the Council, and that would have overridden some normal caution in his approach. Gideon knew it, because he would have done the same if he were in Daegan's overpriced shoes. *Damn it.*

The two vampires on the door were, as advertised, from military stock. He saw it in their bearing, level of attention and how they handled the weapons they carried. It was also in their quick recognition that Gideon had some of the same skills. Gideon forced himself to be deferential, not meeting their eyes to acknowledge what they were as he helped his Mistress out of the vehicle.

She'd brought a red dress with long sleeves and a high neck that clung to her from throat to midthigh like a wet skin. There was a diamond of sheer black cloth at the navel and between the breasts, showing her generous cleavage. Another in the back was so low that it was possible to discern the dimple between her buttocks if a man strained his eyes. He didn't doubt there'd be plenty of eye straining. A jeweled belt rode low on her hips, crafted with chains and glittering red gems. Her heels were red stilettos, a staggering five inches. He had no idea how any woman could walk practically on her toes, but she not only did it, but also managed it with the right amount of swing in the hips, her ass sitting up so high and tight no man could help but look at it. Her sable hair was loose, brushing against that pendulum sway, tempting a man's hands.

At her own club, when she dressed the part of Dominatrix, she was more severely put together. In this outfit, the sexuality still pulsed around her, but it was like the allure of the Holy Grail. A man might hesitate to touch, but he'd do it with just a little encouragement from those lush lips. This look said she was a Mistress, but one still young in her skills, a bit wild and reckless with the sexual vibes. One who might need a strong hand to help her rein them in and guide her. He thought Daegan would admire it as much as he did . . . and still have trouble rolling his tongue back in his mouth if he could see her.

Actually, if this had been the three of them going to a club for their own enjoyment, a disturbingly intriguing thought, Gideon expected the vampire would simply unsheathe his fangs and make it clear anyone who tried to touch her would lose more than fingers. He had a similar feeling himself, but one he had to curb, because that wasn't the role he was supposed to play here. Fuck and double damn it.

As he closed the door, he gave Debra an even look and a nod, which she returned before she drove off, headed to the parking area. It was late enough that the crowd was thinning a little, but music still pumped out of the club like a fountain.

Gideon produced the envelope that Brian had given him and handed it over to the vampire at the door, managing an obsequious nod of his head that let him scan what the man was carrying. Probably a Bowie knife, some smaller knives and of course a wire to decapitate silently and with less muss, laced behind his dark belt. Both men were dressed in black fatigues.

"Welcome, Mistress Anwyn," one of them said with a slight nod of his head, his dark eyes roving over her in speculation. Gideon had to suppress an urge to step in front of her as he saw that despicable game begin, the way vampires tested one another, seeing what the pecking order might be. What they could get away with toward her. "You may prefer to skip the upper floor and go directly to the second level. The public and private viewing rooms there offer our kind more intense entertainments."

"How kind," she said, her voice that throaty purr she did so well. "Actually, I'm interested in all levels of the club, since I run my own fetish club in the States. Club Atlantis? Would the proprietor have the time and kindness to give me a more in-depth tour?"

It was a calculated risk. If Lord Stephen had shared any background on Daegan that might include his involvement with Anwyn, the game was up before she'd gotten out of the car. Gideon watched their reactions closely as the two guards glanced at each other.

"He's on the grounds tonight, but is currently entertaining another guest." There was an unpleasant glint of fang as the two guards shared the private joke. Unfortunately, Gideon was all too aware of the meaning. A flash of heat shot through Anwyn's eyes, a warning of stirred blood, but then it was gone before he could tense in preparation. She was keeping it leashed down damn well. He knew her desire to find Daegan was pumping behind a wall like a dike about to blow.

"However," the guard continued, his gaze undressing her again, "while 'kind' is not a word normally applied to Master Xavier, he might be willing, if you have an incentive to offer him."

Her spine straightened, just enough, and she met his gaze. "I understand the pleasure of incentives . . . for our kind. I might be willing to entertain them, for Master Xavier specifically." She gave a cool smile. "I'll hope he is available, so we can make the tour mutually pleasurable. Until then, I need no guide. I'll enjoy wandering through the club, making my own impressions."

Giving a quick flash of smile, she shifted her hips, tossed her hair back. "If that's permissible, I promise not to bite anyone."

The right combination of promise and denial. Of course, this was just getting in the door. Obviously not forewarned, unless they were better actors than Gideon suspected, the guards had no reason to be suspicious. Why would anyone be rescuing a vampire assassin from the bowels of their club, after all? Since Daegan's capture had been an ambush set up by a Council member, there was no reason for Xavier to be concerned about an obvious fledgling.

Gideon was sure Xavier was blood-connected to his two bouncers, so they'd likely already given him a mental heads-up, a mind "videocam" of their new arrival. While Anwyn had considerable weapons at her disposal, and she was vampire, she couldn't stand against even one of these older and more experienced vamps. Definitely not in those heels. Of course, toe-to-toe, he likely couldn't either. She was the one with the wits; he was the brawn. He'd let her lead until the time came for otherwise.

Let me lead? Perhaps I'll allow you to take over when I know it's wise.

Typical woman. But he was glad to hear her voice in his head with the admonishment. She'd assumed the role, pushing the rest aside for now. That was what they both needed for this to work.

"The hostess will come find you when the owner is free," the one said, handing back the note. Anwyn passed it to Gideon without looking at him, and he took it, sliding it into his jacket. She'd let him keep his dark jeans, but his chest was bare beneath the coat, the scarlet trinity visible on his left pectoral above his heart. He also wore the collar she'd bought for him, distinctive and bold on his neck. Even now, despite the circumstances, it was still capable of giving him that weird feeling.

He'd made a calculated risk by visibly arming himself, counting on vampire arrogance. He waited impassively to see if he'd made a mistake as they had him open the coat so they could see the shoulder harness for the steel knives and gun.

"My servant is protective of me," she noted with an indulgent smile. "But I expect I won't have any problems here."

"No," the doorman said. "There's not much he could do against us. He can keep his pretty toys. Good-quality knives," he noted with a soldier's approval.

Gideon thought of the thirty-six vampires like this smug bastard, the ones he'd staked in a variety of unexpected ways. It helped him keep his expression neutral as he inclined his head and followed Anwyn into the bowels of the Coffin.

It was the typical Goth club with a vampire fetish, almost a cliché, though a classy and expensive one. Lots of vampire paraphernalia, like the useless garlic cloves and many flashing silver and gold crosses hanging from the rafters. If someone came in with a cross, they were encouraged to loop it over the beams, a playful admission that they were throwing any protection for their souls away as they entered. Gideon saw a wide variety up there, everything from cheap pewter costume wear to crosses that might have been given to a kid as a graduation gift and lost in a moment of drunken stupidity. He didn't doubt that among them were crosses the vampires had placed there, sly trophies of actual kills amid harmless props.

True to the modus operandi of a smart bad guy, other transgressions in the club were kept to a minimum. He didn't see any indications of hard-drug users, dealers or professionals hustling the crowd. He didn't suspect these vamps feared law enforcement, though. Police were just an annoying inconvenience that could ruin the sweet deal they'd built here. No kills would ever be connected to this place. They'd be found far from these hallowed doors, if at all. He'd seen enough of this kind of vampire to know right away these guys killed when they wanted to kill, not at Council discretion or in respect of the "twelve human deaths per year allowed" rule. And Stephen covered for them so they'd do his dirty work. Asshole, conniving-prick weasel.

Anwyn had stopped, staring up at the crosses. She grazed her fingers along them, so that they moved against one another like wind chimes. *You'd expect the gateway to Hell to look like this. Childishly whimsical and horrible at once.*

Can you hear him, Anwyn? He moved closer, concerned about the tone of her mind, but she glanced over her shoulder at him with clear eyes, even as she took her hand down, scraped those nails high on his thigh, teasing at his groin.

No. Either he's not answering because he doesn't want us here, or he's unconscious.

Well, tell the bastard we're not leaving until we find him, so if he's awake, he might as well help us out so we're not walking in blind. He dipped his head, kissed her shoulder beneath the cloth of the snug dress, nuzzled until she pushed him away with studied indifference, and moved onward.

As he'd noted, it was a thinning crowd because of the late hour, so it made her that much more noticeable. Anwyn sauntered without any obvious haste, taking advantage of it. As if she were at a gallery, she studied the slaves who'd been hung on meat hooks with leather straps. Most were being tormented in some way by their Doms, or whoever they allowed to touch them. She was granted the invitation to touch by almost every Master and Mistress. Occasionally she took the opportunity.

With a curve of those mysterious lips, she slid her knuckles oh-so-lightly down a male thigh, caressed or weighed quivering testicles in her palm. Once, she bent to touch her lips to the sweat-slick abdomen of a young woman, so near climax that the kiss almost set her off, earning her the whip of her pleased Mistress. No matter the vampire dynamic, the hard-core could tell what Anwyn was. It was like recognizing royalty, and treating her accordingly. When she turned her gaze to any slave, they attuned to her, almost before their Dom or Domme directed them to do so.

It was an admirable strategy. She knew she was under scrutiny, and not by the club patrons. Somewhere, someone was watching, and she was calling him to her as skillfully as any sorceress, challenging a more experienced wizard to come put her in her place.

A dangerous and mesmerizing game, because he knew what she was attracting, and what their endgame was. Gideon divided his focus between her and a constant surveillance of his surroundings, which would be expected since he was already recognized as combat trained. He noted exits, obstacles, crowd groupings. Within them, he separated staff from clients, vampires from humans.

While he did, he said little in his mind, and neither did she. It wasn't necessary. Their minds were in perfect sync, an open radio channel waiting. Of course, thanks to her goading in the car and that synchronization, his body was no less susceptible to her magic than any other slave, hard and aching despite their purpose here.

I've seen the spy shows on television, Gideon. Everyone knows the best covers are those that are the closest to the truth.

That seductive tone, spinning him into her web. Every touch she dispensed, every look she gave, sent a wash of heat through him. He'd moved closer to her, so that her shoulder blades brushed his chest when she shifted. She was aware of him behind her, the protection and the offer at once. He was still just as alert to his surroundings, still cognizant of why they were there, but by falling into her natural role, just as he'd suggested, she'd brought him into it with her.

Turning into him, she threaded her hand through his hair, taking a tight hold, and yanked him down to her mouth for a hot kiss. Her tongue worked his as deftly as if she were sucking his cock, giving him that mental image to fog his antennae before she sank her fangs into the side of his mouth, from inside the cheek and outside, puncturing between the two.

The pain was excruciating, the nerve clusters there dense enough to render him almost insensible for a second, his fingers automatically clutching her hips in protest. Yet he didn't try to pull away from her. Later he would realize he wouldn't have, even if they were standing in the middle of her club at home, no threat to him but how she could make him into this. Her slave, willing to do anything to give her pleasure. She licked the blood away, soothing and abrading the throbbing ache at once, and dropped her hand to cup his balls in the snug jeans, massaging him there.

You know I could just squeeze, crush them and make you a eunuch forever?

What good would that do you, Mistress? He jerked his head up then, met her gaze with fire. Her grip tightened until it became painful, until he had to let out a gasp, which he strangled down to a growl.

You wouldn't ever look at another woman without my permission.

He couldn't have been more surprised if she'd punched him in the face. He'd been watching her kiss the naked slave, and sure, he'd have to be dead not to appreciate the wondrous variety of tits available at eye level every which way he looked. Big, small, jiggling, firm, clamped, pierced . . .

Jesus. He sucked in a breath as that flesh-and-bone nutcracker increased its grip.

"Perhaps," she murmured against his mouth, "I should make you drop your pants, walk with them around your ankles as if you were a shuffling prisoner, and let all these women have equal time to ogle your big cock, your fine ass, and wonder if I might give it to one of them. Or . . . perhaps you should apologize and keep your eyes down, on my feet, until I tell you whether you have my permission to look at *anything*."

He could tell nothing from her mind, because now it was filled with this. The vampire side of her, strong and in full force, a herald of what she would become if she could pull it out so easily now. There was a vicious undercurrent to it that suggested she was letting her bloodlust rise. Or it was rising, whether she wanted it to do so or not. If he assumed the former, since the latter just couldn't happen right now or they were all dead, the question was: Was this real, or was there an ulterior motive? It helped convince those watching that she was absorbed in the pleasures of the club, for sure, and that she was a badass vampire, but the intent he felt pulsing from her was very real. As was the response he gave her.

"I'd rather spend the rest of my life staring at your beautiful legs and ass than at any other woman."

"I said my feet."

"That, too. But my gaze has an unavoidable range, Mistress." He flinched when she caught the back of his nape and sank her fangs into that same spot beside his mouth again. Fuck, if the Council ever decided they needed a torturer as well as an assassin, he'd have a great candidate.

"Your feet, Mistress," he grated out when she released him. "I'll keep my eyes on your feet."

She stroked the hair at his neck with deceptive tenderness. "See that you do. Or I'll shove something the size of your fist up your ass and make you keep it there all night so you remember it."

"Breaking in a servant is always a pleasure and a curse at once, isn't it?"

Anwyn slowly pivoted on her heel, using Gideon's body as a wall, leaning against him. Crossing her ankles, she reached back with both arms to take a nice grip on the part she'd just been threatening, rubbing herself against his cock in a sly little move as she tossed her hair again, lashing his neck with it. It gave the approaching vampire an eyeful of thrusting breast, the taunting impression that she was bound, when she was not.

"More pleasure than curse, truly," she said. "You must be the owner."

"Xavier." The male moved forward from the shadows and Gideon kept his eyes down, though Anwyn sent him a clear enough picture. A big motherfucker, tall as Daegan, but not lean and graceful. This one looked exactly like what he was, the most dangerous possible combination. A thug with a brain, his intelligence showing through the burning clarity in his gaze. "Mistress Anwyn, let me welcome you to my club properly."

He moved faster than she or Gideon could anticipate. One second, they were standing; the next, Gideon stifled a curse as he was slammed against a wall. Anwyn was still in front of him, only now she was mashed between Gideon's body and Xavier's. He had his hand collared around her throat, his thumb forcing her chin up.

"You don't draw blood in my club, fledgling. It attracts unnecessary attention." Bending, he licked the corner of Anwyn's mouth where Gideon's blood had been. Anwyn trembled, managing to pull it off as a shudder of desire, but Gideon knew differently. One blatant movement, forcing her in between the two of them, and those shadow creatures were trying to drag her down, take her back into an alley. The stench of vampires and blood all around her, no escape, no ability to move, seeing what was coming.

I'm here, Anwyn. It's not the alley. We're here to help Daegan. He's just testing you. You know it. Remember, Daegan is here. We have to find Daegan.

Xavier had maneuvered them so quickly, her hands were still gripping Gideon's ass, but now she shifted her grip so her thumbs hooked his belt, holding on for support and reminder, not provocation. Gideon would have given anything to offer her more, but he had to settle for the slightest movement of his thumb along one hip, his breath at the crown of her head, his heart pounding steadily between her shoulder blades. He didn't allow himself to think anything. He couldn't descend into the rage that normally would have taken him over, or get trapped by the helpless fury that he couldn't help her right now. He reminded himself, and her by proxy, that they were in charge of this situation, regardless, because Xavier didn't know why they were here.

You're the scariest bitch imaginable when you want to be, whether you're facing man or bloodsucker.

She got that message, loud and clear. Her finger loosened on his belt, though she continued to hold it. "My apologies, Master Xavier." She tilted her head, her hair whispering over his beefy knuckles, their continued grip on her throat. "Unlike you, we allow bloodletting at Atlantis, under controlled circumstances. Even before I became a vampire. Do you usually handle Mistresses as if they're your personal slaves? I don't think I'd get repeat business at my club if I allowed that."

Her voice didn't shake now. She even managed to convey cool disdain.

Xavier gazed down at her. It was taking everything Gideon had to stay still, be her submissive wall, when that hand still rested on her throat, the male's saliva probably still drying on the corner of her mouth. But it was then he felt it. A pulsing rage coming through her, fuzzy and somewhat disoriented, but unmistakable in its homicidal intent.

Daegan was alive. And murderously awake.

18

His reaction to their presence was also unmistakable, strong enough that Gideon wasn't entirely sure if the rage was directed at Xavier for touching Anwyn, or at the two of them, for trying to come after him. Anwyn's mind was still open to his, so that he heard the flood of thoughts. It alarmed him, how disjointed they sounded.

Run... Don't... Can't protect. Where... How got here... His voice faded away.

He's been weakened somehow. Anwyn's thought, laced with anger and apprehension, stiffened her body against Xavier's touch more than even her cool response should have warranted.

Steady, Gideon warned. He dared more of a caress at her hips, making it look as if he were taking a better grip to brace himself against the insistent pressure of Xavier against her.

"Careful, fledgling," Xavier said. He sounded amused, but nothing in his expression suggested it. "You may be queen of your little club at home, but you're on my turf here. I'll strip you down, hang you upside down on one of those meat hooks and whip your little ass through your panties until they're in tatters, like that unwise pride of yours." He leaned in, his breath an insidious intrusion against her ear, hot and revolting against Gideon's thundering pulse. "There are no rules except power among vampires, little one. No matter what bullshit the Council's been feeding you."

"You can't get panties under this dress." She turned her face so her lips almost brushed his. Arching her back like a purring cat, she curved her leg around the back of Xavier's. It had to press his cock right up against her crotch, because she wrapped her flexible leg so high her knee brushed his ass.

Being in her mind, Gideon witnessed something remarkable. She compartmentalized, as if she were doing summer cleaning and putting things in boxes under a bed, only she did it in a rapid blink. Bam, bam, bam, the alley vanished. Every horrible transition moment vanished, the restraints, all of it. Even that brief glimpse he'd been given of her childhood got contained and thrust into the shadows, knocking the shadow creatures away like bowling pins. All that remained was Anwyn, a Mistress walking into a room and facing down her prey.

She'd learned, too many times now, that there was no way she could control the seizures if they wanted to come. Yet with Daegan in danger, it seemed she was going to refuse to let it happen. The effort of it reminded Gideon of mothers who lifted cars to save their children. The consequences of such an effort, the fallout it would bring, were secondary to her, no matter what happened later.

Leaning her head back on Gideon's shoulder, she angled her chin to nuzzle his neck above the collar. It deliberately exposed her throat. Xavier's eyes crawled over it greedily. "I'm sure you can beat me up or kill me, Xavier. But is fear the only way you'll earn my respect? The man who created all this"—her gaze passed over the club—"has a brain."

Her shifting pressed her ass into Gideon's groin. Of course his was probably nowhere near as excited as Xavier's probably was at her taunt.

Stop this . . . Run.

Shut up, Daegan. Gideon didn't know if he could hear him through Anwyn's mind, but he had to try. *She can't afford the distraction right now.*

A muttering grumble, like a distant storm thunder, but it subsided. *Good.* It suggested Daegan, while somehow drugged, was cognizant. Xavier smiled, showing a wide mouth with a hint of fang. "A tour of the circus means you have to pay for a ticket."

"I'll gladly pay it. If what I see is worth the price of admission."

"I am a pay-up-front man." Xavier eased back enough to let his gaze walk with blatant crudeness down her breasts, to her crotch. "I'm civilized, but I'm also a beast. The beast in me needs to see you sucking my big cock, before I'm willing to prove anything to you." His eyes glowed red in the darkness of the club. "You sashayed your ass in here, and got the attention of damn near every Master and Mistress. You did it to taunt me, and now you pay a price for that. We both know I'm just indulging you. I don't owe you shit. Go to your knees now, show me respect, and then we'll give you that tour."

"You'll have to beat me to unconsciousness in front of them to get me to do that."

Her words cut through Gideon's haze of rage. He wanted to stake him so badly he nearly trembled with it, fury filling him with such strong purpose he knew it wasn't only his own. It belonged to him and Daegan, anyone daring to touch her, to force her. They'd never let it happen to her again, even if they had to torch the whole damn world to prevent it.

However, her statement cut through all that. He felt a deadly calm pass through her mind, stilling the faintest breeze of anxiety or shadowy whisper. It was something he'd never felt from her before, though there was something tumultuous and terrifyingly familiar about it. Like the silence before a tornado came. The largest, most powerful twister possible, one that would turn on her and blast her to shreds if she lost control now. But she was more than controlling it, keeping it at bay. She was fucking channeling it as her own personal weapon, to hold her own against this wall of bloodsucking muscle and every schizophrenic voice in her head trying to pull her down.

"I've met many big and powerful men, Xavier," she said softly, and there was that same dead calm in the tone, something that would catch the attention of even a hardened psychopath, give him a trickle of unease. Gideon knew the hairs on his own neck were standing up at that eerie tone. "The ones that like to threaten, that tell a woman that she's got to be on her knees or else. Those are the ones that wish just the reverse were true. They want to meet the woman who can order them to *their* knees, force them to do it by the will of her mind alone, to punish them for every transgression they've committed against a woman. To heal the sickness in their hearts. They're seeking divine absolution from a Goddess they can't summon before them. One they challenge every single time they abuse a woman, daring Her to come down and punish them."

She straightened, which moved her closer so she and Xavier were facing each other with several inches between them. "Now, are you going to give me a tour of the club and impress me with what you've created, or are you going to continue to try and threaten me with your dick? I've seen plenty of them, and never found them particularly intimidating." A feline smile curved her lips. "A man's mind, his ability to create Rome, to conquer nations, that's power. Not forcing a woman one-third his size to suck his cock on the dirty floor of a sex club."

Xavier stared at her for long moments. The beat of the club's music vibrated through Gideon's feet, in tune with his thundering heartbeat, the pulse of Anwyn's body, so close to them both and yet so distant in a strange way. Her mind was shuttered like a trap, a total darkness that awed and worried him at once. When he dared a glance around, he realized they were almost alone. The other patrons had moved on, as if sensing the volatile nature of what was happening, or encouraged that way by two other vampires who had appeared from the shadows, here to reinforce Xavier's will if needed.

Despite the force with which she'd just taken the reins, a familiar rubber-band-taut apprehension was swirling in his gut. He'd had it twice before, both times right before he'd been captured by a vampire. It made him antsy as hell. He wanted to strike out, fight in some physical way before things became any more claustrophobic. He held steady, though, because she did. Though Xavier saw and felt only the sexy frosting of the ice she was dishing out, Gideon could feel her pulling on his strength with all that she had to keep that chill. They were a unit, one person. He had to remember that.

Xavier shook his head at last, a rough chuckle rumbling from his chest. "Boys, I best watch my step. I might be talking to a future Council member here. You've certainly got bigger balls than most of them. Not a whiff of fear on you." His gaze hardened. "Don't push it, though. Lovely and clever only go so far with me."

For the first time, he turned his attention to Gideon. "This one looks big and mean enough, but you seem to have him towing the line. I should have known you had more than one ace in that tight dress of yours." He proffered an arm. "Shall we take that tour?"

Inclining her head, she laid her slim fingers in the crook of his arm, caressing his biceps with easy familiarity, as if they'd never teetered on a violent edge. "It would be my pleasure, Master Xavier."

∾

He took his bloody time with it. A thorough tour of the upper area, and then the lower dungeons, where more intense, and a lot less legal, play occurred. Couples that liked to push it way past the safe-word route, into play that was far too risky for the body. Asphyxiation, full sensory deprivation, beatings, electric shock. Russian roulette with loaded weapons. Anwyn passed by it all with perfect aplomb, whereas Gideon felt like he needed a shower. What he'd seen in the lower levels of her dungeon had skirted into these areas, but were far better monitored, the boundaries far clearer than he'd realized at the time. Anwyn had no interest in facilitating people with a careless desire to throw away their lives or who cared so little for the trust of their slaves that they'd cause them permanent damage.

While Gideon had shied away from the physical machinations of BDSM, having a difficult enough time with his own strong responses to psychological D/s, he had a new appreciation for Anwyn's firm but intelligent hand on it by the time they reached the final staircase. They were already belowground, making Gideon wonder if the club had once been some type of utility facility, delving this far into the earth.

"If you're a bit squeamish about taking things too far, this level isn't for you, little queen," Xavier said, sliding a finger across the top of her right breast, a casually possessive touch, as if he already assumed he had that liberty. "Typically only very select clientele go into this area."

"Lord Stephen hinted you had such a place." Her gaze gleamed, her lips lifting in a cruel smile. "Why do you think I was so eager to come here?" She glanced back at Gideon as if she were looking at a prized possession, not a sentient being. "Last night, I used a bullwhip on him. Thirty-six lashes, until the skin was hanging in strips off his back." She gave a shiver. "He screamed during the last of it. Then he crawled to me, put his lips to my shoe. I was a Mistress before I was a vampire, but I find I like how much deeper I can take it . . . with fangs."

"I would have liked to see that. I can see why Lord Stephen directed you our way." Eyes gleaming in anticipation, Xavier flourished her ahead. "I have a captive lion below that needs to learn quite a bit more humility. Maybe I'll let you help me with that."

"My pleasure." Anwyn's expression reflected eagerness, with the right touch of wariness. Gideon amended his earlier assessment. She was scarier than he'd ever imagined she could be. However, as she gracefully descended, he had to bite back his irritation and discomfort when Xavier stepped in behind her, leaving him to bring up the rear. The bastard's hand rested nearly on her ass to "steady" her going down the winding staircase.

We're getting close, Gideon. She'd done such a good job of pulling in Xavier, Gideon was relieved to hear her voice, the concern and compassion, speak in his mind. *I can feel him, but I'm not sure . . . I think he's out again.*

All right. We know our plan. Hold to it. I've seen eight vampires in the building so far, and it's a safe bet Xavier's linked to all of them.

This was a dungeon in truth, complete with water dripping from damp walls and stifling, close air. Though he heard nothing, it was like the stone had absorbed past cries of pain and hopelessness. Cold fingers gripped his vitals. As they reached the ground level, Xavier took them down a narrow, poorly lit corridor. Opening a metal door with a security panel code, he swung it inward, gesturing Anwyn ahead of him.

Following them in, Gideon saw several cells. Two of them held small clusters of young women who had obviously been club patrons above. Their clothes were too thin and scanty for this damp level. Some were like junkies, sprawled on the dirty floor or cots in various stages of stupor. Seeing the pallid tones of their skin, their lethargy, he realized they were being used as donors, with no care for how much or how often. When they were husks, their bodies would be discarded.

Others not so far gone huddled in the corners or behind the cots, keeping their eyes down, as if that would keep them from being noticed. He saw bruises and gashes, evidence of other forms of abuse Anwyn would recognize far too well. The pretty clothes they'd donned to entice others and please themselves were now soiled rags that mocked the independent spirit that had brought them to the club doors.

"It's inconvenient to my men to maintain servants, and going out to dinner all the time can be a pain in the ass. Why do that when we have a potential buffet upstairs every night?"

"Indeed," Anwyn murmured. "But don't you worry about human law enforcement?"

"Their disappearances are never connected here. My men talk up the girls, target the ones that come alone, that have few family ties, or are just traveling in the area, not locals. We take a new one every few months, space it out." He nodded to a girl that appeared to be barely breathing, curled in a fetal position in a corner. "That tough little piece of ass, we call her Sarah. She's survived nearly six months with us. If any authority gets too close, it's easy to distract them or make them vanish. That's what you need to understand, fledgling." Xavier shrugged a massive shoulder. "The Council won't tell you this, but as long as we stick to the shadows, we can do as we please. Humans don't want to discover us. They don't want to believe we exist."

"I'm only seeing young girls," she said, with just a touch of boredom. "You promised me a lion." She glanced up at him with an avaricious smile tinged with hope that Gideon fervently wished never to see on her face again. "I saw a bear once, in the States. All pent up in a cage outside a casino. He caught a gawker who got too close. They'd declawed him, the cowards, but he still crushed the man's chest, beat him to death against the bars. It was when I was human, so at the time I thought I was appalled. But secretly . . . it was delicious, in a way."

"Yeah, you have a taste for it, all right. Maybe you should consider staying in our territory for a while." Xavier leaned in with a wink. "You could be my little secret, so I wouldn't have to share you with a territory overlord. I bet Stephen would do it as a favor for me. You could pretend to get on your plane back to the States, but never really go back."

Anwyn laughed. "As appealing as that sounds, I have a club to run there, a lucrative business. Maybe you could come be *my* little secret, hmm?" She winked at him, moved forward with a sashay of hips that was pretty much indecent. Walking down the stairs had worked the dress up around her hips, the lower curve of one bare buttock almost visible, even in the dim light. She adjusted the hem with a finger caressing the cheek, making Xavier growl low in his chest.

"You'll be fucking me tonight, fledgling. No matter what clever words you say or do. Hope you can handle a big cock in that smart ass of yours. I want to make you cry."

"I don't waste my time on anything small." She gave that head toss again. "Where's my lion?"

Xavier chuckled. "Impatient bitch. I have other, more interesting playrooms for vampires beyond this one, but I'll show you my current prize." He moved past the cells to another heavy door and pushed it open.

Gideon tried to brace himself for the next horror he would see. More important, he prepared to brace Anwyn, if it was Daegan.

It was.

She saw him first, because Gideon felt all those carefully packed boxes in her mind swell against their seams, in danger of rupturing as rage entered her mind like a flood. It shoved into every corner of her mind, threatening to disrupt that cool veneer that had carried her this far.

He wanted to get closer to her, give her physical as well as emotional support, but Xavier stood between them. His hand was now square on her ass, fondling the hem of her skirt, meaty finger sliding under it. He'd have it in her pussy in a second, and Gideon knew she wouldn't be able to handle that. Her skin was crawling from everywhere he'd already touched her. The bastard likely planned to fuck her right here. The stench of his arousal was growing.

It was easy to see at a glance why Daegan had sounded so disoriented and weak. He'd been restrained on a steel autopsy table, so that the blood being drained from him flowed down the molded channels. It was a slow drip, but the blood bags to catch the flow were full, another three already lined up where he could see them. There was a refrigerator out in the cell area, so no telling how much had already been banked, or if they were just throwing it away.

Gideon realized the purpose wasn't torture. That was a side benefit. This was to keep him weak. Apparently, even that hadn't been enough, because crude electric wires had been wrapped across his far-too-pale body. The bastards had left the power source on, keeping his body jerking, the smell of flesh burning constant and nauseating. No wonder his thoughts had been coming through disjointed.

For as little time as Gideon had known Daegan, perhaps because his mind was so melded with Anwyn's, he realized he'd unconsciously shared her belief that Daegan Rei would fall to no one. To see him weakened and tortured like this, brought down low by trickery and cowardice, opened something as dark and volatile inside him as what was boiling in Anwyn's soul. He closed his hands into fists just as Daegan's eyes opened, the dark, dull depths struggling to focus. Gideon remembered the man's grace, his deadly speed, the way he'd spoken with such calm about justice. No revenge, no anger, just quiet dispensation to balance the scales.

Sorry, Daegan. I think this calls for full Noah-flood, wrath-of-God response.

"Feel no pity for this one, Mistress Anwyn," Xavier assured her. "He was a lion to take down in truth. Killed four of my men, even though we had the jump on him. He's a very powerful vampire. Centuries old."

"What did he do to earn this punishment?" Her voice was flat and wooden, but fortunately Xavier was caught up in his boasting and didn't notice.

"He offended me. I will drink his blood, let my men drink it, and keep him alive long past when he is a living skeleton, to show my enemies what I'm capable of being. This is what I was saying, sweet fledgling. I am a worthy overlord for you. At least for tonight. Or until I tire of you." He gave an ugly laugh that was matched by feral grins from the three vampires now arrayed at the door. Gideon flicked a glance toward them. It was the two from earlier, plus one more. Xavier had apparently signaled them to rejoin the party. *Shit.*

Anwyn turned on her heel, studying Xavier. "I think it's time to pay that price of admission," she said with a slow curve of her lips, the baring of her fangs. To the completely oblivious, it suggested she was aroused by his display of strength. She unfastened her belt, the jewels and chains catching the dim light.

"You knew I wanted to do it right here. Intuitive little thing." Lust thickened the vampire's voice. Gideon felt the pressure of his knives, gauged the distance to the three vampires. *We're still a go, Anwyn. Do it.*

"Right here." She echoed Xavier's words, a cold and deadly tone entering her soft voice. Then she dropped the belt to the ground with a clink of metal. Threading her fingers under her hair, as if searching for a fastener at the high collar of her dress, she stepped toward the vampire. As he moved to close the distance, she stepped on the belt, the center jewel setting.

The tiny crunch of broken glass made him look down. "Ah, sweetling, you broke your pretty baubles. We'll have to—" He stopped, swaying, his brow furrowing. With a disoriented frown, he turned to his men.

Gideon leaped for him. As expected, the vampires responded instantly, rushing forward to defend their leader.

They crossed right into the invisible fumes now drifting into the air. Thank God it worked fast. They were not as large as Xavier, and fell quicker, dropping to their knees, though one did reach Gideon, tackled him like a front lineman in that rush of movement too quick to follow. Gideon grunted at the bone-breaking impact that would have killed him if he were still human. Now he managed to pull the wooden knives he'd concealed in the lining of his jacket, tearing the seam. He staked the one and lunged for the others, who were scrabbling across the floor, eyes wide and dazed.

Xavier remained on his feet, rocking like a tree in a storm, his eyes flashing with anger and fear at once, his giant fists clenching, trying to fight it off.

Anwyn had shoved away from him in that first moment, stepping out of her shoes lithely to run to Daegan's side. Putting the filter mask she'd had folded inside the neck of her dress over her nose and mouth, she put another one over Daegan's face.

Xavier struggled forward, stumbling, his murderous gaze on her. Gideon shouted out a warning, tried to get past the two crawling vampires, but he needn't have worried about his Mistress.

He never saw a hint of fear. When the big male fell, she moved back toward him, slipping the mask tie over her head to free both her hands. Bending with a predator's grace, she picked up one of her abandoned stilettos just as Xavier crashed to the floor at her feet. Gideon's heart skipped a beat at how close the monster was to her. However, dizzy and fumbling, Xavier was unable to push her away as she straddled him. Her eyes bright with cold rage, fangs bared, she slammed the heel of her shoe into his chest. Fueled by vengeance, she brought her fist down on it like a hammer. The impact was so great she caved in his chest, making sure those five inches of wood went straight into his heart.

She twisted it with a snarl, and earned a dying bellow of pain. Shaking himself out of his moment of pure admiration and adoration for her, Gideon straddled the other two helplessly wriggling males and staked them with the wooden-bladed knives. When he spun around, Anwyn was back on her bare feet, her eyes still wild.

"Think I can't take him with these heels now?" she demanded, her voice muffled by the filter mask.

It took a second to recall his thought about her shoes, barely an hour ago. But she wasn't seeking a response. She was back at Daegan's side, hand on his mask to steady it, to make sure he didn't inadvertently inhale the now-dissipating fumes. Though most vampires didn't breathe when unconscious, Brian had explained the fumes could still enter the nasal membranes or soft tissue in the roof of the mouth if they didn't take the precaution.

Brian's chemical worked on the same theory of high-noon daylight, making vampires more sluggish, the reaction enhanced by a factor of ten. It had no impact on humans. Gideon had wondered if the Council knew Brian was not only researching vampire weaknesses, but making weapons out of them, but knew it was far more likely he was making them with their blessing.

A worry for another time.

He covered the door as she secured the straps for the mask over Daegan's ears. Then she disconnected the battery holding the wires with a competence that suggested she wasn't unfamiliar with electric shock, at least as a BDSM tool. As she pulled the needles out of his arms and throat as gently as she could, she studied the pale face, the closed eyes. "He needs blood, Gideon. A lot of it." Her head came up. "Go into the next room. In that first cell."

～

Gideon glanced at her sharply, as if he'd caught something unexpected from her mind. "You're not suggesting those girls—"

"If it would save his life and not take theirs? In a heartbeat," she snapped. "But there was a refrigerator there, remember? I'm willing to bet they bank human blood in case of emergencies. Go get as much as you can carry. Unless you have some moral objection to *that*."

Knowing she sounded shrill, she closed her eyes, fighting her unreasonable anger with him, out of proportion for the moment. The bloodlust boiling through her, the cacophony of voices in her head, were way too roused by this environment.

When he pivoted on his heel without further comment, going into the next room to find the fridge, she located a fan in the corner. Turning it on, she waited a few key seconds before she took a cautious inhalation without her mask to confirm the fumes had dispersed adequately. Putting a hand on Daegan's far-too-still face, her throat got thick as she removed the mask and stroked his hair, bent to touch his cold mouth. Thank God Xavier and his men hadn't favored human servants. If they'd dropped dead on the floor above at the moment she and Gideon had taken their Masters' lives, it might have brought a larger force of vampires down here. As it was, it was getting too close to dawn. Soon the club doors would be closing, and she was sure this lower level was where Xavier's men passed the daylight hours, probably toying with those poor girls in the next room, and whatever fresh victims they brought down.

Tapping into Gideon's mind, she found her servant had met an obstacle. The girls still aware enough had shrunk back in fear as he came into the cell. He spoke to them quietly, told them they were trying to get them out of there, but they needed to stay put for now. However, Sarah, the girl who had been in a fetal position, apparently was quite tough, as Xavier had said. At Gideon's words she'd made it to her feet, albeit swaying on legs that were far too thin. The feral look in her eye said she was cognizant enough to recognize escape was near, but her mind too altered to hear what he was saying. The twisting agony in Gideon's heart shot pain through Anwyn's when he had to shove the girl back forcibly, closing the cell door. They couldn't risk her running aloft and calling down the others any sooner.

It's all right, Gideon. We'll take care of them all.

Yeah. A little late for that.

His hot hatred and revulsion for vampire kind boiled over into her brain, nearly upsetting that cauldron of simmering bloodlust. She had to fight it down, enough that when he brought her the blood, she could manage only a curt nod. "Watch the door."

His hands were clenched into fists, his gaze on Daegan's too-pale face, but he complied. Anwyn tore the seal off the first packet and brought it to Daegan's lips.

"It's cold, love, but drink. It will bring back your strength. Wake up. Daegan, we don't have much time." She took a deep breath, blasted him in her mind as well as with her low, urgent voice. *We're in danger. I need you.*

He came awake with a sudden snap, his hand clamping down on her wrist in a painful vise that could have broken human bones. As it was, it wrenched a gasp from her, but he was too immediately disoriented to gentle his touch. He was drinking, though, pulling hard at the packet in her hand, draining it. She fumbled to reach the other, trying to pull the seal off it one-handed. Ignoring her curt order, Gideon came back and did the task for her. Sliding the empty one from Daegan when he drained it, Gideon brought the next to his mouth. Daegan's hands closed over Gideon's fingers as he drank. Gideon held that contact until Daegan was able to hold the packet on his own; then he slid his hand free.

Anwyn put a hand on his shoulder, another on Daegan's, drawing strength from the fact the three of them were here, together, and alive. At least for the moment. She didn't know if vampires could drink so fast that it would make them sick, but fortunately it didn't seem to be the case. As Daegan gulped down four of the containers, color started to come back to his face, his eyes growing more alert and sharp on the two of them. By the time he finished pack five, he was sitting up without aid, his feet planted solidly on the floor.

The burn lines of the live wires didn't seem to trouble him, and she assumed they were already healing. Other than that, there were no marks on his naked body, save for a pair of crossed ugly slashes high on the inside of his thigh. A branded X. For that scar to remain, Xavier had seared it with Daegan's own blood, the only way to permanently mark a vampire. He'd wanted Daegan to carry his brand. She wished she'd dispatched the piece of shit in a more painful way.

Could have been worse, cher. *He talked several times about cutting off my cock, putting it in a blender and making me drink it.* Daegan wiped his mouth with the back of his hand and glanced around. "Are my clothes anywhere around?"

Just like that. Fully in command of the situation, now that his sensibilities had been restored, but Anwyn sensed he needed more. "You're not at full strength. You need some fresh blood."

"I've had enough to get us out of here."

"But not enough to finish the job you came here to do." She knew he wanted that, felt it from him in a low-level pulsing fury that matched her own. She didn't care about what the Council would or wouldn't do to her. She wanted those vampires taken down because they'd hurt him, bound him. She didn't have to reach out far to know Gideon felt the same way.

"Getting you both to safety is my first priority," Daegan said evenly. Gideon had found the cabinet where they'd stored his weapons and clothes. Daegan yanked on the jeans without bothering with the torn briefs, ignored the tattered shirt. Shrugged into the duster and loaded it with his weapons. The state of the clothes, the bloodstains on the jeans, told her how many injuries he'd initially sustained when they took him down. He twirled the sword, loosening up his wrist, sheathed the knives.

"She's right," Gideon said. "And it's not just about payback, Daegan. They're holding prisoners in the next room, and half of them won't be able to walk out on their own. If we leave them, they'll kill them before we come back. She's right about the blood, too."

Daegan twisted around as Gideon shed his torn coat, revealing his bare upper body, though he left the collar on. "Take it from where you need it."

Anwyn was surprised, warmed by it. Until Gideon locked gazes with her. *Might as well give it to him before you make it an order. Right, Mistress?*

Gideon excelled at wry humor in high-pressure situations. She knew that. But the deepest layers of his soul were at high tide, darkening any light, and the comment didn't hit her as casual wit. He was horrified by what had happened down here. Female victims were always the most difficult for him to handle. His mind was replaying ten years of layered images, the things he'd seen vampires do to his kind.

His kind. She swallowed. Had she really just thought that? In such a short time, was she already identifying more with the vampire she'd become than with the human she'd always been? Remembering the flicker in his gaze when she'd commanded him to go get blood out of the women's cells, she realized that was what he'd seen in her eyes, what had given him pause. And she couldn't deny it.

Not very long ago, he'd expressed amazement she'd handled everything that had been done to her so well. On that same note, she wondered that he'd managed to get this far at her side without having more moments like this, when his passive angers reared up and struck like venomous snakes.

Regret crossed Gideon's face, apparently realizing how the comment had struck her, but before he could reach out to her, Daegan surprised them both. Picking up the coat, he tossed it back to Gideon.

"No," he said. "I don't need it." When he strode from the room, they exchanged a glance and followed him, puzzled, to the cells that held the women. Anwyn saw the same confusion of fear and hope that Gideon had confronted, but when they recognized what Daegan and Anwyn were, they shrank back again.

"I need to take some fresh blood from one of you," Daegan said in his velvet, sensual voice, the one that stroked frayed nerves. "Not all vampires are like those here. It won't hurt, and it won't harm you. Three minutes, and then I will be strong enough to get you out of here. You will be able to go back to your homes and families."

He moved into the cell. There were no volunteers, of course, but Anwyn was surprised that he moved toward Sarah. But since she'd uncurled from her fetal position, she'd made it obvious she had the most spirit, even if she was weak from malnourishment and blood loss. Maybe Xavier and his monsters had gotten bored with her and used her less than the newer girls. She looked like a wild animal, hair disheveled and no makeup. Anwyn assumed they let the girls bathe, because the stench in here was from sickness, blood and fear, not unwashed bodies. However, when she saw a coiled hose in the corner with a cold-water tap, the image of them being hosed down through the bars made Anwyn feel fury anew.

But Daegan was murmuring to her, as if to a wounded and abused animal, which she supposed was what Sarah was. While her fists were still clenched, her frightened, angry eyes watching him, she was trembling. The others shrank back, made no move to bolt toward the open cell door, as if they'd realized long ago how futile that was, only an amusing game for their captors.

"Your name, child," he said quietly. "Do not fear me."

"They called me Sarah. I don't . . . I can't remember my real name."

As she met his gaze, hers unexpectedly filled with tears at what she saw in his face. Perhaps she saw the truth, that he did mean to help. Anwyn knew Daegan Rei had that effect on a hurting woman.

Then, oddly, the girl's eyes became unfocused, and she swayed forward, toward Daegan.

"Sarah," he murmured. "Come to me."

~

Gideon knew compulsion was a gift that some older vampires had. However, it usually worked only on a human whose blood the vampire had taken, unless the vampire was extremely powerful, like Lady Lyssa. Or in this case, Daegan Rei. As the magic spun its hypnotic web, Daegan drew her closer to his body so she leaned into him, getting lost in the folds of his duster. Her cheek rested on his chest as he stroked her hair to the side and bent his head. When he sank his fangs into the side of her throat, he released the pain-numbing pheromones immediately, for she moved in lazy sensuality against him, responding to it. As he drank, he pressed his arm around her back, stroking her, keeping her still, soothing her. It was probably the first kind touch she'd experienced in months. She certainly hadn't experienced it from Gideon.

He turned away, unable to watch. Anwyn's focus was all on Daegan. Reaching out from his head to hers, he saw the gremlins trembling in the corners of her mind like gladiators waiting for the gate to go up so they could charge the arena. He moved through that center area, going by instinct to help calm her, give her strength against them. He wasn't sure she was even aware of the effort, as everything in her was attuned to the other vampire.

As Sarah's hands relaxed, burrowing into Daegan's coat and the increasing warmth, Anwyn's clenched. Gideon wondered what thoughts were in her mind right now, but his own were so torn up, he couldn't summon the courage to find out, to rise above the insidious gremlin chatter. It was safe there, black and white. His world was easier if he kept it that way.

He'd been there, right in front of him, offering, and Daegan had turned him down. *I don't need it.*

Daegan *had* needed it; he just wouldn't take it from Gideon, though he'd have given him ten quarts of his blood if it got him off that damn table and looking like the Daegan he knew. Untouchable, capable of handling anything, even Gideon's constant barbs.

Just because he couldn't offer blood with fucking enthusiasm didn't mean he wasn't willing.

They'd lost precious seconds convincing and gentling this terrified woman to get the blood Gideon could have given in a blink. Damn it, he'd screwed up. He hadn't meant to give Anwyn attitude at such a stupid time, but it had been knee-jerk. A reaction to what he'd seen rear its head in her mind at that moment, like a fire-breathing dragon, scarier than the voices, because it had been *her*, not them.

Yeah, he knew this environment was taking its toll on both of them, particularly her. She was working her ass off to keep the things in her mind under control, drawing on his energy as much as possible. But unfortunately, he knew the difference between what Anwyn, the tough-as-nails woman, would do to protect her own, and what the vampire blood thought it had every right to demand. Even though she hadn't consciously recognized it, when she told him to go to the cells to get the blood, it was that voice he'd heard and seen.

If she'd thought fresh blood was necessary, she would have made him drag one of those girls in here and open up her vein for Daegan. Or done it herself. She would have stopped short of killing the girl, just as she said, but she would not have been denied. She knew she had the strength to force her will, and she would have used it.

Just as vampires always did when it came to a choice between what they wanted and what a human wanted. He knew his reaction to that was fucking idiotic. They were in a life-or-death situation. If something happened to her, he knew he'd go to extremes to protect her as well, care for her. But this was different. He could see in her mind, so he couldn't tell himself he'd misinterpreted her emotions in the heat of the moment. She hadn't thought of it as extreme. It had simply been an option available to her.

Daegan eased a weakened Sarah onto one of the bunks, drawing Gideon out of his mind, and Anwyn's. The cot was filthy, but since the floor was worse, it was the better alternative. "Stay here with her," he commanded the rest of the prisoners, as if they'd become active participants in the rescue. "We must dispatch the others before we can get you out, so you are safer in here until we have done that." Then he was turning and leaving the cell. He left the cell door closed but unlocked. None of the girls moved, and Gideon didn't blame them.

When Daegan turned toward the two of them, there was nothing remotely human about him. Something had happened while he was drinking. His eyes had gone all the way dark, no whites, though there was a tinge of crimson to them. His movements were so eerily graceful Gideon realized he was moving almost exactly like a feline predator. Now he knew why Xavier had called him a captive lion. It hadn't been an idle taunt.

Was the transformation the result of restoring so much blood so quickly, or was this how he looked right before a battle? Gideon didn't know, but it kept everyone in place, waiting to see what he would do. Even he and Anwyn.

Daegan turned his attention to her now. "Take the west staircase back up to the club floor. They don't watch that one, because it only opens from this side and they don't expect anyone but Xavier or his people to use it. Tell them Xavier finished his tour and you're leaving. You can say your servant already preceded you."

She stared at him, incredulous. "I'm not leaving you. There's absolutely no way."

"Yes, you are." The deadly tone made it clear she wasn't talking to Daegan, but to a warrior who would brook no argument from his troops.

Gideon could have told him that worked better on males. Anwyn crossed her arms and gave him an "I'm not buying it" look that made it clear she wasn't going unless it was kicking and screaming. Gideon might have found some humor in it, but her earlier words, recalled to his mind now, made it no laughing matter.

I won't run. Not ever again. Not when someone I love needs me.

"*Cher,*" Daegan said sharply; then he closed his eyes, sighed. "You have a vampire's strength, but these are trained fighters, who are also vampires. I don't doubt your courage. If we survive this, I promise to train you to be a guerrilla soldier."

"Don't patronize me," she said sharply, but her voice broke, an unexpected snap. Gideon assumed that was the only thing that kept Daegan from roaring at her. Still, he had no time for tenderness. Instead, he stepped up to her, so close he forced her back a step. It also reminded Gideon that the only thing scarier than his Mistress was Daegan.

"You will obey me, so we know you are safe. If we do not make it out of here, you are the only one who has a chance of explaining to Lord Uthe, with the help of Lord Brian, what happened here. To keep Stephen and Barbra from wreaking havoc on the one vampire governing council that has a chance of keeping order among all of the vampires. I don't have time to explain the Territory Wars and everything that went into the structure we have now, but they could dismantle it. I told you to trust me that all this is important. I need you to continue to do it. Do you understand?"

Her jaw was clenched so hard the muscle was flinching. When he put his hand on her cheek, she closed her eyes. Gideon stepped forward then, taking her hand. Thank God, she didn't pull back, so she must have heard his mental apology for being an ass. "You aren't running, Anwyn," he said quietly. "This is different. You know it. There's not a drop of fear in you. This is what needs to be done."

"You said 'we,'" she said at last, a note of sullenness in her voice. "Why does *he* get to stay?"

"He's a veteran soldier, Anwyn." Daegan offered a grim smile. "If you would grant me the use of your servant, I would be in your debt."

"They're coming."

Gideon snapped his attention to the cell. Sarah had spoken in a disembodied voice, and now she pushed herself upright from the cot, staring at him. Whether they'd marked her so they could enhance her fear or some other intuition told her, Gideon didn't question it. Reluctantly releasing Anwyn's hand, he crossed to the other side of the room, where fortunately Xavier and his thugs kept an assortment of weaponry. Apparently they'd been ready in case they were challenged by other vampires. He pulled a pair of loaded crossbows off the wall, verified the firing mechanisms.

"We should meet them at the door," he said. "We might take a couple out in the corridor before they get in. It's a defensible position."

"Go, Anwyn." Daegan pushed her toward the exit-only doorway to the upper level. "Go now."

"Damn it." She started in that direction, then flew back at them both, nipping at Daegan's lips hard enough to draw blood. Then she drew Gideon into a similarly violent kiss. She clutched his shoulders as he clumsily tried not to spear her with the weapons. "If either of you dies, I won't forgive you," she threatened.

Tears were on her face as she turned, and they both felt her frustration, rage and fear for them. As she disappeared up the stairs, Gideon cleared his throat gruffly, but it was Daegan who spoke as he took one of the crossbows from him.

"It's going to be close quarters once they get in the corridor, so speed will be less of a factor. I want you watching my back, getting anyone who makes it by me. I know you can do that."

Daegan lifted his gaze, locked with Gideon's. It was fucking embarrassing, but Gideon felt a flush cross his face, spread out through his chest, as if he were a Spartan soldier who'd just received praise from King Leonidas, right before they faced the 10,000 Persians.

A perfect parallel, since it was going to be the two of them against God knew how many vampires.

"Yeah," Gideon said, managing to sound casual. "I can do that. Unless it looks like we're done for. Then I'll shove you in the middle of them and make a run for it."

Daegan's sensual mouth curved in a feral smile, so devastating that Gideon's groin and heart tightened at the same time, painfully. "You know the saying, vampire hunter. When two friends are running from an enemy, the one in the lead doesn't have to run fast. Just faster than his friend. I think I have you on speed."

They moved to the door, one on either side, watching the short corridor down which Xavier had brought them. "Not if I trip you," Gideon retorted, but then there was no time for further talk.

The metal door at the bottom of the stairwell opened, and five vampires came through it, twenty feet of hallway between them and where they stood.

Here we go.

～

He and Daegan surged into the opening, shoulder to shoulder, and let the crossbows fly. The bolts took out the two in the lead, finding their heart targets dead center.

No time to celebrate, though. Despite vampire speed being hampered in narrow quarters, it still made crossbows effective for only the first shot of a full forward charge. Unless the sniper was hidden, which they weren't. As soon as the shots were made, the other three came sailing over the bodies, like those fierce, fast monkeys they showed on documentaries. Only these were sleek gorillas, combat ready, weapons in hands. Daegan tossed his crossbow to Gideon and moved into the hall to meet them. As Gideon quickly reloaded, and flipped Daegan's crossbow over to use the second arrow, Daegan's blade came up and out, a silver thing of deadly beauty.

The cleanup crew upstairs had apparently requested some rough and brutal heavy-metal music to finish up the night. It pounded and ricocheted down the corridor, telling Gideon these guys had left the door open at the top of the stairwell, or more vampires were coming down.

Shit, shit, shit. There they were. Four more.

Thank God for a small corridor, and fuck, but it was a small corridor. They were moving too fast for him to get a shot past Daegan. So for a few seconds all he could do was watch. And in those few, heart-stopping blinks, he saw why Daegan Rei scared the Council shitless.

Gideon had a clear-eyed grasp of his own not-inconsiderable battle skills, and how they matched up to fighters better and worse than him. Yet there was nothing and no one he'd ever seen that could stand toe-to-toe with the fighting ability he was witnessing now. If he believed in warrior archangels, like Michael or Lucifer, he imagined this was the way they would fight.

Fighting seven to one, Daegan picked up the rhythm of the music, used it. There was no other focus for him but this moment, his body twisting and sliding in the perfect place, at the perfect moment, as artistic and graceful as a divinely choreographed dance. Gideon saw no enthusiasm for the bloodtaking, but Daegan was consumed by his own composition. His blade came down, cut across, as his knife went up for a block. He ducked under an enemy blade, swept right to avoid a shower of blood and spun in a kick that knocked one vampire into the wall. Clean through the wall. He took his head in the resulting cloud of rock dust.

It was awe inspiring, horrible and riveting, all at once. Gideon was seeing the Grim Reaper at work, his victory a calm certainty because it was divinely ordained.

Two more down in the first ten seconds. The second vamp fell with a gurgling noise. When one lunged past, Gideon was ready, firing the crossbow and taking him down before the vampire could get behind Daegan and attack his flank. In that last fatal moment, the speared vampire's eyes found Gideon. An incredulous look crossed his face before his body crumpled.

He'd once told Anwyn that a hunter's greatest danger was a vampire's servant, because it was easy to forget about them in the focus on the vampire, the greater threat. *He* was now the servant who'd been unwisely forgotten. It was a different, somehow satisfying feeling. For that second, he forgot he was only Anwyn's servant and not also Daegan's, watching his back.

Daegan cut down two more with one sweep of his blade, sending an impressive fount of blood arcing across the stone walls, dousing one of the torches. As the two vamps collapsed, he came back up in the follow-through to jam his wooden eight-inch blade under the ribs and deep into the heart of the third. That was the last one. He finished the motion in a half-bent position that looked like a graceful bow to his vanquished enemies. Then he whirled with that same economy of motion. Pulling a cloth out of his coat, he slipped it over his samurai blade, taking away the blood.

Just like that. Done. Bodies littering the hall, and not a scratch on him, though Gideon saw a flash of weariness in Daegan's face, probably because he needed yet more blood, the stubborn bastard.

"I've sent a thought to Anwyn, assuring her she has no reason to be angry at either one of us, as we are very much alive. You might do the same."

Gideon nodded, shouldering his own weapons. He straightened in the doorway, turning back toward the cells. "Some passable fighting out there."

"Some passable shooting." Daegan slanted him a glance, then bent his head to fit his blade back into the coat.

"Yeah, when you cared to let somebody get by. Selfish—"

It was like getting hit in the face sometimes, the sense that something was going to happen right before it did. It had felt that way the day his parents had been hit by a lightning strike. For years he'd wondered why he'd been given a gift that, when it mattered the absolute most, did him no damn good.

Sarah screamed, the others too frightened or catatonic to warn their rescuers. The door that was only an exit, the one Anwyn had used, had opened, and two more vampires stood there. In those few seconds, they'd raised two crossbows and fired. Both at Daegan.

The vampire was moving forward, passing Gideon into the room. Looking down at his sword, tired from his blood loss, he hadn't seen or sensed them.

Since Daegan was too big to stop his forward momentum in time, Gideon simply rammed his back, shoving him aside with everything he had.

The first wooden arrow took Gideon high in the shoulder, the second puncturing his chest, through the heart. It threw him back, so he hit the wall and then dropped to the floor. The metal tip was searing fire, the wooden shaft a tearing agony as it punched out through his back.

Mortal. Holy crap, he was dead. His heart stuttered in panic at the invasion. He'd gone down like a felled tree, just like Xavier had. He tried to scramble for a blade or any other weapon, something to lend additional help to Daegan. It was a warrior's instinct only, or useless pride, because his body was jerking with the loss of motor control. He had no ability to defend himself, let alone anyone else.

Daegan had moved across the room, too fast to follow, a phantasm of light and shadow. If it had been a movie, Gideon thought there should have been more to it, a longer action sequence to justify the suspense, his dramatic fall, death hovering over him. But he'd barely hit the floor himself when two decapitated heads were rolling across it, the bodies hitting stone with a thud, just like Gideon's. The girls who could were screaming, in an annoyingly high pitch.

"How many come here at night to rest?" Daegan demanded, his blade glistening with the blood. When Gideon blearily heard more hysterical crying, he wasn't surprised by Daegan's commanding roar, though it made him wince. He couldn't breathe. His heart had to be a mangled mess. Fuck, this hurt. *"How many?"*

It was Sarah, bless her brave soul, who came up with a coherent answer at last. "It's always fifteen," she stammered. "Always."

That was the right number. Should be all of them, but there was always the possibility of first- or second-marked servants who wouldn't fall at their Masters' deaths. They really needed to get out of here.

Daegan was back over him. With a warrior's brutal mercy, no advance warning and doing it quick, he broke the two arrows, pulled them free from either side and flung them away. "Anwyn is leaving Debra outside. She's coming back down. Hold on."

"No . . . not safe yet. Got to get out of here. I'm dead."

"She is insisting. She felt you fall." Daegan passed a gentle hand over Gideon's sweaty brow. "I am not in a position to stop her. The arrow would have killed me, vampire hunter, not you. The shaft was wooden. But since the tip was steel, you need her blood, if you are going to walk out of here on your own two feet. As I know you must to maintain your fearsome reputation."

"Bite me. No cute jokes."

"I have rarely been accused of cuteness." Daegan pressed his hand against the wound. "I told Anwyn to have Debra contact Lord Brian, have him bring the Council here immediately."

"Think . . . they'll come?"

"Yes. They need to see this. We will wait, make sure Sarah and her friends get home."

Daegan knew. Knew how it was eating at Gideon's gut, seeing those hopeless faces, the lank hair, the blood and bruises in places that no woman should have them. Those pretty dresses, meant to work a guy up but not to do . . . not to do what had been done to them. Gideon closed his eyes. Did Daegan know all that because he knew him better than Gideon wanted to admit, or because Daegan shared his feelings on it? Did it matter?

"Be easy, Gideon. Anwyn will be safe. If there are marked servants here, they will scatter. They are no threat to her or anyone else. When Lord Stephen's role is determined in all this, I expect he will be replaced as Master of this territory. And on the Council. That may be the least of the punishments he faces."

"Maybe you'll get to be the one who takes him out."

"If the Council does not authorize it, I will take care of it, regardless." Daegan's mouth was a firm line, his face resolute in a way that Gideon wholeheartedly supported. "He will answer for what he did to Anwyn."

Gideon tried to move, and choked on the vicious wave of pain that squeezed his chest in a vise. "Jesus."

"Shhh. Easy. Do as you're told for once and stay still. She's coming." Daegan shifted so Gideon's head was braced on his thigh, his hand still pressed on the wound in a way that comforted and reassured, even though Gideon told himself he didn't need coddling.

"You know"—Daegan studied the opposite wall with great interest—"you could have held back, let the shot find its true mark. Then you would have had her to yourself. I guess you didn't think of that in the heat of the moment."

"No, damn it, I didn't." Gideon coughed, had the remarkably horrible sensation of his own blood bubbling up into his throat. "But . . . time machine . . . handy, I'll go for the . . . do-over."

Daegan looked down at him. "If I'd been at my full strength, I would have seen them. Your noble act would have been unnecessary."

Gideon shook his head. "Still think you're invincible. How'd they get you . . . on that table, Superman?"

Daegan grimaced, his lips twisting. "Snipers were already hidden and in position when I arrived. I might have sensed them, but the girls' plight distracted me. Though I don't think that was part of their plan. They don't know what mercy is, and wouldn't have expected it from another vampire. However, they took me through the chest, the throat and the stomach with their arrows, and the arrows were poisoned. It was enough to debilitate me temporarily. Then they set upon me, beat me into unconsciousness, and used a similar form of narcotic to keep me incapacitated, along with the titanium chains and electrical charges. Most drugs have no effect on me, so I'm sure Brian will want to test my blood, see what it was."

"Might be good . . . not to give him your Kryptonite. She's going to need you . . . for a long time."

"She will need us both. Don't even think of dying, vampire hunter. You are not getting out of this that easily. She responds to your temperament far better than mine."

"Can take out . . . ten vampires, but can't handle one . . . vampire fledgling . . . shrew. Going to tell her." Gideon closed his eyes, though, and was mortified to feel wetness on his face. "Not tears. Pain. Fuck, this hurts."

"I know. It will be all right."

Gideon managed to shake his head. "I screwed up, Daegan. She . . . already knew I didn't belong, but I convinced her of it, for real. Too much happening here, and yet . . . I couldn't put it aside." This time the coughing almost vaulted him off Daegan's lap, but the vampire's arm was around his chest, bracing him. The male was curved over him, pressing his jaw against Gideon's temple, keeping his head from exploding.

"Enough," Daegan said, with stern firmness this time, easing him back down. "Emotions run high in battle. It changes afterward. Shut up and save your strength."

Gideon indulged him, though he told himself if it didn't feel like an elephant was slowly depressing his wide gray ass on his chest, he would have talked about anything he damn well pleased. Then he noticed Daegan studying him in that intent, disturbing way he had, the way that made it hard for Gideon to meet his eyes, but he couldn't look away this time.

The vampire stroked his hair back along his temple. It wasn't the gentle touch of Anwyn's slim fingers, but the caressing strength of the large hand didn't feel bad, so he decided not to complain about it.

"No one has ever saved my life before, Gideon Green. I thank you for it."

"Don't . . . get all mushy. You'll try to kiss me. Fag."

A light smile touched Daegan's firm lips, but his gaze slid over Gideon's mouth like a caress, or the kiss Gideon claimed to fear. "You'd be in a poor position to stop me, if I wanted to do so."

"Haven't brushed this week. Onions for breakfast. Healthy dose . . . of garlic." He wheezed then, and more bloody froth gathered at his lips. "I would have . . . you know. Given you blood. If you needed it. Wouldn't have been thrilled, but . . . you know."

"Yes. Rest easy." Daegan's eyes darkened and he wiped the froth away, cradling Gideon's face. "She's coming. Hang in there, Gideon."

He sent a follow-up into Anwyn's mind then, so strongly that Gideon received it.

Hurry.

~

When Anwyn arrived and knelt beside him, her blue-green eyes were hard, her mouth taut with worry for him.

"You shouldn't have come back," Gideon managed for form's sake. "Wasn't safe."

"Shut up." She glanced at Daegan. "What does he need?"

"Just your blood, *cher*. I'll tell you when to stop." Daegan began to draw his knife, but before he could complete the motion, Anwyn had her wrist to her mouth and punctured open a vein. Swiftly, she brought it down to Gideon, her blood welling up fast and bright.

As always, the smell of it activated his taste buds. He'd assumed that was part of the bonding between them, but he'd had a similar reaction in the past to Daegan's blood. He was too tired right now to deny it.

Putting her wrist to Gideon's lips, she shifted to take Daegan's place when he rose. Though he watched over them, he moved a few feet away to talk to the women, give them an idea of what was about to happen. It gave them some privacy, so Gideon could focus on Anwyn's beautiful face. Her hand cradled his jaw, helping to steady him as he drank, and that brief touch was blissful. He inhaled her through all his senses, though his eyes closed as he did it. He still couldn't handle the reflection in her eyes, the way he looked, taking blood from her arm. Nevertheless, strength and health flooded back into him, in addition to an absurd, lazy arousal. It never failed to amaze him, how her nearness, or putting his mouth on her flesh, could do that, no matter that he couldn't have gotten to his feet, let alone gotten anything else up right now.

She was withdrawn, pensive. Maybe just worried, as Daegan had said. Her hands were gentle, firm, but she could have been twenty miles away. He didn't have the strength to really plumb her mind, see if she was near a seizure.

"Mistress . . ."

"Shhh, Gideon. I'm fine. I want to take care of you. Just drink."

Anwyn stroked Gideon's hair as he obeyed, relieved to feel the chest wound under her palm closing. The shoulder puncture was likewise healing. Daegan's gaze kept flicking to her, so she knew Gideon wasn't the only one who sensed something amiss. It didn't matter. She was locked down right now on purpose. If she loosened the latch on her emotions at all, she was going to become shrapnel, flying out and striking everything within reach with lethal intent.

They'd assume, rightly, she was a little overwhelmed by everything. Though she ran a BDSM club, Atlantis was, after all, all about consensual pain and pleasure. While it tapped into the most raw and volatile areas of a person's psychology, it was in a controlled, civilized environment with rules, and the underlying rule was love and respect, or at least healthy lust. Even that, while sometimes bordering on violence, was never criminal or evil in its intent.

She'd experienced the evil of her uncle, of Barnabus and his cohorts. But seeing something like this, where evil was a daily practice, a method of operating that connected closely to the vampire propensity for domination and brutality . . . she'd known they were going to face something terrible tonight, but perhaps it was good she hadn't expected this to be as truly heinous as it was.

Exposure to it made her comprehend better what Daegan and Gideon faced in the profession they'd chosen, with two such different perspectives. Still, whereas Gideon dealt with the fallout with entertainment tabloids and bitterness, Daegan had exorcised his demons in the time he spent with her. It had merely amused her in the past, the pleasure he took in the smallest things. On her days off, his favorite pastime was to lie on the sofa and watch her read. Requiring nothing other than that she indulge his regard. Sometimes she could tell he was just listening to all the minute sounds of the apartment. Her breath, rising and falling, the tick of the clock, the hum of the refrigerator, and probably myriad other things she couldn't hear with human ears.

If this was what his life was like when he wasn't with her, she would never again feel amusement with his need for such tranquility. Only tenderness, and gratitude that the gods had brought him home to her once again.

She definitely wanted to be gone from this place, gone from Berlin, and back home. But there was more to her pensiveness than that. She'd heard some of the things Gideon had said to Daegan, and those words had twisted a knife in her heart. He was right and wrong at once. Right, in that he'd convinced her tonight he didn't belong, would likely never belong. Wrong, in that he thought she'd come to the realization because he'd screwed up. She wanted to push away the painful knowledge lodged in her breast like Gideon's arrow, avoid the pain of pulling it out, exposing it to scrutiny. But truth was truth, however it happened.

She would have used her vampire strength and will to force him or the girls to do whatever was necessary to restore Daegan's strength. She would do the same for Gideon if he was injured. Through her transition, she'd been "becoming" a vampire. Tonight she truly was one, and she could no more change that than Gideon could change what he was. Even now, Gideon's eyes were closed so he couldn't see what she was doing, unable to handle seeing himself as a servant. But his mind was an open book to her, and what she saw on the pages of his soul broke her heart.

Everything she and Brian had discussed, everything she'd known since the beginning about Gideon, that she'd learned about vampires through Daegan and now herself, had come to the surface in this most brutal of moments. Gideon was right about that part, too. But it still wasn't his fault. She couldn't bear for him to blame himself, and hoped that when she had the courage to cut him loose, she could do it without making him feel it was. She'd rather have him hate her than hate himself, more than he already did.

Bending to her task, her hair curtaining her face from Daegan, she let Gideon drink. She held on to the miracle that they were all alive and let that be enough, for now. It was as she'd always known, always believed and tried to practice as her one enduring faith.

It was always best to live in the moment.

19

LORD Stephen had disappeared, confirming his guilt and cowardice. Lady Barbra was nearly meek in the subsequent review of events. It was a wise choice, considering her head could be on the same chopping block. The Council shake-up, the renewed debate of whether made vampires serving on the august body was a dreadful mistake, rendered the question of Gideon Green serving as a fledgling's servant, or Anwyn's state of mind, much less high-priority issues.

Gideon was intrigued to hear through Daegan that the Council thought they could pressure Lord Mason, the second-oldest vampire after Lady Lyssa, to take Stephen's slot. Lyssa, having a long history with the antisocial Mason, would find that pretty amusing.

In short, when Daegan firmly indicated they would be departing for home, the Council simply waved them off. Uthe, with dry humor, indicated they would trust him to monitor his domestic situation and advise the Council if there were any problems. Though Gideon still felt Daegan had taken an excessive gamble, it had paid off. The exposure of Lord Stephen, and Daegan's dispatch of Xavier's potential threat in the Council's very backyard, had restored their full confidence in their personal assassin. For now. He had no illusions about the consistency of vampire loyalties.

Any short-term conflict they faced going forward wouldn't likely come from the Council, though. The most immediate problem appeared to be that still-unthawed wall of ice Anwyn had erected around her, threatening to freeze him to death every time Gideon came near her.

He studied her now as the Gulfstream leveled from takeoff. She'd chosen a seat diagonally from him, which prevented any casual contact. She'd touched him very little during the past twenty-four hours, except for disgustingly neutral Mother Teresa–type touches of his brow or pulse, making sure he was recovering well. It wasn't like she was angry. She was just . . . withdrawn. Deep inside herself, chewing on something he knew didn't bode well.

"I don't know whether it's reassuring or scary to find out that vampire governing councils can be just as fucked-up as human ones," he observed, making another foray.

"I think Daegan handled the situation capably. It left no doubt in their minds that you and I are in good hands," Anwyn responded, her gaze not leaving her laptop screen.

Yep, still in full passive-aggressive mode, which made it impossible to penetrate or aggravate her. So far she'd stayed impervious to any attempt to draw her out, though he'd withheld some of his more obnoxious tactics. None of them wanted more issues to address until they were safely on home turf. She'd made it to the car that night before she had a full-blown seizure, one that had pretty much rendered her insensible for half a day and destroyed the interior of Brian's Mercedes, which Daegan promised to have restored. Thank God for the Council's distraction and Brian's discretion.

From Daegan's speculative glances, Gideon suspected the reticent bastard understood what was going on with her, but he wasn't talking, either. Gideon hadn't yet sunk so low he'd go begging for answers.

He suppressed a sigh as she kept on working, obviously intending to pass the trip home immersed in her backlog of paperwork from the club. Membership applications to review, invoices to process and approve, proposals for a renovation she'd been planning for some time. That VIP weekend thing. Anything to keep from talking to him.

Damn it, he missed her. It was stupid, because it had been only a matter of freaking hours, but ever since he'd gotten that third mark, bonded with her over that and so many other things, he'd gotten used to the feeling of closeness . . . emotional, physical and all points in between. Easy touches and warmth, even barbed comments or her Mistress coolness. He couldn't help comparing this moment to the trip to Berlin. She'd sat next to him for part of that flight, doing the same thing she was doing now, but telling him about it, sharing things about her business as if she wanted him to be a part of it. Leaning against him so her shoulder brushed his, giving him absent smiles, both of them responding to Daegan's comments as he read the paper.

As he shifted, he stifled a quiet curse, finding himself stiff and tired again. He'd walked out of the club standing in his own boots, as Daegan had predicted, thanks to Anwyn's blood, but his body was going through lethargic cycles. Lord Brian, after a quick examination, had noted he'd be fine, but should rest whenever his body demanded it. While he was impatient with it, it wasn't the first time he'd had to make himself do what needed to be done to recover as quickly as possible from an injury. All in all, it was pretty nifty. Take an arrow through the heart, drink some blood, rest a few days, and he'd be good as new. The metal tip on the thing was the only part that made the injury serious enough to prevent a faster recovery.

If the arrow had stopped in your heart, instead of puncturing out the back, it would have killed you within seconds, Lord Brian had offered cheerfully. Of course, he'd seemed pretty cheerful about everything since Debra had returned. When Gideon had visited him for the quick checkup before leaving for the airstrip, he'd come into the lab to find Debra pouring something into a beaker, Brian right behind her. He had his hands planted on either side of the counter, lips on her neck, hips firmly pressed up against her pretty heart-shaped ass as she smiled and tried her best to concentrate on what she was doing.

Yeah, he knew what that was like. Shit. There seemed to be no cure for the heavy weight that Anywn's self-imposed distance seemed to be placing on his heart. His limited experience with women told him that there was little he could do except be as ingratiating as possible until she decided to let it go or vent. He didn't ingratiate himself very well, but he'd give a lot right now to put his head on her thigh, feel the absent brush of her fingers in between typing e-mails. Hear her voice as she fussed about someone's incompetence, or shared a funny story that Madelyn had e-mailed her about a client. God, he was pathetic.

Gideon pushed his seat back into a reclining position, turned his face toward the window again and tried not to think about it anymore. He couldn't be anything more or less than what he was. If she had a problem with that, she'd have to deal. Though he wished to hell he knew what to do to make it better.

Anwyn looked up from her computer when Gideon's even breath, the relative stillness of his agitated mind, told her he had succumbed to sleep. He'd done that frequently in the past day, making her realize how rarely the man actually slept. When they'd first returned from the Coffin, he'd refused to give in to it, to go to their rooms. Not until he was certain Daegan would emerge, safe and sound, from the Council chambers. She'd learned that from Brian, who'd watched over her until she regained consciousness. Vincent had reported that the vampire hunter had dozed against a column outside the great hall, his arms crossed over his broad chest, face pressed against the stone, jacket still stained with his own near-mortal blood. It had apparently made an impression on Belizar's majordomo. Of course, Gideon had that effect on people.

Setting her computer aside, she shifted over to the seat next to him. She studied his handsome features, the lines around his eyes, the rugged toughness overlaying the fresh handsomeness of the far more carefree young man he'd once been. Swallowing, she feathered her knuckles over his brow, down along his cheek, a hard burning in her chest. She'd almost lost him. She'd heard what Brian said as well. Gideon would have died in that horrible place. She thanked whatever god's genius insight had made vampire and servant mortality affected by different weapons, so the same could not be used against both.

Still, when the arrow had taken him in the chest, she'd doubled over in the car. Debra had twisted around as Anwyn cried out, grabbed the back of the seat for support, her hand pressed to her chest. From Debra's expression, Anwyn had experienced a moment of total terror, thinking this was what the girl meant about knowing when one's servant had died.

Daegan, however, had quickly caught her spinning mind in his sure grip, sending her what was happening, even as he was shielding Gideon from further attack.

She didn't know Gideon's favorite color, or if he preferred his eggs scrambled or boiled. Brian might say it was all biology, the blood connection, that made it feel as if a vital part of her heart resided within his powerful frame. But it didn't explain why he'd attracted her long before he'd become her servant, or why, when he'd spent his life moving toward solitude and sure death, that he'd finally joined his life to hers.

Maybe it had been desperation, his soul reaching for something his mind and heart were too far gone to accept. Too little, too late. The truth was she couldn't keep him. He'd always known it. Now she knew it, too, and she wouldn't risk his life, or her heart, any further.

Bowing her head, she let the pain of it wash over her, and slid back into her chair. Glancing up, she saw Daegan watching her. While there was pain in his expression, telling her he heard her thoughts, she shook her head. She couldn't handle any advice that would be a balm on the obvious. At the moment it hurt too damn much. All of it hurt too much, and it was all the wrong kind of pain.

~

"It's time for you to choose, Gideon."

Gideon jumped as he came out of the bathing chamber. She'd startled him.

Anwyn bit her lip at his reaction, another tiny pain amid many larger ones. Even though she'd gone up earlier with Daegan to do a nighttime round of Atlantis while Gideon showered, Gideon usually stayed locked into her whereabouts, a comforting presence in the back of her brain. However, given that she'd been shutting him out the three days since they'd been back, she couldn't fault him for withdrawing some. Hell, he'd probably been relieved not to have to walk on eggshells around her for at least a half hour.

He'd tolerated her treatment longer than she would have expected. Gideon Green wasn't a doormat, and his patience was zero. Maybe he'd sensed what was coming and wanted to delay it, as she did. Or maybe it was because he would let her abuse him in a way she'd never permit anyone else to do, a shameful thought.

He hadn't completely avoided it, though, like she had. On the first day back, he'd approached her with heartbreaking tenderness, asking her point-blank what he could do to fix whatever it was he'd done. But she, who had stood up to the Council, who'd faced down Xavier in his club, surrounded by hostile vampires, couldn't tell him. At least she hadn't lied. She'd said it was something she was working out and she'd tell him in her own time. Told him to focus on recuperating and stop worrying about her.

At night, she stayed busy in her home office, leaving them to watch television or do whatever men did. Practice weapons or martial arts. Daegan even started teaching Gideon how to use a bullwhip, something she'd been almost tempted to go watch, and give tips, but had stopped herself.

That first dawn, and each of the two dawns after, she'd gone to Daegan's bed and hadn't invited Gideon to join them, as she might have before. She'd shut her mind like a trap, unable to handle his confused and hurt reaction. She couldn't even look at his face as she vaguely encouraged him to use her bed rather than the couch for his comfort and recuperation. Day or night, she'd said carelessly, whichever suited his sleeping schedule best.

He slept on the couch, refusing her bed. He couldn't handle her scent there, without her in it. When she saw the thought in his mind, she almost broke, so she tried not to listen to anything else, pouring more energy into that screen between them than she ever had before. She knew she'd successfully been able to keep him out of the part of her mind dealing with this issue. He'd probed hard a couple times, and she'd set him back on his heels for it, so he'd quit, with a mutinous look, but he didn't know what the worried look in his eyes did to her heart. She felt like a multitude of cracks were starting to run through it, the prelude to a full shattering into dozens of pieces.

It had made her even crueler. When she'd needed blood, she'd asked him—or rather the wall in front of her—to drain it into a cup and mix it with wine for her. She knew how he anticipated the intimacy they shared when she took her preferred position in his lap and brought her lips to his throat. She'd denied him even that. The first time she'd done it, he'd left it on the kitchen counter, reaching out into her mind to let her know it was ready, and then left the apartment for several hours.

She couldn't risk any of it. Couldn't risk his thoughts, sharing a bed or drinking from him. It wasn't deliberate cruelty; it was resolve. If she twined herself around him, touched him, allowed herself his body, she'd rationalize herself away from the truth. Pleasure was a poor substitute for what she really wanted—his heart and soul.

On day three, hurt had begun to shift to his familiar bitter anger, his mind twisting in ugly thoughts. As she prepared to leave him for the dawn, headed for Daegan's bed, Gideon had demanded she tell him what the fuck was going on. She'd felt numb, because she knew it was time. She told him she wanted one more day.

Daegan wouldn't help or hinder, damn him. She hadn't asked his opinion, but she would have welcomed it. However, when she came to his bed that morning, she'd seen in his eyes he knew too well what was happening, and that he knew this was her decision to make. Instead, he let her spoon inside the shelter of his body, curl in a ball. He'd folded himself around her, giving her shelter but no sanctuary from her own thoughts.

When she rose for the evening, she found Gideon had fallen asleep on the couch. She'd wanted to slide onto that lean body, twine around him, hold him close to her heart, but she couldn't bear it. She'd gone up top upon rising, with Daegan, to do rounds. She'd worked upstairs, cognizant of Daegan's presence, his watchfulness, and then she'd asked him for privacy when she went back down to face what she had to do.

~

So here she was. She'd come back in, heard Gideon in the shower, taken a seat in her wing-backed chair. Allowed herself to slide into his mind fully for the first time in three days and almost sobbed at the pleasure of it. Experiencing the roll of water down his body, watching his hands rise to slick the hair back from his skull. Feeling the loneliness in his mind warring with irritation and anger at her treatment of him, the confusion and apprehension.

He always sensed her in his mind, so it spoke keenly of his state that she'd startled him when he stepped out of the bathroom.

She knew what he saw. A Mistress in full regalia, no softness to her. A corset and snug skirt, high boots, hair slicked back. She'd greeted some high-dollar clients tonight, introduced them to the staff members who would pleasure them, but that wasn't why she'd dressed this way. Gideon reacted to her remote and tempting appearance, his barely leashed irritation rising again, a cloak for more jagged emotions.

He knew, as she did. Except he thought there was something to fight about, but there wasn't. She wished there was. There was nothing to change or fix.

"What do you mean, I need to choose?" He spoke stiffly.

When she let her gaze course down Gideon's bare chest, the arrow of hair that disappeared into the towel, she heard his hopeful, hungry thought that maybe she was ready to make up, ready to take him into her body, use his as she wished. It made him despise himself, made him feel like he had no pride.

It made her despise herself, because of how desperately she wanted to accept less than what they both deserved, so she wouldn't have to face this moment.

"Sex is the great anesthesia, isn't it?" She cocked her head. "For men at least."

His brow furrowed. She felt him reach out to her on instinct, but she kept that wall steady between them. She was becoming better at making her screen opaque, possibly a cumulative effect of Brian's serum. She wanted to celebrate how much control she was reclaiming for herself, but not only was Gideon a cornerstone of that control; she actually missed the intimacy of giving him easy access, letting him share her thoughts, something she'd never thought she'd appreciate with anyone.

"Anwyn, what's happening?" His voice stayed wooden, though, his expression already closing against her.

"I'm letting you go, if that's what you want," she said. "I don't care about the Vampire Council, what they say about not releasing a servant. As far as they're concerned, I'll just say you travel for me a great deal."

He reached for the jeans he'd left over a chair, yanked them on and tossed away the towel with a jerky movement. It gave her only a second to enjoy bare flesh, though she was hypercognizant that he put no briefs on. Only thin denim separated her from him. Thin denim and a chasm only he could cross. And wouldn't.

"I guess I knew this was coming." He shrugged. "Whatever."

Anwyn rose, her eyes on his face, though he wouldn't meet her gaze. Didn't he know she could read everything in his mind, feel his pain and betrayal rising to the forefront to tear him apart, even as he used it as his only defense?

"You're not listening, Gideon. You have two choices, and neither one is wrong. I'm not angry with you, I promise. This was never your decision, becoming a servant." She pushed aside her own anguish. "While becoming a vampire wasn't mine, it's one I can live with."

"I've been here. I've been fucking doing what a servant is supposed to do. I haven't asked you to be different—"

"Do you know what I notice about you?" she interrupted quietly, stepping forward. He pulled on his shirt, raked his hands in his hair, and rocked away from her, avoiding her outstretched hand. Anwyn dropped it, firming her lips. "You won't refer to yourself directly as my servant, except when necessary for the perception of others. You close your eyes when you feed, when I feed, because you can't handle seeing yourself feeding or being fed by a vampire. At the Coffin, you couldn't accept the part of me that would have forced those girls to feed Daegan. You considered it a great and noble sacrifice to offer Daegan your blood, because it was still something you were deeply reluctant to do. When he refused, it angered and hurt you, but there was relief as well."

"Doesn't sound like there's a choice anywhere in there," he said gruffly.

"If you wish to stay with me, you accept three things. You accept me as a vampire, not as a victim of one. You accept yourself as a servant, with me as your vampire Mistress. If I see in your mind that you can accept that right now, then you can stay."

"Fine, I accept it. That's only two things."

She arched a brow at the obvious lie. "You accept Daegan. Feed him tonight, and let him take you to his bed, without me."

He stepped backward involuntarily, though he tried to catch himself. "See?" She nodded with a sad smile. "Your mind rejects all those requirements, Gideon, perversely because your heart and soul *don't*. It's exactly what they want, but your mind is the guard at the prison gates. You won't free yourself until you're ready." Her emotions spiraled upward, like there was a geyser in her heart, needing to release pressure, but she fought it back down, kept her voice steady. "Remember that first session between us, when I walked out because you wouldn't give me your real name? This is that, all over again. I need you to admit what you really want, surrender that to me."

"That isn't a choice. And this is bullshit. You're just ready to be done with me and choosing a chickenshit way to do it. Hell, Anwyn, it hasn't been that long. I can't just change overnight—"

"No, you can't. But I can't change at all. You were right, what you saw in my mind in the Coffin. I am a vampire, Gideon, and that will continue to grow stronger inside me. I hope it won't change certain things about me, but it has changed other things, and will continue to do so. Gideon, I need a true, dedicated servant." *I need you.* Though she held that yearning thought back. "A servant is my link to my humanity, to the values and beliefs that have guided me throughout my life. I'm going to need those. I need to hold on to some of what I am, figure out what parts are really, truly me. I need a servant to help me do that, but one who will, at the same time, accept whatever I'm becoming fully."

She took a step forward, holding him in her gaze, suffering, wanting to hold his rigid, angry body in her arms, soothe all those tense muscles. "When a person gives another time to change, Gideon, it's because they *can't* see into their head. They're just nursing hope that something about that person will alter. I can read your mind, your thoughts. Hating and killing vampires, seeing their excesses and violence, is something trapped so deeply inside of you."

"And what about those gremlins in your head? You know I'm the only one—"

"I'll manage. I have serums to help, and Daegan will help. I don't need you for that."

His features tightened as if she'd struck him. Anwyn swallowed the pain with the lie, tried to steady her voice again. "I could give you more time, both of us more time, but my heart won't take it. I already care so much for you. It may be selfish and cruel of me, but as you said, that's what vampires are. I don't want to wait. I want it all, and I want it now, or I want you gone. If you come back, you come back to me forever, with full commitment to those three things, no matter what. I know this hurts." Her voice quavered, despite her best efforts, and his gaze snapped to hers. She was going to die inside in another few moments. She managed the rest in a whisper. "But doing this now will be less cruel, to both of us."

"Fine. If you want me out, I'm out. Go back upstairs with Daegan. When you come back down, I'll be gone." He stepped forward, but she shifted, moving in front of him.

"I'm not done. I need to say something else to you, something I think you need to hear."

"I don't need your psychoanalysis," he snapped. "Just get the hell out of the way."

"No," she said, her tone becoming even softer. "When I'm done, I'll move, but you'll hear me out. I know you, Gideon. You won't strike out at me."

He planted his feet, his face hard as granite. "Fine. Say it so I can get the fuck out of here."

It almost stole her breath, the vicious anger in his voice, the fact that for a moment, he *had* wanted to hit her, strike her down, knowing she'd get back up without a mark on her, because a vampire couldn't be wounded, not by a lowly human. The shadow creatures in her head stirred restlessly, anticipating. Soon he would be gone, and the battle to fight them would be hers and Daegan's alone. They could do it. They would have to, because she couldn't bear this.

She made herself pull out the harder edge of the Mistress she knew she could be. He needed it now, but more than that, it was the only way she was going to get through this without breaking down.

"It isn't that vampires repulse you, or that you can't let go of what happened to Laura. The largest part of it isn't about that anymore. It's because you *want* to be my servant. You want to belong to me, and more than that, you want to belong to us. Both of us. It scares the shit out of you. The only way you can handle that is to keep acting like a foster kid forced to be part of a family he knows he really can't do without. So he pisses and moans about how he hates them, even as he hopes they'll always be there."

His jaw flexed and he crossed his arms over his chest, walling himself off to her. Deliberately, she curled her fingers over the rigid forearm on top, felt the quiver of reaction. "Surrender is your choice, Gideon. That's the thing you want the most and can't accept. If you ever accept it, you come back to us. But until then, we're done playing Mommy and Daddy to you."

"Go to hell."

Anwyn thanked all the years she'd had to practice a neutral expression in volatile circumstances, because she had to draw on it as she never had before when the venomous words pierced her. His mind was pure roiling emotion. She could handle all that, the usual rage and fury, but not the sudden panic beneath the anger. He was realizing that she really meant it. Except he believed she truly *wanted* him gone, because his mind wouldn't accept her words.

Oh, Gideon.

He recoiled from her touch. "I was around when you needed a nursemaid, or a big brother, or a quick fuck to scratch your itch," he spat. "I was your babysitter for Daegan. Now all you need is each other. You don't get to make yourselves feel better by telling me it's for some fucking magnanimous reason. You're tossing me out of the nest because that's what you want, what's easiest for you both. Well, you didn't have to come up with some sentimental excuse. I told you I'd eventually leave."

She moved in again; he moved back again. One more step, and he had nowhere but the corner, unless he wanted to knock her down. She lifted her chin so their faces were inches apart. His body was vibrating with fury, and a heartbreaking need to reach out, to offer something to her to change her mind. She visualized herself encased in solid ice, and was glad Daegan wasn't here, because she didn't think she could handle any acknowledgment of the pain she was feeling.

"I wanted to do the same thing. Rationalize it, tell myself to give you more time, the time you say you need. It was a comfortable idea. You've lived your whole life under one belief system, and it's difficult to change. You've never doubted your instincts as a hunter. It's what you know best. This transition threw me off, but somewhere along the past three days, I remembered that, as a Mistress, I never doubted my instincts. And I shouldn't have forgotten that. You're ready to make this decision, Gideon. This is a thorn that has to be drawn out immediately, no matter how much pain it causes. Leaving it in, hoping it will work itself out, will only lead to festering, infection. For all of us."

He was staring at the ground to the left of her body, closing himself off to her. But she could tell from the cock of his head, the thrumming tension of his body, he was listening to every word. Probably looking for a way to change her mind, refute her logic, but he'd remember the words later. She hoped.

"As I told you from the beginning, you're not a submissive, Gideon, but you are a servant. You serve. That's your deepest dream, to protect and serve the love and needs of another to the fullest extent of your soul. And I think Daegan and I are the ones you wish to serve. But you have to believe that yourself. A Master or Mistress can help you with your belief. It doesn't have to be perfect from the very beginning. But you have to accept it exists before we can do anything else.

"I think I told you once it's easier for some submissive males to be forced. You give them the safe word they'll never use, and then you have a license to beat them, chain them, drag them to you by their balls, no matter how much they fight or struggle or curse you. Because nothing is more frightening to them than being forced to face the fact they need, they suffer. They love."

He was drawing darkness around him with every word, shoving her away from his mind, shoving her back from him. She stopped, bit her lip, gave herself a full moment before she spoke again. He stayed silent, waiting. Waiting to escape.

"Go, Gideon," she said. "Because you're not a submissive, I won't grant your wish. You're my servant. I want your obedience and surrender, freely given."

Stepping back now such that she drew his attention to her face, she hardened her tone. "And I want it for both of us. You give it to me *and* Daegan, belong to us both the way I know your cock, heart and soul want to, or you don't come back. We are a family," she said, her voice laden with emotion. "But one of choice. You no longer have my permission to dishonor that with lies to yourself. Choose, or go with my love and best wishes."

∼

Choose. Yeah, right. With her three freaking bullet points, she'd set an impossible bar. Probably because she knew it was impossible. They didn't want him here. But for a few moments, he was paralyzed. He guessed he'd known all along. The pain had been building for these three days, so now her words froze every nerve ending, made it hard to breathe or even function.

She'd turned on her heel without another word, and left their quarters. Leaving him to pack up his few belongings and get out. It took only minutes, something that felt like hours. When he was done, he didn't let himself look at anything. Not the morning paper Daegan had left on the sofa so Gideon could read it, a new routine they'd adopted, or the silk robe Anwyn had draped on the back of her vanity chair, visible through the open door of her bedroom. The fabric would smell like her, and he had to fight the desire to steal it, ball it up and stick it in his bag to take with him.

The stuffed gremlin he'd bought her was sitting on her bed, staring at him in a way that felt smug, not cute. Which just confirmed he was about two clicks from losing it.

All the items in these rooms had meanings and significance, things that identified them as Daegan's and Anwyn's. He'd seen into their minds, when they'd let him, and he'd had a precious few weeks to experience being a part of them. Maybe being one of those items, in a weird way.

For just a minute, he wished he had direct access to Daegan's mind, so he could figure out . . . something. Appalled with himself, he realized he was doing exactly what she'd implied, appealing to one "parent" about what the other had done. Besides, Daegan had damn well known this was coming. That was why he hadn't said anything. Oh yeah, he'd say some reasonable bullshit, too, only for Daegan it would be about giving Anwyn the free will to handle her choice of servant the way she saw fit. But either way, he no longer had to share her with Gideon, did he?

Shut up. He swore at himself viciously. None of that made any sense, but he knew empty lies to himself to keep him pissed off were better than acknowledging the truth, the pain he'd seen in her face, the tears threatening behind her eyes. The quiet sadness he'd caught in Daegan's expression these past few days, as if the vampire would change the outcome if he could.

But Anwyn had made it clear. Only Gideon could change it. Damn it, this was the way he was. If they couldn't accept that, then fuck them. He was done. He could be whatever she needed, within certain boundaries, but that wasn't what she wanted. She didn't want him.

More lies.

Though it felt like he was going to his own execution, Gideon left the apartment, let the door close behind him. Walking up the corridor through accounting and maintenance, he avoided the higher-traffic areas, headed for the alley exit that would take him out of Atlantis and the strangely welcome reality he'd found there.

Home and family.

Bullshit. *Bullshit.* He summoned the rage, but it didn't hold against the other shit. Hell, she was right. He'd never been cut out for this, and though it hurt like hell to leave her behind, she'd been the smart one, right? She was going to be fine now. She and Daegan both. They didn't need him. She'd gotten through the Council. Yeah, maybe she'd still have the seizures, but . . . Fuck it, she'd said she could do without him, so fine. Her well-being was no longer his concern, right?

He put his fist into the brick wall, was somewhat amazed when it crumbled, though his knuckles vibrated with the pain of impact. There. He'd made his mark. Maybe sometime she'd be out here, feeding her cats, and her hand would drift over it, feel his lingering presence.

Damn it. Yeah, he was mad right now. But he did care. He wasn't that much of an ass. When push came to shove, it was the right thing. He'd always known it. Maybe one day he'd even be okay thinking about them, and it wouldn't feel like this, like he wanted to howl and rage, tear something apart. Only he couldn't figure out what.

~

As Gideon shouldered his duffle and headed out the side alley, the alley where he'd found her that terrible night, Anwyn watched him from the second-story level of the club, her office on the main floor. When he put his fist in the wall, she flinched.

She guessed she'd advanced to the head of the class on hiding her feelings from him, because inside she was beating on the bars of her own mind as violently as she'd fought her restraints during her transition. That part of her was begging the cold, efficiently closed-down part of her to lift the gate, let her say a better good-bye. It was like watching her heart walk away.

It was no surprise to feel Daegan's hands close on her shoulders. She didn't let herself break, though, just quivered under his touch and watched the tall, dangerous-looking man walk away and disappear around the corner.

"He wouldn't listen. He's telling himself that we've rejected him. That I don't want him." She laid her hand on the glass, over the receding figure just before he vanished.

Daegan's hand covered hers, his fingers pressing to the pane between the spaces. "You knew he needed to leave us to make up his mind, *cher*. You saw it in his mind. He needs time. You both do."

He was so fucked-up, their vampire hunter with so much rage and a heart of gold. She was his last sanctuary. Hadn't Daegan said something like that? But she'd just sent him out into the cold, knowing all he'd face was his own desolation, and he might not have the ability to work his way through it.

She locked her jaw against the fear, the threatening tears. She couldn't keep him, couldn't protect him from himself. Not until he wanted that, was ready to accept it. To deal with that pain, she would ruthlessly shut that curtain between their minds, dedicate herself to reinforcing it until she at last perfected a complete block. The best way to deal with a drug was a full withdrawal. If she couldn't hear his thoughts anymore, the pain would fade. She could handle it. She would. She wouldn't worry every waking moment about what he was doing, if he was okay. If she'd sent him to his death, the kind of death that came with blank despair.

The shadow creatures laughed.

And kept laughing, getting louder and louder, until she did her best to tear them out of her head, using her hands or whatever solid surface presented itself. She knew she made it worse because she struggled to keep her mind closed even as she fought those monsters, but she didn't want Gideon to know. If he came back to help her, she'd only give in, do the wrong, easy thing, and be forced to reenact the same scene again, a few months down the road. Then it would be even worse, though she couldn't imagine anything that felt worse than this now.

As she screamed and thrashed, Daegan took over the wall, made her understand he'd cocooned her mind so she didn't have to worry about Gideon knowing. Then she let go, let the blackness take her.

A few bloody and violent hours later, she found herself with Daegan, back in her apartment belowground. He held her between his knees on the floor. With his arms tight around her, she buried into him and sobbed, trying to ignore the frightening fact she'd let an essential part of her soul go.

She wasn't sure how much soul she had left to spare.

20

Soon after leaving, Gideon felt a disturbance from her. Before he could respond to her distress, an instinct he didn't question, he'd felt something else. Her destructive and excessive effort to keep him shut out of her head, a clear message that she didn't need his help. Then a block, a sense of Daegan that told him he'd helped her.

Once the dust settled, the connection with her remained, even though it was like an abandoned room, whispering with past voices, nothing left of the present. To get away from it, the first thing he did was drive halfway across the country. He knew that most vampire mind-link ranges were within a thousand miles, much less for a fledgling, so as he kept a loose hand on the wheel of the old Nova, he let the rhythmic thump of the asphalt beneath the turning tires drown out the whispers in that abandoned room. As they died away, it made it easier not to strain to hear them, to see if maybe one of those whispers was talking to him, asking him to come back.

There was a vampire in Seattle who'd taken twenty kills the previous year, and that was his first target. Once he got into town, found the usual dive where he could sleep and plan, he set up his prey as he always did. A couple of weeks later, he made the kill, then threw up afterward. It made him savagely angry, such that he destroyed the shack where he'd cornered the vamp, tearing down boards and risking electrocution from the faulty wiring before he set it on fire, a wooden pyre on top of the body.

It wasn't long after that he had the insidious, tempting thought. He should kill another vamp like Trey. Daegan would come looking for him. Gideon could see him, maybe smell Anwyn's lingering scent on the vampire, feel the warm touch of her mind one last time before Daegan ended him. Losing a servant had been described as leaving an aching hole in a vampire's soul, but Gideon was sure she'd fill it with someone far more appropriate in no time.

He refused to think about the things she said, but he wasn't stupid. In hindsight, Gideon knew she'd done what she thought was best, even if he couldn't bring himself to face or believe the reasons she'd given. He knew it had hurt her. As a result, him being taken out would likely be for the best. Then she wouldn't have to suffer guilt or anything else. He didn't want her to worry about anything, not ever again. He was too fucked-up for anyone, anyhow. He'd just forgotten that for a little while, and it had made him mad to be reminded of it. Really wasn't her fault.

His brother called several times, but Gideon never answered. One night he tossed the phone out the car window and watched it shatter on the gravel shoulder. He didn't know who or what to be anymore, so he'd just be nothing and nobody. A shadow even more ghostlike than Daegan himself. A being that wanted no name, no soul, nothing that would make him feel or care or suffer loneliness. He'd reached the end of the road. The only thing left was what kind of cliff he'd drive over.

Daegan paused in the sitting room doorway and considered the woman on the couch. He pushed down his frustration, knowing it wouldn't be useful. She was making steps backward, showing little interest in going above, and it was not all because of her grief over Gideon. Whether that was the catalyst, or the lack of Gideon's steadying physical balance as her servant, the convulsions were back to at least once a day, sometimes twice, the emotional stress overriding Brian's best efforts. She was losing the newborn confidence she'd just started to have.

He knew several ways to address her issues, but he expected none of them would meet her approval. Of course, her will be damned, he was fast moving into territory where he would railroad over her if he needed to do so. She'd been reading the same damn book for the past hour, and hadn't turned a page. He could look into her mind, except it was usually in the same place. A vacant drifting, as if she'd become an oblivious kitchen wench, tending a simmering cauldron of her anguish. The shadow gremlins, as she called them, were eager children, dancing about and waiting to tip it over once again.

Last night, she'd immersed herself in what seemed like better thoughts. The touch of Gideon's mouth, the sweep of Daegan's hands over her back, the feel of them inside her, grounding her to earth, holding her connected to them so she wouldn't get lost . . . But she'd drifted away to dreams rather than turn to him.

Her shoulders stiffened as she realized he was there, and that irritated him most of all. It was time to take this bull by the horns, on various fronts, but he would start with the most immediate one.

"You need to consider a new servant," he said, taking a seat at the end of the couch so she had to look at him directly if she raised her gaze. She didn't. "He's been gone a month, Anwyn. Give yourself that gift. James is a prime candidate. He's a widower, and he knows what you are. And he's trained. At least a second mark, to start."

"I didn't do the right thing, Daegan."

"Yes, you did."

"No, I didn't." She surged off the sofa in a sudden movement, throwing the book aside. "I was so pissed off at him for rejecting me, rejecting us, keeping us at arm's length. He was right. I forced him to choose before he was ready. God, he had no time to adjust to any of it, and I threw him out because of my own selfish hurt. I was just as bad as he was. He needed us. I felt it in everything he did. That's what he was fighting, and instead of giving him that time—"

"Anwyn, goddamn it." He rose as quickly as she did, forcing her to look at him despite the fact she bared her fangs in an aggressive, instinctive reaction. He held her by the shoulders, waiting until she got it under control. It tore at her, as it always did, the inescapable truth that part of her mind didn't belong to her anymore, that it could make her do violent things she didn't expect. Before she sent Gideon away, she'd been learning to accept that, not exacerbating it as she was now by keeping herself on too tensile a leash. With Gideon, she'd trusted herself more.

So while Daegan suffered for her, he couldn't help being vampire, which meant tolerance wasn't limitless for him. He gave her a quick shake, snapping her attention to him. "You're doubting yourself because you're hurting, but you thought about it for days before you gave him the choice, *cher*. Hell, from the very beginning you resisted making him your servant for those very reasons. Even if your emotions coated your decision, it wasn't why you made the decision you did. You're a Mistress before you're anything else, even a vampire. You know that."

She closed her eyes, but he refused her that, tipping her chin up roughly enough to bring her focus back to his face, the truth there.

"That skill told you he was ready to face the choice. Learning how to deal with the acceptance, and the acceptance itself, are two different things, and it was past time for him to face the latter. You knew it. You know better than most women what drives a man, what makes him break and run, what brings him to his knees.

"What makes you an incomparable Mistress in Atlantis is you're like the damn Three Fates. You always know the right timing. You know *when* a man needs that catalyst, to force him to let it all go and be the essence, the very best and worst, of who he is. To face it, accept it and walk out of the doors of Atlantis a more whole man than he walked in.

"You let him go, because in addition to being a Mistress, you're a vampire. You could see deep into his mind, and knew if you kept him here, he would kill his soul and yours, trying to fight that edge in himself and 'settle' for you as a vampire."

She shook her head. She'd put her hands on his chest to push against him, but now her fingers dug into his shirt, held him as an anchor. He relished the far-too-infrequent instance of a spontaneous touch even as he ached at the pain he felt behind it.

"As a Mistress, I relied more on intuition, what I 'felt' from a man. As a vampire, with Gideon as my servant, I had the option of delving into his mind. Maybe I didn't give him a choice. Maybe I took it. Because I saw the way he thought now, and believed that's what he'd always think. I didn't listen to what Brian told me. All of us, we're always evolving in our opinions and beliefs, based on wants and needs that change and grow. It's something fluid . . . intuitive. I could know everything in Gideon's, and still miss it. There's a part of him he has to give to me willingly, or I'll never understand it."

A soft smile touched Daegan's mouth then as he gazed into her suffering eyes. "Something I realized about you a long time ago, *cher*. It took me seven hundred years to learn what you have learned in less than a handful of weeks." But as despair gripped her expression, he gave her another little shake.

"He hunted vampires for ten years. His first true love was killed by one. He will not lose that edge of anger, or come to terms with that overnight. You didn't expect that, weren't asking for that. However, if he truly wants to be with you, with us, he must start with acceptance. He didn't have that. You respected his freedom to choose by cutting him loose, and exerted your will over him as Mistress by forcing him to face that. You were both Mistress *and* vampire. You did what was right, Anwyn. Do you want to know why it's really tearing you apart so much, why you're losing your objectivity?"

"Because I failed."

"No. Idiot." That got a reaction, a flash of temper he didn't mind needling. "You put a lot of energy into every man you took on personally inside Atlantis, but you didn't give your heart to any of them. Gideon was different. You offered what he was too afraid to take, because of what he might do to it, with what and who he is. You gave him your faith, and it's tearing you apart because you know he truly loves you."

His voice lowered, his gaze holding hers. "I know that feeling very well. You didn't throw me out, but you refused to surrender to me, knowing that I didn't deserve the gift yet. You did the same to Gideon, in a different way."

"I sound like a real bitch, then."

It startled a harsh chuckle out of him, but he couldn't stand to see her tortured expression. Loosening his grip, he stroked his fingers through her hair, pulling it down from its pins so it was tethered in his fingers. She shuddered, because she'd denied herself any type of physical comfort, stiffening beneath his touch so often that he'd almost stopped offering. He was good at reading a woman, at least this woman, and had known she needed some time. Just as he knew she was reaching the breaking point, where she needed his demand, his override of her refusal. Which was fortunate, because he was approaching a breaking point himself. To his knowledge, abstinent vampires didn't exist in Nature.

"It's the greatest irony, that it's a slave's submission that frees a Master or Mistress to offer their own hearts. It's a delicate chicken-and-egg game, when love is involved. I chose to love a woman who was almost as Dominant as myself, and had no one but myself to blame for that. If you want a queen's heart, you have to earn it by offering your own first. We played that game with one another so long, but when it came down to it, it was as simple as the second I saw you in that alley."

He didn't want to take her to that pain, but he thought he could give her something that would lay a soft curtain over it, change one part of its meaning. He reeled her back into him by those silken strands, patient but inexorable when she tested him by balking, her eyes glittering with the unspoken sexual tension instantly created with her resistance, his demand. But there was more in her eyes, too, things that gave the coil around his cock a deeper bite, higher up, closer to his heart.

"When I found you in the alley, none of it mattered. All I thought, all I felt, was that something sacred, vital and permanent to me had been harmed, something that mattered to me more than anything had ever mattered. It enraged me, not only that it had been done, but that it took a hideous, shameful act of violence against you for me to drop all pretenses and shields to offer you my heart. Whether or not you cut it up and threw it back to me, it couldn't hurt more than thinking I'd never loved you fully before this terrible thing had happened, something that might hold your trust and love from me forever. You've forced Gideon into his own alley, and he has to seek that answer for himself now. What he values most."

When he saw her reluctant acceptance of the harsh truth, he swallowed and offered his heart to her again now, making himself vulnerable to her. "Have I lost your love and trust, Anwyn? Did Gideon hold that for us as well? The longer he's gone, the more you close yourself off. You give your body to me as you've always done, but it's an even more shallow pond than what we had before him. At least before, you gave me hints of your heart, but when he was here, I tasted it fully. I can demand nothing less from you now. You're killing me with your omission."

He'd rarely felt fear in his life, and yet in such a short time, he'd experienced it several times. In the alley, when he hadn't known if he was too late to save her. In Xavier's dungeon, when the arrows punched through Gideon's far-too-fragile body. And now, in this moment, waiting for her answer.

~

He was breaking her open, the bastard, and he knew it. Or hoped for it. Anwyn closed her eyes, pressing her forehead into his shoulder. God, loving had so much pain and loss attached with it, the promise of great joy and utter desolation coming hand in hand. But he was right. It was so ludicrous to pretend it was anything else.

"I miss him," she whispered. "I feel like a part of me has died, and so I've kept that closed off from you. I was afraid you'd think I didn't love you as much. I couldn't bear to lose you both, but by losing one, I *am* going to lose both, aren't I?"

"Oh, Anwyn. Only if you don't allow yourself to feel." Daegan closed his arms around her, held her as if he'd never let her go. "I don't care if you rage and storm, strike out at me and wish me into Hell a hundred times to deal with your missing him. Give me everything going on in your heart, *cher*. I will never leave your side. Not ever."

Tears burned beneath her lids as Daegan whispered the next words against her ear. "As I told you before, I was never jealous of Gideon Green. It was so clear, his meaning to us both. You have seen the many ways that love and desire manifest, Mistress, yet you're such a traditionalist. You can't see how the three of us became whole together? Even though it was right in front of your face, every time he took off his shirt?"

She stilled, her mind riveted by the memory of that mark. When she'd asked him about it, long ago, Daegan had said a vampire's mark was a mysterious thing. *No vampire really understands it, but there is almost always a meaning to it.*

The scarlet trinity. Three tears of blood. It was so obvious. How had she missed it?

"I do not value your love any less if it is shared between Gideon and me. Not if it makes it richer and deeper, stronger and more enduring." He paused, and she sensed his struggle to say something that might be hard for him. Because she knew him better than he realized, she said the words for him.

"Not if it's a reflection of how you yourself feel."

His lips curved in a feral smile, pure desire and emotion combined in a way that curled in her chest like liquid fire. "You think so, *cher*?"

"Yes." She whispered it, her chest still tight with a wealth of backed-up emotions. "Your feelings for him are no less strong than mine. You're right. Somehow it's him that ties us together. The missing part of our heart. Daegan, what are we going to do?"

"We go on with our lives, knowing that truth. He will come back, *cher*. It may take far longer than we wish, but it's inevitable. I know it."

She would have risen on her toes, put her mouth on his, but his hand settled on her throat. His fingers clasped her there, with enough firmness to stir her blood, make it pump a little faster through her heart.

"You have not directly answered my question, *cher*. I am selfish, and want to hear it. Have I lost your love and trust? Are we back to the beginning?"

Anwyn parted her lips, her breath caressing his mouth where he wouldn't allow her to touch. For the first time in quite a while, she let a seductive smile curve her lips, even as her eyes softened, filling with love and letting him see her heart.

"Daegan Rei, I was yours the first time you walked into this club. I belong to you. Gideon and I both do. Until he decides to come back and prove it to you as well, I'll offer for us both."

"Hmm. For that, I'll take it out on his ass in my own way. For now, you answer only for your own self."

The part threat, part promise did a great deal to reassure her, in a way that she knew most the world wouldn't understand. As a Mistress, maybe she herself didn't understand her surrender to Daegan any more than Gideon did. Unlike Gideon, though, she knew the freeing power of surrender.

Daegan brought her to his mouth, taking over the kiss, taking the reins away from her, telling her with the strength of his arms, the demand of his lips, that there was no need for her to be anything but sensation in his embrace. She could trust him with everything else.

She prayed that was true, and chose to believe it.

21

PERFECT. There he was. Allan Walker, a vampire in a nice suit, strolling into the coffeehouse. He wasn't there for a cappuccino, though. He was stalking his annual kill.

There was no way around learning who a man was when you were setting up his surprise execution, though Gideon had spent less time on Allan than he had on previous targets. There hadn't seemed to be much point. He knew that Allan had no servant. He was a financial analyst, a job easy enough to coordinate at odd hours and via technology, rather than out in the light of day. He was a quiet member of his territory, not interested in vampire intrigues. He continued to embrace his human life as much as possible. That might be because he'd had no sire to integrate him into the vampire one. He'd been made nine years ago by a vampire Gideon had killed last year, Clarence Wilson, a seventy-five-year-old vamp. Clarence had turned Allan but then, for whatever reason, had abandoned him shortly after the transition to let Allan find his own way. Usually, such an early abandonment made a fledgling easy prey for other vamps.

Not Allan. He'd figured it out, though Gideon hadn't been around to witness how. All the better. He had no room for admiration for the man's character. He doubted Allan's prey, a young man named John Whitcomb, currently checking his e-mail in the cafe, would have any, either. Whitcomb was working on his bachelor's degree in environmental studies while contemplating a career with Greenpeace, or the Peace Corps, or some other idealistic shit, but Gideon had found even the peace-and-love types didn't find room for "love thy brother" when that brother was sucking the life out of your body.

He had noticed Allan was far more alert to his surroundings than most made vampires like him, suggesting a military background. This one wouldn't be oblivious enough to chase a young junkie into an alley. Fortunately, John liked to seek out quiet places to take pictures, because he was an amateur photographer. So Gideon planned to lure John Whitcomb into this abandoned warehouse, several blocks down the street from the café. Allan would think he'd gotten an easy killing ground, John simply scoping out his next shooting location, but Gideon would be waiting. There wasn't much cover in here, but he didn't need it. He'd set snares to trip the vampire up, cause him confusion. It was more risky, but doable.

He was doing what he should be doing. He had his focus again. His time with Daegan and Anwyn had been one of those odd forks off to the side, a detour that tried to make him believe something different, when he knew there was nothing different for him. There were other vampires, within fifty miles of this area, who deserved death far worse than Allan Walker. Those who preferred to live in the shadows, preying on the weak, doing things that skirted or overstepped Council law when they assumed eyes like Daegan Rei's weren't watching. But Daegan would handle those. The John Whitcombs and Morena Wilsons of the world needed Gideon to handle Allan.

Gideon squeezed his eyes shut. Before the night he'd walked into Atlantis, his gut had always been in knots except during the kill, when he'd trained himself to go into a no-feel zone. Sometimes the actual killing had been the closest he'd felt to peace, because he hadn't needed to think. A temporarily release that could easily turn into a psychopath's addiction. Knowing how fucked-up that was, he was never surprised when, after it was over, he had an overwhelming urge to stab himself in the arm or some other less vital place, cuts that blended in with the battle scars. It was a form of score keeping, tics on the side of the container that held his diminishing soul.

Jesus, enough. This was the right thing to do. It couldn't be right to stand by and watch someone kill an innocent, just because they needed their blood to live. If he accepted that, then he accepted that Laura's death was nothing more than a cycle of nature, a cheetah calmly walking into a gazelle herd and plucking a fawn out of a depression in the ground, none of the others stopping her, because of course no gazelle could hold its own against a cheetah. How could anyone accept that? What kind of fucking God came up with that as the natural order for a gazelle and a cheetah, let alone a nurse and a vampire?

His stomach was cramping, damn it. He fumbled for his wallet, opened it up. Saw Laura's picture gazing at him, but it was like he was looking at the picture of a stranger, the attractive model someone had hired to sell a frame. She was gazing at nothing but a camera lens, not seeing him. Not even knowing him, because the Gideon she knew had died with her.

Son of a bitch. He couldn't afford this right now. He ducked back into the warehouse, took up his vantage point. As soon as John left the café, headed past here to return to his loft apartment, he'd make his move. He wanted to remain alert, but he had to squat down low, breathing hard, squeeze his eyes shut. He was not having a goddamn panic attack, like some kind of rookie.

Instinct. It was always instinct that saved him, his precognition, but now it failed him utterly, because his enemy had walked right up on him. A familiar hand stroked through his hair, the fabric of a duster brushing his back. He had two seconds to think, *thank God*, his earlier denials forgotten, and then he'd sprung to his feet, his knife in hand, a snarl on his lips.

Daegan countered the lunge, drawing the katana in one smooth moment that Gideon couldn't follow. He knocked the shorter blade completely from his hand, followed it up with a reverse thrust that knocked him in the chin with the hilt, hard enough it sat him back down on his ass. He would have jumped back to his feet, ready to go another round, but Daegan was ten feet away, his shoulder braced against a beam scrawled with graffiti.

He wore his hunting gear of solid black, and his dark hair had grown out a little so it was feathering over his brow. It made Gideon remember how Anwyn had said she'd love to see it longer. *Women.*

Except his eyes were on it as well, following the hard lines of

Daegan's warrior face, those dark, fathomless eyes, the firm line of his mouth as it spoke his name. "Gideon."

He would have answered the brief greeting, but he couldn't. It was caught in his throat, too hard to say it aloud. Far too many times, he'd woken with both their names on his lips, for embarrassingly the same reasons. The most humiliating dreams weren't those where his dick was hard, needing the relief of his hand, though of course his wayward imagination had concocted way too many unlikely scenarios of that. It was that half-dream state where he was in a bed with them. Anwyn curled between the two males, all of them twined together, arms, legs, the intimacy of feet touching and overlapping as they slept. At peace with one another's proximity, with the easy caresses of sleep and half wakefulness, the simple affection of belonging.

Something altered on Daegan's face, watching Gideon's. When he took a step forward, Gideon pulled out the nine-millimeter. It wouldn't stop a vampire, but it hurt enough to give him pause. He fired before he gave himself time to think.

Daegan was gone. Just long enough for Gideon to feel a moment of panic; then he felt him right behind him. No more than an inch between their two bodies. His long-fingered hand came forward, sliding down Gideon's forearm, teasing the wrist gauntlet under his coat sleeve, closing over his knuckles, white and hard, holding on to the gun. The motion put them even closer together, because they were of similar heights, though Daegan had slightly longer arms, something Gideon noticed for the first time.

What other things would he notice if he had time, all the time in the world?

"I ought to beat the shit out of you," Daegan murmured. "Drop it now."

"Make me."

"No. Too easy. You drop it, because I told you to do it. Do it, Gideon."

His hand began to tremble, and that cramping in his belly turned into something else, no more controllable. Daegan waited, a still, deadly presence at his back, dangerous for so many reasons, at so many levels.

Slowly, Gideon lowered the gun to his side. Daegan's fingers loosened it, took it away, put it on the ledge behind them. "I'm hungry, Gideon."

Everything inside him stilled. He wanted to cry; he wanted to scream and rage. He wanted the soft touch of Anwyn's hand, her reassuring smile, but this was between them. It had to be between them, because that was part of what she'd known, right? In some cloudy part of his mind, he understood it. He didn't want Anwyn's hand alone. He wanted Anwyn's touch with Daegan's. In this still, abandoned place that was ugly with the things that lost men did—graffiti, the stale smell of urine and vomit, garbage they'd left behind when they found a night's uneasy rest here—he faced it. It was a fitting place for Daegan to find him.

Even more slowly, Gideon shrugged out of his jacket, let it fall between them. Closing his eyes, he tilted his head down, his chin tucked toward his shoulder, baring the artery. He could hear it beating in his ears.

"Tell me, Gideon."

"Do it. I'm . . ." He couldn't continue, could only shake his head. "Do it," he repeated. "Please."

Daegan set his fangs to his neck, his other hand sliding over Gideon's shoulder to collar the base of his throat. That alone made Gideon hard, his hands clenching with the need to touch. But he didn't. He held still, waited. They both knew a woman's desire, how to pleasure her slowly. Watching Anwyn grow aroused was a burning pleasure worth killing or dying for, worth taking the time. But men's pleasure worked differently. Fast or slow, it burned just as deep. A woman desired to be teased; a male desired to penetrate, to take. Conquer . . . or be conquered.

Still, it was unexpected when Daegan bit down, his fingers tightening, pelvis moving in against Gideon's ass. Gideon strangled on a moan at how aroused the vampire was, and at how quickly more blood shot into his own cock in response. The heel of Daegan's battle-toughened palm pressed against him, rubbing, slow and easy, but that was all it took. Whether it was the self-deprivation or how responsive he was as a third-mark, or some combination of both, Gideon came, shamefully as a teenager. He fell to one knee with the force of it, his hips jerking, but Daegan followed him down with graceful power, shielding him under his body, keeping up that slow massage, milking him to the end as he drew Gideon's blood into his mouth, his tongue flicking the artery. His other hand still gripped Gideon's throat, making him think of

Anwyn's collar. He imagined it, ribboned with some claim of Daegan's as well, holding him captive to their needs and wants through the next several centuries . . .

He bowed his head even lower, hunching over at the pain. A slight burn at his throat told him Daegan had given him something more. A mark.

"Just the first one," Daegan murmured as he slowly withdrew, making Gideon shudder with the painful and pleasurable sensation of those fangs pulling out. The vampire still had his hand on Gideon's cock, continuing to caress and knead despite the completion of his orgasm. It made it clear he was doing it for his own pleasure, not Gideon's, and he wouldn't be denied. The organ was sensitive, so Gideon jerked in his unrelenting embrace, but he didn't fight the mastery. "I'm tired of tracking your ass when I need to find you," Daegan added.

"Lazy prick," Gideon managed, his voice too strained. He couldn't stand it, now that the feeling was washing past him, leaving him behind, bereft, adrift. But Daegan's arm locked around his chest. He pulled Gideon down so he sat on his ass on the dusty boards, his body braced between Daegan's powerful thighs as the vamp held that half-kneeling position.

"You went as far as you could go to get out of range of her mind, Gideon." His voice was that silky murmur against his ear. The longer hair brushed it, a caress. "You are unnecessarily cruel to yourself. If you had stayed closer, we could call to her now, and she could come into your mind, show you how she might be in your lap, kissing your mouth, rubbing her beautiful, soft ass against your cock, making it hard again. Teasing you with the give of her sweet breasts against your chest. Demanding you open your mouth to her, let her strip you down and ride you, possess you as she was meant to do. You are hers."

"She doesn't want me; you don't need me. She has you."

"Yes, she does have me," Daegan acknowledged, in an arrogant tone that made Gideon briefly consider stabbing him through his excellent-quality shoe. "But we don't have you. And we both want you. Need you."

Abruptly he yanked Gideon's head back, hard enough that tendons and bones groaned. When he covered Gideon's mouth, made him submit to the heated kiss, taste his own blood on Daegan's tongue, Gideon strangled on a half sob.

"I'm fucking broken," Gideon choked out in his embrace. "I'm lost, Daegan. I'm just lost."

He couldn't believe he was admitting it so baldly, like some little kid, sitting in this warehouse almost near tears, for Christ's sake. But he didn't know what else to do, and Daegan . . . Well, hell, Daegan just brought this shit out of him.

"No, you are not." Daegan's arm tightened around him. "She found you, Gideon. She found us both. You can heal. It is only you standing in the way of that."

Daegan slid his fingers down into Gideon's T-shirt, found the mark with unerring accuracy, tracing the three small scars. "Use your brain instead of your dick. Think about what this means. I had to point it out to Anwyn as well. Daft humans."

He pressed his fang back against Gideon's throat, not breaking the skin this time, just letting him feel the enamel, the wet, hot promise of it again. "She needs you . . . and so do I. Come home when you're ready, but come home. And when you do, I'm going to make you pay for every tear she's shed for you."

He straightened abruptly, though his hand lingered along Gideon's nape long enough for Gideon to confirm he could sit up on his own. He realized that was why Daegan had done it, cosseting him. But before he could form words, Daegan shifted in front of him. Gideon stared at his shoes, the dark jeans. He wanted so badly to look at all of him, but he was here, on his ass, and it would be like being on his knees . . . wanting to be on his knees.

"Thank you for the meal, vampire hunter."

Gideon dropped his forehead onto those knees, stared between his own shoes. Daegan was taking off. Of course. "Yeah, sure. Me and Mc-Donald's. Drive-thru open all night."

He was startled when those long fingers slid under his chin, jerking up his head, not so gently this time. "You're not doing this." Daegan nodded toward the window, where Allan was moving past. John had already gone by, Gideon's opportunity to save his life lost. "For one thing, you should have realized Allan Walker was a Ranger before he was a vampire. He would have killed you." Daegan held Gideon's gaze, wouldn't let him shift away, even though Gideon felt his cheeks begin to burn with the knowledge there. "Though obviously you know that."

The vampire's firm lips tightened, a flash in his eyes reminding Gideon of the seemingly long-ago time when Daegan had pinned him in the weapons room and fucked him for the first time, a sensual and savage reproof for a death wish. "Regardless, you will not punish others in a failed attempt to reclaim a belief you no longer have. You're better than that, Gideon Green. Deal with it; accept who you have become. Understand what you are being offered and be courageous enough to accept it."

His tone softened slightly. "If you have the courage to do that, perhaps you can rely on Anwyn and me to help with the rest."

Then he was gone, with that Holy-Transporter-Beam speed that irritated Gideon mainly because it was so damned impressive. He thought about getting up. Getting his gun, if nothing else. Instead, he let himself fall back to the warehouse floor. He covered his face with his arms to hide from the truth he couldn't bear to face in himself, but that didn't stop his heart, neck and groin from throbbing, still stirred by the impressions Daegan had left on them.

22

BLOCKING Gideon out of her mind was something Anwyn had integrated into her daily routine, her usual disciplines. When he'd been out of geographic range, she hadn't had to devote any energy to it, and maybe she should have been grateful he'd done that for the first month he'd been gone. Now, though, he was back in range. The first second she'd been aware of it, it had been an amazing relief, like when she was a little girl, staying beneath the water of the swimming pool as long as she possibly could, then surging up to savor the sweetness of oxygen.

Careless of who saw her, she'd raced back to their apartment with all the fledgling speed she had. Finding him not there had been a crushing blow. Realizing that all it meant was he was within a few hundred miles of her made her furious with herself, her weakness, so she'd made a new resolve. She would keep her mind blocked to him at all times, no matter how close he was. He could come find her if he wanted something, though of course he wouldn't. That was the whole problem.

Remarkably, despite her self-imposed boycott, just having the connection active again had diminished the power of the voices in her head and the severity of her seizure episodes. She should have been happy at the evidence that she might not need his immediate proximity to help with that, but she wanted that proximity too much.

Keeping that checkpoint between her mind and his, not allowing herself to set one toe over it because she knew she wouldn't be able to bear it if his mind was crying out for her, was every bit as difficult. As he got even closer, Kentucky, Tennessee, she immersed herself in the now-ongoing club renovations, but stressed herself out too much. Though Gideon's nearness might have helped the strength of the seizures and the volume of the voices, her frayed nerves could still increase the frequency with which she had to deal with them. She and Daegan had several near misses, where a seizure began when she was among staff personnel. After that, she forced herself to work in cautious increments, and kept her mind fully open and connected to Daegan when she was outside their rooms.

It was a limited existence, but he'd warned her it would be a long while before they had enough of a handle on it that she could trust herself to manage fluctuations in her stress and not have the convulsions. Brian was continuing to work on an improved injection, but that was in the future. He and Debra had stopped by for several days on a research trip to Texas. Daegan had left her for two days then, indicating he had to finish up a small bit of Council business. But other than that, he hadn't left her at all. She knew that couldn't go on forever.

Though they'd had more than one struggle of wills over it, Daegan encouraging her to mark James, she refusing, she knew she'd eventually have to choose a new third-mark servant and get a grip on the stress. If for no other reason than it wasn't fair to Daegan. He needed to have the freedom to resume whatever role he wished for the Council, though he pointed out that was an expectation she was setting, not him. He'd indicated he had no interest in lengthy assignments that took him away from her.

She had no intention of turning into a long-term burden, though, even if he refused to view it that way. When she finally forced herself to think over her choices, she knew he was right, that James was the likely candidate. Still she hedged, until that sense of Gideon told her that he was getting farther away again, headed toward New England. Then she broke down and did it. Partially. She gave James the first and second marks.

Right afterward, she'd had to flee to their quarters, running straight to the cell, knowing that the jagged pain in her chest was going to explode in her head, the gremlins tearing her apart from the inside out.

She'd locked herself in, refusing Daegan's help, and fallen to the cell floor, hated tears flooding anew as she writhed and screamed.

It was giving up, the first, definitive step to truly letting Gideon go. Accepting that he wasn't coming back anytime soon.

Daegan had explained, unnecessarily, that she didn't have to worry that James could cause her the same pain as Gideon. Most vampire-servant relationships, while physically intimate, were not the emotional bond she'd formed with Gideon. It was just a different level of employee/employer relationship.

She'd managed a dry, humorless laugh at that idea. As Daegan had said, James was willing to serve her. When they'd initially talked about it, the staid and quiet male had shocked her—not an easy feat—by saying he thought he could handle the demands of a servant in vampire society, if ever she wanted to give him that third mark and she and Daegan needed to travel or entertain vampire company.

She wasn't sure if he knew what he was saying, but at least on its face, he was appropriate on all levels, right? He was her security chief after all. While his insight into her shifts of moods wouldn't be as good as Gideon's precognitive sense, with the marks he could anticipate the seizures well enough, and he had the training and dispassion needed to put the restraints on her. She had Daegan for love, and in the vampire world, the strength of her feelings for Gideon, a human, weren't appropriate, even if he wasn't an infamous vampire hunter.

But she still couldn't bring herself to give James that third mark.

Despite Daegan's pressure in that area, she sensed he was more reluctant about it than he wanted her to know. When they were intimate, curled up in his bed together, hands interlaced, his body moving on hers, eyes clasped in hers, mind open, she knew he felt the emptiness around them in the shape of a person that should be there, as she did. They didn't want anyone else. They both wanted Gideon.

She wondered if the powder keg that represented her feelings about Gideon would eventually explode her brain, so she wouldn't have to face the aching truth. Needing him wasn't a choice. She didn't know how or why he'd become so vital, but she wasn't sure if she would survive without the balance of his presence beside her. On those days, she knew if she could go back in time, she would have kept him on whatever terms or lies were necessary. They would have ended up hating each other.

That said, she wasn't sure if what she felt was joy or murderous fury when she woke early one evening, emerging from her daytime slumber, and sensed Gideon sitting in their living room, waiting for them both to wake.

~

She didn't raise that curtain between their minds. It had been down long enough that it was weighted with her emotions, rusty and inflexible. She wasn't ready to talk to him yet. In the late-afternoon hours, she'd risen from Daegan's bed, come back to her own as she often did, to lay and stare at her ceiling in a lethargic drift of thoughts, needing that time to collect herself for the day ahead. It took so much energy to handle those voices. Sometimes she wanted Daegan to cut off her head so she wouldn't have to listen to their damn noise anymore.

Now they were quiet. Waiting, like Gideon was. As she always did, she went to her shower, let the water wake her up fully. Brushed her teeth and hair. Slid a silken wrap over her shoulders and then turned her feet toward her doorway. She stood there for several moments, wondering what she would have done if he'd left while she was pulling herself together to face him. Probably run him down like a one-woman pack of wolves, even naked and dripping wet.

He was quiet out there, too. All through her shower, his mind touched her, a caressing knock she refused to answer. It was as if he were leaning against the door, stroking the wood, flattening his palm against it. Waiting her out. She didn't give herself to fear, but he was the match to that powder keg, perilously close. She trembled in the grip of it when she put her hand on the door, forced herself to stop and take a breath.

Willing submission. That means willing dominance as well. If he's offering himself, I take him back because I want him, desire him, not because I think I have no other choice. I refuse to be that weak, that person who needs another so desperately I would beg to keep him.

~

He rose from the couch when she opened the door. Daegan was already there, though from his damp hair and his open shirt, he had only recently emerged as well. She hadn't heard voices, and she understood, just from looking at them, that nothing had been resolved between them. Daegan had a particular code on this matter. Gideon was her servant. It was her right to confront him first. She suspected the men had done little more than exchange nods. Now Daegan gave her a searching, reassuring glance, and took a seat in her desk chair. Stretching out his long legs, he watched them both.

"Mistress." Gideon cleared his throat.

He looked tired, was her first thought. He'd often looked tired when she'd seen him, never an easy sleeper with the many internal struggles he couldn't seem to resolve, but there was a difference. The struggle going on with him right now was somehow very much in the present, as if his worries and apprehensions centered right here, not on the past. It gave her a cautious hope, but she held her tongue and her expression. She'd basically told him to get the hell out of her club until he could get his shit together and accept what he was being offered. It wouldn't do for him to see that she doubted she'd have the strength to let him leave her side again, even if she had to employ chains to keep him there.

Daegan's brow quirked, his lips twitching at the provocative mental image. She was too involved in the moment to send him the searing glance he deserved.

Gideon shifted. "Guess it would be cowardly to ask you to read my mind to know what's there, rather than me saying it aloud."

"Yes," she said coolly. "It would."

He nodded, his jaw tightening. He almost slid his thumbs into his pockets. She'd missed that defensive, sexy hip-cocked stance that said he wasn't to be fucked with, but it was also an emotional defense. One he recognized because he caught himself, leaving his hands at his sides, staying open to her. She imagined her feet glued to the ground, a steel bar up her spine, to make herself hold position, unbending.

"Being near you two . . . it's like being near magnets. We feel right, drawn together, and when we're apart, there's a pull to bring us back together. The three of us."

That was the rehearsed part. She could tell preparing to say that much had been difficult for him. Still, she raised a brow, not giving an inch. But she sent out some tendrils of her own, enough to find he was agonizing over her frosty exterior, knowing everything he wanted was beneath it, hoping she would willingly give all of that to him if he did the right things, offered all of himself to her. She knew it was the hardest thing anyone could ask of him. But that was why he was here. He was resolved to do it, just . . .

"Fuck, I don't know how to ask," he burst out, his fists clenching. "All the way here, I thought of how to say it . . . I know what I want, what I want to give you. But I don't know how to do it, Mistress. I don't know the right fucking combination of words to tell you that I feel like a fucking empty husk away from both of you, and I'm so completely fucked-up about that. I know I want to be with you, whatever the hell that takes or means. I know I want to be your servant. The idea of not being around when you need me, when I can help take care of you, love you, worship at your fucking feet if that's what you need, it's torment.

"I thought about ending it, you know." He gave a bitter half chuckle, missing the slip in her mask, the fear and anguish when she read it true in his mind, but Daegan saw it, coming to his feet to catch her gaze in reassurance.

I would never have let him do it, cher.

"But you know what happened?" As if the two men she loved were synchronized, Gideon glanced toward Daegan. "He came and said I couldn't go after anyone, because he knew that was what I was thinking about. Hell, any other time, I would have done it as a big fuck-you to him, just to be contrary. But . . ."

Gideon gave that strangled laugh again. Anwyn knew it was a near sob, and it pulled her a step closer to him. He seemed oblivious to them both now, though, his fists still clenched, fighting himself and his words so hard.

"All I could think was you hadn't given me permission to kill myself. That you'd be really pissed. And he probably would be, too. I started thinking about why that was, and all of a sudden I was more scared than I'd ever been in my whole life."

He was now staring at the floor, but everything in him was focused on her, on Daegan, longing for them both. She could feel it like a dense energy field between their three bodies.

"You remember how Daegan said he didn't make you his servant because he figured out asking you to be what you couldn't be would destroy what he loved most about you?"

She nodded, surprised he knew that. It made her realize anew how much he'd understood from her mind that she hadn't revealed directly. "Well, when I left, I was pissed, and thought you were asking me to be what I wasn't. But eventually I figured out that you never would have asked . . . demanded it"—he swallowed—"if you hadn't known that's actually what I am. What I wanted to be."

She wondered if her heart could swell to the point it could hurt her rib cage, because her chest was aching at the look on his face, his eyes trained on the ground between her feet. "When it came down to it, I don't think I let you send me away because I didn't want to be your servant. It was because if I finally had a real reason to live, I'd have to deal with all this other shit, the stuff that's been rolling around in my gut like a cancer for so long it feels like that acid is part of me. I don't know how to fix it, what to do. And that scares the shit out of me, because I might never be enough for you."

He lifted his baffled gaze back to her. Anwyn was frozen, seeing something she'd never thought she'd see in Gideon's face. Long ago, tight, stingy tears had squeezed out when he'd spoken of Laura, the love he'd lost. But now his eyes were brimming full. As she watched, the tears broke free like a dam held back too long, tightening his face in anguish. It was the boy of long ago, who'd lost so much, surging forward.

"I'm so fucking scared of loving someone again with every part of myself, and yet it's too late. I've already done it. I know it sounds stupid, but I really thought I'd never have to risk that again. That I was done with it. Jacob, what he became. Laura. All of it hurt worse than anything to have that taken away from me, and now I can't . . . I need your help. I need you to love me." He drew a deep, shuddering breath, bowed his head, and whispered it, staring at the floor. "Both of you. But I don't know how to ask or give, or do anything but stand here and fucking beg for something I don't even understand, that I may not even know how to do anymore. I want to belong to you. Both of you."

A hard shudder went through his body. In a moment that seemed to move in slow motion, he sank to one knee, then the other. Anwyn couldn't bear it. In the next blink, she had her arms around his great shoulders, head bent over his. The second she touched him, his arms flew around her, almost as fast as a vampire would have done. He banded them so tightly around her he might have hurt her if she had human bones. As he buried his face into her midriff, that dam completely shattered. Hiding his shame in her soft, womanly flesh, he couldn't hold back too many years of loss and blood. They crashed over him, wracking him so violently even her strength couldn't hold him steady.

But Daegan's could. He was here, crossing the room toward them swiftly. Anwyn was glad, because she was pretty sure she was about to shatter as well. She couldn't bear the thought of this moment being lost to a seizure.

We are both here, cher. He put his hand on her face, against her neck, steadying her, as he brought the warmth of his presence behind Gideon's kneeling form. *Those devils in your mind have no power over this moment.*

We'll kick their ass if they even try. I've been playing a lot of arcade games.

She choked on a sob, realizing she'd dropped her defenses without even thinking about it. Her subconscious knew it was okay, that she didn't have to shut Gideon out anymore. Oh, how she'd missed having him in her mind, and she wondered that anyone could ever find it invasive and unwelcome, to have that intertwined mind-to-mind connection. The pleasure of it seared through her, a sacred experience.

Daegan put his hands on Gideon's shoulders, knelt behind him, laying his jaw on Anwyn's hands and against Gideon's skull, holding him steady between them. Which was why she got to see the brief shock cross Daegan's face when Gideon at last drew breath to say more.

"I want your permission . . . I want Daegan to third-mark me, too. I want to close the circle. The way it should be."

Daegan curled his hand in Gideon's hair, tightened so he had to drop his head back to look at the other male. Gideon resisted, still embarrassed, but Anwyn took the silken corner of her robe, pressed away his tears. Then she leaned down, kissing the rest away before brushing his mouth, just a taste of what she wanted to devour. Gideon felt the same way, but anticipating it, Daegan's grip tightened so his Mistress could sample and tease.

She felt it descend, that delicious emotional power joining forces with the overwhelming physical needs of three people. Needs that hadn't been fully met for nearly two months. She and Daegan had never been more in sync, in their absolute ravenous hunger for the man who'd just given himself to them. Whether he knew it or not, he was making it worse, because their usually laconic hunter was still talking.

"I want things I never thought about wanting. I don't really care . . . that you're male." He dared a glance over his shoulder this time, before staring back at Anwyn's midriff. "That's not what it's about. But it's as if something happened deeper than the bodies, and now—hell, I don't look at any other guy and want his dick, but I want everything about you, including that. It's damn confusing to me. I want to give you something of myself, the way I give to Anwyn. I want to feel you . . . Shit, damn, fuck, I sound like an idiot. Let me up."

Gideon tried to pull away from them both, but he'd given away his choices. His Mistress and Master, eager to seize them, were now determined to teach him what he claimed not to know. Daegan took advantage of his surprise to kiss his mouth, fisting his hand in his shirt. Gideon's passion-starved body responded instantly, his strong hand curling around Daegan's wrist, as if to throw him off, but he didn't. Instead, he held on, a growl in his throat as Daegan flicked his tongue back out over his lips, slid his hand down to cup him with blatant demand.

"You want to feel me inside you, the way she is inside you," the vampire finished for him. "That intimate connection that says I have had your body as thoroughly as she has."

Tell him, Gideon. Anwyn met his midnight blue eyes, knowing her look could strip him even more bare, though she'd never seen him so emotionally naked.

Gideon wouldn't loosen his grip on her waist, but he did shift and let go of Daegan's wrist so he could look at the male vampire more directly, summoning a warrior's courage. "You remember the night we went to the tasting and you told me about Laura?"

The vampire nodded. "I shouldn't have told you then."

"No." Gideon shook his head. "In the beginning, it pissed me off, something else you'd handled far better than I could have."

"But now you saved my life, and you're feeling a bit more smug about yourself."

"No. I guess now . . . I just feel like . . ." Gideon shrugged, uncomfortably, and would have risen, but Daegan put a hand on his shoulder, fingers near his throat, caressing him there.

"You can tell me anything, Gideon. In a matter of moments, I'll be in your mind, your soul. It would mean a great deal to me if you gave me the gift of your trust now." He gave him an implacable look. "Tell me."

"You know, it still freaks me out, the way I feel when either one of you does that." Gideon didn't say what "that" was, but it was there in his mind, and on his face. The way it felt when they commanded him.

"Yes, it unsettles you. And arouses you. And makes you glad to belong to us, no matter how that also discomforts you. We're glad you belong to us, Gideon. Tell me."

Gideon looked down, then made himself meet Daegan's gaze again. "It makes me feel like you were looking out for me, even then. Like my dad, or older brother, or . . . Shit. I don't know what to call it. I wish it could have been me, but you made sure he wouldn't take anyone else's Laura. Thank you."

Daegan paused a long moment, and Anwyn felt her own throat tighten at what she read in both of their faces. "While it was not my motive then, I think I might do anything for you, Gideon Green. You and Anwyn."

It was a powerful admission, a quid pro quo, and Daegan did it with unwavering resolve, making it clear how significant a statement it was. Gideon tightened his jaw, lifted his hand and closed it over Daegan's forearm again.

"Same goes. Well, except maybe shining those fancy shoes you have. Or ironing your shirts, or wiping your—"

"I'd let you stake me first."

Gideon gave a half chuckle, then mortified himself further when his voice broke. This time it was Daegan who embraced him, palming his head to hold him against his heart.

Anwyn had seen the vampire be tender with her before, but it moved her more than she could say, to see him use that gentleness on Gideon now. Knowing it was likely to be gone in a matter of seconds, she filed the picture away in her heart to savor as only a woman could.

"For so long you felt alone, watching out for others," the vampire murmured into the crown of his head. "Now you have both of us. Just as we have you."

Then Daegan pulled back, made Gideon look at him with two immovable hands on either side of his head. "As far as what I am to you, you know exactly what to call me."

"Let go, you bullying asshole," Gideon muttered weakly.

Daegan ignored him. "I have been alone most of my life as well, Gideon, until you and Anwyn made me feel like I belonged to a family. You both give me that. Now give me the greatest gift of all. Let me hear you say it, and then you can touch us, take your fill of both of us, the way you wish, with no condemnation of yourself."

"I don't know . . ." Gideon cleared his throat, put his eyes back on the ground at their feet, because his cheeks were burning. "I do better when it's the two of you taking your fill of me."

~

Everything about this was a dreamlike haze, something that had overwhelmed him in imagination for so long, and here he was. In this whole new place, scared shitless as he said. But also thinking maybe something better than his miserable existence was possible, was truly being offered to him. He'd come here, not sure he believed it, but he hadn't been able to forget Daegan's words in the warehouse, or how they connected to Anwyn's, the day she sent him away.

Now the charged pause was enough to cloak him with the heat of their responding lust, possession and desire. If they didn't start touching him, or letting him touch them, he was going to go crazy. He should have known they wouldn't make it that easy.

"So you're saying you're ours, to do with as we will. You serve us." Anwyn's voice, a Mistress's voice.

"Yes," Gideon managed in a low voice. "I belong to you. Both of you."

"Then call us by name." Daegan repeated it, that most difficult of all demands. At least they didn't make him look at them, though he had a feeling one day he could, if he could say it now.

He was a vampire hunter, a soldier, a loner. A man who'd always said he wouldn't respond to any authority greater than his own. And he'd given up on God a long time ago.

"Mistress," he managed in a throat that rasped. Drawing in a deep breath, he lifted his gaze after all to meet Daegan's dark eyes. "Master." It tore something inside him to say it, but it was a good pain.

Anwyn slid the tie of her robe free, drawing his attention. When it opened, her bare breasts were level with his avid gaze. "Suckle me, Gideon," she murmured. "Show me your devotion."

He seized the opportunity. If he had to express any more of his feelings, which were as painful as wounds, he might lose it. He latched onto her brutally in the first moment, as unthinking as a starving infant. However, the press of Daegan's fingers into his shoulders recalled him. He eased his bite, turned it into an urgent laving. He would have used his hands, crept up to her hips, but Daegan's firm grip was already on one of his wrists, Anwyn's on the other, drawing them back until Daegan took over both of them, making him clasp his opposite elbows, boxing his arms behind him. Then Daegan began to wrap him with Anwyn's sash, starting at one wrist and working across until it reached the other, binding his forearms together at the center of his back.

A deep shudder started somewhere in his knees, rammed up through his testicles and lower belly, accelerating his heart. Always before, when one or both of them had tried to dominate him, the internal struggle had been one of resistance. This moment, the willing surrender, was far fiercer than that, and it shook him to his foundations, the overwhelming, paralyzing power of it. It was something close to divine bliss, a tranquility painful in its truth, tearing him away from the violence and turmoil with which he'd framed his life. It put him somewhere where he floated, unsure of anything, having to trust them both in a way he'd never trusted anyone, not even himself.

He remembered that night long ago, when he and Jacob had shared Lyssa. It had taken him a while to recognize the key difference in dealing with his two Dominant vampires. The one being shared between the twosome of their particular threesome wasn't Anwyn, but him. Like everything else, it had been initially hard to accept, but now, letting go, it overwhelmed him to be so desired by the two of them, rendering him helpless, mindless. He wanted to feed them both, wanted that light-headed feeling of giving his blood to them, and how crazy was that? He wanted the different feel of their hands, Daegan's stronger, broader grip, Anwyn's slim fingers, her polished nails digging into his flesh.

A long time ago, a much younger, far more innocent version of himself thought he'd be saying forever to the woman he asked to be his wife. Yet when Anwyn had put him in her collar, the one he'd left behind and yet wanted to wear again, he remembered wondering if that was what marriage felt like, that commitment to forever. He thought it was. To both of them.

Anwyn sucked in a breath, overtaken by his thoughts as much as by the sensual hunger he was exercising on her nipple. While Daegan was binding him, Gideon hadn't let up, leaving a trail of wet heat as he switched to the other one. She made a soft moan on his first contact with each of them, acknowledging how very much she'd missed his mouth, his body, those callused hands. She ran her hands over the broad shoulders, now taut with his arms drawn back in restraints.

Opening the windows of her mind wide so Daegan could feel everything their servant was feeling, see what images were flashing through his mind, she knew from the emotion in Daegan's eyes that this was a defining moment for him as well. He'd understood it, and so had she, though she'd let her worries blind her. This was the link they needed to fully belong to each other, what they'd always needed. Three tears of blood, forever marked on Gideon, proved it.

"Second mark, vampire hunter," Daegan breathed against his flesh, hearing her desire and answering it. His hands came around, curled in the front of Gideon's shirt. With an ironic flash in his dark eyes, he ripped it free like paper, taking it behind the vampire hunter and down his arms so it added to the bindings on him, baring those beautiful shoulders, the wide, scarred chest that bore her mark. Daegan brought his mouth to Gideon's throat as Anwyn held Gideon's head to her breast, her hips pressing urgently closer to his body. Both of them could smell her arousal, hot and needy. Under the press of her leg, Gideon's cock was enormous against the jeans, struggling for escape. When Daegan pressed his own erection against the vampire hunter's muscular ass, there was a flex of acknowledgment, of apprehension and pure lust, that seared through Anwyn's awareness, because Daegan's mind was open to her as well. A trinity in truth.

～

As Daegan's fangs sank in, he exulted in Gideon's guttural response, an animal cry he made against Anwyn's generous curves. Her servant bit her in reaction, marking her breast with a red imprint of his teeth. Her hand tightened on his hair as Daegan released the serum that would give him direct access to Gideon's mind, no longer only through the lovely conduit of Anwyn's. It unfolded inside Daegan like a gift, two entwined sets of thoughts of lust and longing, of sanctuary and need.

It was a welcoming circle, giving him a sense of home he'd never realized he needed until he felt it now. One touch and he knew he'd never want to be without it, that he would defend both of them with every deadly skill and vulnerable emotion he had to keep them safe and bound to his heart.

Sliding his mouth free, he turned Gideon's head again, capturing his lips to make him taste his own blood and the residual of that serum, and spoke for the first time, mind to mind. *It's time to pleasure your Mistress, vampire hunter. Then we'll finish it, make sure you both belong to me.*

Gideon opened his eyes, the first time he'd ever dared to do it while their mouths were so intimately involved. Daegan saw that warrior's response in their depths that stirred and drew him at once. *As you belong to both of us. Ours to protect as well.*

It was a startling challenge and offer at once. At Anwyn's soft, determined agreement, Daegan realized his life was likely to change in ways he had not anticipated. But he'd lived on the unpredictable edge of violence; he wouldn't mind indulging the unpredictable edges of love, freely given.

He gave Gideon another hard kiss to remind him who was in charge, his hand tightening over the marks on his throat. *I think we'll need another collar, Anwyn. One with a bit more bite to it, to keep our servant aware of who he answers to.*

She gave them both that mysterious female smile she did so well. Her thoughts, though open to them, tumbled like the mystery of clouds and rain, sunshine and rainbows, perfect, simple and yet too beautifully complex to ever unravel. Reaching down, she unbuckled Gideon's belt, slid it free, then brought the tongue up in a caress over his nipples that had his muscles tensing all along Daegan's torso where their bodies touched. She wound the belt around Gideon's throat, threaded it, drew up the slack and then began to tug, making it clear she wanted him to follow her.

"You can get to your feet, Gideon," she said, in that sultry voice that could coax a man's cock to jet with the velvet caress alone. "I don't need a man to walk on his knees to prove I own him."

With a wry smile, Gideon rose, though Daegan knew the man's usually strong thighs were trembling. It moved his heart and got him harder at once, so that he rose with him, putting a steadying hand low on his hip, his thumb caressing his buttock. *He's overdressed*, cher.

So he is. Would you take care of that for me?

Daegan knew that Gideon was offering him their trust, but he also understood the instincts of a street fighter, as Gideon had been for so long. Therefore, he moved that reassuring hand to his shoulder, drawing his eye to what he was doing before he did it. His switchblade flipped out in his hand, and with swift, light pressure, he cut through the side of the denim, moving from the waist down to his ankle, letting the tip touch the flesh so there was a faint sting that Gideon registered, the edge of danger. Then Daegan moved to the other side and pulled the now-ruined jeans away from the snug briefs beneath. The thin fabric was straining, unable to contain his cock, the crotch showing dampness where he'd already spilled some of himself there.

"You know, clothes don't have to be ripped or cut off." Gideon spoke offhandedly, though there was a crack in his voice. "Most people don't buy new wardrobes every time they have sex."

"You have stayed away from me for months," Anwyn noted, that steely glint coming to her eye that Gideon recognized. His cock jumped in immediate response, even as his fingers dug into his forearms under the wraps of the robe sash. Daegan closed his own hand over them, enjoying the taut resistance, as well as the tone of Anwyn's voice and Gideon's reaction to her words.

"I'm exacting a biblical retribution," she continued. "For the next forty days and forty nights, when you're in these rooms, you'll wear no clothes at all. My punishment, and my pleasure, as well as Daegan's." Her fingers trailed down Gideon's chest, across to the nipple, her nails scraping hard enough he sucked in a breath, a response that Daegan felt in his own testicles. God, he loved to watch her work. And he loved watching Gideon surrender to it, all that fierce passion rising up to meet her, fire for fire. "We'll have the joy of seeing your beautiful body from any angle we wish, and you'll be readily accessible whenever either one of us wishes to fuck you. Or enjoy your response when we fuck one another and force you to do nothing but watch."

Anwyn went to her toes, sliding her body oh-so-lightly against his almost bare one, her thighs playing with the hard organ beneath the briefs. Gideon made a low, needy growl in his throat, trying to surge forward, and found himself unable to do so. Daegan had moved his grip to Gideon's biceps, anticipating him.

"You have put me through hell, Gideon Green. You deserve the punishment. But it's not only about that." Her touch gentled unexpectedly, tracing the line of his face, and Daegan watched the way her eyes and mouth softened. Could Gideon see the sheer adoration in her eyes, how she wanted to cherish him, torment him, love him beyond all sense and reason?

"I see in your mind how badly you want to surrender to us, and tonight you'll do that. But tomorrow, you'll resist, because that's your way, because you're a long way from healing, trusting us completely and giving up your anger. So for those forty days, you will be brought to climax, over and over. You'll wear a plug and a cock harness more often than not. You will do things for me and Daegan that you've never contemplated, that you would have refused without a second thought. I am going to train you to surrender to our pleasure, in whatever form we wish it. And when I'm done, you may find yourself begging for forty more days of the same punishments."

She stretched up on her toes, brushed his mouth, wouldn't let him have more than that brief taste. He seemed frozen by her words, however, held in a stasis of apprehension and anticipation. "Somewhere along the way, you'll learn that letting yourself completely go like that will take you to a place of perfect balance. Where wounds will heal, where pain will no longer be feared. Where you will never doubt my love or Daegan's, or your own capacity to return it in full measure."

She was a sorceress, and every word wove its magic. Not just around Gideon. It wove around all three of them as she backed up another step, the robe still open to show the firm quiver of her breasts, the jut of her aroused nipples, well suckled by Gideon's mouth so the damp imprint remained. Her hand was wrapped in the belt collaring him. Perfect to her desires, and to Gideon's, the vampire hunter didn't immediately come when she started to pull. He forced her to give it a sharp tug, drawing it tighter around his throat so that he resisted her as they moved forward.

It made the feeling between them even more combustible, and Daegan had to smile, showing his fangs in dangerous appreciation of Gideon's insight into his Mistress's pleasure, as well as his own. They liked his fight, and would always welcome his need to do it, as much as he welcomed their arousal from it.

She brought them into her playroom, only this time they weren't here to take care of her seizures, or deal with a vampire's transition. Tonight they were handling the breaking of a cherished slave, a servant who would be like no one else's.

They wouldn't have him any other way.

23

Anwyn moved into a chair with a split footrest, putting her feet onto it in a way that allowed her to spread her silken legs. The robe fell down between her knees, hiding what lay between them from view. As she settled on the chair specifically designed to allow a woman to be fucked comfortably in a partly reclined position, she drew Gideon down to her mouth while Daegan held his hips.

Daegan was too stirred now to let her lead the game. She was teasing them, which he recognized as a challenge to him, so he took up the gauntlet, as naturally as Gideon's resistance had come to him.

Use your mouth to lift the robe over her thighs. Show me her pussy.

His voice in Gideon's head was resonant, authoritative. In Gideon's bent position, it was easy for him to take that hem, draw it up and to the left, letting it fall to the outside of her leg. Then he bent to do the right.

Daegan's gaze lifted to meet Anwyn's. *Put your arms over your head,* cher. *Display yourself to me.*

There was a smile in her gaze, laced with her trembling desire. She obeyed him, allowing their servant to complete his task. Gideon revealed the lips of her cunt, wet and already damn near dripping, a sight that had both men salivating. Their gazes coursed greedily up her body, across the soft stomach and upwardly tilted rib cage to the heavy breasts, slim throat and lush lips. There were so many things they wanted to do to her, so many images that flashed through both minds that a sexy whimper escaped her throat, even as she took one foot and placed it on Gideon's abdomen. "Cut off his underwear," she said. "Please."

Daegan obliged her, though this time he moved up close behind Gideon so his ass was pressed solidly against Daegan's erection, letting Gideon feel how engorged he was, what he would be feeling inside his ass very soon. He threaded his arm under Gideon's, and now both men watched as Daegan let the blade tip drift down his belly, leaving a red line as he went toward the pubis. Gideon went very still, his heart pounding up into his throat.

Daegan almost heard the rush of blood that added to the painful state of Gideon's cock. It fired both Dominants' desire, the obvious evidence of Gideon's response to the threat of pain administered as foreplay, from them at least. Daegan kept his hand very, very steady as he went over the line of Gideon's cock, following it down, parting the strained fabric easily. When he reached the large testicle sac, he nicked him deliberately. Gideon quivered, but didn't move. Anwyn reached forward, loosening the garment and letting it drop so he was fully naked before them.

"I will take you into her, and when I do, you will be guided by my hands, my pace," Daegan said quietly. "But right now, I want you to turn around, drop to your knees and put my cock in your mouth. Make me slick for your ass."

By the end of those forty days, Anwyn would accomplish what she said. Gideon would truly have surrendered everything to them. The beginnings of the slave they saw in him now would be honed to a fine point. But Daegan wanted this from him now, before then. It was the cruel edge of a vampire's power that could not be dulled, that Daegan wanted to make sure Gideon understood was part of the package.

Gideon pivoted on his foot, met Daegan eye to eye. They held that way several charged seconds as Anwyn watched them, her sable hair framing her intent face, her mouth soft, the lips that had also been on Daegan's cock in times past. She sat up then. Curling her fingers in the ties of the sash holding Gideon's arms, she exerted a gentle pressure that brought the three of them together again, helped Gideon's knees to bend. He went down.

For the first time in centuries, Daegan damn near disgraced himself at the surge of pleasure watching it. Because they were both tall men, Gideon had to dip his head, but when he took him in, he did it with no hesitation or reservation. His mouth encompassed Daegan, deep-throating him, sucking hard immediately . . . with rough male desire.

Anwyn reached into the discreet drawer of the small table next to her chair and withdrew the lubricant. As Daegan put his hand on Gideon's head, digging his fingers into his scalp, controlling his movement, Anwyn drizzled the lubricant in the dimple between his buttocks, and then smeared more of it on her fingers, taking them down the crease. As she began to massage his rear entry, Gideon made an incoherent noise against Daegan's cock, a vibration that made the vampire convulse and mutter an oath. Gideon flicked a glance up at him. Daegan was pretty sure it was a cocky expression, one that said Gideon was getting an inkling of the true power of a slave. While it was a pleasure to see it, Daegan tugged at his hair roughly, giving him a warning growl.

"Don't get too self-assured down there, vampire hunter. The harder you make me, the less likely I am to be gentle. In fact, I'm pretty certain I intend to fuck you so hard you'll have trouble walking afterward."

Gideon's cock jumped at the sensual threat, heightening the anticipation for them both. Anwyn's fingers slid inside the hunter, along with the slender tip of the lubricant tube as she got him nice and slippery. Gideon gasped against Daegan's cock.

At another time that broken rhythm would earn a punishment, but now he was just too damn hard. At Anwyn's nod, Daegan pulled free, suppressing a groan at the tantalizing suction of Gideon's hot mouth; then he turned the man, levering him to his feet, and onto the kneeling bench between Anwyn's knees.

"This chair puts your Mistress above you when she is fucking you, keeping you on your knees, so you remember that she is your Mistress." But even as he said it, Daegan remembered the night she'd let Gideon lie down upon her. That would happen again, he was sure, just as he could easily see the three of them entangled in more intimate couplings in his large bed, falling asleep in one another's arms. With a deep, pleasurable surprise, he saw a flash of recognition in Gideon's mind, a yearning dream recalled.

"Later," he murmured, touched. "Right now this is a marriage, a ritual surrender, an understanding of who and what we are to one another."

Though he could imagine many such scenarios, including one where he might lay Anwyn down upon Gideon's body, letting their servant cradle her from beneath. Cupping her breasts, Gideon would offer them up to Daegan's mouth as the vampire slid into her cunt. Gideon would pleasure her ass, her soft body sandwiched so close between them. The possibilities were endless. Tonight was just the beginning.

Anwyn had resumed her reclining position, her fingers drifting down to touch herself, spread her moisture even further over her lips as Daegan watched. Taking her fingers back up, she fed them to Gideon one by one, letting him suck them greedily. She then brought him to her lips for a tongue-sucking feast. While she did that, Daegan opened his jeans, let his cock stretch out, long and hard, brushing the tip over Gideon's ass.

When Anwyn at last pushed her servant back, her eyes glittered. "I wanted to taste Daegan on your mouth," she breathed.

Daegan knew then he could wait no longer. From the raging lust in Gideon's mind, he didn't think he could, either. His own cock was high against his belly, Anwyn's weeping pussy so close. All Gideon needed was her command to come into her, the craving for it taking over his mind. Well, partly. It was twofold. He wanted, needed, would perhaps even beg, to be filled by them both.

God, Daegan had to have him now, wanted to be in Gideon when his cock slid into Anwyn's slick channel. Daegan pressed up against the male, guiding his cock to that well-lubricated entry. "Relax," he murmured. "Push against me; let me in." As he put the pressure there, the cant of his body leaned Gideon into Anwyn, so he knew Gideon's cock was brushing that heated entrance. A shudder ran through him as Anwyn's lips curved, knowing what she was doing to him. But she was trembling with her own need as well. "There you are, that fine, tight ass."

He slid in slow, easy, knowing that Gideon's ass was still pretty virgin. He was the only one who'd had it, and possessiveness streaked through him at the thought, so strong it surprised him.

Why does it surprise you, my love? Your need to own both of us is part of your love for us.

Anwyn's desire-filled observation in his mind brought him all the way to the hilt in Gideon. Before the man could get too caught up in the burn, Daegan clasped his hips, holding him tight and flush against him, feeling the press of his bound arms across his lower abdomen, the sliding clutch of Gideon's fingers against his sides where he could reach. Then Anwyn reached down, closing her fingers around Gideon's cock, and made him do a controlled glide into her.

~

It was indescribable. They were letting him into their minds, so Gideon could see and feel how synchronized they were, mind to mind, two Dominants controlling his movements with tormenting pleasure. As he sank into Anwyn, her body arching up to his, Daegan moved with him, until they were fitted together, the three of them, Gideon high and tight inside her as Daegan was inside of him.

Utter, perfect bliss. Anwyn met Gideon's gaze and then his mouth with her own, wrapping her arms around his shoulders, her hands caressing Daegan behind him as well. Her legs rose to encompass them both, heels resting on Daegan's bare hips. Gideon was held between them, his arms bound, directed by Daegan's movements, more physically helpless than he'd ever been in his life because he was emotionally helpless at the same time, rolling on the ocean they'd created with no direction to go but where they took him.

Daegan withdrew partway, then slid back in, increasing that burning pleasure at once. He took Gideon with him then, pulling him back, pushing him into Anwyn as she made wet sounds of need with every thrust. Gideon thought he was going to die from it. Her cunt sucking on him, caressing him with every stroke. Daegan's cock rubbing those dense nerves inside, hitting them with perfect accuracy.

The male set his teeth to his neck once again. Gideon knew he was about to mark him, but for the first time the tension that spread through him was all anticipation, something he wanted, maybe needed. It was crazy, but he was past questioning it.

Having Daegan in his mind, along with Anwyn, was yet another way he'd thrown off the lines and taken himself out into the sea of their own making, absorbing every thought and command, whispered emotion and physical response.

Beg him to mark you, Gideon. Give us the gift of your need.

He didn't allow himself to think, merely let the thoughts flow out from a part of him he didn't even know he had, an infant emotional trust that he knew she would bring to full maturity, with Daegan guarding his back.

Please. Finish it. Bring us together . . . Master.

Maybe he'd be embarrassed as hell to say it aloud, but right now Gideon felt it with everything he was. Anwyn met his mouth in a kiss. As Gideon groaned into her mouth, Daegan bit down.

Though he couldn't see it, he knew it was an ethereal blue serum, like a piece of sky melting and flowing through the veins with the power of fire. Unlike the acid of the rushed third mark he'd received from Anwyn, something he knew she regretted for the pain but he no longer did, it roared through him with fiery, erotic pleasure. As it built with the orgasm, he couldn't wait for the permission their minds were demanding of him. He tried, but oh, fuck . . . he couldn't stop.

He bucked in their embrace, his mind tumbling between theirs. It felt like he had dropped deep into each of their souls. Then Daegan was pulling his head back, letting him smell the nick the vampire had made at his own throat. Gideon put his mouth to that heated skin and took his first draught of Daegan's blood, willingly locking the manacle of the third mark firmly around his soul. Binding himself to them both.

You can come for us, Gideon. Give us all of yourself.

He didn't know who uttered the command, or if it mattered. He released with no choice otherwise, convulsing between them, his movements spurring theirs so he had the roaring pleasure of feeling Anwyn's cunt clamp down on his pulsing cock, her own orgasm rippling over him. They cried out together, holding on against the impact, bucking and savage, as the power of it stole away all sense of time or surroundings, except for the steadying power of the male vampire holding on to them both. Daegan kept up with their movement, called out in primal encouragement at their release. Then, on the receding tide of their response, the straining shudder of his body warned he could hold out no longer. Anwyn dug her heels into his hips and Gideon clamped down on him, bringing Daegan his release. The vampire let go with a deep-throated groan that pushed them up and over an even higher edge of climax.

It was a perfect joining, a perfect release. A perfect homecoming. A perfect trinity.

24

"**S**o if I'm the exclusive entrée for both of you, should I have a perma-nent stash of cookies and juice standing by?"

Gideon turned his head into Anwyn's hand, for she was idly strok-ing his hair. They had the gas logs going, the only light in the living room. She lay on the couch, temporarily sated, her lush body draped again in one of those silky robes she liked. Her small feet were folded together between Daegan's splayed legs. The vampire wore a pair of jeans, carelessly undone at the waist as he sat propped against the other end of the sofa. One leg was bent and leaning against the sofa back, behind Anwyn's legs and hip, the other long leg braced on the floor, his bare foot next to Gideon's flank.

For his part, Gideon sat on the floor next to the large sofa, one arm loosely corralling his own bent legs. He was trying to decide if the soft throw rug felt good or odd on his uncharacteristically bare ass.

Daegan swirled the last bit of his wine in his glass, giving him a direct look. "You want me to feed from you?"

"Well . . ." Gideon shrugged, looked toward the wall. "I guess that's part of the marking deal, right?"

Having two vampires in his mind could be a pain in the ass. Having two vampires who wouldn't let him get away with any dissembling, any avoidance of his own desires . . . It sucked, but then again, it didn't. Like the ass on the carpet, it was . . . good and odd at once.

"Mmm." Daegan's long fingers overlaid Anwyn's as he leaned forward, snagging Gideon's attention. "You want me to feed from you, vampire hunter? You want my mouth on no other human? Do not look away from me."

"Thought you guys didn't like humans looking you in the eye. Part of the whole subservient thing."

Daegan's brow arched, his touch descending to Gideon's jaw. It was so different, to be touched by them both at the same time, the female and male fingers caressing him in different ways, Anwyn's stroke through his hair a seductive pull, Daegan's stronger, even more demanding tug.

"Except when a servant is doing it to avoid his own feelings."

"Jesus. Here I thought you were a badass, and you're one of those sensitive types who likes to yammer about feelings. What a turnoff."

Anwyn's chuckle didn't change the set of Daegan's expression at all. He held Gideon's gaze, his lips unsmiling.

"Yeah," Gideon said. "Yeah, damn it. Don't really want you using anyone else other than me. It would piss me off. Happy now?"

"Ecstatic." Daegan let Anwyn take over the stroking again and leaned back, releasing Gideon from that way too intuitive stare.

It was like opening a floodgate, though. Gideon wondered if he could get them to gag him before he humiliated himself further, but he had to say this part. And there was no gag for his mind, after all. "I should have fed you then, that night in Xavier's. I wanted to."

His gaze shifted to Anwyn. Sometimes it was easier to meet her gaze. "If you hadn't been so pissed off, you might have seen from my mind that I did. It freaked me out that I wanted it. Which was why I acted like I didn't."

"I was a little too busy worrying about our lives to plunder your mind," she said dryly, but her eyes softened and she brushed his cheek.

"But she wasn't too busy to get pissed off about it," Gideon offered to Daegan. The vampire grinned but gave Gideon a mental heads-up so that he dodged before Anwyn could smack him with the pillow she'd pulled out from beneath her. Since it would have hit him with the force of a basketball, he gave Daegan points for male solidarity. As it was, the pillow took out a lamp behind him. Gideon was on his feet and caught it with a swiftness that took him by surprise. "Wow."

"A side benefit of a third mark from an older, stronger vampire," Daegan noted. "As Anwyn increases in strength and speed, it will enhance you further."

"Enhance me further, hmm? I'm not sure if she can handle anything more enhanced than what I've already got here."

Anwyn rolled her eyes as Daegan snorted. "It can only stand improvement. It was good I was there to satisfy her, this latest time."

"Hey, if I pitch strikeouts the first seven innings, I can afford to let you finish out the last two."

Anwyn saw the flash in Daegan's eyes, the way his lips pressed together against a smile. The past twenty-four hours had belonged entirely to the three of them, and she'd loved every minute of it, hope growing inside her with every touch, every whisper of a smile, every sensual laugh, every quiet moment where they simply absorbed the bond they'd accepted. Every passionate moment that had taken them over that edge again.

Gideon would never be easy. Daegan would always be impossibly arrogant. She might always deal with shadows in her head. But together, she was less afraid of any of it. And she believed that bond would last. She and Daegan had kept their minds mostly open for these blessed hours, an unspoken agreement to give Gideon temporary access in the more intense moments they'd shared, to reassure him. To help him believe what was still so new and doubtful to him.

"Gideon, did you know that Daegan was willing to abandon us, let me have you all to myself?" She slanted Daegan a playful glance, recalling their far more somber conversation of weeks before. "He said if you were able to fulfill all my needs, he didn't want to be in the way."

"Oh, hell, no. You're not getting out of this that easily. Jesus, her mood swings make PMS in a normal woman look like a picnic with a dozen naked Hooters girls."

Gideon tried to duck her swat, but she put enough speed on it to tumble him, which he managed lithely and in a very distracting flex of bare muscles. "See what I mean?"

"I'm sure I only said such a thing to appear charming and sensitive." Daegan shrugged. "You could never possibly meet all her needs."

As they continued bantering back and forth, she could tell a wrestling match was pending. There'd already been two so far, like lions tussling. She was going to have to set down a firm rule that roughhousing was only for the weapons room or playrooms. She had too many breakables in here, and eventually their reflexes or hers wouldn't be quick enough. But for now, she indulged them. "We never answered his juice and cookies question," she broke in, bringing their attention back to her. "We'll usually stagger our feedings on you, Gideon. If we took from you at the same time, it might temporarily weaken you."

"But it might happen occasionally," Daegan said, a deceptively languid look in his dark eyes.

In fact, they'd already done it once in the past few hours. The memory brought a pleasurable flush to her body. However, it reminded her of something else.

"Don't think I've forgotten," she mentioned, curling her fingers in a loose strand of Gideon's hair, tugging to cause a bite of pain. He gave her an arch look, but she wasn't fooled by the guileless eyes. For one thing, she suspected Gideon had never had a guileless day in his life. For another, he was so well tapped into her mind, she saw the combination of trepidation and reluctant fascination as he realized what she was referencing.

"There were three requirements. One was that you would submit to Daegan taking you to bed, without me there. I'm too greedy right now to let you out of my sight, but I won't be forever."

Gideon pressed those firm lips together, moistening them, telling her he was keenly aware of Daegan's predatory gaze, resting on him with lazy pleasure, like a tiger contemplating his dinner. And that contemplation was arousing the male vampire anew.

She could tell it made Gideon's cock respond as well, such that he gave them both an exasperated look. "I'm going to the kitchen," he grumbled. "Anybody want anything?"

"Gideon." That one word arrested him on his heels before he could straighten. If that hadn't reassured her how he felt about her third requirement, his next act did. Her servant met her gaze, covered her hand and lifted it to his mouth, nuzzling her with a heated, moist seduction of tongue and lips. Then he glanced at them both. "I'm yours, however you want me," he said quietly. "Whenever you want me."

Then he cleared his throat and got to his feet, giving Daegan his typically cocky look. "I don't plan to go down easy though, so you better come at me with your A-game."

"Count on it." That predator's look became hot and dangerous, enough to raise her blood temperature. She wondered that she'd be able to stay away from watching such a match of wills.

Gideon gave him a quick, feral grin, then glanced back at Anwyn. "What do you want from the kitchen, Mistress?"

You. But she *was* thirsty. "Some more wine would be good," Anwyn noted, and Daegan nodded.

Gideon could feel their gazes following him as he moved across the room, naked as Anwyn had demanded. While he wanted to protest their unrelenting sex drive, his cock wasn't any better behaved. It was already getting hard at that reminder of them both taking blood from him. Daegan had pierced his femoral, holding his legs spread open to his will as Anwyn straddled Gideon's face, making him lick at her cunt while she suckled from his wrist. As Daegan drew blood from his thigh, he'd worked Gideon's cock, slid a finger inside him, making it near impossible for Gideon not to come before he serviced his Mistress. But he'd done it, damn it all. Then sprayed like a fountain, amazed and humbled when Anwyn bent lithely, her wet pussy over his face, and took all of him in, swallowing him down. Daegan had drawn back, but only to lean over her, press his lips to the fragile curve of her spine. He'd left a faint imprint of his mouth there, outlined by Gideon's blood.

There were other things, even more than the soul-shattering sex, that had reduced him to tight-throated silence these past hours. They'd all taken a break in Daegan's bed, dozing, but Daegan had slept. Slept deep in her and Gideon's embrace, in a way Anwyn had whispered she'd never seen him do. A true act of trust.

Of course, Gideon did doubt he'd be asking for forty more days of this, like Anwyn thought. He wasn't sure if he could overcome his embarrassment about walking around like their sex slave on demand. Of course, he couldn't seem to stop being reluctantly turned on by it, either.

"Daegan, are you going to keep hunting for the Council?" He called the question from the kitchen as he looked for clean glasses, considered the wine choices. Jesus, how many bottles of wine did anyone need? He chose one at length, mainly because he liked the dog printed on it. "You don't have to stop. We're going to be okay. There are three of us. We handled ourselves pretty well at Xavier's."

"Yes. You were nearly killed, and Anwyn came close to being violently raped. It went very well."

Gideon grunted, unimpressed. "You would have been staked if I hadn't been there. Or drained of blood if we hadn't come at all."

He pulled the cork. Though he didn't see it, he could feel the forbidding clouds of Daegan's thoughts gathering. It was clear from his actions that he was the most protective and dominant of the three, and would take command of any situation he felt was necessary, a sense of superiority over the two of them that was not as overbearing as Gideon initially thought it would be. It was more like having a general of their small army, or maybe that was just the best way for Gideon to handle thinking of it.

I'd love to see you salute him. Anwyn's amused thought.

"Yeah, that'll happen," Gideon muttered. He wasn't about to let the bastard intimidate him, ever. Anwyn was one thing, but she was a girl. Girls were allowed to be intimidating. Her laughter and Daegan's grunt made him smile as he pulled the pizza box from the oven.

Are you saying you want to hunt with me?

The thought came to him straight from Daegan, and he suspected it wasn't one he was sharing with Anwyn, though of course Anwyn could hear it in his mind . . . unless Daegan was distracting her. A quick check on that, glancing toward the living room, showed that Daegan had drawn her over to him, pulling the loose neckline of her robe aside to tease her breast with his lips. All in the midst of conversation, as casually as if he'd picked up his wineglass. It was a general's reminder, he guessed, that he would take from them when he wished, and yet make it well worth their while to surrender to him.

He wanted to shy from that thought, big-time, but every muscle in his body was deliciously sore from the frequency of the lesson. And he was willing for him to do it all over again.

Anytime you need a backup, I will. Gideon put down the bottle, stared into space. *But otherwise . . . I think I'm done with that, Daegan. Guys like Trey . . . I can't really say I'm sorry for that, but I think I know it was kind of fucked, and that's a part of me that's going to take some time to handle. You said it right, at the beginning. My job now is to protect Anwyn, be here for her.*

He was unexpectedly warmed by the relief he felt from Daegan, the words he spoke in his head. *It would ease my mind greatly, to know you are at her side when I cannot be.*

Gideon took a deep breath. So many changes, so fast. His mind wasn't wrapped around them all yet. But in a weird way, he'd never felt freer to say and do whatever he wanted. Pain and shadows would linger, like those shadows in Anwyn's head, but she and Daegan were just as good at helping him deal with them. And that, too, was new. Letting someone in, letting someone help.

Like all of it, it seemed to be beyond his understanding, but he could rely on his intuition to guide him where his dense brain couldn't.

There was one thing he wasn't going to let stand, though. Taking advantage of Daegan's absorption with Anwyn's arched body, the wet, taut nipple he was teasing with his mouth, he left the wine and pizza and strode out of the kitchen, right back up to the vampire.

Leaning down, he cupped Daegan's head as the vampire looked up, and planted one of those fast, hard kisses on his mouth. Daegan did those kinds of moves better and more smoothly, of course, but the flash of surprise in his eyes was worth it. "You can get your panties in a twist about our coming after you at the Coffin," Gideon said, holding his dark gaze, "but you're going to have to live with the fact we're going to watch over you just as much as you watch over us. Servant or no, I'm not going to stand by and let you go into situations where the numbers might be against you. Neither will Anwyn."

He pivoted on his heel and strode back to the kitchen. *And don't be staring at my ass.*

Though Daegan scowled at the man's presumption, his mouth eased at Anwyn's chuckle. "Not even forty days is going to change that stubborn rock head of his," he decided.

"He's rough around the edges, but he's perfect. And he's right. We both love you. You'll have to accept what that means, just the same way we do."

"Hmm. His kissing technique leaves a bit to be desired. He's much nicer to you."

"I'll help you teach him," she promised, laughter in her eyes. Gideon returned then, wine bottle and pizza box in hand, both strategically placed to hide the embarrassing movement of his genitalia. In sync, the two Doms made him put down the box and wine bottle, return to the kitchen and come back unprotected, underscoring the lesson that he must be open to them at all times. It was a sensual demand that had his cock stiffening under their pleased regard anew, though he sat down with the box and a narrow look.

"All-powerful vampires or not, I *am* eating before you do anything else to me. I may not be able to die of starvation, but having your backbone rubbing against your stomach while being fucked is *not* pleasurable."

"How will we pass the time, then, while you're stuffing your face?" Anwyn used her toes to tease his nape. Her servant swatted at her, but then captured her foot, bent his head and touched his mouth to her instep, bringing those midnight blue eyes to her face for an equally pleasurable caress.

"Twenty Questions again?" he murmured. "Though I think you've far exceeded twenty. Just ask them to Daegan. I want to eat."

From his significant glance, she knew there was an ulterior motive to it, but she didn't disagree with it. As much as Daegan had given them tonight, there was still a reserve to him they both knew was likely to remain in place. According to Gideon's thoughts, that was how older vampires were. However, Gideon was giving her a sly reminder that they might be able to take advantage of his mellow mood to learn more about the male vampire they both claimed.

However, that reserve would no longer make her doubt the feelings that existed under the dangerously still waters. Or if they did, that doubt would be removed hastily. Even now, as Daegan gazed at them, obviously aware of the drift of thoughts between them, she saw his contentment and devotion to them both, his amused indulgence. There were no doubts tonight.

"Besides, there's no point to Twenty Questions with me anymore," Gideon added. "You can both pluck any information right out of my head."

"And your life is appallingly tedious," Daegan observed. "For the past ten years, the same thing, day after day. Brood, stalk, eat, sleep, sh—" At Anwyn's jab, he gave an unrepentant flash of teeth. "Really, was there no time to take in a film festival? A book?"

"I picked up the occasional *Penthouse*."

"Or *Martha Stewart Living*," Anwyn riposted.

Gideon shot them both a grin, an unusually open gesture that riveted Anwyn. It was the first time she'd ever seen such an expression on his face, and though it was quickly gone, buried in another slice of pizza, she held on to it as another gift of the extraordinary day, seeing how handsome her vampire hunter truly was.

"While I'm still not happy with the two of you risking yourselves to come to my aid," Daegan noted, giving them both a sharp glance that promised sensual retribution in the future to remind them of that, "I do appreciate your courage and fortitude that night. I've had vampires try to ambush me before," he said thoughtfully. "But this time I was so much more concerned about the two of you, about Anwyn's safety, and proving something to the Council. I expect this bond between us gives me a new level of distraction I'll have to accommodate."

"It can be that way at first," Gideon said slowly. "But I think, in time, a family also gives you strength to do the things you know are right. Vampires like Xavier need to answer to someone. You should do what you want to do, but you shouldn't quit because of us. You know the Council needs all the help it can get, and you don't let them bully you. They need that."

"Perhaps your brother and Lady Lyssa will need my services at some point, and we can arrange a visit," Daegan suggested.

Gideon scoffed at that. "If you know anything about Lyssa, you know what she'd say to that. I can almost hear that sultry, scare-a-man-shitless voice. 'Thank you. I prefer to gut the bastard myself. Soon as I put a garden glove over my perfectly manicured nails.'"

"Sultry?"

"In a very non-appealing way," he assured Anwyn with a smile.

Despite his longing for the pizza, she was warmed when her servant let her drag him up onto the couch between them. She gathered him in so he leaned against her body between her bent thighs. As she pushed his head down onto her shoulder to stroke his hair, the width of his shoulders, he took full advantage of the position to tease her throat with his mouth, nuzzle her sternum so the neckline of the robe was pushed an inch or two farther from her ripe breast.

The position leaned him against Daegan's leg as well. When the vampire laid a hand on his lower back, giving him an absent caress, he didn't tense, too sated and loose to think to do so. It would take time before a man's touch wasn't unusual to him, but she saw this unguarded moment pleased Daegan as well.

She suppressed a sigh of contentment. "So tell us something we don't know about you, Daegan. Something important," she amended.

"Mmm." He was quiet for a bit, drinking his wine. Dropping his touch from Gideon, he caressed her foot, curved around Gideon's hip and pressed against Daegan's splayed knee. "My father was an angel."

"Yeah, I'm sure that's what your mother said." Gideon snorted against Anwyn's throat. "Until she saw you."

At the vampire's silence, Anwyn lifted her head from where she'd dropped it back to give Gideon's lips better access. She studied Daegan's face. "You're serious."

Gideon straightened then as well, turning in her arm span to look at Daegan. The vampire lifted a shoulder. "It is what she told me. He was an angel. Wings and everything." He cleared his throat. "It explains my speed. One time, when they were together, he took her on a flight that circled the globe in only an hour. He said he'd gone slower than usual, so as not to overwhelm her."

Gideon grunted. "Who'd have thought it? Angels try to impress girls just like other guys."

She didn't have Gideon's gift for smartass quips to cover her nonplussed reaction. Daegan gave them both a wry smile, though. "You see why I wouldn't tell many about this. You would doubt my sanity. I don't doubt my mother was telling me the truth. It was before she got the Ennui, when she still served the Council."

"Are there other things you have . . . like the speed?"

"I can exercise compulsion on humans not blood-linked to me, as I did with Sarah. And I'm not entirely sure a stake can kill me. The sun doesn't harm me as much as other vampires, though it does give me pain and significant discomfort."

"How do you know a stake can't—"

"It's not something I've tested. Just a theory I have."

"Well, I'm glad that Gideon was there that night at the Coffin so you didn't have to test it," Anwyn said firmly. "Though I would have rather you both been unharmed."

Daegan gave her an absent smile. "Nothing makes permanent scars on me, either. Even my own blood." He tapped his inner thigh, and though he was wearing the jeans, she recalled with a start she hadn't noted the "X" Xavier had tried to cut into his flesh, not since the rescue. At Gideon's blink of surprise, she realized he'd missed that as well. Of course, given how much had happened that night and since, it made sense that both of them, usually so detail-oriented, had forgotten about it. Particularly since there was no evidence of it left.

Setting the wine aside, Daegan focused his gaze on Gideon now. "I also can see the quality of a soul. When I have been dispatched after vampires and others, I know if there is good there, making him or her worth salvaging." His expression tightened. "Or if I am an instrument of justice. Karma coming home to roost."

"Which was why you always reserved the right to turn down an assignment," Anwyn recalled.

"Yes. Fortunately, while my mother was alive, she convinced the Council to heed my judgment, and seek other ways to change a vampire's path, if I said that execution was not the proper method."

It all made sense, Anwyn realized, but it was somewhat of a large idea to put her head around. Gideon was the same. She sensed the turmoil in his mind, possibly greater than her own. He'd decided a long time ago there was no higher power. However, perhaps he would rediscover faith in love. After all, everyone knew love was the largest proof of Divinity there was.

Daegan gave a half chuckle, as if bemused by his own reluctance to speak his feelings. He met Gideon's eyes again. "When I began tracking you, it was why I began to feel . . . how I feel for you. Your heart and soul . . . No matter the damage that has been inflicted on it, I felt a kinship with it, a bonding with you that began as a sense of brotherhood, and then became more, particularly when Anwyn brought us together."

He extended his hand, a curious gesture with Gideon sitting there, not a stitch on, but the vampire hunter—or former vampire hunter, Anwyn was pleased to correct herself—met it, the two clasping forearms. "You have my respect, Gideon. I will always watch your back as well." A light smile touched his mouth as he gave Gideon back his part threat, part promise. "And Anwyn's."

She saw Gideon's face tighten in unexpected reaction. His battered soul was barely able to absorb it, all of this emotion and feeling. It overwhelmed him, in a good way, but she knew they needed to help him. Daegan gave her a slight nod, acknowledging her desire to change the subject before Gideon's nakedness wasn't the only thing that would embarrass him again.

"I do have one more question for you, Gideon," she said. "You won't think of it without being asked. Therefore, it's not something I can just pluck out of your head."

He cleared his throat, managed to speak in a steady voice. "So I need to concentrate really hard and make sure I don't think about all those other women I've had?"

"Neanderthal." She pinched his ass, hard enough to make him jump, though she curved her leg over his hip, holding him to her. Daegan's fingers slipped along her calf, teasing the back of her knee, making her increase her grip, pressing her still-damp sex against Gideon's lower abdomen. But since she wanted an answer to her question, she pushed away the silky swirl of lust, in her mind and theirs. There was time for all of it. That was what made it so worth the wait.

"You've been doing what you do for a long time, with no rest. Is there one thing, something you haven't done in a long time, maybe, that you'd like to do?"

As she expected, it came into his head, a bright fruit on a tree of memory, the first thing that flashed. It startled him, she could tell, because it came so easily. He'd never entertained such a question, though he'd apparently revisited it in his subsconscious a thousand times.

"I haven't been to the beach in years," he said.

A simple wish for a complex man. Running her knuckles along his strong jaw, she gazed at his beloved face. "We can do that. We couldn't be with you during daylight, but . . ."

He shook his head. "I always thought the beach was pretty at night." Looking at her, he added softly, "Now it'll be flat-out beautiful."

Anwyn lifted a brow. "Having Daegan there won't make it beautiful?"

Gideon raised an eyebrow, glanced at the vampire. "Sometimes you have to take the ugly-assed weeds with the flowers."

The tackle was expected, even though she shrieked and had to use her vampire speed to get out of the way.

"In the weapons room," she commanded loudly, waving her arms at them. Gideon countered Daegan's attack with a few lithe moves that quickly became quite an impressive display, seeing as he was wearing no clothes, and Daegan was wearing very little. Then he landed a sharp elbow in Daegan's jugular that had her wincing. Gideon bolted for the weapons room, the vampire in close pursuit.

Taking another leisurely sip of her wine, she trailed after them. In the doorway, she folded her arms and watched them hit the mats, a light smile on her face, bright joy in her heart, contentment settled in every pore.

No woman in her right mind could underappreciate what she was watching now, the two men she was certain would become more irrevocably lodged in her soul every day, just as she would in theirs. She knew it not only because she was in their minds, but because she was in their hearts, every double beat met with a resounding one of her own.

She had Daegan, Gideon and the world of Atlantis. Tragedy had taken her down roads to wondrous places never imagined. Those places didn't replace or make up for the tragedy, but they underscored that there was sweet mystery to life she'd never dismiss or underappreciate, whatever shadows or gremlins she met.

Gideon and Daegan would help her make sure of it.

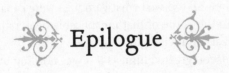

Epilogue

THE ocean waters glittered in moonlight, the white curve of sand private and long, stretching into the night shadows. As he drew the smell of clean saltwater into his lungs, Gideon realized not only had he not smelled the ocean in a long time; he hadn't really breathed deep and easy in a long time, either. It was amazing how emotional pain cramped one's breathing, without even realizing it.

The night Anwyn had asked him about this, he'd also remembered why it was his favorite memory. Ironically, the last pain-free day of his life had been the day he'd lost his parents. They'd been on a beach, he and Jacob, playing in the waves, making sand castles, running along the shoreline, wrestling.

Because Anwyn knew his heart so well, he didn't know why it surprised him now to look up the beach and see three figures—two adults, one carrying a child—joining Anwyn and Daegan. He'd left them relaxed on a blanket, next to the picnic basket of food for him and good wine for them.

Though instinct had him briefly tensing, scenting for danger, a part of him already knew who it was. A man with his own stride and set to his shoulders separated from them and came down the beach.

He'd talked to Jacob a few times by phone these past couple of months. Some of it had been hard, covering ground that should have been covered years ago, but he'd done it. Jacob had wanted to come see him then, but Gideon had put him off. It had been too difficult to explain that he had to wait until he was allowed to wear clothes. There were some things he was not going to share with his brother, though he expected Jacob knew all too well what vampires were capable of doing to their servants in the name of that inexplicable ownership he now embraced like a bizarre but vital gift.

"Hey, Gid." Jacob greeted him, as if it was nothing unusual for him to show up on a beach miles from his home.

"Hey." Gideon studied him as his brother came to a halt. Slightly leaner than Gideon, with their mother's reddish brown hair, they nevertheless shared those midnight blue eyes. And without rancor, he admitted Jacob had always been prettier. Anwyn and Daegan didn't seem to mind the rugged cut of his face, though, the scars he carried. Jesus, he had changed, if he cared about something like that.

With a slight smile, as if reading his thoughts, Jacob moved in, took him easily in a hug. It was awkward at first; then Gideon let it go, banded his arms around his little brother, held him tight. It was okay; his face couldn't be seen. He sensed the vampire in his brother, the strength restrained, and yet Jacob conveyed in his embrace the love he'd always bore for him, that Gideon had kept at bay for far too long.

When Jacob drew back, he had a wider grin on his face, though a suspicious brightness to his eye as well.

"Don't go all Irish on me," Gideon warned. "We haven't even started drinking."

"You either." Jacob reached out with a casual thumb and startled Gideon by taking a track of moisture off his own cheek.

"Yeah, well, hanging around a woman will do that to you. Makes you soft."

"I wouldn't know." Jacob wryly glanced up the beach, toward Lyssa and their son. His slender, dark-haired mate had Kane on her hip, but even the maternal picture didn't take the regal set from her shoulders or dim the aura of power that both intuitive brothers could sense. Gideon chuckled.

"Well, women who don't happen to be thousand-year-old vampire queens. It's good to see her. You treating my nephew good?"

"He's running us ragged. In a moment or two, she'll put him down and you'll get to see how much fun it is to keep track of a toddler who can already move at a gazelle's speed. Kane thinks it funny when you're trying to catch him. I've suggested hobbles on his ankles until he's ten."

"Good thing you became a vamp, then."

"Yeah." Jacob studied him. "So I met Daegan."

"Yeah." Gideon looked out at the ocean uncomfortably. "They're kind of a package deal. They do good together, but they seem to need me. I keep them a little bit more human."

Jacob's mouth quirked. "So you're the sensitive one?"

"Knew you'd pick up on that and laugh about it." Gideon snorted. "Lesser miracles have been known to happen, you know."

"Not many. They seem good for you, Gideon. Both of them."

Gideon turned back to his brother's shrewd blue eyes. "They are. It's . . . not what I expected. Guess I wasn't sure what you'd think. I mean, I know you've been part of this world, but some part of me is still who we were, you know. Before we knew about any of this. Couple of middle-class kids in a pretty traditional world."

"Yeah. That part of me was shocked." Jacob gave him an easy grin, though. "But I think the rest of me accepts it pretty well." He sobered then, put his hand on his brother's shoulder, fingers curling against Gideon's neck in deep affection. "They've given you peace, Gideon. It's all over you. Whatever they did, I accept them, and what they are to you, into my heart without question. Be easy on that, in every way."

"Okay." Gideon cleared his throat. "Same goes. In case I haven't said it the way I should. I get it now, Jacob. I really do. I'm sorry I didn't for so long."

Jacob shrugged a shoulder. "Well, I'm not surprised. Your head has always been dense as a rock."

"Yeah? You know, I hear vampires sink in water. You keep shooting off your mouth, you're going to find out what it's like to be a big paper-weight."

Jacob laughed, but then Gideon was on him, grabbing him around the midsection and taking them both into the waves with a resounding splash that had him spluttering. Jacob recovered fast, though, flipping over to exact retribution. He didn't use any more of the vampire powers than Gideon had third-mark strength, but then even the techniques of the two trained warriors melted away, the years melting with them.

They were wrestling as they had as boys, holding each other under, twisting free, splashing and shouting, laughing.

When they stopped at last, flopping on the warm sand under the moonlight, they stared up into the sky. Those disappearing years had closed in on other memories, such that Gideon felt the ache in his chest. "We're far away from the dreams we had as kids, aren't we?" Regret for things lost passed through him, even as he accepted what he'd gained.

"I don't think so." Jacob watched a shooting star cross the sky, a smile playing on his mouth. "I think we start with a boy's dreams, like pitching for the major leagues or being an astronaut, and then we get a man's dreams. Those are about being worthy, being loved, being content and happy. When you're a kid, if things are the way they should be, you already have that. When you grow up, no matter what else we think we're seeking, that's the heart of all of it. I think we found that, didn't we?"

As usual his poetic brother had taken it, put it into the right words. They were both cognizant of the vampires nearby, loving them enough to give them this time together.

No, not vampires. Family.

As they looked back up the beach, toward Kane and Lyssa, Daegan and Anwyn, Gideon felt the force of a thousand poems, written by a thousand different poets, fill him. In that moment, he knew any words of his would honor the truth as much as those flowery sonnets.

"I think we did at that."